Praise for *The Puritan Princess*

'A powerful and superbly researched historical novel'
Andrew Taylor, author of *The Last Protector*

'A genuinely moving portrait of the tragedy of the Cromwells at the height of their power, and Miranda Malins handles the tumultuous drama of the last days of the Protectorate with incredible aplomb'
S G MacLean, author of the *Damian Seeker* series

'There is much to enjoy in this evocation of a family whose lives are so upended by the convulsions of history'
The Times

'The extraordinary, revealing and moving relationship between Oliver Cromwell and his daughter Frances is brought to vivid life in this masterly historical novel'
Paul Lay, author of *Providence Lost*

'Miranda Malins is a real and fresh new talent. This is beautifully written, exciting fiction from a writer in full command of the history' Suzannah Lipscomb

'Totally gripping – grab it now. There's a new Cromwell on the shelves!'

Minoo Dinshaw, author of *Outlandish Knight*

'This engaging novel brings one of the most momentous but least well known periods of English history vividly to life'

Carolyn Kirby, author of *The Conviction of Cora Burns*

'A fine and compelling debut novel . . . Miranda Malins creates a cast of three-dimensional characters, vividly imagined against a deeply researched historical background. A joy and an education to read' Rowan Williams

'A beautifully written and captivating true story of personal love and loss . . . Malins inhabits her characters and brings them convincingly to life'

James Evans, author of *Emigrants*

'A thrilling debut novel, packed with expert scene-setting and juicy details, bringing to life her characters with aplomb' Michael Scott

'Malins' easy and graceful style makes for a thoroughly enjoyable read . . . It is high time we reclaimed this hidden piece of our history'

Linda Porter, author of *Mistresses*

'A fresh look at the Cromwell family' *The Punch*

'Simply brilliant . . . At times I was in floods of tears'

Rachel Phipps, blogger

'A love story played out against a colourful, fascinating historical backdrop' For Winter Nights blog

'An outstanding novel' Versus History blog

'The writing is lovely . . . Miranda Malins is one author to keep an eye on' Hayley's Book Room blog

'Authentic and beautifully researched'
Jaffa Reads Too blog

'This book has absolutely stolen my heart'
Vicky Lord Review blog

'Unforgettable characters, beautifully written . . . Intelligent and engaging' On the Shelf Books blog

Miranda is a writer and historian specialising in the history of Oliver Cromwell, his family and the politics of the Interregnum period following the Civil Wars. She studied at Cambridge University, leaving with a PhD, and continues to speak at conferences and publish journal articles and book reviews. She is also a Trustee of the Cromwell Association. Alongside this, Miranda works as a commercial solicitor in the City and began writing historical novels on maternity leave. She lives in Hampshire with her husband, young sons, and cat Keats. *The Puritan Princess* is her debut novel.

MIRANDA MALINS

An Orion paperback

First published in Great Britain in 2020 by Orion Fiction
This paperback edition published in 2021 by Orion Fiction,
an imprint of The Orion Publishing Group Ltd
Carmelite House, 50 Victoria Embankment
London EC4Y 0DZ

An Hachette UK Company

1 3 5 7 9 10 8 6 4 2

A CIP catalogue record for this book is
available from the British Library.

ISBN (Mass Market Paperback) 978 1 4091 9481 1
ISBN (eBook) 978 1 4091 9482 8

Typeset at The Spartan Press Ltd,
Lymington, Hants

Printed and bound in Great Britain by Clays Ltd,
Elcograf S.p.A.

www.orionbooks.co.uk

For my boys

CAST OF CHARACTERS

THE CROMWELL FAMILY AT COURT

Oliver Cromwell, Lord Protector
Elizabeth Cromwell, his wife, Lady Protectoress
Bridget (Biddy) Fleetwood, their oldest surviving child
Charles Fleetwood, Bridget's second husband, Major-General of the army and Councillor
Richard (Dick) Cromwell, the Cromwells' oldest surviving son
Dorothy (Doll) Cromwell (née Maijor), Richard's wife
Elizabeth (Betty) Claypole, the Cromwells' second daughter
John Claypole, Elizabeth's husband, MP and Master of Horse
Mary (Mall) Cromwell, the Cromwells' third daughter
Frances (Fanny) Cromwell, the Cromwells' youngest child

THE CROMWELL FAMILY IN IRELAND

Henry (Harry) Cromwell, the Cromwells' second surviving son and acting Lord Deputy of Ireland
Elizabeth Cromwell (née Russell), his wife

THE WIDER CROMWELL FAMILY AT COURT

John Desborough, Cromwell's brother-in-law, Major-General of the army and Councillor
Elizabeth (Liz) Cromwell, Cromwell's unmarried sister
Lavinia Whetstone, Cromwell's niece
Richard Beke, her husband, Major and Captain of the Protector's Life Guard
Sir Oliver Flemyng, Cromwell's cousin and Master of Ceremonies

OTHER MEMBERS OF THE COUNCIL OF STATE

John Lambert, Major-General of the army
Nathaniel Fiennes, Commissioner of the Great Seal
Sir Charles Wolseley, his brother-in-law
Henry Lawrence, President of the Council
Sir Gilbert Pickering, Lord Chamberlain
John Thurloe, Secretary of the Council and chief spymaster
Henry Scobell, Clerk to the Council and Justice of the Peace

Robert Rich, grandson and heir to the Earl of Warwick
Earl of Warwick, his grandfather
Countess of Devonshire, Robert's grandmother
Bulstrode Whitelocke, MP and Commissioner of the Great Seal
Roger Boyle, Lord Broghill, MP and courtier
Marchamont Nedham, writer and editor of the newspaper *Mercurius Politicus*
John Milton, poet, polemicist and Latin and French secretary
Andrew Marvell, poet and deputy in the Latin and French secretariat
John Dryden, writer and civil servant in the Latin and French secretariat
Edmund Waller, poet and composer
John Hingston, Master of Music
Master Farmulo, Cromwell's music teacher
Samuel Cooper, painter
John Michael Wright, painter
Thomas Simon, chief engraver at the Mint
Dr John Hewitt, clergyman
Hugh Peters, chaplain
Jeremiah White, chaplain
Katherine, Frances's lady-in-waiting
Anne Grinaways, Mary's lady-in-waiting
Anthony Underwood, Gentleman of the Bedchamber
Sir Thomas Billingsey, former Gentleman of the Bedchamber
Nicholas Baxter, Gentleman of the Horse
John Embree, Surveyor-General of Works

Philip Jones, Colonel and Controller of the Household
George Bate, physician
Master Hornlock, tailor
Master Riddell, jeweller
Assorted singers and musicians including two boy trebles

VISITORS TO COURT

Thomas Belasyse, Viscount Fauconberg, courtier
Francisco Giavarina, the Venetian ambassador
Antoine de Bordeaux, the French ambassador
George Fox, founder of the Quakers
Margaret Fell, Quaker
Sir William Davenant, opera composer
Mountjoy Blount, the Earl of Newport, former courtier to King Charles
Sir Thomas Billingsey, former courtier to King Charles

PROTECTORAL OFFICERS AWAY FROM COURT

Edward Montagu, General-at-Sea and later Councillor
Robert Blake, General-at-Sea (jointly with Edward Montagu)
William Lockhart, Cromwell's ambassador to France and later commander at Dunkirk
Robina Sewster, his wife, Cromwell's niece
Philip Meadowes, Cromwell's ambassador to Denmark
George Monck, General in command of the army in Scotland

IN PARLIAMENT

Sir Thomas Widdrington, Speaker of the House of Commons and Commissioner of the Great Seal
Sir Arthur Haselrig, republican leader
John Lisle, regicide, republican and Commissioner of the Great Seal
Sir Christopher Pack, proposer of the new constitution

THE RUSSELL FAMILY AT CHIPPENHAM

Sir Francis Russell, second baronet
Catherine Russell, his wife
John Russell, their son and heir

THE RICH FAMILY AT LEIGHS PRIORY

Lord Rich, Robert's father
His second wife and young daughters

IN YORKSHIRE

Thomas 'Black Tom' Fairfax, former Commander-in-Chief of Parliament's army

OPPONENTS OF THE PROTECTORATE

Edward Sexby, former Leveller and conspirator
Miles Sindercome, former Leveller and conspirator
Thomas Harrison, regicide and Fifth Monarchist

OVERSEAS

Charles Stuart, son of King Charles I, living on the Continent with an exiled court
King Louis XIV of France
Cardinal Mazarin, his chief minister
Queen Christina, former ruler of Sweden

All of the characters in this novel are real people.

THE CROMWELL FAMILY IN 1657

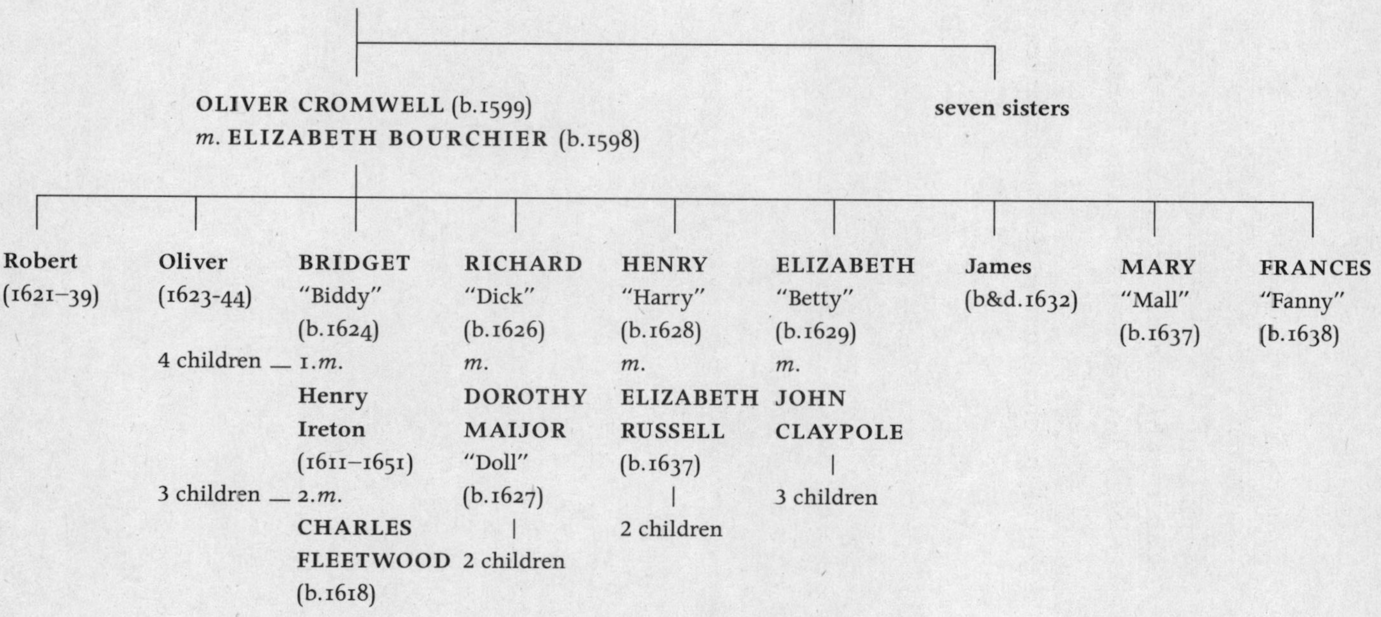

PROLOGUE

30 JANUARY 1661

We stand together, shoulder to shoulder, skirt to skirt, like a chain of paper dolls, come to see our father's execution.

Our hoods are pulled low over our faces although, in truth, few in the crowd would recognise us without our finery: we grace no coins, no medals or prints, and it is hardly likely any of them would have seen our portraits hanging, as they had, in the palaces of Whitehall and Hampton Court.

A frosted blast of wind whips around my cloak and sends the three nooses hanging from the gallows before me swinging as if the condemned men already danced their deaths. I stare at the gibbet in blank horror. It is a terrible thing, vast and three-sided like a triangle, designed, Father once told me, to hold twenty-four souls at a time.

'Why did it have to be here?' I speak sideways to my sisters. It is somehow worse, much worse, that this is happening at Tyburn, the dirty, eerie crossroads outside London where they hang common felons: highwaymen, thieves, murderers. 'Parliament settled on treason as the crime, so it should have been the Tower.'

'They wish to make a point, I suppose,' Mary answers. 'Some warning against men rising so far above their station.'

Fear creeps up my back like a spider and I feel it crawl along my arm and onto Mary's. She shivers against me.

'We shouldn't have come,' I say.

Mary stiffens. 'We were right to come, Frances. Father would want us to be here; we were his soldiers too.'

Her words conjure images of the russet-coated Ironsides of the old days and, as I watch them march through the air, I am surprised again by the resolve Mary has shown in these past days; it used to be me who was the brave one.

'We are here for Henry too,' Bridget says quietly on my other side, her voice breaking over his name.

And that is when we hear them coming. A slow drumbeat parts the crowds and a dragging, catching sound behind it takes me back instantly to my early childhood when the boys drove the ploughs up and down the marshy fields outside Ely. But this is no plough. I know, without turning, that it is a hurdle, a great gnarled gate on which the horses have drawn the prisoners all the way along Holborn. It is a strange route to take from Westminster Abbey but, once again, symbolic – a final pretence that the men had come not from the sanctified chapel of kings but from Newgate prison, as most come to Tyburn.

The crowd begins to swell forward, nudging us closer to the scaffold. I smile in the sudden memory of what my brother-in-law Charles had reported Father saying to General Lambert, the day their great army marched north to fight the Scots. When Lambert had remarked on the cheering, massing throng waving and wishing them success, Father had quipped that the crowd would be as noisy to see him hang.

How right he was.

But as I peer from beneath my hood at the faces around me, I realise that Father was only partly right. As many are here to see him hanged, it is true, but they are not cheering and bustling as they had been to see him lead his army. Nor are they laughing, drinking and pinching each other with the holiday mood that I understand usually accompanies public hangings. They are solemn, watchful, nervous.

For this is no ordinary execution. This crowd has come to witness something grotesque; an act outside the conventions of normal society, a violation of God's law, a performance of pure, visceral vengeance by their so-called 'merry monarch'. This would be a traitor's death for men beyond the reach of the law, beyond the reach even of the king; a second death for men already with God.

For these prisoners are already dead.

They are not living men that the hangman and his assistants now unstrap from the hurdle and haul upright to stand, propped awkwardly beneath each noose, wrapped in their death shrouds. They are corpses, disturbed from their consecrated sleep, taken from their allotted square of earth. Robbed from their Christian graves.

John Bradshaw, president of the court that tried the young Charles Stuart's father, the tyrant King Charles.

Henry Ireton, Bridget's husband and the fiercest, cleverest man in Father's army.

And Father, Lord Protector of the Commonwealth, Oliver Cromwell.

At the sight of Henry, Bridget's hand creeps into mine and I think how, though she had taken a long time to accept Henry as a suitor, she had grown to love him deeply. Something in the gesture – in the childlike feel of her small hand in mine; her, my big, brave sister, so much older than me, so strong, so sure of herself and of her nearness to God – breaks me.

'Father!' I blurt out the word though I know better. 'Our Father . . .' Louder now. Heads turn towards us.

Mary seizes my hands and bows her head: 'Our Father which art in heaven, hallowed be thy name, thy kingdom come . . .'

I remember myself and mumble along with her. The heads turn back to the gallows.

I watch, cold tears tumbling down my cheeks, as the hooded bodies are strung up with a great fanfare and a proclamation condemning the traitors is read to the crowd, the wind whisking the words away from all but those closest to the steps. The accused men cannot stand on stools to await their fate, of course, neither can they be hanged without their shrouds for risk of their bodies disintegrating on the scaffold. And so the swaddled, decaying bodies are hoisted up instead to swing aimlessly in the air, no kicking and jerking convulsing their shapes but instead a still, almost serene acceptance.

They are not there, I tell myself. They are with God. No one can hurt Father now.

We stand there for hours, numb from the cold, until

with the winter sun slipping towards the horizon the corpses are cut down, falling with a dull, muffled thud onto the ground below. With the corpses at his feet, the executioner draws a huge axe from beneath the straw and instinctively the crowd pulls forward for a closer look. Still in their green-moulded death shrouds, the men are arranged like animals on a slab before a butcher. The executioner paces before the bodies, tilting his head to examine the angles and cuts which would produce the best joints. Satisfied and with a last stretch and cricking of his neck and shoulders, he sets to work.

The heads are struck off first, the swaddling grave clothes dulling the axe's impact so that it takes eight violent attempts to hack off Father's head, almost as many to remove Henry's; each blow followed by a gasp from the crowd. The executioner holds each head aloft, not bothering to keep them at arm's length, certain for once that no fresh blood will fall on his jacket. His assistants join in and toes and fingers are attacked next, those nearest to the scaffold scrabbling forward for a grisly souvenir. Bridget grips my fingers with her own and we lace our bones together fiercely as if, by this, we can counteract the dismembering playing out before our eyes.

When, at last, the butchers grow bored by their labours, the three headless trunks are thrown unceremoniously into a deep pit on one side of the gallows, dropping through the air to land on top of one another with a hideous muffled thump like sacks of flour thrown down from a mill-loft. The heads remain above ground, spirited into a bag from which they will no doubt be taken to sit atop spikes in the time-honoured way. I watch in horror as the distance between the heads and bodies grows. I have been told that the old king was made whole again after his head was struck off: that it was carefully sewn back onto his body before it was lowered into the holy crypt of the chapel at Windsor castle. There will be no such happy fate for our beloveds, forced to spend eternity headless in an unmarked pit of thieves and murderers.

I can look no more, turning my eyes instead on the men, women and children pressed around me. Each face is caught, fixed in a moment of horror like a smashed clock. Could there be one among them who is not thinking of the moment on this same day twelve years ago when the traitor king's head had been held out above the scaffold at Whitehall? Mary and I had not been told of it for months. We were mere children and a conspiracy of silence attempted to keep us that way; broadsheets were hidden, letters thrust hastily into pockets and servants hushed. I look across at Bridget. She had known of course – she had been a new bride then, starting her family with Henry. She was in the crowded gallery at the king's trial and Henry had signed the death warrant; ninth on the vellum. Bradshaw first. Father third.

I close my eyes and savour the silence. When men come to write of this – the chroniclers, the gossips, the hacks and government newsmen who even now press against the scaffold, notes and pens in hand – they will say how the people cheered to see Old Noll, the great usurper, strung up and cut down to size; how justice was done and how God smiled on this day.

But we will know the truth. We are here too.

PART ONE

Four years earlier, January 1657

CHAPTER ONE

They want to make my father king. King of England, Scotland and Ireland. King Oliver – the first of his name.

I have heard this before, when Father was first made Lord Protector three years ago, again in '55 and then at my cousin Lavinia's wedding last year. What a day that was. I had never seen anything more beautiful than the bride who shimmered with happiness in her gold-edged gown as she planted a kiss on my cheek. The newlyweds laughed and whispered and the candles in the huge sconces along the Great Hall here in the Palace of Whitehall burned low as we feasted and danced into the night. At seventeen, it was the first time I had been allowed to stay up so late, the first time too a man had held my hand as he led me through a dance.

I had danced first with my brother Richard and after him with my brother-in-law Charles Fleetwood, Bridget's second husband. But then Robert Rich, grandson of the great Earl of Warwick, had asked me to dance and something about the pressure of his hand on mine sent my eyes after him for the rest of the day as he drank and supped, weaving among the other guests. Later, once the corners of the room had receded into the dusk, I found my feet following my eyes and I hovered behind a Plantagenet suit of armour listening to Robert as he joked with his other noble friends.

'You have to hand it to Cromwell, he throws a fine wedding party,' a young courtier had said, spilling fat drops of red wine over the rim of the cup he pressed to his lips.

'Ha,' Robert had scoffed, eyes dancing above a long, aristocratic nose. 'Surprisingly regal affair for a lot of East Anglian farmers.'

Another had chuckled at that. 'True. The court becomes less starched and stuffed by the day, fewer soldiers about too. Perhaps King Oliver might not be such a bad idea after all.'

That brought a swell of fists as the men clunked their heavy goblets together, candlelight flashing on the pewter.

I had shrunk back then, slippered feet pressing into the alcove. Tears threatened to come but I swallowed them down. I was my father's daughter; no man would make me cry. Robert had come to find me later to ask for another dance but I had turned my marble-white shoulder to him and talked to my sister Mary instead.

I was hurt by his insult to my family of course, though hardly surprised. A man cannot rise from obscurity to become Head of State as my father has done – his wife and children scaling the mountain in his wake – without attracting the hatred and envy of others. There is no greater vice than ambition, after all, and it is a charge Father is particularly sensitive to; the sin of pride being so foreign to his nature. But these insults never stick to him for long as Father, far from denying his humble stock, glories in it. It is he who speaks of being nothing but a 'good constable' to watch over the people. It is he who tells the courtiers, ambassadors and envoys who press in to see him each day that our family name should rightly be the humble 'Williams', not the grander 'Cromwell' assumed by my great-great-grandfather to reflect the glory of his uncle, King Henry's chief minister Thomas Cromwell. It is he who would have Master Cooper paint him 'warts and all'.

No. Those words stung as they always did. But it was the laughing young man's mention of *King* Oliver that had unsettled me. I had come across the notion before, breathed on the lips of an ambassador or stamped on a pamphlet. And I had felt its consequences for us, even finding myself referred to as 'princess' once or twice, though usually by a servant whom I had taken to know no better. But I knew that Father was quite content to be Lord Protector. I knew too that the word 'king' could stir men into a frenzy of passions: could drop them to their knees in a storm of tears, weeping for the 'martyr' King Charles who had died on the scaffold, or rouse them to their feet in a furious clamour for a pure Commonwealth of free-born men. Why would Parliament risk reigniting these dangerous fires to make Father king? Heir to the dead tyrant's corruptible crown. It was this thought that had caused my face to fade to alabaster at the young courtiers' idle talk.

And now today, here we are again. It is my older sister Elizabeth who whispers it to me as we sit with the family before the court, Betty's children perched and tumbling around us. She is always the first with gossip, usually from her husband John Claypole who, as Father's Master of Horse, is one of the most senior officials of the Protectoral household. Though, in this case, it is in John's capacity as Member of Parliament for Northampton that he has heard the news.

'John says some MPs are now talking openly of offering Father the crown.' Elizabeth leans close to me, her familiar rosewater perfume scenting the air. 'It's John's friends, his allies, who want Father to become king – John's all for it.'

'But why now?' I ask, removing my little niece's sticky hand which is clutching the satin folds of my dress where it drapes over my knees.

Betty cocks her head at me, her eyes dancing. 'Because at last John Lambert and the other army leaders are on the back foot. They have failed in governing each region directly – they are out of money and deeply unpopular. Father set up this rule by the Major-Generals as an experiment; an emergency response when it looked like the royalists were rising up again. But the threat has passed now and the people don't want a lot of armoured generals like Uncle Desborough marching around spouting the Old Testament, closing alehouses and pulling down maypoles in Father's name. And between us,' she puts her hands over her daughter's ears, 'Father does not want it either.'

This surprises me, for Father counts many of the Major-Generals not only as fellow visionaries of a reformed society but among his closest friends. These are the heroes who won the late war for Parliament and changed the world, the brothers-in-arms to whom Father would entrust his life – my own uncle and brother-in-law Charles Fleetwood within their ranks – and they guard their revolution and the power it brought to them jealously. 'He actually said that?' I ask.

'Well, not in public, and certainly not in Charles's hearing. He told me privately.'

I know all too well Father's fondness for late-night confessionals with Elizabeth and feel the usual pinch of envy at their closeness. I push the feeling away and concentrate instead on piecing the puzzle together, eager to prove myself Betty's equal in understanding for all the nine years between us.

'And if the Major-Generals' regime is dismantled,' I say slowly, 'there will be a chance to establish something else in its place; a more traditional government with power returned to Parliament.'

'Exactly.' My big sister beams at me and I bask in the warmth of her approval. 'A new constitution drafted by Parliament, with Father king and the country back on familiar ground. But we are not out of the woods yet; the army leaders will fight it, you'll see.'

I look over to the far end of the presence chamber where Father sits on the dais and scrutinise his expression for some hint of the sands shifting beneath us all. But I cannot read his face as his stocky frame leans forward from his gilt chair, head bent over the velvet cushion a kneeling figure holds up before him. The figure – who I know to be Master Simon, the engraver – appears to be pointing out various features of the object he is displaying in answer to Father's studious questions. After a few minutes Father grasps him warmly by the shoulder and bows his head to him in respectful acknowledgement of a job well done. Sitting back in his chair he claps, the rest of the court following his lead. I smile to myself, forgetting the unease of moments earlier: I would know the round thick sound of the pressed air, the precise pace of his clapping hands anywhere; can still pick out his rhythm even once a hundred more join it in one swell of noise.

And so I hear rather than see Father stop clapping to wave Master Simon over to us. Smiling politely, he bows low and approaches Mother, who sits on the other side of me from Betty. We all strain to see the offering Master Simon makes to Mother and I catch the tang of wine on my brother Richard's breath as he leans forward from where he stands behind us. And there it is, nestling in the creases of the crushed crimson velvet like a goose's golden egg. The newly minted twenty-shilling broad coin, the arms of the Protectorate pressed proudly on one side and, I see as Mother turns it over, Father's head gleaming on the other. I gaze in wonder at Father's familiar profile – captured even down to the prominent wart on his chin – crowned with the laurel wreath of a Roman emperor, the great expanse of naked neck where his collar should be, oddly effeminate. He is a king already, I think, as I examine it closely and reflect with awe that, from now on, Englishmen from Bude to Berwick will carry the image of my father in their pocket.

'I still cannot fathom how it has come to this.'

'Keep your head still,' my sister Mary chides me in the mirror. 'How can I comb out these knots if you keep shaking your head?'

I smile at her in the glass, her reflection as dear and familiar to me as if it were my own. Mary is only a year older than me and the two of us, born to our parents so many years after our other siblings, have always lived as twins – our two lives one shared experience.

'There, finished.' Mary drops a kiss on the top of my head. 'My turn.'

We swap and as I take the comb to Mary's curls, I tell her all that Elizabeth had said earlier.

'Father, king?' Mary looks up at me with surprise.

'Yes. Well, possibly.'

'But that is extraordinary. Father is just Father; not a king, not a prince of royal blood.'

'I know.' I smooth Mary's hair one last time before placing the comb on the chest. 'But Father *is* extraordinary. Indeed I have begun to wonder if he was ever ordinary at all.'

It is a thought I have long struggled with, yet something I doubt troubles my much older brothers and sisters in the same way. For they remember Father as an ordinary man, at his lowest point nothing more than a tenant farmer. They were on the cusp of adulthood when Father strode onto the world stage in his forties to answer Parliament's call to arms; and fully grown up when his star ascended in the later years of civil war and the struggle for a peace settlement that followed.

It was different for Mary and me. When we were children Father was the ruler of our small world and by the time we grew up, he had become the ruler of everyone else's. It felt almost as if, as we had grown and our world had expanded, Father in turn had expanded to fill it. He had been my horizon when he was merely the cathedral's tax collector of Ely and he is still my horizon now as Lord Protector of the whole country. I can never outgrow him or leave him behind as I imagine the daughter of a normal man would.

'You realise what else this means,' Mary says

thoughtfully, chewing the bottom corner of her lip and bringing my attention back to her. 'It means that our marriages, when they come to be arranged, will be matters of state. If we become princesses we can expect not just Father and Mother to have a say in who we wed but Secretary Thurloe, the Council and even Parliament to weigh in on the matter, to debate the most useful alliances we could make for the nation.'

I quail at the thought before a more customary resentment takes over. 'What you say is that the higher Father climbs, the less control we have over our own futures; if he takes the crown, what little choice of husband we may have had before would vanish entirely. Mary, how can you speak of it so calmly?'

'I merely accept things as they are, dearest,' Mary replies, her soothing tone so like Mother's.

'Well, I don't,' I counter, and hear Father's voice answering Mother's in my reply.

We stare at each other as we stand at the foot of Mary's bed, firelight flickering on our nightgowns. Then, without further talk, we do what we do every night: hitch up our hems and sink onto our knees, elbows propped on the bed, fingers laced together and heads down.

'Who shall we pray for tonight?' Mary whispers after a few moments have passed.

'Ourselves,' I mutter, shutting my eyes tightly.

It is too much to expect to sleep with such thoughts to unsettle me. Returned to my own room, I lie in bed for hours, too awake to slide fully into sleep, too tired to run my eyes along the lines of Aristotle's *Politics*. The book lies open across my stomach, my thumb hooked under it still keeping my place even though I know I will not lift it up again tonight. Still, something in the pressure of the pages, the weight of the expensive binding on my body, calms me. Books are my companions and always shared my bed even in childhood when Mary used to lie beside me with her doll and the books in our house were fewer, more precious possessions.

My oldest brother Richard – who would always choose a ride out with his dogs over an afternoon's reading – used to tease me for being bookish, but this was more than made up for by Father's ready pride in my quick mind. 'My little scholar' he took to calling me and his praise sent me in search of more and more books, convinced I had found a role for myself among his multitudinous offspring. Father always appreciates talents in others that he does not possess himself and as I would read at his feet by the fire after supper, he would tell me of his misspent school days.

'I was never of a scholarly bent, Fanny, not like you. Master Beard would try his best but I was always too much rooted in the soil, too busy living in the real world. I didn't want to think about other countries or other times. This is God's country, here, now: the Promised Land for his people. And it is our duty to make the best of it. I was too busy thinking about how my father should invest that year's rent money or who should stand for the town council. I lived in a world of acres, bills, lawsuits, not one of great philosophy or grand theories. And then I had but a year up at the university in Cambridge before my father died and at eighteen I had to go home and manage the household: business affairs, a mother and seven sisters to marry off didn't leave much time for reading, apart from my Bible of course. Ha, I should say not!'

I would laugh then as he wanted me to. Make some joke about all the many women in Father's life, of whom I – the youngest of his four daughters – was but the most recent addition. But I knew Father's levity masked the truth of a difficult time and, from across the fireplace, Mother's weary smile as she pinned a patch to the elbow of one of my brothers' shirts spoke volumes. How Father must have leaned on her when he brought her home as his bride three years later.

And harder years lay ahead for them: a decline in Father's fortunes forcing them to sell up his properties in Huntingdon and take a farm tenancy in St Ives; seven babies to birth and raise; a crisis of faith. But then, after sixteen years, God turned back to Father. A legacy came from an uncle – some modest properties and a position as tithe collector in Ely – and Mother and Father began to live and love once more. Mary and then I were the unexpected results of their new life: 'a second family', so Father's friends teased him, and eight-year-old Betty was the baby of the family no longer.

From the gallery outside my room, I hear the telltale scuffle as the retiring soldiers, tired from their shift, shuffle away; the scrape and stamp of the new men, fresh and alert as they settle into comfortable positions. Still sleepless, I huddle down under the thick fur coverlet and think of the dead King Charles. My room here in Whitehall Palace used to be his study and I often hear his soft slippered steps pacing around my bed, the Scotch lilt of his voice dictating a letter to his secretary. Sometimes

I can even smell the sweet perfume his pageboys have rubbed into his hair and pointed beard. How different this royal chamber is from our children's bedroom in my first home – the timbered tax-collector's house in Ely. There, on frosted nights like this one, Mary and I would chafe our fingers together against the cold under the patchworked blankets on our rickety bed, listening to the tangle of chimes as the cathedral bells interlaced with those of St Mary's next door.

When I was three, the king and Parliament went to war, taking Father away from me one morning, my earliest memory his tan boots high above my face as he bent to kiss Mother from his horse. He was of little importance then, an obscure MP who raised a local troop of horse and led them to the war. But he showed a raw talent for battle and rose through the officer ranks, moving us all to London when I was seven and war was giving way to politics. Our first lodgings in a townhouse on Drury Lane seemed the height of sophistication to me and, though Mary and I still shared a bedroom, there were no more rough walls with damp patches or fenland frost inside the windows; we did not have to creep barefoot down flagstone stairs to the kitchen for our darned stockings dried above the kitchen fire.

Then came the long-drawn-out peace negotiations with the king, another burst of fighting, a trial and then a cold January morning when King Charles stepped out of the Banqueting House to an executioner's block. I was ten when England was declared a Commonwealth; a republic, with no need for kings or lords any more. Parliament was supreme and I was in awe. But we were not at peace: royalists kept harrying the edges of the fledgling Commonwealth and the government dispatched Father with the army to Ireland and then Scotland to put an end to the fighting once and for all.

He was away two years and, though Mother tried her best to keep us cheerful and occupied with the gentlewoman's diet of sewing, singing, reading and polite conversation, we longed for Father and the lively chaos he sprouts around him, as over-wintering seedlings miss the sun. When, finally, he returned home in triumph, he found Parliament bickering and prevaricating in search of a lasting settlement, and me, precocious and restless as ever, demanding audiences of his friends and colleagues to explain affairs to me. There followed a busy time, with Father and his allies working till all hours, and so we moved to rooms in the old Cockpit within the wider estate of Whitehall so Father could walk to Council meetings or to Parliament in just a few minutes. For me, the move brought new levels of luxury: my own room and a maid – Katherine, a war widow pensioned by Father – to wait upon Mary and me and help us grow accustomed to the corseting clothes of young ladies.

But little did I know how my life, already so different, was about to change for ever. Father and the other senior officers of the army lost patience with their political masters and in '53 dissolved Parliament at musket-point. The godliest men were nominated to govern in an assembly but they could only look up at heaven or down at their navels – never straight ahead. The assembly split into factions and the army council went to Father to ask him to rule. And so we had a new government by a Lord Protector and Council of State working with Parliament. I was just fifteen when we became the first family in the land three years ago. We were to move into the royal apartments of Whitehall and Hampton Court, I was to have many maids and ladies-in-waiting, tutors in music and languages and a dress allowance to spend as I pleased. And best of all, the royal library to plunder and the finest minds of the court with whom to discuss my loot. People began to curtsey to me; other girls dropped their conversations as I drew near; young men circled. I remember the first time a servant called me Highness and I didn't know to whom she was speaking.

My older sisters Bridget and Elizabeth made much of the stark contrast of this life to their apprenticed womanhood, where supper with our neighbours was the highest social occasion and Mother allowed them each a few pennies a month to spend on ribbons or other dainties. But their attitudes to the greater opportunities open to Mary and me were typically different: Betty helped me to spend my dress allowance, cooing over the silks and satins and teasing me for affording what she could not at my age; while Bridget warned me sternly not to slide into sinful vanity and bid me attend to the lessons I was lucky enough now to have.

They were both right in their own ways, as they always are, but as I listened to them battle over my soul, I could not help wondering what the ultimate purpose of my newly exalted cultivation was to be. If my fate was merely to marry a man approved of (if not even chosen) by my parents, would my expensive clothes and new mastery of the humanist curriculum bring me fulfilment or serve simply to enhance my value on the marriage market? Perhaps I would suffer for being prized more highly, seeing me sold as a princess to the highest bidder in a diplomatic alliance where, a decade ago, plain Biddy and Betty Cromwell could take a more natural course and simply fall in love with family friends.

It took four months to ready the palaces for us as they had fallen into such disrepair in the years without a king. So it was April '54 when we finally moved in, the spring blooms bursting from the beds beneath the deep-bayed latticed windows of my new grand bedroom, the old king's study. I basked in the excitement of it all even as it left me nervous and bewildered, though others were not so easily impressed. My grandmother, Father's mother, who moved with us, clucked and clicked her tongue in distrust at our new grandeur: 'There are those who'll hate us for it,' she said time after time, 'Oliver's friends as much as his enemies.' Since she was then in her ninth decade, it felt to me that the madness of these great changes was too much for her; and she died a few months later to be buried incongruously in Westminster Abbey, unable to escape her son's staggering ascent even in death.

And madness can be the only way to describe the course our lives have taken. Mother tells me I have never known normal times; that the ever-shifting ground on which I first learned to walk, used to stay still. That my normal was, for everyone else, a world turned upside down. And so I returned to my books, peering into the pages of the past searching for parallels for our extraordinary times. For without precedents, where else can I look for guidance? There is no teaching in an age without rules, no textbook for revolution.

Everything is history now.

A log hisses in the grate when suddenly a volley of

shouts and screams tears through the night-time silence. A furious knocking wrenches me out of my half-dream. In another moment, the guards burst into my bedroom, falling over each other in their anxiety to reach my bed. Through the open door behind them I can see torches flying through the air of the passage underneath running feet.

Instinctively I pull the cover up to my chin, the fur hot and silky against my skin.

'You must come with us, Your Highness. Now if you please.'

Fear steals over me like a blanket of frost. I know not to question them, and scramble down from the bed, sliding my bare feet into slippers and grabbing a thick shawl to wrap around my nightdress. They bustle me from the room and I find myself slotting into a stream of other night-robed figures snatched from their sleep and hurrying through the palace corridors. I glance around, looking for Mary. Or Elizabeth, Mother, Father. But I see none of my family, just the familiar faces of courtiers, servants and officials swept along in one rapid current. Suddenly, my maid Katherine finds my hand and I clutch it gratefully, her small palm always so warm. There are shouts and calls from the guards, wails from children, but, for the most part, people press forward in silence, faces set with only one fixed thought: to get out of the palace.

We emerge suddenly, erupting into the court like the jets of water that surge from the mouths of the bronze fishes on the great fountain Father had installed as the centrepiece of the privy garden at Hampton Court. I expect utter darkness but instead the sky lightens as if it is already dawn as the palace servants bustle around the enclosure lighting every lamp and torch there is. Everywhere candles and lanterns spring to life in clutched hands illuminating the underside of anxious faces. A lone blackbird starts to sing from the roof of the Great Hall, its sweet song eerie in the moonlight.

It is then that I see Mother and the rest of my family on the far side of the courtyard surrounded by the unmistakable grey-and-black liveried backs of Father's Life Guard. The sight of Father's personal bodyguards is a relief and I press forward towards them, Katherine following.

'Mother, what's happened?'

'Frances, thank the Lord.' She squashes me to her bosom, unsupported in her loose white nightgown. 'We're not sure. When they came in to us they said it was a bomb in the chapel.'

I look back towards the chapel, although of course it is blocked by the towering roof of the Great Hall. I notice they have brought us away from the chapel to the palace gate by the Banqueting House.

'Is Father hurt?' Mary asks, her voice shaking. 'Is he safe?'

'Your Father has gone with Secretary Thurloe and members of the Council . . .' Mother tails off, looking around us abstractedly.

I gather my scattered thoughts. So this wasn't simply an attack on Father – he has faced assassins before. No, if it was a bomb in the palace, it could have killed any of us: my mother, my sisters, the children. I know there are men out there who hate my father, even if I struggle to reconcile this with the loving parent I know, but I had never thought there might be men who hate us too by extension. Men who wish to see us all die. This attack is something altogether more terrifying than any threat that has come before and I feel my heart thumping, blood coursing through my veins. I look around the anxious faces of my family and wish, not for the first time, that my brother Harry was not in Ireland. His is always the coolest head in a crisis, a glimpse of what Father must have been like as a young man. I turn to my other brother Richard as the next best thing. 'Who has done this, Dick?'

Richard runs a hand through his hair, sandy curls snaking through his fingers. 'Royalists most likely. They are constantly plotting against us, scheming to bring the dead king's son back. But we all thought the threat was passing. If it is them, this will play right into the army's hands. Father can hardly dismantle the rule of the Major-Generals if the royalists are on the move again.'

'I heard it's the Levellers,' Elizabeth interrupts, her beautiful chestnut locks loose over her shoulders. 'Thurloe said so to Father.'

'Well, they hate Father just as much as the royalists now he is the one to rule.' Dick smiles ruefully. 'More perhaps, as only those who once fought for the same cause can. Nothing is so bitter than the falling out of friends.'

Their words unsettle me with the picture they paint of enemies gathering around us on all sides. Could Father really have done anything so terrible to drive a former friend to this? To turn a man who fought shoulder to shoulder with him in battle into one who would kill him as he slept? Father is the same man he ever was: so how can he now be judged a bad man where before he was judged a good? And what of me? Is it my fate to live or die by his reputation even though it was made on muddy battlefields hundreds of miles away from me when I was only a child?

I look around in confusion and see people cradling their most precious possessions, snatched as they ran from their rooms: a courtier carries a silver clock even as his stockings slip down around his ankles, a lady clutches her perfume chest. One of the cooks is staggering under the weight of a great cheese. Somewhere further off I hear a child crying.

'It will be those Fifth Monarchy men, sir,' Katherine says, fear making her forget her place. She pulls her faded brown shawl more tightly around her, digging her fingers under her armpits. 'The ones who say His Highness must be removed for the kingdom of Christ to come again. A few of the men in my poor William's regiment have gone that way. I've heard,' she adds quickly, before we accuse her of consorting with such lunatics. I know she is thinking of her husband, killed only a few yards from where Father sat on his horse, on the field of Marston Moor. She searches for my hand and I take it, as I always do, feeling it small and warm in mine.

'Are they many? Are they still here in the palace?' I look around nervously, half expecting to hear shouts and howls of pain; the sound of fighting.

'Scores of them!' My younger nephew Henry, Elizabeth's boy, thrusts his head between us, clutching at his mother's nightdress. 'And one had his hand cut off in the struggle!'

'Not his hand, stupid, his leg.' His older brother Cromwell pushes him and grins up at us.

'I heard it was his head.' Elizabeth leans down to them and they shriek gleefully, hopping from foot to foot.

'Betty, please.' Mother's tone is firm and she smiles gratefully as the graceful, black-gowned figure of John Thurloe, Secretary to the Council of State and – everyone knows – Father's chief spymaster, drifts noiselessly towards us.

I wonder how it is that he is fully dressed when no-one else is.

'Highness.' He bows to Mother. 'Let us fetch you all out of the cold. The guardroom beneath the Chairhouse would perhaps be safest.'

He takes Mother's arm and leads us across the courtyard as calmly as if he were taking us into dinner. The crowds part to let us pass, some bow and curtsey – deferential even in this night-time panic. I pause to watch them but Richard hurries me under the great Holbein gate, and we turn up the stone steps into the guards' room.

Having made us as comfortable as he can in the spartan barracks, Thurloe stations several household guards outside the door and dispatches Katherine and our other attendants back to our rooms to fetch our clothes and to pack our things.

Thurloe closes the door behind them, bright hazelnut eyes darting into the furthest corners of the room. Reassured we are alone, they settle at last on my brother Richard as the oldest male member of the family present. 'Highness.' He addresses Dick in his customarily soft, quiet voice, quite unshaken by this tumult. 'I suggest that you take the family to Hampton Court as soon as it is light enough. It is Friday today after all so you would be making the journey in any event and it can do no harm to go a little earlier than usual. I will have the royal barge readied for you, with an extra troop of the Life Guard. His Highness will follow you later today; I have already agreed the matter with him.'

No one questions this. We all know that it is Thurloe who takes charge in an emergency; he whom Father trusts above all others.

There is nothing to do then but wait.

A few hours later, as the first pinks of dawn tint the edges of the clouds, I clamber into the barge and settle, huddling against Mary, on the cushioned benches, swathed in three of my cloaks and a soft wool blanket. The bargemen push us off from the landing stairs and take up their rhythmic row, the muffled sound of oars patting against the swell of the Thames which breaks around us in dark inked waves. We sit in silence. Laying my head on Mary's shoulder, I watch the great jumble of the palace fade from view, the tiny figures of the guards swarming over it like ants over crumbling headstones.

I am not sorry to come early to Hampton Court. It is my favourite place in the world; a rural paradise far from the busy streets of London. I spent my childhood under the big sky of the fens, which explains perhaps why at Whitehall, in the centre of the noise and smells of the great city of Westminster, I find myself longing for the quiet river, privy garden and endless deer park of Hampton Court. Our life there is quite different. Where Whitehall is Father's place of work – the site of state occasions, meetings with Parliament, the reception of envoys from foreign princes and the sitting of the many committees that manage the day-to-day administration of the nations – Hampton Court is our home.

It is only here, away from the public eye, that Father can indulge his gentlemanly tastes for sport, music and fine classical statues; tastes which would provoke the disapproval of his most puritan Bible-waving subjects. None of us will ever forget the time an outraged iconoclast Quaker cook took a hammer to Father's statue of Venus and Adonis, calling it a wicked heathen image. Father himself spent hours watching anxiously as the court masons did their best to repair his beloved statue but he insisted the Quaker be sent away with no more than a flea in his ear: 'I will not punish a man for acting out of his faith,' he said. 'His way is the equal of mine.'

And so at the end of each week, we travel here to Hampton Court for Father to relax, far from the glare of Whitehall. Of course the court comes with us – the everyday meetings and business of government must continue – but we live more simply, more informally, with Father hunting and hawking and sharing his treasure trove of stories with us over a laughing supper. Elizabeth tells me we have invented something new by dividing the week this way, with two days of rest following five of work, and that others have now begun to do the same; she is delighted whenever we begin a fashion.

Father follows us upriver later that day, as Thurloe had promised, though I do not see him as I would expect to. He does not go out to ride, or come to our family rooms for dinner and a cuddle with Mother. Instead he is closed up in his private study, talking late into the night with Thurloe and the fifteen or so members of the Council of State, working through supper and sending the servants for more candles. The atmosphere even here is tense and rumours of the conspirators fly along the corridors and across the long tables at supper. There have been arrests and Thurloe's messengers travel up and down the river between Hampton Court and the Tower of London, their faces grave under broad-brimmed hats, letters taken out and pressed into their hands through half-opened doors.

Mother retires early with a headache and I follow her, climbing into the bed beside her, a child again in my fear. She whispers nothings into my hair, slowing the beat of my heart into sleep so that it is there that I wake at dawn, wondering if Father had slept in the great bed of the state bedchamber, finding his own private bed usurped, or if, indeed, he had come to bed at all. I lie for some minutes moving from the twisting thoughts of my dreams into the uncertainties of a new day and feel my resolve hardening as pale sunlight slips around the edges of the yellow curtains. I must consult Mary at once.

I go straight from my parents' chamber to Mary's, hurrying along the long gallery, wondering absently if Katherine will be worried when she comes to wake me and finds my bed untouched. Mary is still asleep and her room thick with darkness – her lady-in-waiting Anne not such an early riser as Katherine. I pull the curtains a little apart, enough to light the room gently, and walk around the bed until I am level with Mary's head, her dark curls, fluffed with sleep, stirring now on the pillow.

'Mary, we must take control of our lives,' I say; simple and to the point.

'Hmmm?' She keeps her eyes closed.

'We must start living our own lives. Today.'

'What time is it?' Mary turns away from me, burying her face in the pillow.

'Time that we understood things for ourselves.' I am pacing now, warming to my theme even as my bare feet feel the morning chill. 'We know now that we could be murdered in our beds at any moment. And if Father becomes king, the danger only greatens. If we are expected to run these risks, I think it only fair that we gain something from the bargain – more choice over our futures.'

Mary abandons sleep and turns to face me then, her grey eyes bleary as she props herself up on her elbows. 'Please don't talk of our being murdered in our beds, I am frightened enough as it is.'

'I'm sorry.' I take her hand then and kiss it before bowing low to her in an approximation of courtly love; despite being the younger of our pair, I always play the man when we act out our romantic hopes. She slides over in the bed to make way for me and I pull myself up and sit next to her, snaking my arm around her shoulders, my head thrown back against the carved oak headboard.

'Think of the brightest, best ladies at court,' I continue, Mary's head heavy on my shoulder. 'The ones who proved themselves in the war – defending their homes from besieging troops when their men had gone, taking up causes, protecting their families. Think of Bridget working with Henry Ireton and Father on the peace terms the army put to the king. I know she had a hand in them; she's told me enough times when scolding me for idleness. She was here at Hampton Court when they presented the terms to the king – she met him, dined with him twice; can you imagine that? And it's not just women of our station who have been empowered by the war. Think of the ordinary women out there in the city – the preachers and printers, the Leveller wives and their petitioning. They don't sit around all day sewing and waiting for a man to speak to them. Why should that be our fate?'

'I can see you now, Fanny, preaching hellfire at St Paul's Cross with the other Quakers.'

Mary giggles and I poke her in the ribs.

'I'm not saying I want to preach to anyone, Mall,' I say, answering my nickname with hers, well aware what a Ranter I sound with this speech. 'I don't know what I want . . . But I do know that we won't have any choices at all if we are married off to some wealthy widower or foreign duke who only wants to set us in a display cabinet along with his other treasures. If we can pre-empt Father's match-making and find companions of our own choosing, we can search for fulfilment on our own terms.'

When Mary stays silent, I turn my thoughts to our older sisters, always setting the parameters. 'Betty was seventeen when she married John – a whole year younger than me.'

Mary twitches her lips and I can see she is counting in her head. 'Yes – but Biddy was two years older than I am now, remember? She was twenty-one when she wedded Henry, twenty-seven when she married Charles.'

'That doesn't count.' I shake my head. 'Bridget is a challenge; Father probably couldn't get her off his hands any sooner.'

Mary slaps my wrist in mock reproof.

'Anyway, that was ten years ago, before all this.' I gesture at the grandeur of the room, its silken tapestries now shining in the morning sun as it rises over the great deer park. 'It is our time now.'

Having fixed on the idea, I cannot shake it from my head. It seems so clear to me that love must be the answer to fear, and a life lived to the full each day the best defence against death. Mary might be cautious but I know Father would agree with me. No one values love of all kinds greater than he – the love of wife and children, of kin, of friends and brothers-in-arms – though I know that he would urge me to seek the love of God in all of them. Mindful of this, later that morning I go with Katherine in search of our chaplain, Jeremiah White. He is a young and eager man and a great deal more charming than most in holy orders. Where others walk with God with the dragging steps of a penitent, Jeremiah gambols along beside Him like a dancing master. It is this joy in his faith, this lightness of spirit that endears him to Father, who cares far more about a man's passion for Christ than his style of worship – how else could he count both former archbishops and dissenting Quakers among his friends, enjoying a glass of wine and spirited discussion with each, sometimes in the same evening?

I find Jeremiah in the Great Hall listening to the singing boys rehearse, servants busily clearing the remains of breakfast from the tables around him. The boys' soaring trebles stop me at the door and I too listen with great joy to their sound, looking up past the mounted stags' heads into the vaulting beams as if I can see the voices as they wing and swell into the vast space overhead. They finish a motet and John Hingston, Father's Master of Music, plays a chord on the organ to check their tuning. He glimpses me as he turns to speak to the boys and waves; Mary and I take weekly singing lessons with him and he has become a good friend.

Jeremiah jumps to his feet at our approach and, brushing breadcrumbs from his gown, gladly follows us to our family's private rooms. We talk easily of the music as we walk, of its closely knitted harmony and sweet sound, and it is not until we are settled in the deep blue-cushioned chairs of the balcony room, Katherine dispatched to summon cups of sweetened hot chocolate for us, that I come to the point.

'I seek your advice, sir,' I begin, a little embarrassed now at the topic ahead of me. 'I have been . . . I have found myself very upset and fearful following the attack at Whitehall.'

He inclines his head towards me. 'I too, Your Highness. Grieved, in particular, that the villains hid the device in His Highness's chapel.'

I nod in sympathy though I admit to myself that this aspect of the offence hadn't occurred to me. It was the proximity of the bomb to me and to my family that shook me to my core. It was not like the attempts taken before on Father's life – the pistol pointing from the crowd. This attack could have killed us all, much as the Gunpowder Plotters had planned to blow up the king and his court assembled in Parliament half a century before.

'But can this be God's intention for us? For me? Before I have done anything of worth with my life?' My eyes flick to Katherine as she re-enters the room and comes to sit beside me, taking out the sampler of needlework she always keeps in her left pocket.

'I am sure that it is not God's plan for you, Lady Frances,' Jeremiah says, placing a hand on mine, his voice soothing as lavender oil. 'He will intend a great deal of joy for you and your sister, I have no doubt.'

I relax with his words even as the warmth of his large palm covering mine unsettles me. I press on. 'I am glad that you speak of joy for I have been thinking that the search for happiness is the best and proper answer to the wicked designs of our enemies.'

'A fine thought, my lady Frances, and well said.'

Encouraged, I lean towards him. 'And I wondered if you could give me any guidance on how I should set about this search?'

'Well, my lady.' Jeremiah shifts a little forward in his seat and settles his green eyes on mine. 'God informs us that the greatest happiness available to man or woman is to be found in marriage. And, indeed, this is a state of happiness I have long wished to enter into myself.'

This is not the reply I expect and it is my turn to hesitate. I smile to cover my embarrassment, aware anew of his hand on mine and of the quickening of my pulse. Out of the corner of my eye I see Katherine's needle pause mid-stitch.

Before I can take another breath, Jeremiah has taken my hand in both of his.

'Perhaps we could find such happiness together, my lady,' he says softly, eyes locked on mine. 'We have long found a happy accord in our conversation and share a delight in music. Might this not be nourishing ground in which to grow a fine, lasting love?'

The room spins. Dizzy, I am reaching around in the blank spaces of my mind for an answer when the door opens smartly, revealing no less a figure than Father himself. Jeremiah, Katherine and I freeze, fixed in a canvas of painted shock.

'What's this?' Father's voice crosses the room like a cannon shot. 'Do you make love to my daughter, sir?' His eyes bore into the unfortunate chaplain.

I drag my gaze from Father back to Jeremiah and watch as the full horror of the situation floods his face. I dare not speak; it is Jeremiah Father has addressed, not me. Softly, slowly I slide my hand out of his and fold it underneath the other on my lap. The motion seems to waken Jeremiah and he springs to his feet, turning to face the Lord Protector.

'Not at all, Your Highness,' he says, his voice higher than usual. 'This is not how it may appear.'

'Then enlighten me.' Father strides towards us, his weathered forehead crumpled in a frown, a marksman's eyes trained on the chaplain. Though I know Father's quick temper better than most, I am surprised at its ferocity.

Jeremiah looks back to me but I have no inspiration to help him. Helplessly I glance sideways at Katherine but she is watching the scene with the same blankness. Jeremiah turns back to Father with a sudden torrent of words.

'Sir, I wasn't seeking your daughter's favour as you may have supposed but . . . rather, seeking your daughter's intercession on my behalf with another lady.'

'Another lady?' Father raises a sandy eyebrow.

'Yes!' Jeremiah dances forward. 'Your daughter's

lady-in-waiting, Mistress Katherine here.' He gestures unnecessarily to Katherine as if Father cannot see her for himself.

Katherine's sewing slides off her skirts and onto the floor. I gape at her before composing my features into an expression of agreement, though I am sure I do not fool Father; I have never been able to dissemble with him, he reads people too easily.

'Mistress Katherine,' Father repeats, turning his gaze on her, though his eyes catch mine for an instant as they sweep past me and onto her and I see them begin to dance as his mood shifts with customary speed. 'And why, Mistress Katherine,' he addresses her directly, his voice stern, 'have you so rejected my good and worthy friend Chaplain White so as to drive him to seek help from my daughter?'

Katherine rises to her feet at this but is struck dumb.

My wits suddenly returned to me, I stand up beside her. 'Please, Father, this is a delicate matter. You know how Katherine loved her poor husband.' Jeremiah shoots me a look of desperate gratitude, though Katherine remains as still as one of the garden statues. I know I have said the right thing as Father's frame softens and he takes a few steps closer to us.

'William was a good man indeed, and as fine a captain as ever I served with. You know the love I bore for him, my dears,' he says softly, his voice carried to the far-off place he visits when he is reminded of the men lost in the war. But Father summons himself back to us and sets his face in a sincere smile as he takes Katherine's hand. 'You know too that it is my love for him – for you both – that saw me take you into my household on his death; where you have been happy, have you not?'

Katherine nods silently and I see the beginnings of panic steal across Jeremiah's face, a panic echoed in my quickening pulse.

We all wait on Father's next words.

'Well, then,' he grins. 'Let us have no more worrying about this. William would wish you to be happy and it will be a fine thing to see you settled again, Katherine. You will do well with the chaplain here. Will you not have him with my blessing?'

I gape at him, at her, amazed at how this scene has swept away from me, not knowing how Katherine could possibly respond when her fate is snatched away from her in an instant.

'I will, Your Highness, gladly.' She smiles then, a faint rose blush spreading across her cheeks. I look at her closely and reflect that though Katherine is nearer thirty than twenty, with a thickening waist and eyes edged with lines, she is quite pretty. I look at Jeremiah, who is staring at her much in the same way, rapidly assessing her worth in the manner of an unsuspecting winner at an auction.

But what else can he do?

'Come.' Father sweeps his grin over us all, dazzling as the arcing light of a lantern. 'I will see you both married, here and now!'

'No!' Mary almost bursts as I reach this point in the story. 'He couldn't! He didn't!'

'He could. He did,' I reply, as we pass through the

grand west gate of the palace and turn in the direction of the stables.

'So what happened then?'

'Father summoned Chaplain Peters and a Justice of the Peace and they were married there and then. He's promised them £500 as a wedding present.'

'Good God. Chaplain White must have turned the colour of his name. And for Katherine to be married off like that.'

I laugh nervously then grimace, the strain of the morning spilling out of me in a jumble of emotions and noises. 'Oh Mary, it was awful! To see her future decided for her on a whim, because of my foolishness. Katherine went into that room a widow and came out of it a wife without the least notion that any such thing would happen. I don't know how I'll ever face her again.'

'Was she upset?'

'Well, no,' I concede, the thought cheering me a little. 'Actually, she seemed rather pleased with herself.'

'No!' Mary said again, eyes widening with each new revelation.

'She did! Of course she was shocked and dazed at first – we all were – but you have to admit that Jeremiah is handsome and very charming. She could do a lot worse.'

'Frances.' Mary's eyes narrow at me. 'You did not want him for yourself, did you?'

'Of course not,' I say quickly, but she holds my gaze until I know I must tell all. 'But I confess I found the feel of his hands on mine, the pretty words he spoke, rather thrilling. I could imagine how the same touch, the same words of another man might send my head spinning.'

Mary grins, her smile so like Father's; of all of us girls,

it is she who resembles him most closely in her features, yet also least in temperament. 'Well, we must find a way then to become better acquainted with the gentlemen at court.' She takes my arm and we walk some way lost in our own thoughts. The pungent smell of the stables drifts towards us on a strong breeze and we draw closer together against the chill, hurrying along the driveway and plunging with relief into the straw-bailed warmth of the stable block.

The stables are a riot of colour and noise as liveried grooms and footmen bustle about, fussing over the horses, cleaning tack and carriage parts. I see the master of this domain and our brother-in-law, Elizabeth's husband John Claypole, leaning over the farthest stall, in close conference with a groom, his dog Badger worrying at his boots. Another gentleman completes the group, standing with his back to us, dressed in a beautiful silk laced coat of deep evergreen.

'John!'

He turns towards us smiling, his dark curls springing around his rosy cheeks.

'Hello, girls,' John says brightly. 'Come to see the new mare?'

Mary pulls forward eagerly, her passion for horses an abiding love where mine, a brief childhood infatuation, has long since burned away. It is she who insists we visit each new addition to Father's stables.

'An Arabian!' Mary says, admiring the large grey tossing its head before us. 'From Africa? Fourteen hands by the look of her. Will Father breed her?'

'I should think so,' John answers. 'She's the best specimen yet. Though we need more like her and stallions too if your father is ever going to see the breed take root in England as he wishes; they're the best bloodstock for racing horses, he says.'

I catch up with Mary then and incline my head to acknowledge the gentleman in green who has bent his own low before me. When he sweeps up straight, shaking his tawny hair much as the horse does, I see that it is Robert Rich, the arrogant young courtier who danced with me at Lavinia's wedding and then laughed at my family behind my back. The wide smile that is always my instinct shrinks into a shallow, polite curve and I fold my arms across my body, gloved hands lost under my sapphire blue shawl.

'Lady Frances, I trust you are well.' Robert pours his copper-rich voice on me and I cannot help but hear a sharp, metallic edge.

'Perfectly well, thank you.' I return my gaze to Mary and John, indicating that we should listen to their conversation rather than have our own, though I find myself hearing instead the words Robert spoke about us at Lavinia's wedding even as I watch Mary and John's lips moving.

They talk a little more of the horse. How to acclimatise her to England's weather. Her feed, mixed oats with a little bran until she is settled. But then the arrival of a liveried messenger with a packet of letters from Westminster halts the discussion. John scans the handwriting of the small squares of paper before making his excuses.

'I'm sorry, girls, but I must attend to these at once. We've a fight on our hands if we're to defeat your Uncle Desborough's bill.'

I am listening now, the memories of Robert's insults

pushed aside by a subject more to my taste than oats and bran. 'A fight, John?' I ask.

'A battle.' He nods. 'Your uncle and the other Major-Generals who govern the country are short of funds and he is proposing to raise the taxes on royalists to plug the shortfall. If his Militia Bill passes, we'll be living under martial rule for years to come.'

'Poor Uncle,' Mary interrupts. 'He still mourns Aunt Jane; her death upset him greatly.'

I look at her fondly. Mary always brings the political back to the personal; always thinks of how people feel before she considers how they act. Indeed the recent death of Father's sister Jane Desborough had upset all of us. Not least Father who, as the only boy, never lost his feelings of responsibility for the women in his family even once most of them had married and left home. Still I struggle to summon much sympathy for my uncle John Desborough, always so stern and forbidding, with no time between God and his soldiers for his silly nieces.

John Claypole inclines his head. 'That may be, Mary, but it doesn't stop your uncle being wrong about this. We can't keep the army in power over us.'

'And this bill is your best chance of killing off the rule of the Major-Generals for good?' I say, remembering Elizabeth's words yesterday.

My favourite brother-in-law takes a moment to smile at me. 'You have the nub of it, Fanny, as always. We have the numbers in Parliament to block the bill but it will be tight. And so I must leave you. Girls,' he nods to us each in turn, winking as he does it, 'enjoy the mare. Though, Robert – see that my sisters-in-law don't take it upon themselves to ride her.'

Whistling to Badger, John hurries away and Robert chuckles with the air of a man of leisure content to watch the industry of others. He pats the mare's neck which now hangs steady over the edge of the box, her thick rubber lips exploring Mary's palm. 'She is lovely,' Robert says, smiling at Mary as I watch from a few feet away. Still patting the horse's neck, he glances over his shoulder at me. 'Are you tempted to a ride, Lady Frances? Will I have to restrain you as your brother-in-law commands me?'

'Frances takes little interest in horses.' Mary is teasing me.

'Oh really? And what is Lady Frances interested in?' Robert looks at me but I set my lips.

'My sister is a great scholar,' Mary says, her tone shifting from teasing to proud, 'with a fine knowledge of history and the classics. Though her love of books does not preclude an enjoyment of the outdoors,' she adds quickly, eager I can see to paint a rounded portrait. 'In the summer months she likes to read and walk in the gardens.'

Robert raises an eyebrow. 'Then she must take care not to fall. It is a particular hazard of walking while reading.'

Mary laughs at that. 'Not if you know these gardens as well as she does.'

'Of course.' He inclines his head to us both, allowing Mary the point.

'I hear that I am to congratulate you on the recent and very sudden marriage of your lady-in-waiting.' Robert drops his hand from the mare then and turns to face me fully.

I am amazed that he should have heard the news so quickly. He must be woven into the web of court gossip like a spinning spider. Though, I reflect, with a noble name but no offices to occupy him, he will have plenty of time on his hands for idle conversation.

'Indeed,' I reply. 'A most happy event.'

'Of course,' Robert says again and I wonder if this is what he says whenever he means precisely the opposite. 'I love weddings. Would that there were more at court like your cousin Lavinia's last year; a most spectacular affair.'

I bridle at his mention of that day, calling to mind our brief intimacy, but Mary seems not to notice.

'Wonderful, wasn't it? Though I'm sure my sister's would be every bit as fine.'

I curse her inwardly for walking into his trap.

'I do not doubt it,' Robert chuckles. 'And who is the fortunate gentleman to be?'

Mary colours at that, realising at last that we are straying into an intimate topic. I feel my blush rising too and though with anyone else I would bat my eyes and manoeuvre a way out of the conversation, Robert inflames me to haughtiness: 'I am yet to make my selection, sir. Though,' I add, 'I will be sure to inform you the moment that I do.'

He bows to me. 'Please do. And perhaps I can be of assistance to you in making that choice? If your candidates are the young gentlemen at court, you will find none who knows more of them each than I.'

'Oh really?' I scoff, hardly believing the brazenness of his words. 'You offer your advice to me on this most personal of subjects?'

'I can think of none better.'

'None better than an idle gossip,' I agree.

His shoulders shake with laughter at that, a wolfish grin spreading above his collar. 'None better than a young man well connected and popular at court, against whom you have – for some reason – formed an evident dislike and who would not, therefore, feature on your list of prospective suitors.'

I stare at him, shocked into silence while Mary laughs nervously as she glances between us. 'Come, Mary,' I say when the power of speech at last returns to me. 'Dusk approaches, we must return to the palace.'

I gather her to me and walk hastily away from Robert Rich, the low baritone of his chuckles following us.

'Consider my offer,' he calls after us as we hurry out of the stables, knocking into a mortified stable boy in our haste to reach the palace gate, looming now out of the twilight.

CHAPTER TWO

Returning from Hampton Court on Monday, we find Whitehall in a state of nervous tension. The conspirators languish in the Tower and, though we know Thurloe to be busy questioning them, few details of their plot leak out of the thick stone walls of the Norman fortress. I feel an increasing unease as I walk around the palace, the sense of security I had felt in our country refuge slipping from me as I round each corner. While the doubling of the guards at every door should reassure me, the sight of so many soldiers only heightens my anxiety.

Father, meanwhile, remains preoccupied with affairs of state – chiefly with the troublesome Militia Bill my uncle, Major-General Desborough, is trying to push through Parliament against the staunch opposition that John has marshalled. He has the unenviable task of keeping the peace around the Council table as Uncle Desborough, my brother-in-law Charles and the great Major-General Lambert rage against the civilian Councillors like the young moderate MP Nathaniel Fiennes, his fresh-faced brother-in-law Sir Charles Wolseley and the slippery Secretary Thurloe, who, they are sure, are all working quietly with Parliament against them. With each day, the conflict over Parliament's bill seems to assume a greater meaning and I sense from the chatter along the tables at dinner and the conversations I see snatched in doorways that we are in for a bumpy ride.

For us, there is nothing to do but wait, anxiously, for news. Thus it is a taut, fidgeting Cromwell family that Thurloe visits in our private rooms in Whitehall on 19 January.

Foretold of his intentions, we have assembled around the fire in the privy dining room. Mother and Mary sit either side of me, our voluminous skirts overlapping on the narrow couch. Opposite us, Elizabeth and John recline close together, splendid in the latest fashions which I can admire closely as, for once, no children, servants or horses circle around them. My oldest brother Dick and his wife Dorothy have also joined us, again without their brood, and now promenade along the room arm in arm, speaking in low voices. Even Bridget has come from the townhouse she shares with her second husband, Major-General and Councillor Charles Fleetwood, and their patchworked family of shared and step-children. The oldest sibling living, she takes up a commanding position in a high-backed chair, stern and serious in grey silk. Charles himself paces behind her, his military frame coiling and snapping with energy, his presence too big somehow for the room. My eyes are drawn to him in the same way they are to Father and I think once again how very similar they are – something which explains their intense friendship.

And so we are almost a complete set, all present and correct save for my brother Harry and his family who are, of course, living in great state in Ireland, which he effectively governs, having taken over the administration of that troubled and exhausted country from my brother-in-law Charles. I sigh, wishing beyond anything else that he were here too, and I resolve to write to him later – I have left his last letter unanswered for two weeks now.

At the appointed hour, Father enters, Thurloe slipping in behind him like a sharp summer shadow. Father takes a seat beside Elizabeth and, patting her hand reassuringly, motions for us all to hush so Thurloe can speak. Charles, Richard and Dorothy settle in their chairs.

'Your Highnesses.' Thurloe bobs a semicircle before us, his back to the fireplace, face dark against the glow. 'His Highness desires me to brief you all – together – on my findings into the late attempt on the palace before I make my report to Parliament later this afternoon. He is of the view, which I share, that this latest attempt on his life, occurring as it did within the palace, concerns you all and that you each have the right, therefore, to be fully informed.'

I find Thurloe's pattern of speech strangely soothing: so lawyerly and fluid, layering clause upon clause like pastry. The effect of his voice is that my breathing slows, despite the violence he speaks of. Dick, now seated, leans forward, elbows on his knees.

'This is what we know. The conspirators – we know of at least five – are disaffected Levellers; former soldiers for Parliament who want radical reforms to level society.' It is clear that he adds this description for the benefit of Mary and me, though we read enough of the newspapers to know who the Levellers are. I look at Bridget as she shifts uncomfortably in her seat, her narrow face with its wide-set eyes pink and pinched. I know that she, an army bride in her youth, has some secret sympathy for such men – will this latest outrage change her mind?

'These men wish Your Highness removed from office,' Thurloe goes on, 'and the Rump Parliament restored to its former power.'

He means the Parliament which sat all through the war, I think, the rump of whose purged members tried the old king, then sat on for four more years, refusing to disband and call free elections until Father forcibly dissolved the Parliament in '53.

'The conspirators planted a bomb in the chapel with the intention of destroying the whole palace by fire.'

Mary tenses and Mother puts her hand on her arm.

'But how did they get in?' Charles asks sharply, his dark blue eyes glaring at the secretary above his fine, high cheekbones.

Thurloe answers smoothly, unperturbed by Charles's tone. 'As you know, General, members of the public can enter the chapel at certain times of day and it seems, furthermore – and I regret to say this – that the group had some help from a member of His Highness's personal life guard.'

We all gasp at that.

'Who?' John and Charles are both on their feet now, competing almost for the higher personal outrage: Charles as one of the leading officers of the army, from whom the life guard are recruited; John as one of the principal heads of Father's household, to which the Life Guard belong. Though it is surely their commander, our cousin Lavinia's adoring husband Major Richard Beke, who will be held to account, I think as I watch them.

Thurloe pauses. 'I would prefer not to reveal his name for now as it was he who betrayed the conspiracy to us and I may have use for him yet.'

John and Charles look at Father but he merely nods, content as always to place his security entirely in Thurloe's hands. His silence unnerves me. Bridget takes Charles's hand and pulls him gently to sit back down beside her. 'So they have been planning this for some time, Master Thurloe?' she asks.

'In truth, Mrs Fleetwood, this outrage was planned in haste, which explains in part why my informants were not alerted to it. We had been tracking some members of the group for months and knew that there had been other attempts on your father's life.'

I watch tears trickle down Mary's cheeks; of all of us she is always the most fearful for Father's safety. Mother knows this too and I feel her stiffen beside me: she will yearn to comfort Mary but won't do so in front of Secretary Thurloe.

'God's blood.' It is Dick who curses and he leans back in his chair, his face glazed. 'What means have they tried?'

'Mostly the pistol, when they can get close enough. Though our precautions have not made it easy for them – His Highness's guard and the variations we make to all travel plans. It seems the closest they came to the Lord Protector was in Hyde Park some weeks ago, though, in that instance, it was your father himself who was the unwitting foil for their plans. One of the men was waiting his chance when His Highness, passing close by, noted the man's exceptional mount and actually called him over to compliment him on his horse, at which point the villain lost his nerve.'

Thurloe's words are swallowed in a thick silence for one moment, then two, before an eruption of deep-throated laughter brings all eyes to Father. 'Ha!' His whole body convulses as he shakes his head over and over the same two words: 'His horse!' He looks to John, hoping it seems to share the equine joke.

John's laughing eyes meet his. 'Well, you have always had a keen eye for the nags, Highness, I cannot deny it. Though I had never thought it would save your life!'

Mary giggles through her tears and I smile, though more with pleasure that the joke could not be better fitted to cheer her, than through any great merriment. A few others of the family chuckle nervously and we all breathe again, relieved at the temporary break in tension.

It is Charles whose stern voice brings the meeting back to order. 'These men, Thurloe. Who is their chief? Who are their backers?'

'Their commander, I regret to tell you, General, is Edward Sexby.'

'Sexby.' Father's face falls at the mention of his former friend. The man who had served in Father's own regiment of Ironsides during the late civil wars. The hero whom Father had chosen to take news of his great victory at Preston to Parliament. The mercenary whose debts of a thousand pounds were met by Parliament only on Father's intervention.

'I'm afraid so. Backed by Spanish gold, aided by exiled royalists – a more unholy alliance it is hard to imagine.'

Father looks ashen, all mirth about horses drained from his furrowed face. Betty places a ringed hand on his arm.

'You must not shrink from this, my dear,' Mother says, her voice gentle but firm. 'You must not let Sexby and the others cause you to doubt yourself or the good you do.'

Father smiles at her in thanks, though the smile does not reach his eyes. Every one of us in that room knows that Father's self-doubt runs to oceans, where most of ours fills only a garden pond. I have come to believe that this is the unwelcome companion to his closeness to God: the insecurity he feels in himself when he cannot fathom the Lord's intentions matched only by his blazing certainty when he can. Only in this way can the man who thundered onto the battlefield with God's breath in his lungs and strength in his sword be the same man who trembled with indecision each time Dick asked him to settle his gambling debts.

'But some good has come of this, Highness,' Thurloe says softly. 'We finally have the evidence we need to move against Sexby. And once we have done so I hope – I pray – that all of you will be a good deal safer.'

'There, Father,' Betty says, her voice cheering. 'Master Thurloe has words of comfort at the end. And perhaps more good may yet come of this once Parliament has been told all.'

Wordlessly, Father takes her hand from his arm and tucks it under his elbow, dropping his heavy head so his chin sinks onto his chest. I – and perhaps only I – see the glance of encouragement Betty then exchanges with her husband.

'Indeed, Highness,' John continues seamlessly. 'There are many in the House who would see the country placed on a firmer footing and believe making you king the best way to achieve lasting safety and stability. This latest danger may be the call to action they need to gather support for the idea. Do you not agree, Master Secretary?'

Thurloe spreads his hands in a gesture of practised ignorance, though something in the tilt of his head suggests quite the reverse. I watch him carefully but he gives nothing away.

'Nonsense,' Charles snaps before Father can answer. 'The best guarantor of the realm's safety is strong government by the Major-Generals, and it would be madness to withdraw the army from the localities just as our enemies rise against us.'

He rises from his chair as if to emphasise his point and paces purposefully but without aim around the room. As my gaze follows him, I cannot help thinking how loath Charles would be to lose the great power he has acquired as Major-General of the eastern counties: he governs a vast territory stretching from the outskirts of London up to the Wash and from Oxford across to Norwich. Even if, for the most part, he likes to keep to the corridors of power in Whitehall and leave subordinates to deputise in his place, still it is he who makes the key decisions and only Father can challenge his rulings.

'Besides, Father would never countenance such a thing.' Bridget's clipped voice brings me back to the room as she looks past Father to scowl at John and Elizabeth. 'This Protectorate is bad enough but to end the republic entirely is unthinkable.'

I cringe at her words, not on my own behalf so much as on Father's. No one speaks to challenge her; we all know that Bridget, schooled in the radical republican politics of the army as Henry Ireton's wife, struggles with our family's elevation. But always the love and affection Mother and Father bear for each of us in our differences allows her to speak her mind freely.

'Biddy speaks truly,' Charles says, striding back to his seat and brushing a speck of dirt from it before sitting. 'The army would never tolerate it.' He shakes his head firmly, the fair curls at his neck brushing back and forth over his high white collar. 'The Lord has passed judgement on the office of king and we would all do well to listen.'

I look from one sister and brother-in-law to the other and glimpse a fragment of the abiding conflict between the army and Parliament refracted before me like sunlight in a broken mirror. I lean towards Betty and John as I always do when I observe these arguments. I cannot help myself: I am so much closer to Betty. We are so similar, both accustomed to life as the youngest child, both so like Father whom we adore and draw towards, where Mary cleaves more naturally to Mother and Biddy sails her own enigmatic course. But this time I check myself, remembering that I should not believe the Claypoles' reasoning to be right simply because of my partiality; my tutors would hardly approve of such childish irrationality.

I wonder if Father shares my difficulty and turn to him, expecting him to speak honeyed words and smooth ruffled feathers. But he is lost in the forest of his own thoughts and that night, after I have written to Harry to tell him all we have learned of the plot, Mary and I pray to God, not for the first time, that he finds his way back through them.

I had thought little of Robert Rich since his impudence in the stables and so find myself caught unawares when he glides across to Mary and me towards the end of supper one evening a few weeks later. We are in the Great Hall of Whitehall Palace dining with the court, the rich aromas of roasted meat, cheese and wine rising from the long tables like steam from a hot bath, the sounds of laughter, chatter and the scraping of cutlery on pewter bubbling around us. It is a Thursday and so Father has gone, as he often does on this day, to dine with his officers at Somerset House where – I imagine – war stories, toasts to victories and tears for the fallen will cause him to drink more wine than he can hold.

In his absence, Mother is presiding at supper, the nerves she always feels when she does so visible only to me who knows so well what the finger she runs under the pearl necklace that sits beneath her smiles really means. Watching her now I have to pinch myself to remember that she is the same mother of my childhood, who used to make her own candles and darn our stockings before the fire to make ends meet.

This evening, by contrast, Mother is entertaining the French ambassador Monsieur Bordeaux while the rest of us deploy our charm on members of the Council of State. It is an uphill task, however, with the Council still bitterly divided between the army leaders and their civilian counterparts, the former smarting from yesterday's defeat of the Militia Bill in Parliament by one hundred and twenty-four votes to eighty-eight. Indeed, I notice that Uncle Desborough is not among his fellow Councillors but sits further off, directing the occasional glower at John for masterminding the downfall of his beloved bill. No doubt he wishes he had chosen to dine with the army instead.

My uncle is a carthorse of a man. A man built for

the outdoors, whether farm or army camp, who always seems uncomfortable at fine court occasions like this; too big and blustery for anything more luxurious than the fireside of a coaching inn. I am sorry to see him out of sorts but remind myself that there is no solace he would accept from me, being nothing to him but a chit of a girl.

John, in contrast, is in a buoyant mood, either oblivious or unconcerned at his wife's uncle's stares. In his gaiety, he fills my glass of wine far higher than either of my brothers would.

'Doesn't it bother you?' I ask him as I sip the claret, motioning with my glass down the table to Uncle Desborough, now attacking a wedge of game pie with his knife.

'I believe in being cheerful while I can,' John replies, his words muffled as he chews. 'Mark me, there'll be worse to come. This is but a skirmish – the prelude to a proper battle. Wait until we have drafted the new constitution, then there'll be blood on the field.'

There is to be music after supper and it is in the movement and rearrangement of people and the scrape of chairs that always precedes this that Robert Rich approaches us with lively dancing steps. He is dressed this evening in a pale blue suit, his choice of soft buckled shoes rather than riding boots marking him out as a young man of fashion reacting against the warlike garb of his elders. A tall young man with brilliant fair hair and an upright bearing hovers at his side. I recognise him as Anthony Underwood, one of the gentlemen of Father's bedchamber – his closest attendants.

'Ladies.' Robert bows low with his customary courtly

swagger that, to me, betokens amused irony as much as deference. 'May Mr Underwood and I join you?'

'Sirs,' Mary says, her encouraging smile a mirror image of my own insincere expression. 'A pleasure.'

'The pleasure and the honour is mine, Lady Mary, Lady Frances,' Anthony Underwood says in the soft burr of the West Country.

He is a handsome man and I cannot help but sit a little straighter in my blue silk, congratulating myself for whatever foresight led me to choose one of my finest dresses that evening; conscious too of its low lace-trimmed neckline showing me to my best advantage as the men stand before us. I catch Robert's eye and pray that he has no gift for reading my thoughts; it is embarrassing enough to have him attempt to match-make for me. Worse than embarrassing, I decide as I return his look; infuriating. I wish to meet young men on my own terms and substituting Robert Rich for my parents as a marriage negotiator hardly helps me do this.

'You are off duty, Mr Underwood, with my father at Somerset House?' I ask, ignoring Robert and turning my attention to his companion as the two men sit on the bench opposite us.

'I am, my Lady. I welcome the respite, though of course,' he adds quickly, 'I am most fortunate to be so much in His Highness's company.'

I smile at this, always pleased to hear Father appreciated.

'It must be a demanding post though, Anthony, however prestigious,' Robert says, leaning back in an attitude of languor. 'Whatever my respect for your father, my ladies, I'm not sure I would care to spend so much of the day running his errands, dressing and undressing him and attending him on the close stool.'

Anthony Underwood colours at this but an awkward smile draws my eye from his reddened cheeks. 'I assure you it is nothing but a pleasure to attend on such a great man. He knows how to inspire loyalty.'

'And has a keen eye for spotting talent,' I add, turning my pointed gaze on Robert. 'Perhaps we should recommend you for such a post, sir, so that you might understand the honour fully for yourself.'

'Haha!' Robert laughs. 'It is generous of you to seek to further my career, my lady, but I prefer the freedom to come and go from court as I please. And besides, I should miss the time I can spend at my books. Your duties will not leave you much time for reading, eh, Anthony?'

'Indeed not,' he replies.

I narrow my eyes at Robert, now examining me closely over his cup of wine. His reputation as a gambler and lover of fine living is an established one; I very much doubt he spends his days in the library. 'Ah, the joy of reading.' I give an elaborately happy sigh. 'You will have read Harrington's *Oceana* then, sir, now that my sister Elizabeth has prevailed upon Father to sanction its publication. I myself find much to agree with in Harrington's admiration for the political institutions and wisdom of the ancient Greeks and Romans. What is your view?'

He won't have read it. My gauntlet thrown down, I wait for Robert's answer, the silent seconds that spread between us more delicious to me than the sweetmeats the servants are now laying before us. He leans backwards, the pewter cup swilling in his hand, and I imagine his thoughts scampering after an answer like hounds after a hare.

'I too admire our ancient forebears,' he begins slowly, 'but we must also avoid their mistakes. Harrington cautions against the private interests of men, does he not? It is a government of *laws* not of men that he advocates.'

Anthony Underwood shifts in his seat and I pause, caught halfway between annoyance and pleasure at Robert's confounding my expectation, before addressing the real subject of his remarks: my father.

'True. Though it is warring factions of men that I take to be his chief concern.' I gesture around the Great Hall, assuming him astute enough to take my meaning. As if on cue, Uncle Desborough rises from his seat and barges from the room, knocking into a knot of courtiers gathered about Secretary Thurloe and John Claypole on his way to the doors. Instinctively I look to Father's chair before remembering that he is not here and I am instantly aware, as never before, of the delicate balance of men that Father alone holds together by the sheer power of his presence and his diplomatic skill. I turn back to Robert: 'Harrington acknowledges the need for lawgiving sovereigns to check these conflicts – if they themselves are constrained by an effective constitution, of course.'

Robert smiles. 'An effective constitution, you say? A subject you'll find on every pair of lips at our court at present. But remember the Romans thought their constitution the pinnacle of man's achievements; they imagined they had designed it to withstand and defeat the over-mighty and ambitious. And yet the republic barely survived Sulla and it could not survive Caesar.'

I bridle at this and drop all pretence that we are discussing the ancient world and not our own. 'Whatever my father is, sir, he is no Caesar.'

'Oh listen, Frances, the music is starting.' Mary places a hand on my arm and attempts to direct my attention to the group of viol players whose first twinning and weaving string notes thread towards us. I am aware of Mr Underwood's awkwardness, as he has watched my exchange with Robert as a helpless spectator at a card game, but though I know I should make some effort to include him in the conversation I am too set on having the last word with my adversary.

Keeping my eyes on Robert, I drop my voice to a stage whisper as I lean across the table angrily: 'Caesar, Sulla, Augustus. They were men who lusted after their own glory. Men of conquest seeking power, not men of God seeking peace.'

'Of course.' Robert inclines his head, a smile tugging at the corners of his mouth as he reclines languidly, refusing to meet my anger with his own. Despite the two concluding words through which he delivers his familiar note of gracious superiority, I sense for the first time a hint of admiration.

Our duel concluded, I mean to lean back in my chair, determined to lose myself in the music, but Robert is not quite finished with me.

'You are wise to search for wisdom in the past, my lady,' he whispers, leaning across the table to meet me so that our faces almost touch beneath the candles: his smiling and mine simmering back. 'We have much to learn from the classical world. The search for *eudaimonia* for instance – the well-being and happiness that comes from realising one's true nature.'

'And what is your true nature?' I fire back instantly, unsettled by his intimate tone.

'Ah.' Robert chuckles, something in his auburn hair and self-satisfied smile putting me in mind of Aesop's fox when it has flattered the unsuspecting crow into dropping its cheese. 'That you must discover for yourself.'

At the end of the week we return to Hampton Court in time to take advantage of a spell of unseasonably warm weather. I sense a slight relaxation in the court but it feels temporary, as if the factions in the late dispute over the Militia Bill have withdrawn into their respective camps to draw up their battle plans. But still it does everyone good to come away from the nervous intensity of Whitehall and when, over supper in our private apartments, Elizabeth tells the family that she is with child once more, the happy news is a further tonic to us all. Despite my many nieces and nephews, I still find these announcements embarrassing, the unfamiliar acts of love that they conjure in my mind's eye irreconcilable with the siblings and spouses who sit so sedately around the dining table.

Happily I am distracted by Father who leaps to his feet to dispense kisses, clasps and handshakes; his guise as doting grandfather and paterfamilias fitting so snugly with his role as father to the nation. Keen to find more beneficiaries for his largesse, Father sends servants to summon his closest friends to smoke a celebratory pipe and compose verses with him and John after supper – Mary and I can still hear their lusty attempts as we ready ourselves for bed later that night and we add Master Hingston to our list of prayers, hoping the music master is fast asleep and unable to hear the tuneless din.

Despite his late-night revels, the next morning Father rides out early to hunt, John and Dick too along with Robert and a number of the gentlemen of the court. It is such a fine, clear morning, the snowdrops under the great beech trees heavy with dew, that Mary and I ride with them; our custom on such occasions is to ride around the edge of the great park while the men hunt the deer across it and rejoin them at the end of the sport for a glass of Rhenish wine.

Although I am no fine horsewoman like Mary, I enjoy the ride, the watery February sunshine warming my skin and sparkling on the river that bends wide around the park, a light breeze skimming my horse's mane as I sift my gloved fingers through her coarse hair. Time passes quickly with the whole park to gaze upon and Mary and our ladies-in-waiting for company. I catch up on gossip with my beautiful cousin Lavinia, before talking idly with Katherine, whose glowing cheeks and sprightly rising trot reassure me that her sudden marriage to Chaplain White has not been altogether displeasing to her. When, later that morning, we see the hunters regroup and turn back to the palace we cut across the park to join them. Seeing us, Robert breaks away from the pack and brings his grey horse into step beside mine. I glance across at him and see the breeze whisking his hair as it curls beneath his feathered hat, the tawny tips flashing red-gold in the sunshine.

'You ride well, Lady Frances, despite your indifference to horses. Did you learn on your father's farm?'

I pull the reins a little tighter as his words bite into me like midges. I don't know why he must always cut me down to size; why any compliment needs to be delivered with his back hand. Robert Rich may be of a noble house but his grandfather, the powerful Earl of Warwick, commanded the navy on Parliament's side in the war and fought beside Father, who counts him a firm friend. If the earl can adjust to our exalted status, I don't see why his wayward young grandson can't do the same. But I will not rise to his bait, nor challenge the satire of our impoverished origins among the yeomanry he so obviously enjoys.

'Oh yes.' I keep my voice light, dancing over the words. 'We girls had to work in the fields and forage for food when we were but a few years old, else we did not eat. We are but a family of East Anglian farmers, as I have heard you say before.' It is an exaggeration of course: even in the family's leanest years when Father had sunk from the ranks of the gentlemen to the status of a tenant farmer, there was always food on the table. And our luck turned for good before Mary and I were born. But I never risk giving the impression that I am inflating my upbringing; far better to own our story and to be proud of it in the way Father does.

He has no answer to me and we ride the final yards towards the palace in silence. 'What did you make of Anthony Underwood?' Robert tries a new subject on for size. 'A fine fellow, nobly bred, though not bookish enough for you perhaps. Never mind.' He smiles reassuringly as he scans the flushed and windswept riders who mass and weave before us like the shoals of tench that swell the fen rivers around Ely. He gestures to Nicholas

Baxter, a Gentleman of the Horse and John's deputy in the stables, who has dismounted and is directing the grooms and pages who filter between the steaming flanks of the horses, taking reins and helping the less nimble to dismount. 'What about Nicholas? He's a good horseman and a devil at billiards. Nick!' Robert calls out to him. 'Come and help Their Highnesses dismount, would you?'

Nicholas strides towards us, long-limbed, his cheeks ruddy from the exercise, a streak of mud on his forehead underneath wisps of red hair. He helps Mary down first, as the elder, and then does the same for me, catching my waist in his broad hands as I slip from the saddle. I thrill at the brief feeling of his strength and push my hair out of my eyes, sweeping a stray ringlet behind my ear. I see Mary watching us in the corner of my vision and wonder, in a rush of excitement laced with concern, if this is a man we might both admire. A servant hands me a glass of wine and I gulp it quickly.

'Highness.' Nicholas smiles at me before bowing and hastening off to some other duty.

'Aha. More success here, I believe,' Robert whispers, leaning down so close to me that the feathers at the back of his hat tickle my shoulder. 'Though, on second thoughts, Nick may be a bit too wedded to his horses for your liking. Perhaps he may suit your sister better.'

I flinch, turning my shoulder away from him and looking around for Father.

Laughing, Robert bows his leave. 'I will see who else I can throw into your path at next week's entertainment for Parliament.'

'If such sport pleases you, sir,' I say without looking at him. 'Though I would not wish to take any of your valuable time away from your studies.' Catching Father's eye, I push my way towards him, longing suddenly for his warm, straightforward company above all others.

The entertainment planned for Parliament is indeed an exciting prospect. It has become Father's custom, whenever Parliament is sitting, to invite all its members to dine with the court in the Banqueting House once or twice in each session. These occasions are sumptuous and Father has instructed his Master of Ceremonies, his cousin Sir Oliver Flemyng, to spare no expense this time. Four hundred dishes of meat are planned and all of the court suppliers – the brewers, butchers and fishmongers, purveyors of wine and spices – have been stretched to meet our orders. The palace kitchens, cellars and slaughterhouse are a hive of aproned activity. Above stairs, Master Hingston has composed some new pieces which he has been rehearsing with his musicians, and a number of additional performers have been hired from the City for the occasion. Finally, of most excitement to us, the court tailor Mr Hornlock has made new dresses for Mother, Elizabeth, Mary and me, though Bridget declined his offer.

My gown is cut in the latest Spanish fashion with sleeves so full and bunched I can barely see my arms within them. I feel with pleasure the eyes of the other young women at court follow me as I move around the Banqueting House, the ceiling painted with Master Rubens' great adulation of the old Stuart King James soaring noisily over my head in a riot of jewel colours framed with shining gold. We are all dressed finely this evening but I fancy the oyster-pink shade of my dress has the edge over Betty's mint green and Mary's sapphire blue; and I feel a sudden and almost frightening confidence, as if my whole body is charged and primed like a musket.

In stark contrast to our joyful surroundings, all talk is of the trial of the Whitehall assassin, the Leveller Miles Sindercome, which took place a few days ago in Westminster Hall and every moment of which has been related with relish in the newsbooks. Speaking of this while standing in the Banqueting House, I cannot help my mind slipping back to the scenes I have imagined of another trial that took place beneath the ancient hammer-beamed ceiling of Westminster Hall – that of the tyrant King Charles and of his execution on a scaffold just outside this very room; Rubens' celebration of his father's divine right to rule and ascension to heaven almost the last thing the traitor king saw on this earth.

'But to be hanged, drawn and quartered.'

Mary's visceral words bring me back to the present. 'It is horrible, barbaric.'

I shiver at the thought, picturing the man writhing and screaming as he is dragged to Tyburn on the hurdle, the instruments of his torturous death shown to him as he is strung up on the gibbet. However much I hate Sindercome for the violent deaths he imagined for us when he planted his gunpowder in the palace chapel, I cannot help wishing his own were more peaceful, his life snuffed out quietly like a candle.

'But that is the way it must be, Mary,' Dick says, his voice placid. 'Rich, don't you agree?'

Robert Rich, passing close by us with an entourage of younger Members of Parliament, pauses. 'Highness?'

'Sindercome.' Dick sips his wine. 'He must have a traitor's death. My young sisters would prefer him to live a quiet life of retirement here at the palace.'

I shoot him the exasperated look that only an older brother can provoke, though I know his jesting masks real concern for us.

'He must indeed, Your Highness. It is a horrible thing to contemplate, ladies,' Robert says, turning to us. 'But I'm afraid it must be so; it is the only way to ensure your continued safety.'

His gaze rests on me, his expression set in such a serious cast it occurs to me that these are the first words I have heard him utter plainly, loosed straight as an arrow.

'Well said.' Dick grins at him. 'But come, Rich, I must tell you of this horse race I'm sponsoring in Winchester. I've given thirty pounds for the winner. It'll be fine sport – the first to be had now the ban has lapsed. You must come down and watch it with me. I've heard talk of a fine gelding due to run . . .'

The talk is lost in horses then and I in turn lose all interest in it.

The feast itself is magnificent and, sitting between Mary and Dick, I thrill to look up and down the long tables at so many active and powerful men gathered together, the government of the nation their meat and drink. We eat course after course as the wine flows and I find my stays growing uncomfortably tight as the evening wears on. But it is too hard to resist the extraordinary dishes placed before me: there are pies and pastries, poached salmon and potted shrimp, roast chickens dripping with fat and great haunches of beef and mutton on beds of steaming vegetables. There is goat's cheese, sheep's cheese, candied fruits and walnuts, lemon ices, apple jelly and a new delicacy called gingerbread which leaves a fine dusting of sparkling sugar across my fingertips and a warm fuzz on my tongue. But the crowning centrepiece of the banquet is a large fruit, shaped and scaled like a pinecone, presented to Father on a silver platter as the first ever brought to England from the New World. He is delighted at the novelty and sends it up and down the tables for us all to admire before it is cut. I am one of the lucky few he gifts a precious sliver and I savour the exotic taste of the sweet, tart flesh.

The effect of the hundreds of candles, banked along the colonnaded walls of the Banqueting House in mighty sconces, is overpowering. Massed in this way they give off a powerful heat against the winter night and when finally the meal ends and Father rises from his chair in search of amusement, I follow suit, moving over to one of the great latticed windows to cool myself. I try to peer outside into the evening bustle of White Hall Street, but the candlelight is so strong that the fog-fringed glass simply mirrors the swirling dresses and colourful suits of the courtiers behind me as they shimmer among the flames like butterflies and fireflies in a jar.

I only have a few moments to myself before I feel a light hand on my bare shoulder and cannot but smile at a familiar, lilting voice.

'Principessa.'

It is Signor Giavarina, the resident ambassador from Venice.

'Ambassador, you know you mustn't call me that,' I smile, always pleased at the company of the dark, courtly Italian.

'And why not, my dear? As a proud republican I have made a particular study of the monarchs and courts of Europe in my travels. And none is quite so regal, so divinely monarchical as your dear father, despite his best efforts at the contrary.'

I chuckle at that. 'Come now, Ambassador, you tease me. I am no more a princess than the King of Spain is and besides,' I lower my voice conspiratorially, 'you will be well enough informed to know our royal or non-royal status to be a delicate subject at court at present.'

Giavarina laughs and raises an eyebrow. 'I do enjoy these events. They are the only times I ever set eyes on "King" Oliver, thanks to his guard dog the "little secretary" Signor Thurloe but I can also enjoy the company of his delightful daughters. And the youngest, naturally, is the most delightful and, I might add, the most astute.'

I am pleased with this compliment though try not to show it too much. 'Do I infer that you still have had no audience with my father, Ambassador?'

'Not since our last meeting, when he promised assistance in our war with the Turks. It was unfortunate that I have suffered some illness myself precluding my further attendance, but nor have I received anything in writing. It is your father's most regal attribute to reserve issues of foreign affairs for himself and Signor Thurloe, and to make promises he will never keep. It is a gentle, regal hypocrisy, seen in every royal court in Europe.'

'Ambassador,' I say quickly, embarrassed at Father's neglect, 'if my father promised assistance in your war, I'm sure . . .'

'*Bella Francesca*,' Giavarina chuckles at me, his dark eyes dancing as he leads me over to a quieter corner.

'How little you know of my world. Why would your father sacrifice his dear, fine English soldiers to the gaping jaws of the Turk? How dearly our republic would appreciate his assistance but I am under no illusions. See how I wander the banquet alone? Look with me.' Giavarina guides my vision around the room where the MPs and courtiers attempt to stroll off their supper, mingling, forming knots and breaking out of them in a swirl of copper-coloured candlelight.

'See your brother-in-law General Fleetwood at the window, talking with his ally, the French ambassador Bordeaux. And there, look: Signor Thurloe sits with our friends from the Swedish embassy, telling them no doubt of his great plans for a league of Protestant nations. They each speak where their sympathies lie. General Fleetwood,' he nods again at Charles, 'who believes in this alliance with France so many years in the making. England and France allied! Such a thing . . . And there General John Lambert, your latter-day "Hammer of the Scots".'

Giavarina takes my eyes now to the tall, spare figure of Lambert, who is stalking alone around the edge of the room as if he is patrolling one of his encampments. 'Lambert, who hates France and would ally with Spain. And all the while England makes enemies of its most natural allies in the Dutch Republic and Denmark, all in the name of protecting its precious trade in the Baltic. Is it any wonder that your father will not discuss foreign affairs in public at court, or that he will not entertain me? His Council is so riven with disagreement. It is the Lord Protector who must achieve the daily feat of keeping them together and, through them, keep the army and your Parliament from coming to blows. But there are more storms to come, mark my words. It takes an outsider at the court to see it.'

Beside us a curl of smoke spirals from a guttering candle before a liveried footman pounces to replace it, hot wax splashing onto his white gloves. I catch the first discordant notes of the orchestra tuning their instruments on the dais at the far end of the hall.

'You do not think much of the Council members, Ambassador?' I ask quietly, leaning close to him so he catches my words. I am so used to hearing these great men praised to the skies: tales of Major-General Lambert – second only to Father in power and popularity – and his brilliant conquest of Scotland; stories of Charles's ruthless ruling of Ireland; and accounts of Lord Commissioner Nathaniel Fiennes's efforts at negotiating a peace with the king. It is refreshing, if unnerving, to listen to the ambassador's frank views.

Giavarina tuts into his wine cup. 'Not one of these men is a true diplomat, not one understands the subtlety of our craft. Not one understands where England could place itself in the world if it chose to.'

'And is that not then the role of my father?'

'Exactly, my dear. The role of a king – though I know this too is the cause of great disagreement within your government. Your father tried to mediate between the Council factions several years ago, with that pitiful compromise fighting Spain in the Caribbean. The Western . . . I forget.'

'Design. The Western Design,' I answer.

'Precisely.' He gives me a little bow. 'And now, after many lives lost, England clings on by her fingertips to some small godforsaken diseased island called Jamaica which the Spanish will doubtless retake at any moment. Foreign affairs require leadership and the making of decisions. And I hope soon that your father will begin to make them – for England's sake, not mine, you understand. You truly will be a *principessa* when that happens.'

And what if I become a princess in name as well, I wonder, as I search the Italian's bronze face for further wisdom. What would this mean for my freedom?

'Signor Giavarina.' The wine-soaked voice of Bulstrode Whitelocke slides over us as he approaches on light, prancing feet. 'My friend, you must cease boring the most beautiful woman in the room with your chatter. Highness.' He bows and grins at me.

Giavarina smiles at him. Bulstrode Whitelocke – lawyer, MP, Commissioner of the Great Seal and Father's great friend – was once an ambassador himself, representing Father at the court of Christina, the former Queen of Sweden. Because of this, I know Giavarina has more respect for him than most of the politicians of our court. I myself am pleased to see my friend Bulstrode who, though he has known me since I was a child, has never treated me as one; we have long had the measure of each other.

'I was merely restating that Christendom itself must be defended,' Giavarina answers Bulstrode smoothly, without missing a beat. 'Venice cannot be expected to keep the borders of Europe secure on her own. The Turks' new Grand Vizier is giving them renewed fire and I do not see how we can hold the Dardanelles against them; it's only a matter of time before the Ottomans will look to Greece, Austria and then who knows. And, for myself, I do not have the funds to wait at this court for many months more. His Highness must decide soon.'

His voice is smooth and congenial though his eyes darken under the hat which only he and the other ambassadors in the room are permitted to wear in Father's presence: a symbol that they represent his only equals, the other heads of state.

'I will speak again with His Highness and Secretary Thurloe, my friend,' Bulstrode reassures him, his own uncovered head thick with waves of black hair that sway gently as he beckons to a servant to fill up Giavarina's glass.

Keen to help smooth the conversation, I ask Bulstrode about Queen Christina, famed for her learning and love of the arts. Long a heroine of mine, Christina abdicated the Swedish throne and now travels around Europe collecting artists in what seems to me an impossibly glamorous fashion.

'Did the queen really refuse to marry?' I ask. 'Give up her throne rather than be forced to marry where she did not wish to?'

Bulstrode smiles, his unusual coal-black eyes dancing in a face I cannot help thinking rather too small for his large features. I know well his love of gossip, flirtation and the chance to tell a witty anecdote.

'Do you know, Highness, I heard Her Majesty say once that it takes greater courage to marry than to go to war.'

I laugh at that before sinking into more sober thoughts as I contemplate the campaign that lies before me. 'Did she really? She thought women as brave as men?'

'Indeed.' Bulstrode strokes his narrow beard, thumb and index finger meeting at the point. 'Though I liked to think her admiration extended to bridegrooms too as then my three marriages rendered me especially brave in her sight.'

He grins at his joke and waits for our laughter to trickle away before dropping his voice to a conspiratorial whisper. Signor Giavarina and I lean towards him.

'When I told Her Majesty I had had three wives,' Bulstrode continues, 'she asked me if I had had children by each. Then when I answered in the affirmative, do you know what she said to me? *"Pardieu, vous êtes incorrigible!"*'

We laugh heartily at this, Signor Giavarina too, his crusading warships momentarily forgotten. Flushed with my conversational success I look around, hoping to catch Mary's eye, or those of my parents, but the only gaze I meet is that of Robert Rich, who smiles and raises his glass to me from across the room.

Robert comes to find me later after the concert of entertainment has finished, while I am still basking in the music. Master Hingston's new compositions were sublime and every piece on the mixed programme – from the choral to the instrumental – held the vast room and its hundreds of listeners spellbound. Father was particularly delighted and his beams of pleasure, cheers and claps led the audience in its reactions. Of all the performances, it was that of the two boy trebles of the court that stirred me most, their voices calling out from the dais and swirling around the columns of the room like a pair of nightingales singing in a silent wood.

'We must ask Master Hingston if we can learn that piece,' I say to Mary as we sit with Dick's wife Dorothy, eating lavender cakes in a pool of evening candlelight.

'I would dearly love to hear that, Your Highnesses.' Robert bows before us, flanked by some of the young Members of Parliament I saw him with earlier. They all look flushed with wine. I have no words to answer his, always caught off-guard by the courtesy Robert shows to me when others can hear.

Robert introduces his parliamentary colleagues and a conversation about the entertainment strikes up. I open my mouth to contribute but find Robert lowering himself into a chair on my other side, forcing me to turn away from the others as he speaks to me alone.

'I have brought you some more potential suitors,' he winks, nodding at the MPs now thronging around Mary and Dorothy. 'Just tell me if you like the look of one of them and I'll engineer a private conversation.'

I look at him coldly and he smiles back, helping himself to a cake. 'Very well, Highness, I will confine myself to more polite topics of conversation. I think it is delightful that you and your sister should so enjoy your singing lessons. It is a charming way for young ladies to pass their time.'

'But not young gentlemen?' I ask, drawn as always into our discordant duet.

'Oh no. Frightful waste of time, music. I have little interest in it.'

I gape in horror. 'You cannot mean it! How could anyone dismiss one of the finest pleasures known to man or woman? My father would cast you from court for such heresy.'

He tilts his head to one side, a cheekbone catching the light from the great sconce beside us, his auburn hair glinting. 'Well, I will admit that Hingston has a fine ear, even if I do not. The harmony produced by the countermelody of the first piece was exquisite and, in the last, the way the line of the bass viols mirrored that of the second treble voice quite transported me.'

I tut in irritation at his games. 'You are confounding, sir. Do you delight in appropriating and professing opinions which you clearly do not hold?'

Robert grins. 'A gentleman must have some occupation.'

'At last!' I exclaim. 'Something on which we can both agree. And pray, tell me, what is your occupation to be? Besides drinking, playing billiards and posturing. I was raised among busy, industrious men – men who believed that honest, arduous work is the greatest way to honour God.'

I think of Father always toiling, thinking, planning. And of Harry learning at his elbow. Even Dick, for all his love of hunting and horse racing, was no shirker of hard work when it was allocated to him. What could this spoilt brat with his smooth hands and aristocratic vowels understand about work and responsibility?

'Oh, it hardly matters,' Robert laughs, though I catch the effort with which he attempts his casual tone. His levity angers me. I imagine life has always been a game for him, while every day of mine has felt precarious; we Cromwells know we could lose everything in a second.

'You are right,' I smile. 'It hardly matters what you choose to do with your life when every option under heaven is laid at your feet.' It is my turn to draw him out now.

'Every option?' He sits forward, looking at me intently. 'You mean the ceremonial offices of a courtier where I run errands and process through the palaces in brocade?

Or a seat in Parliament where I can sleep the afternoons away? Perhaps I should join the navy and sail off to the West Indies to join our General-at-Sea Robert Blake in harrying the Spanish treasure ships. I hear they're seeking another new governor for Jamaica – I could die of plague like the last one. Or a commission in the army where I am forced to listen every day to the heroic war stories of the radical old veterans I would have to command?'

'Ah.' At last I think I begin to understand him – to discover his true nature as he challenged me to. 'We come to the root of it. It is jealousy that you must overcome, not indolence.'

His mouth twitches. 'Do enlighten me.'

I look down at the satin pink of my lap and twist the pearl bracelet at my wrist, steeling myself to speak my true understanding, as my father would do. 'You are jealous of the extraordinary times that have just passed. Our fathers' generation turned the world upside down, proved themselves on bloody battlefields, spoke, fought and died for their principles. You are sick of listening to men only a few years older than you talk of "their war". You feel shut out of it; that anything you achieve, now you have come of age in peacetime, will pale by comparison. And that being so, you would rather not bother.'

Robert stares at me, all his former composure gone.

'You speak harshly, my lady,' he says at last, after taking a gulp of wine. 'But the very fact that you imagine such feelings for me suggests you have some sympathy for them.'

'Sympathy?' I smile in my amazement. 'How you can

imagine that as a woman I could feel sympathy for any man at the lack of opportunities open to him is astonishing. Please tell me, sir, what chances I am likely to have to prove myself worthy of my father? Besides marrying a man of his choice, bearing children and passing my time with music and other hobbies you have identified as charming occupations for ladies though you count them a waste of your own time. Whereas you,' I look at him, resplendent in a suit of red velvet, silk ribbons at his knees, perhaps only seeing him fully for the first time, 'you can do whatever you wish with your life. What I wouldn't give to be in your buckled shoes: a young nobleman with my life before me. Bright and vital. Vivid. Handsome, some might say. Clever – though you pretend otherwise. Charming, when you choose to be. Sympathy? No, sir, I have none for you.'

I stop, my mouth hanging open at the rashness of what I have said. I do not believe I have ever spoken to anyone besides my sisters in this way, my thoughts forming free and uncensored into words which pour from me without check. My heart races with a nervous excitement. I glance at Robert and see I have unsettled him. He smiles at me politely but I can see his mind working feverishly, weighing and storing my words so closely that he has no spare capacity for speech. We sit in silence for a minute, the room buzzing about us oblivious to our confessional.

'So you too wish to rebel,' Robert says at length, his voice much quieter now. 'But how do we rebel against our parents when they rebelled against the world? If they who were the rebels are now the rulers, where does that leave us? The old rules don't apply to us, yet we know not what the new rules are.'

I move his words around in my head like pieces of patchwork. He is right: how does our generation find a way to measure up to the previous one? What is left for us to achieve? Gradually the patchwork pieces settle and knit together in an answering pattern.

'We don't rebel against our parents,' I begin slowly, as if I am carving each word from stone. 'We take up their beliefs like a battle standard and advance them further even than they could have imagined. We take their victories for liberty and apply them to our own lives. The freedom to find fulfilment. The freedom to shape our futures. The freedom to choose whom we love.' I think of Queen Christina choosing a life of her own outside marriage and of Katherine having no choice but to marry a man she had probably never spoken to on a whim of my father's.

'I cannot remember life before the war,' I go on, 'but my sister Bridget tells me that the war changed the lot of women: took them out of their kitchens and parlours and onto their battlements, into the printing houses and onto the streets around Parliament. This is a new age for women and I want my part of it.' I pause, taken aback by the clarity of my thoughts and, even more so, by the fact that it is Robert Rich who has drawn them from me.

He smiles at me then. A broad, honest smile, not the smirk that usually curls his lips. 'You are most enlightening, Lady Frances. I must confess to scant knowledge of modern women and how they think about such issues.'

His playfulness has returned and so I reach for mine in answer.

'You do not discuss the views of modern women with your lady friends?' I ask, my allusion to his dissolute lifestyle as pointed as a rapier.

'Ha ha!' Robert laughs as his wine-flushed cheeks deepen in colour. 'My *lady* friends, as you call them, concern themselves solely with the contents of my . . . purse.'

It is my turn to blush at that. 'And you do not discuss such things with the women in your family?' I ask quickly, keen to cover my embarrassment.

The smile fades from his handsome face. 'No, I do not. My mother died when I was four. I only have a few, fleeting memories of her. Her smell, like woodland violets after a rain shower. A curl of her blonde hair dangling above me in the morning light. A sea shanty she used to sing to me.' Robert is lost in thought for a moment before he pulls himself back, continuing quickly in a matter-of-fact tone: 'And my stepmother takes as little interest in me as my father does. I have two half-sisters who I am fond of, but they are only little girls.'

I feel a rush of sadness for him, a sickness swelling within me at the thought of life without my own mother or sisters. I am struggling to find a reply adequate to his revelation, when Elizabeth appears before us, prompting Robert to spring to his feet and offer her his chair. She smiles at him gratefully, her swelling stomach just visible under the generous cut of Master Hornlock's new dress now that she is in her fifth month of pregnancy. Without a word, Robert bows to us both and melts away into the crowd. As his crimson back disappears into a sea of candlelit colours that seems to reflect Rubens' swirling heavens themselves, I lean back in my chair, my mind scrabbling to make sense of what has passed between us.

*

That night, while the court sleeps off the excitement of the day and the last revellers finally fall into their wine-cushioned beds in the early hours of the night, somewhere deep in the bowels of the Tower, Miles Sindercome kills himself with poison reportedly brought to him by his sister. I wake to the grim news, my own head sore with the poisonous effects of wine, and yet it gladdens my heart to think that he has escaped the worst of all possible deaths on the scaffold. Mary is even more forgiving; that night she adds Sindercome to our prayers. 'He had a soul too,' she says when I protest.

A week later, Father's deliverance from danger is celebrated across all three nations with a day of national thanksgiving: apprentices are excused work, servants sent home to their families and the taverns run dry of ale. I give thanks again for my family's safety and pray fervently that we shall face no more danger. And I am not alone in my unease: the celebrations cannot prevent the continued hysteria in certain quarters of the press nor smooth the furrow between Secretary Thurloe's brows. Other plotters – Sexby chief among them – remain at large, aided by our royalist enemies. Worst still, the papers claim Spanish and Irish troops are being mustered in Flanders ready to sail for England with the 'king' in exile, young Charles Stuart, at the head of the fleet. Thurloe sends letters out to every militia up and down the three nations placing them on the highest security alert; Father and the Council sit late into each night; and the country holds its breath.

CHAPTER THREE

I am quite happy to be distracted from these anxieties by a more pleasant thought: I am certain that Mary has taken a shine to Nicholas Baxter, Father's Gentleman of the Horse. I catch them speaking outside the chapel at Hampton Court after the Lord's Day service and again the next day when he sees us into our carriage for the return journey to Whitehall. Each time, she rises up on her toes a little as they speak, her dark head a fraction closer to his red one. I have never seen her do that with a man before.

Mary denies it of course, though she does not meet my eye as she does: 'If speaking with a gentleman above a few times qualifies one as being in love, then I would assume you to be in love with Robert Rich.' She smiles at that, pleased with herself.

'Oh no.' It is my turn at vigorous denial. 'He is an arrogant layabout and quite infuriating,' I go on, though I find myself lapsing into more favourable thoughts of him in the silence that follows. He had revealed so much more of himself in our conversation at the feast, and had appeared interested in my own thoughts. Were we, perhaps, becoming friends?

Mary and I are in the Claypoles' nursery in our family's private apartments at Whitehall, playing on the floor with our nieces and nephews while Elizabeth, Mother, and Father's spinster sister Aunt Liz have gone for a drive in St James's Park. We love spending time with the children, of course, but our real purpose is to catch John the moment he returns from Parliament with news of the newly proposed constitution with its rumoured suggestion of Father's kingship: a change which would affect us all.

The children tumble and fight sweetly, toys and tears jumbled in one long burst of energy. As the afternoon wears on, I am prevailed on to draw a horse and carriage, a tree and an angel while Mary works her magic with the dolls; always her playthings of choice. Our ladies Katherine and Anne, attending on us, sit in the corner and gossip quietly over their sewing. Watching them, I wonder if they are swapping notes on married life, conversing in the foreign language of wives which is unknown to me.

When the others return from the park, we have wine and cakes in the withdrawing room next door and talk, nervously, of Parliament's proposals.

'But why would Parliament wish to make Father king?' I direct my question to Mother. 'Doesn't he already have a king's powers as Protector? More, even.'

'Yes, my dear,' she says, wincing as she wiggles her right foot out of a pinching shoe. 'In effect. But this is not about your father's powers, so much as the principle on which they rest.'

'Exactly.' Elizabeth cuts in smoothly. 'Remember, the constitution which founded this Protectorate was drawn up by John Lambert and the other army generals, not by Parliament. But the Major-Generals are unpopular with the people and their power is waning with the defeat of Uncle Desborough's Militia Bill. It makes sense that now the country is more stable and settled, Parliament would wish to replace the army's constitution with one of its own creation, based along more traditional lines and so more likely to attract the wider support of the public.'

'Our brother-in-law Charles would not be pleased to hear you speak of the army so.' I arch an eyebrow over my glass.

'Charles can raise the matter with God, as they are on such close terms,' Elizabeth replies shortly. 'Biddy too.'

'Betty.' It is Mother's turn to scold. 'Charles and Bridget only want what is best for the country and for your father, as we all do. They are bound sometimes to take a different view from you and John on how this is to be achieved; they are so closely involved with the army, just as you and John are with Parliament and its representatives at court.'

Elizabeth smiles in apology; her disposition is as June sunshine, never clouded for long, and Mother, like Mary, can always make any of us friends again with only a few words.

'Would it help to keep Father safe if he is made king?' Mary asks, stroking Betty's little girl who clutches a doll on her lap.

'It might help to keep us all safe,' Elizabeth replies. 'It is no accident that Parliament proposes this in the wake of the assassination plots – it wants a lasting settlement, with Father king and the succession secured.'

'That's another argument I heard from Bulstrode

Whitelocke at the dinner for Parliament,' I say, determined to seem knowledgeable. 'He took a lawyer's view, saying that with Father king, all men would know their restrictions, but also their rights. The people understand what a king is, what rights of theirs he guarantees, and what befalls them if they plot against him. And, what's more, they trust what they know. Whereas they don't understand the role of Lord Protector, they don't trust it, don't know where they stand . . .'

As my words tail off I cast my mind back to the Protectors of the last two hundred years: Somerset, brother-in-law to King Henry VIII, who governed in Henry's son King Edward VI's minority and ended his days on the scaffold; before him, Richard, Duke of Gloucester, another uncle, who it's rumoured killed his nephews in the Tower of London when he seized the throne; and before that, the succession of dukes who ruled as Protectors in the bloody civil wars between York and Lancaster. These were not happy precedents, neither were they enduring; in each case a protector had merely kept the throne warm for a king.

'I know John takes that view,' Betty says before sitting up in her chair. 'And he can tell you himself, I hear him in the antechamber.'

The next moment brings John in to us, his basset hound Badger as ever at his heels. The boys run to the dog as John removes his gloves.

'Well?' Elizabeth crosses the room to her husband and kisses him on the cheek, handing him a glass of wine.

John greets his mother-in-law with a kiss, bows to Aunt Liz and grins at Mary and me, before collapsing onto the couch and drinking off half his glass in one go.

'Sir Christopher Pack proposed the new constitution and the House is to debate it over the coming days. There are many who will be for it, I think.'

Elizabeth lowers herself beside him. 'And the main components of this constitution?'

'Three.' John holds out a hand and nonchalantly checks them off on his fingers. 'A second chamber for Parliament to replace the House of Lords that was abolished with the monarchy in '49. A new national church instead of the many styles of free worship we have now. And . . . your father to become king. They are already placing bets on it in the City. Even odds now, I believe. Perhaps I'll see if Dick fancies a bet.'

Mother frowns in mild disapproval and we sit for a few moments in silence, all of us working through this list in our heads.

'Your father may accept the first element,' Aunt Liz says, folding her thin hands in her lap. 'It's the old way of government he likes best. But he will struggle with the second. Freedom for people to worship as they choose has been a passion of his since he was a boy.'

'Toleration is his cornerstone,' Mother nods in agreement. 'He won't have the corrupt bishops returned by the back door to rule over their congregations again, demanding attendance, telling men how to worship and punishing them if they do not. He used to believe he could restore a national church, broad enough to welcome all Protestant faiths, but the intolerance of the Presbyterians in Parliament has put paid to that.'

I look at the two women, trying to imagine their life in Father's household when he was the young head of the family. How his every opinion, every action must have mattered to them and how they must have sat, just as they do now, for hours on end poring over his views.

I return my thoughts to the present. 'But the crown?' I ask, captivated as always in equal parts excitement and terror by the idea.

'That,' John says, 'is the great unknown. Your father has always professed a liking for monarchy above all other systems of government. It was the tyrant King Charles he fought against, not the office of king itself.'

'But with he himself as the monarch?' Elizabeth parries her husband's words, doubt edging her voice.

'Aye. That's the rub. Well.' John sits forward, placing his empty cup on the side table. 'Though we don't know the outcome, we must prepare for the change in case it comes. It would affect all of us; you girls above all,' he adds, looking pointedly at Mary and me.

I know full well what he means; I have seen my future written in Signor Giavarina's dark face. My nerves spill over into irritation: 'I love you well, John, but I wish you would stop calling us girls. If we are but girls, you can hardly be alluding to our marriages as I know you are.'

John laughs good-humouredly and inclines his head at me in supplication. 'Very well, Fanny. But there is another descriptor which we would apply to you and Mall were Oliver to become king, that of "princess". And if you become princesses then there will be all sorts of nobles after you – foreign princes, even. My Betty won't benefit though, I'm glad to say. She's stuck with me!' He kisses Elizabeth then, a warm kiss, full on the mouth, one hand flat over her rounded stomach.

I watch them longingly, wondering if I will find as

much love in my marriage as they have. Elizabeth has been lucky with John; they fell in love with their parents' natural approval. It was only because of this that Father could bring himself to give his consent when his beloved Betty was but sixteen.

Bridget and Henry's match was a little more contrived, I believe, as he was Father's army deputy at the time. But there must have been a real attraction between them and I understand they found an intense, almost religious love together – Biddy was certainly struck down with grief and rage at his death. But her second marriage to Charles? Another match with an army colleague of Father's? I could never tell what love lay there. Bridget married Charles so quickly, still a raw widow, and Charles's own first wife had been laid in the earth only six months earlier – just a few days separating her and Henry's deaths. That made for an unusual wedding. But then Mary and I have always secretly wondered if Bridget hadn't welcomed her marriage martyrdoms, embracing her own contribution to Parliament's precious 'Good Old Cause' against the king; the cause which had claimed the blood and sweat of Father and Charles and, in Henry's case, his life itself.

That night, after we have brushed each other's hair and prayed together, Mary and I share a bed for the first time in years – each aware, though we do not say it in so many words, of how suddenly we could be torn apart if we are sent away to marry.

'If we become princesses,' I whisper to Mary in the darkness, knowing from her breathing that she lies sleepless beside me, 'then our value on the marriage market would soar into unimaginable heights. There would be no limit to who Father could wish us to marry.' I should be excited at the prospect but instead I feel only fear. 'What will happen to us?' I ask, seeking Mary's cold hand under the counterpane.

'We will do what is asked of us,' Mary replies quietly. 'We will marry where we are told and play our part in furnishing the country with peace and prosperity.'

Though I hear her fine words, I also feel her shiver alongside me, her arm goosebumped against mine.

♛

We find ourselves back in the Banqueting House the next day, 24 February, for the traditional ceremony to appoint a new ambassador. Philip Meadowes – Master John Milton's former assistant in the Latin translation office and one of Thurloe's protégés – is to lead an embassy to Denmark. His mandate is to further Father's efforts to keep the peace between our Protestant cousins Denmark and Sweden and to secure our access to shipping supplies in the Baltic. It is a bold approach from Father; the kind of strong, decisive foreign policy of which Signor Giavarina would approve. Is England finally beginning to find its place in the world? Does Father's renewed confidence suggest he may be contemplating becoming king?

I watch as Ambassador Meadowes accepts the commission gracefully, his right hand, still scarred from the gunfire aimed at him by an angry Portuguese on his last diplomatic mission, swept across his knee as he bows before Father's dais. I tip my head to gaze at the Banqueting House's astonishing ceiling, running my eyes lovingly over the twisting bodies, cherubs and flower garlands now so familiar to me. It is a bright, clear morning and pale sunlight streams through the vast windows to lay a parade of bright rectangles on the floor. The ladies and gentlemen of the court step in and out of the beams as they press closer to watch the ceremony, murmuring quietly to each other behind their hands.

Looking at them, I am surprised to feel more of their eyes upon me than ever before. Do I imagine the hungry glances of the young, single men of the court, thinking no doubt on the possible elevation of my status? These thoughts send my heart racing but I am pleased to be able to hide my disquiet in conversations on foreign affairs; discussions for which my recent conversation with Bulstrode Whitelocke and the Venetian secretary has prepared me well. I am just repeating Bulstrode's anecdote about the former Queen Christina's views on marriage to those gathered around me – Chaplain White and Katherine exchanging knowing glances – when Robert sidles up to join us.

'Sir.' I greet him, pulling my thoughts away from marriage. I haven't seen him since the entertainment for Parliament ten days ago. The memory of the intimate conversation we shared then momentarily unnerves me and I wait with heightened anticipation to see which Robert Rich will speak to me now: the confidant or the courtier.

He smiles proudly at me, his lips curled as he sweeps into an elaborate bow. 'Highness.'

So it is to be the courtier. I try not to show my disappointment.

Jeremiah and Katherine bow and move a little back to allow Robert and me our conversation and I am suddenly very aware of how our standing together must look to the rest of the room. I flutter my fan nervously though there is no need on a cool February morning.

'What do you think of Master Meadowes' embassy?' I ask, my tone neutral as my eyes scan the room rather than meet his. 'I think it a fine endeavour.'

'A fine endeavour indeed,' he agrees. 'A noble and idealistic enterprise.'

'By which you mean one that is doomed to failure,' I reply stiffly, annoyed at his mocking tone and once more seeing criticism of my father hidden in his words.

'Perhaps. It is not an easy role to play the peacemaker. *To find peace through war* – is that not your family motto?'

He is playing with me as ever. I turn my shoulder a little towards him but keep my eyes on the room, where they settle on my father as he talks closely with his new ambassador and Bulstrode Whitelocke, who is no doubt advising Meadowes on the views of the Swedish. 'But, as I have reminded you before, sir,' I say, picking my words with care like seashells from a pebbled beach, 'ease alone should not be the determining qualification for action. My father and the Council with him are championing the Protestant cause in Europe and the cause of peace. Ease should not come into it.'

'Of course you are right to chastise me,' Robert says, inclining his head towards me, his hat swinging in his hand.

He is never still, it occurs to me, feeling every move of his beside me as if each changes the currents in the air itself.

'But I merely wished to enter a note of reality into the enterprise.' He is continuing. 'Your father has a lot of difficult choices to make: to support Denmark or Sweden? To side with royalist France or Catholic Spain? To work with or against our rivals the prosperous Dutch republic, now the most similar regime to our own? In each case, he must weigh religious alignment with commercial interests and balance England's power abroad with her safety at home. As I understand it, the Council is divided on all of these questions and, under our constitution, they must agree to your father's choices; he cannot simply do as he pleases as our previous kings could.'

I am pleasantly surprised to find that Robert shares my interest in foreign affairs and am struck by his astute analysis. *Our previous kings* . . . As I sift his words for meaning, my eyes glaze and my mind reaches back into the past, which it always longs to visit. Robert's mention of the Council's split opinion on our aligning with France or Spain calls to my mind our Tudor forebears who, only a few generations ago, wrestled here at Whitehall with exactly the same dilemma: King Henry famously played the two much mightier nations off against each other for most of his reign where his daughter, the bloody Mary, married into Spain – the famous Armada the terrifying legacy of this for her sister, brave Queen Elizabeth. These thoughts bring to mind another topic about which I have long wished an opportunity to remind Robert, though I doubt the subject often strays far from his thoughts:

'You are indeed knowledgeable, sir.' I smile politely. 'I wonder you do not offer your expertise to my father, hitching the Rich horse to the Cromwell wagon as your ancestor did a century ago. Did not the lawyer Richard Rich, the founder of your noble house, secure his fortune by entering the service of my great-great-great uncle Thomas Cromwell, rising to the top of Henry VIII's court on the hem of his cloak before betraying him on his downfall?' It is perhaps a little cruel, but faced with his cool expression, I smart, remembering how much of myself I revealed to him the last time we spoke. Now it is my turn to remind him of the murky origins of his own noble heritage; justice of a sort for all his jibes about East Anglian farmers.

'I cannot account for the sins of my forebears,' Robert replies carefully, his voice even against my taunt. 'Though I would remind you, my lady, as the keen student of history you are, that your great-great-great uncle's fall from King Henry's favour was hardly the fault of my great-great-great-grandfather.' He counts the 'greats' with elaborate nods of his head, emphasising the passing years.

'That may be.' I incline my head. 'But doesn't patronage in turn deserve loyalty? Thomas Cromwell did not abandon his sponsor Cardinal Wolsey on his debasement. And he could perhaps have expected the same loyalty meted out to him from his protégé Richard Rich.'

I see Robert take in a breath before turning away from me, his eyes now the ones focusing on the middle distance as he shifts his weight from foot to foot. 'It is a long time ago now, my lady. And besides,' he continues, speaking softly, his voice smooth as if to calm a restless horse, 'the lesson I draw from our families' tangled past is that, under propitious circumstances, an alliance between a Rich and a Cromwell is a formidable partnership indeed.'

His words stop all noise from the room for me and I am flattened by the wall of silence. I hear my breath loud beneath my stays, feel my breasts swell over the lace-edged top of my corset. I am struck by a sudden desire to reach out and touch his face, to run my finger along his jaw and turn his noble profile to face me. The urge unbalances me and I bury it in anger. I cannot let him see the effect his words have had on me. Who is he to sneer at me or make love to me? I cannot tell which this is but either is astonishingly presumptuous.

I paste a smile onto my powdered face. 'I believe my father will be considering our family's alliances even more carefully now that there is the possibility of his becoming king,' I say quickly. 'Were I to become a princess, indeed, I may find that the noblemen of England – perhaps even the princes of Europe – pay suit to me, enabling me to dispense with your most generous matchmaking services.' I glance at him, hoping to see evidence that his supercilious attitude to me and my family is for once bested.

Robert, still gazing over the crowd, stiffens and stills; his veneer, buffed always to the brightest shine, dulls. 'To become a princess may be your girlish heart's desire, Lady Frances,' he says sideways to me, his voice hard and quiet as a sword's blade cutting through the air, 'but I would not be heard boasting of such a happening. The army will never let your father accept the crown: the generals would resign, the men rebel. You may mark my words.'

Robert turns towards me then, sweeping into a low bow of farewell. As he rises out of the gesture, he concludes his rebuke, blue eyes piercing mine:

'Your Highness would do well to remember God's

warning that pride goes before destruction, and a haughty spirit before a fall.'

And with that solemn invocation of Scripture, so strange to hear on his honeyed lips, he is gone.

♛

Robert's words haunt me at night and hound me into silence in the day. I toy with confessing them to Mary, or perhaps to Katherine, but I am too uncertain of the rightness of my own behaviour; aware more and more with each passing day that my own imagined fears of Robert's disdain caused me to stain myself red with false pride, just as he had said. Kneeling beside Mary night after night, I pray silently for God's guidance and wonder if this is the first time I have offered Him an unspoken prayer, directly from my thoughts to His and hidden from Mary.

I have never felt so confused and so exposed, have never before argued with anyone outside my own siblings, and hardly ever with them. Without Mother to arbitrate, wiping cool tears and pressing hot brows, I am at a loss how to proceed. I am chastened further when I learn from Bridget – paying her weekly, private visit to us at Whitehall – that Charles and ninety-nine other army officers had gone in force to Father to persuade him not to take the crown. Father, she tells us, did not react well to such an intervention, hotly demanding what right the generals had to interfere in politics.

Robert had been right.

We are all, thus, in a fractious mood as we travel down to Hampton Court – this week by road in our heavily guarded coaches – glad to leave the tense atmosphere at Whitehall and Westminster behind us for a few days.

While Parliament is locked in its debates on kingship and the army leaders fume at Somerset House, we close members of the family and court will escape to read and sew, sing, sup, hunt and hawk. In our midst, Father and his Council of State grind on with the daily business of government: considering charity endowments, grants for schools and universities, pensions for soldiers and their widows, the renewal of leases on government property, knotty problems brought from Ireland and Scotland, requests from our overseas territories. A stream of traffic passes across Father's great desk: notes and letters, tax tariffs and schedules, government accounts and balance sheets, contracts, maps, building plans, petitions . . . His work is endless.

I look for Robert as soon as we are settled and unpacked, but he is not in the Great Hall for dinner, nor in the chapel for prayers the next morning. Kneeling in front of my pew I squeeze my eyes shut as I seek God's forgiveness once more for the hot pride I have shown; a vanity and care for worldly status that He would abhor and that would appal my parents. As the service meanders on, I glance up to where Father sits in the royal box floating under a midnight ceiling speckled with stars: if he can remain humble at his great height, I should not struggle to do the same.

Mary and I pass a pleasant day, singing with Master Hingston in the morning and practising our languages with Master Marvell in the afternoon, pleased in my case at the distraction. I am conscious, as ever, of our rare fortune among our sex to be so educated and determined that my training will not be wasted in a strangling marriage to an unenlightened husband. It is not until late the next evening that I come across Robert, playing billiards with my brother Richard and our brother-in-law John Claypole in one of the long galleries that stretches between Father and Mother's private apartments and my and my sisters' lodgings. I can tell that the men have been drinking heavily, their cheeks pink in the candlelight, shirts a little open at the neck. No doubt they are playing for money too, for all Father's disapproval of gambling, particularly on a Sunday: Dick is always short of funds.

Robert sees me coming along the gallery, in spite of the concentration he is evidently expending on his shot. He shoots quickly, missing the ball he aims for, and straightens up at once. Before I have had a chance to greet him, Robert is shaking hands with my brother and brother-in-law over the table and coins are passing between them. He takes his leave, a nod of his head in my direction as he passes through a gilt door his only acknowledgement of me. I am pricked by disappointment and forced to admit that I am missing his maddening company.

Over the next few days, rumours swirl around the palace with the blustery March wind that Robert and his cohort have left court to drink and whore around the locality: Hampton Wick, Kingston, Richmond. I know that Father will be displeased when he hears of it, disapproving as he does of such excesses on the part of his courtiers. I too find the notion of their behaviour distasteful and feel my mood sink whenever I picture him and imagine the things he may be doing. Sometimes I allow myself to wallow in these feelings. At others, I convince myself that, after the uncomfortable guilt I have been feeling towards Robert, this is a welcome return to my usual disapproval of him which has quite cheered me up.

My brother Richard is cheerful too, having won a tidy sum in the billiards game with Robert and John. Yet his cheerfulness is short-lived when he finds himself the centre of attention at Whitehall the following week. In its debates on the newly proposed constitution, Parliament has resolved another change: that Father rather than Parliament will be able to name his successor – something he was not empowered to do before. It is hoped that this will provide another safeguard against our enemies who, it is said, believe that while there is no person named to succeed Father in the government, they have only to assassinate Father to plunge the nation into anarchy and civil war. All eyes have, of course, swivelled to his eldest surviving son, though I sense that Dick himself finds the idea rather frightening as he wanders around the palace like a stag awaiting the hunt.

We discuss it at supper in our private dining room, overlooking the privy gardens. Father is not with us, his Council meeting having run over, and neither is Dick, who is chairing a late meeting of the charity committee to raise funds for the Protestant Piedmontese following their massacre by the Duke of Savoy; a project which Dick had resented when Father first assigned it to him but which is now a great passion of his.

This at least frees the rest of us to talk about them.

'I assume Father will name Dick,' I say, looking to Mother for confirmation.

'I would hope so, dearest,' she replies.

'Hope so?' I repeat. 'But as the eldest, surely it would be Richard.'

'It does not have to pass down our family line though, Frances,' John Claypole says, dropping a piece of his cutlet to Badger waiting patiently beneath the table. 'This is a new system of government and not necessarily modelled after a hereditary monarchy. Your father was chosen to rule; he could choose another who is best suited to it in his turn.'

I had not thought of this. 'Such as?'

'One of the army leaders – many are speaking of John Lambert. He is the next most powerful and popular officer after Oliver. Though it could be Charles, even.'

'Charles?' Betty's voices bursts with his name and I am reminded that there is no great love lost between them.

'Why not?' John counters his wife. 'Either of them would be a popular choice with the army and have plenty of direct experience of government as Major-Generals and members of the Council of State. And Oliver loves them both dearly.'

'As he does you, John,' Elizabeth says sweetly, placing her fingertips on her husband's sleeve.

'I know, my dear, of course, but I am not in the same position.' John smiles reassuringly at her, though we all know that relations between him and Charles Fleetwood are not always the easiest. They are as different as wine from water and it is an unfortunate consequence of the loyalty and friendship Father inspires among men of all shades – and now the power he wields too – that those closest to him fall into competition for his affection.

'There is another candidate, of course,' John continues,

again stooping to feed Badger and avoiding our eyes. 'Though I don't know how Dick would take it.'

We wait for the name, though I sense it before he says it.

'Harry.'

Harry – my dear, dear brother away from us so long now as the governor of Ireland. The man most like Father in looks and spirit of any living. I feel a pang for his strong arms and good humour; the way he calls Mary and me 'his little wenches', just as Father did when we were young.

'Father couldn't choose a younger son over an older, surely.' Mary speaks, voicing our collective surprise.

'But if the younger son has more experience of government than the older?' John counters. 'And is better suited to the role?'

'Richard has a fine grasp of affairs of state,' Mother interjects, her maternal feathers ruffled. 'Both the boys do. Harry is perhaps the more outgoing, the more commanding by nature, the more experienced in the army, but Dick has done well in Parliament lately and has chaired all his committees with skill and diplomacy. It is not his fault that we raised him to be only a country gentleman before all of this.' She gestures vaguely around the opulent room, the words dying from her lips.

I can see the truth in Mother's words, whatever her attempts at fairness and, considering my two dear brothers, think of another obstacle to John's idea. 'Besides, Harry adores Dick,' I add. 'He would never step over him to power.' *And Charles would never have it* I choose not to say out loud. We all know the prickly relationship between Harry and Charles that comes from their uneasy time working together on the settlement of Ireland after its harrowing conquest by Father's expeditionary force.

Certainly Father does not like to speak of his time there and I do not ask; he does not recall the glories of it around the fireside as he does Marston Moor or Naseby. I do know that a new ruthlessness entered the war after the king's execution, when the conflict flared up for a third and most bitter stage. Ireland was the most devastated and divided of all the nations and the Commonwealth government sent Father to bring the Irish royalist rebels to heel. This he did, though I believe a great many innocents died in the process. Father was gone a long time first fighting in Ireland, then in Scotland, while Mother, Mary and I waited at home for news from far-off places like Tipperary, Cork and Lothian.

When my brother-in-law Henry Ireton who governed the newly conquered country died, Charles Fleetwood was dispatched to take his place and Bridget swapped one husband for another. Charles was a ruthless ruler in his own way, I believe; my brother Harry has told me of the reprisals Charles would order against communities that shielded rebel leaders. And so Father, by then Lord Protector, sent Harry to be a moderating influence: first to command the English forces and join the Irish Council, working under Charles; then, when Charles returned to London to take his seat on Father's Council, effectively governing in his stead. Things are, I believe, a little better now.

But Father, conscious of Charles's bitterness at what he saw as his replacement by Harry, has not confirmed Harry's powers and he is left having to defer to the absent Charles. Charles, in turn, takes every opportunity to tread on Harry's toes and make trouble for him: dispatching quarrelsome letters instructing him in his business and always weighing in against him when Ireland is discussed by the Council. Harry complains of this in his letters to me, venting his frustration that Father's government does not give him enough support, speaking bitterly of the mopping up of misery he is left to do. It is a mess and I cannot help but think Father does not manage it well. Surely he can see that it is his approval above all that his son and son-in-law do battle over?

'Harry would step over Richard quickly enough if Father wished him to,' Elizabeth says, her eyes sparkling in the firelight over her glass of wine as her words bring my wandering attention back to the conversation. It is always Father's wishes that count with her.

'Well, I am glad Bridget is not here to hear such talk,' Mother says, drawing an invisible line under the conversation. 'How she will react to all this I don't know.'

'Perhaps that depends on whether her husband becomes Father's nominated heir,' I cannot help saying, though I know my words are unfair to Bridget, if not to Charles; no one has less worldly ambition in her bones than Biddy.

Mother looks at me sternly and I hang my head at her unspoken reprimand.

We move into the withdrawing room and Mary plays the harpsichord for us, the notes tinkling around the candlesticks. Afterwards, I decide to use the time to write to Harry and settle at the writing desk in the corner of the room with pen and paper before me. I do not repeat exactly what was said of him over supper, of course, but

I find a way to fish for his thoughts. *Parliament is now proposing Father choose his own successor,* I write, *though none is quite sure who this would be. I imagine there are some he could choose who would be less welcomed by you than others, but let us hope Father is too wise for that. If it were my choice I would nominate you, dearest Harry, so that you would have to come home . . .*

I feel a hand upon my shoulder. It is Father, passing through the room on the way to his study, a sheaf of papers under one arm, two guards trailing behind. Pausing by my chair, he leans down and whispers for me to come and see him when I have finished my letter.

A few minutes later, smoothing the silver yards of my skirts, I slip from the room in the direction of Father's study. I pass along the privy gallery, the formal square hedges of the gardens looming through the windows towards me, until I reach the guards at Father's door. Pausing before I knock, I am caught suddenly by an old but vivid memory of waiting, just like this, to enter Father's room of business at my childhood home in Ely. Then, of course, Father's office had been the beamed tithe room at the back of the house, bursting with the town's tax payments: its floor piled high with musty sacks of flour and grain, tables loaded with baskets of firewood, layers of fleeces and animal hides and bowls of eggs, purses of coins counted and stacked, the air itself powdered.

There, just as here, I had known that the opened door would reveal Father hunched over a paper-strewn table, pen in one hand, the other snaked through his hair. But this is not the shabby back office of a town tithe collector, but the privy study of the ruler of England deep in the heart of the royal palace. The power of the memory knocks the breath from my body and I grip the door frame at the contrast. Sometimes our rise to power frightens me in the scale of its sheer ascent, especially when I pause to look down from the summit onto the death drop below. If the great Thomas Cromwell, Earl of Essex and right-hand man to the king, feared how far he could fall, how much further could King Oliver Cromwell and his children?

I knock.

'Enter,' my father's voice says.

I do and, seeing the same ruddy, rustic father of my childhood before me, his lace cuffs sweeping with his pen over the ebony desk, I am aware more acutely than ever before of the strange, almost fantastical fortune of his life. The room is dark, light falling only around the two candles on the desk and one on the deep stone window ledge. It is a simple space, almost sparse: nothing but the desk and armchair and a couple of cheap spindled chairs at the edge of the room beneath the only decoration: a rich allegorical tapestry with maidens dancing in a forest.

This is the way of all of Father's private rooms: fine textiles and fabrics, a great love of his – the best of the dead King Charles's tapestry collection saved by him from sale – our own Indian sheets on the beds; but otherwise, little furniture, no plate (all now melted down in the Tower for the coin so desperately needed after the war) and few fine objects; no clocks, no mirrors. But the tapestries remain and I wonder, gazing at the one that hangs here, if it is something in the very texture of them, their truth and craftsmanship, that Father likes and also in the sight of classical and biblical stories made real.

True too for his beloved statues scattered throughout the gardens.

'Do you remember this, Fanny?' Father's warm voice brings me back to him and, standing before his desk, I take the small letter he hands to me, stiff in its square, folded creases.

I smile, smoothing the paper with my thumbs. 'Of course. I wrote this to you during the war.'

He nods, smiling fondly. 'It reached me at Marston Moor and I remember well the comfort it gave me to have a little piece of home amid all that horror. I missed my little wenches every day that I was away. I missed you all.'

I scan the letter, reading the trivial news from home I tell him: how the hens are laying, that Mary has a new doll, how Harry has grown a full five inches. The scribbles are foreign to my eyes – the letters large and round, Father and his horse Blackjack drawn in one corner, the hens in another – like they were made by someone else in a different time. As if this is a piece of another's history. 'It looks so childish,' I laugh, embarrassed.

But Father doesn't see it this way. He reaches to take the letter back from me. 'It did not look childish to me but accomplished. You were always so quick with your letters, my little scholar,' he says proudly. 'All of my girls are cleverer than I am, cleverer than their brothers I dare say! But of the four of you, it was my Fanny who was so keen to get ahead, driving herself hard every day to catch up with her siblings. Look – here's Mall's from the same packet and your writing is quite the equal of hers, though she was a year older. But don't tell her I said that!' He takes one last look at the letters, almost breathing them in, before folding them carefully and replacing them in the letter chest on his desk.

I sense the shift coming in his tone even before he speaks again.

'But you're not my little girl any more,' he says softly. 'Here.' He stands and fetches one of the spindle-legged chairs and brings it around the table for me. 'I want to talk to you about the future, not the past.'

I lower myself into the chair and cross my legs, quite at a loss as to what he is going to say. I often feel this way when we are alone: excitable but apprehensive, my senses heightened, my mind whirring like a printing press to prepare the best responses to his words. I know this is not because we are uneasy together or because he intimidates me as so many fathers do their daughters. Rather it is because I love him so strongly that my desire to please and impress him overwhelms me. I steady myself as I wait, letting him come around to the point in his own time as he likes to do.

'You know what is afoot here at the moment, Fanny,' he begins at length. 'This new proposed constitution, perhaps even the crown.' He gives an involuntary shudder at the word as if he has blasphemed. 'Well, it is time we began to make plans for you and Mary too.' Father leans back in his armchair, lacing his fingers together in his lap. 'Secretary Thurloe and I have drawn up a list of potential suitors for you both and we will begin to sound them out shortly.'

It is just what I feared. The moment my life is taken out of my hands and I am moved across the chess board. If Secretary Thurloe is involved, this will be a match not only suggested by my parents but negotiated by the government itself. A political union, not a personal one. A marriage to suit England before it suits me.

'Don't worry,' Father puts a hand out towards me as if he has heard my thoughts, 'we will not agree anything without consulting you. And, I will make sure you have plenty of opportunities to get to know anyone we consider seriously. You will have your say.' The hand goes up again even though I have not interrupted him, almost as if he is arguing with himself. 'And I will do my best to accommodate it.'

'And Mary?' I ask, wondering why he has not summoned us both for this conversation.

'I will tell all this to Mall too,' he says. 'But I wanted to speak to you first, to set my mind at rest on one particular matter.'

If his mind is restless, mine is reeling. This is what I had always expected would come, of course, what I had wanted, even. And yet I feel strangely hollow. I have spent my life straining to be allowed to grow up. And, for a woman, growing up has always meant marriage. But hasn't the war changed everything? It has turned Father from tithe collector to Head of State; could it not take me to unimagined places too? And that may include marriage, of course, but a marriage on my own terms.

I wait for his next words, my shoulders tensing. He is looking at me strangely, his greying brows knotted above knotted hands at his chin, as if I am a terrain to be mapped before a battle. I have no idea what can be troubling him.

Father licks his lips. 'I have heard talk . . .' he begins slowly, rising now from his chair – needing to move, as he always does, when he tackles a difficult subject.

'Talk that you have formed an attachment with the Earl of Warwick's grandson, Robert Rich.'

'No! Certainly not!' The words burst, blustering, out of me with an almost animal instinct, more words pressing behind them, waiting their turn. But they are instinctive words, void of meaning – tasteless in my mouth.

'Good, good,' he says quickly, his tone mollifying. 'I am glad to hear it. Then the remainder of my speech hardly matters.' He is watching me carefully, eyes narrowed.

'Perhaps not,' I say, careful to lighten my own tone. 'But I would hear it anyway.'

Father sighs. 'Very well. What I wished to say was that I could not see you married to that young man, whatever my love for his grandfather. His own father, Lord Rich, is as inept in his private affairs as he was inconstant in the war – supporting the king then defecting to us. Not that I begrudge him that in itself; there are many former royalists that I trust now with my life. Men like Lord Broghill, for instance. But Lord Rich is not an estimable man.'

I think of the passing reference Robert made to his father when we spoke after the feast for Parliament: *my stepmother takes as little interest in me as my father does*. I remember the sweet lines of sadness etched on his face, and the protesting words which march up my throat to continue my denials die on my tongue, with no true thoughts behind them to give them life. 'Father?' is all I can say.

He turns away from me then and walks towards the window, his mirrored face candlelit in the glass. 'I fear Robert Rich takes after his father and not his grandfather, my dear. He has a bad reputation, as a drunkard and a gambler . . . and worse.' Father coughs over his embarrassment but I know he is alluding to the rumours of Robert's recent visits to the whorehouses of Surrey.

'He does not apply himself to any occupation,' Father goes on. 'I fear he is not steady, either in his manner of living, or in his love of the Lord.'

I think of Robert using the Book of Proverbs to warn me of my pride, and wonder at the exact colour of his faith.

'And, Fanny.' Father has turned back to me now, his large hooded eyes fixed intensely on mine. 'I could not in true conscience see you married to a man so unworthy of your spirit, however noble his house. Marriage is a serious business. It needs love, of course, but also strength of character, resolve, care and devotion and mutual respect. It is the parents, at one step removed and with the wisdom of years, who can see how well their sons and daughters could fit with others – just as God knows what is best for us, His children. Be assured I am long-experienced at the art of a happy match: I helped each of my sisters to their husbands and have done the same for Biddy and Betty and for my nieces too. Lavinia and Robert Beke for instance, and look at them – cooing like a pair of turtle doves. And, of course, I myself am lucky enough to live within the happiest of marriages every day. I know you, my little scholar, down to each hair on your head. I will make sure to find you a true partner. I will have all my girls happy.'

I am honoured: Father has marshalled all of his famous weapons of persuasion and turned them on me. I am a congregant listening to the sermonising of a great lay preacher, a Member of Parliament silent before his sovereign, an eve-of-battle soldier taking comfort from the glorious certainty of his general. I bathe in the outward warmth of Father's words, even as I feel their concealed blade. Wilting under his shrewd gaze, I have the sensation I am gliding along a dark passage towards a dazzling shaft of light. With every moment I draw closer to the realisation which dawns on me only as Father speaks his very refusal to my marrying Robert: that I care deeply for him.

It is all I can do to nod and rise from my chair. 'Of course, Father, thank you for your guidance,' I find myself saying though the words have no connection to the thoughts in my head. It is the first time in my life that I must hide my feelings from my father, act the courtier to his sovereign. But I do not hesitate: I will not fight this battle now when I barely understand my own position. My sole desire is to end our conversation quickly and to be alone with the torrent of feeling sweeping through every inch of my body.

I am saved by Secretary Thurloe, who slides into the room with a bow and apology for interrupting.

Father beckons him in and Thurloe approaches us, brandishing documents. 'The evening's papers to sign, Highness, a briefing on the French ambassador's latest treaty proposals and a schedule of your appointments tomorrow. Lest you may have forgotten, it is the day you have appointed to hear the poor men's petitions brought by the Master of Requests . . .'

Curtseying, I slip through the study door and run along the carpeted gallery, wings on my heels flying me to my room.

♛

Safely back in my chamber, I clamber onto the bed and draw the heavy curtains around me, wanting the smallest possible space free from distractions within which to think. I throw my head back and stare at the canopy. Is it possible that I do not hate Robert Rich? That I might in fact like him, even want him for myself? In spite of all his taunts and games, his arrogance and presumptions, his condescension. His laziness and entitled attitude, so at odds with that of me and of my family. Or were all of these features an illusion? The screen of smoke that masks a dampened fire? Where the professed opinions he always leads with paint him in this way, the words that often follow reveal him to be clever and well-informed. And his behaviour thoughtful and courteous, even. Or perhaps I tell myself this to justify an altogether less edifying reality; that it is his very infuriating qualities that attract me, speaking to the Cromwell spark deep within me that flashes and flares at the thought of a just rebellion.

But then again, I think, his actions contradict much of his posturing. If he really feels the disdain for my family I credit him with, how could he live at court and play the courtier? Why would he seek out my company so often, and that of Richard and John? And most of all, how could he speak to me of an alliance of Rich and Cromwell? My heart pounds at the remembrance of that moment. Was he indeed alluding to a marriage between us as I suddenly hope he was? That had been my instinct in the instant he said it, yet my embarrassment and fear that he mocked me still had prompted my spiteful response. I think back to our conversation after the feast, to the way that in our sparring we had moved together towards a greater understanding of our shared heritage and of the rebellion we wanted to effect in our own lives.

I take a deep, slowing breath, willing myself to think rationally. I cast my mind back over my interview with Father and must acknowledge that I had not recognised these feelings for Robert until Father had told me I could not marry him. Do I really care for him? Or do I want him now only because he is forbidden? Or – a third alternative occurs to me – do I select him now that I know marriage for me is imminent, because he would be my own choice and not my father's? It is no use. My thoughts dance around in circles like girls around the May Day maypoles that are slowly coming back now, their streamers circling, twirling and weaving. I close my eyes against the dizzying colours.

When I open them again, my balance restored, I know what I must do. I cannot know – I will not know – the truth of my feelings until I see Robert again with this fresh perspective. All the time we had spent together in recent weeks, I have not been looking at him in this way; I have not been assessing his true worth, merely playing his parlour games. And, more than this, I must see him urgently. If Father and Secretary Thurloe are indeed reviewing candidates for my hand, there is not a moment to lose. Before a few days or a week have passed, they may have assigned me to another noble, perhaps a political ally or an army colleague of Father's. He could be old, a widower, a former royalist even. Or, if Father does indeed becoming king, perhaps I will be bargained to a foreign prince in a treaty of alliance, sent to wed some peacocking German or oriental potentate I will not see until my wedding day. I think of old King Henry, flinging his fourth wife – the 'Flanders Mare' – from his bed when she failed to live up to Master Holbein's miniature portrait, and shudder: it was for arranging that ill-fated match that our forebear Thomas Cromwell went to the block. Paintings of Father's unknown candidates for my hand shuffle before my eyes like a pack of playing cards, the deck only coming to a still when I hear Katherine come into the room.

She does not speak, assuming me already asleep perhaps, but I listen to her footsteps criss-crossing the chamber on her usual night-time tasks: laying out my nightgown; collecting my gloves, or fan or ribbons from where I have left them on the floor; taking out my comb. In that moment, I have an idea.

'Katherine.' I pull back a curtain and beckon her to me.

'My lady? I thought you asleep. Shall we say our prayers or have you done them with Mary already?'

I shake my head in irritation: Katherine was never so attentive to my prayers before she wed the chaplain. 'No, not that. I was thinking. I need you to deliver a message for me. Can you fetch me my writing things?'

She puts down the dress draped over her arm and brings me my writing set. Taking it, I sit back against my pillows and smooth the blank page waiting on the board.

'I need you to find out if Robert Rich is at Whitehall and, if he is, to have one of the boys send him a message arranging a meeting.'

'Fanny!' She has used my nickname so rarely since our elevation that I know she is genuinely shocked. 'You cannot possibly go and meet him privately at such an hour. What if you are seen?'

I hesitate, her shock rubbing off on me. She's right, I cannot risk it. If I were seen it would be the end of my good reputation and that of the whole family by extension. Perhaps worse, it would damage me forever in Father's eyes. But then Robert appears before me, standing in the stables at Hampton Court stroking Father's new mare, his face hidden beneath his extravagant green hat. He is chuckling, pleased with the conversational trap he has led me into as he presses me for the name of my intended. *'I am yet to make my selection, sir.'* I hear myself reply. *'Though I will be sure to inform you the moment that I do.'*

An idea begins to form in my mind.

Quickly, before I can think better of it, I dip the pen and write a few lines, fold the paper and press it into her hand.

'*I* will not be seen,' I tell Katherine slowly, emphasising the first word as I climb down from the bed. 'Robert will expect to meet *you*. And if I wear your hat and cloak, anyone who happens to witness our meeting will think they see you and not me: they'll think I am Lady Frances's companion, running a late errand to the laundry, fetching a hot drink from the kitchen or taking a short cut to her husband's lodgings.'

Katherine's eyes widen in alarm. 'You forget – I am a chaplain's wife now!'

'Please.' I take her small, warm hand. 'I just need your clothes.'

The guards pay little attention to me as I walk quickly along the privy gallery. Pulling Katherine's cloak tighter around me, I pass through the last room to the top of the Adam and Eve stairs. I go down the steps carefully and quietly, hitching up the overlong skirt so I do not fall. At the foot of the stairs, again I find two men of the household guard, but they do not question me, their job being to prevent intruders from gaining entrance to our privy apartments, not to prevent ladies-in-waiting from leaving them to go about their business. I emerge into the sharp cool of the gardens, each heavy breath forming before my face. I peer each way before plunging forward, out of the shadow of the stairwell and into the gardens.

To my right, I can just see the outline of the Holbein Gate rising out of the dark, looming over the long wall that separates our private gardens from King Street beyond. Candles glow in the windows of the great Chair-house within it and I think briefly of the Tudor kings who used it as their private study and would peer out of the slitted windows to watch their unknowing subjects bustle about their daily lives. Even though it is late, I can hear some of this same bustle from the street as it carries over the clipped hedges towards me: a carriage rolling by, some men shouting to each other as they leave a tavern. But, as I weave my way between the hedged gardens towards the sundial, these human noises fade until all I can hear is the crunch of gravel under my feet and the low hoots of a little owl from the orchard beyond which punctuate the still, night-time air. There is no one to see me as I walk but the ghostly figures of the marble statues who stand sentry-like at the centre of each square of grass.

I see Robert before he sees me. He is enveloped in a dark cloak, leaning against the huge sundial, scuffing the toe of one of his buckled shoes in the dusty gravel. I cannot see the expression of his downcast face, hidden beneath the wide brim of his familiar feathered green hat, but something in his overall attitude appears dejected, lacking the usual vigour evident in his limbs even when standing still. Robert peels himself upright when he hears my approach and, after a shallow bow, crosses his arms in a lacklustre posture of defence.

'I do not know what your lady is about, Mistress White, summoning me to meet you in such a clandestine fashion,' he says wearily.

I bob a curtsey from a little distance away and let him continue, keeping my face lowered under my hood.

'You can tell her from me that I do not have the slightest interest in which young gentleman her eye has alighted on, nor do I understand her need to inform me in this way,' he goes on, in a tone trying to convey boredom, though I think I catch a painful edge to it.

I hardly know what to say; for all my planning of this meeting, I have not prepared my speech, could not have prepared it as it was not until I met Robert again that I expected to know my own feelings. Even now, the clarity of thought I had hoped to gain in his presence does not come; there is no sudden sunshine breaking through the fog. But what there is instead is the pure, physical sensation of his voice, with its familiar drawl, enveloping me like the sudden warmth of a friendly hearth cast over a winter pilgrim.

I draw towards him and lower my hood, raising my face until my eyes fix on his.

'I apologise for the theatrics, sir, and for the inconvenience caused to you, but I fancy you have been avoiding me of late.' Looking at him now, I realise how much I have missed him since he has kept his distance from me; how it is only when I am with him, when we talk together, when I meet the conversational challenges he throws down before me, that my own thoughts crystallise and I come fully to know myself. 'I would not have you prevent me from honouring my word,' I continue, my head clearing. 'I promised you in the stables at Hampton Court that I would inform you as soon as I had selected a suitor and so, having done so, I am here.' I speak clearly, straining every fibre to keep my voice level.

Robert gapes at me, mouth open, eyes staring in amazement. Moments, minutes seem to pass before I see him regain control of himself, the smallest muscles in his face and hands twitching him back into life. He pulls off his hat and bows, drawing himself up again much straighter than before, his hat hanging limply in one hand.

'Your Highness, I . . .'

'Hush.' I put my finger up to his lips, desperate suddenly to prevent him taking a false position as he has done at the start of every conversation we have ever had. I know that if he does, I will lose my bearings just when I can see the pole star.

I look at the stars now, framing his face as he gazes down on me uncertainly, like specks of candlelight around a mirror. With such a sight before me, I have no more words, no witticisms, only an ageless instinct. Softly, I slide the hand at his lips around the side of his face until my little finger weaves into the hair above his ear. Rising onto my tiptoes, gently, I pull his head down to mine until our lips meet. For one heartbeat, then two, they press together without moving, like bound books pushed up against each other on a shelf. But then Robert opens his lips and I dissolve into him as he brings both arms around me, his hat dropped in the dust, his hands rising up into my hair and down to my waist, shoulders bowing forward over mine. We clench together, joining every last inch of ourselves until I think we have fused like the nearby sculpture of Venus and Adonis, while every night-time sound of the gardens around me is drowned in crashing heartbeats and a thunder in my ears.

We kiss and explore each other for a seeming infinity until, at last, a mutual need for air pulls us apart. I press a hand to my pounding heart while Robert staggers back a little way, hands balled on his hips while he regains his breath, his eyes never leaving mine. Eventually the power of speech returns to me.

'You were going to say something, sir, before I stopped you. What was it to be?' I smile at him, my eyes dancing with a heady new-found confidence.

Robert laughs, shaking his head from side to side like a colt. 'My lady, I am afraid you took the words from me, I cannot say what was in my mind. Indeed,' he grins, 'I cannot recall anything that has ever been in my mind before the last few moments. In this instant, I am not even sure of my own name.' He reaches for me again then, this time taking my hand and drawing it to his lips.

'You are Robert Rich, grandson of the Earl of Warwick,' I say, my turn now to laugh. 'Courtier, drinker, gambler, lover of fine living and shirker of hard work, and the clever, kind man I choose to love.'

He stops laughing at that, the grinning smile he has pressed to my hand falling away into a look of pure wonder. 'The man you choose to love,' he repeats, his voice bewildered as he pulls me towards him and takes my face in both hands. 'And the man who chooses to love you – Her Highness, Lady Frances Cromwell.'

Her Highness Lady Frances Cromwell, I think, hoping it is truly me as I have always been and not my exalted status that he loves; if Father can rise so high, he could fall just as low again. But I lose these false thoughts as Robert kisses me gently and I feel his eyes shut tight, his eyelashes flitting against mine like butterflies. Then he moves his mouth into my hair and I feel him breathe deeply.

'I only knew my true feelings this evening,' I say, marvelling at the speed with which my life has changed. 'How long have you known?'

'Ah,' he chuckles with a hinted embarrassment. 'Much, much longer than that. But you humble me,' he says, his tone becoming serious again.

'Humble you?'

'It took you a mere matter of hours to act on your knowledge; to seek me out, to take the leap of faith. While I . . . I have danced around my love for you, played with it, played with you. Darting towards my love, only to spring back from it again. You have your father's cavalry courage, I see it.'

The compliment could not please me more, yet the warm smile where his lips have just left mine fades from me as I remember my earlier conversation with Father.

I cannot reveal all he said about Robert, knowing his confidence to be of a thinner, softer metal than it first appears.

'We must tread carefully,' I whisper into his collar. 'Father and Secretary Thurloe have other plans for me than this.'

'I know,' he says, stroking my hair in reassurance. 'I will speak to my grandfather, ask him to approach your father on my behalf. But we have a difficult road ahead of us. The situation will worsen if your father becomes king, making his youngest princess an even more glittering prize than she is now.' He tightens his grip on me as if, in doing so, he can stop any other taking me from him. 'But know this my love,' he says as our heartbeats slow to each other's rhythm. 'Now that I have you, I will not let you go without a fight.'

CHAPTER FOUR

Mary is astounded when I tell her, though at the brazenness of my actions, not at our love, which she had long suspected. She takes a shameless glee in being proved right, though the laughter we share soon gives way to doubt. Father has spoken to her about his list of suitors, just as he did to me, and so we have drawn together, planning our strategy as if at a council of war.

'But what of Nicholas Baxter?' I ask her as we sit together sewing, cousin Lavinia and the other young ladies of court who have joined us sitting just outside earshot. 'I know you have a liking for him.'

She looks away from me, her eyes straying out of the window, fingers loose on her pattern. 'I do like him, but that is all. I haven't spent the time with him you have with Robert, haven't formed such a strong attachment. And I think now that it is wise I don't.'

'Oh, Mary,' I say, leaning forward to stroke her hand.

'No, it is for the best. It is not too late for me, as it is for you,' she says, looking back at me now, her face set. 'I have not yet lost my heart and will now endeavour not to do so. All I want,' her words slow for emphasis, 'is a contented marriage and children of my own.'

I look at her full of admiration. She has always been so sensible, so fair and considered, just like Mother and with a maternal streak to match. I have long found an irony in that – that while of all of us sisters, Mary is the one who looks most like Father, she is most like Mother in temperament; a perfect fusion of our parents. I often wonder where their balance lies in me.

In the following days, we wait nervously for Father or Secretary Thurloe to say more of their plans but, luckily, they and indeed the rest of the court are distracted from any thoughts of us by the war that is to come. After weeks of heated debates, the Council and Father have finally broken the deadlock Signor Giavarina outlined to me and agreed to join with King Louis XIV of France in his war against the Spanish. Charles – the greatest advocate for this policy on the Council – is delighted while the angry lines on General John Lambert's high forehead speak another story. Thurloe explains another benefit of the alliance to me in a rare unguarded moment as we watch a servant laying a fire while the little secretary waits to regain Father's attention:

'The French king will have no choice now but to expel the lurking Charles Stuart from France. The "Sun King" can hardly entertain the pretender to your father's throne now he has allied with him, even if Louis is the young prince's uncle. And that, at a stroke, removes the threat of Charles Stuart launching an invasion of England from across the Channel.'

Statements like this still have the power to amaze me: to hear Father mentioned in the same breath as the godlike King of France and Charles Stuart, who was our much-worshipped Prince of Wales when I was a young child. I think of this as I watch Ambassador Bordeaux of France and Father sign a great treaty to cement the agreement. It is an elaborate but intimate spectacle held in Father's grand state bedchamber, as was the custom of the old Stuart kings, with only the ambassador's secretary, the Council and Secretary Thurloe and my family to witness it. Never before have I felt so keenly the power of symbols and ritual. Never before have I felt such a princess. Once again, I sense Father take a step closer to the crown.

I long to discuss all this with Robert, but he is taking care not to be seen too much with me, his longing looks and smiles whenever we are in the same room having to suffice for now. As the days pass and the nights drag while I lie sleepless reliving every moment of our tryst, I begin to wonder if it was in fact a dream, if he does in fact feel for me as much passion in the light of day as he did in the moonlight. Anxiety and frustration build within me, layer after hot layer, and so I feel an odd affinity with Father, whom I notice daily bowing and bending under the increasing pressure of the two lobbies warring over his becoming king. Every day he is subjected to new and more impassioned arguments from all about him as around his rock, a whirlpool of strong feelings rages at the court, in Parliament and the army, and even spilling onto the streets of London.

God himself is drawn into the debate when the Puritan congregations of the city issue a protestation entreating Father not to accept the crown. This, I see, wounds him deeply, by resting on the greatest fear that Mother tells me keeps him from his bed at night: that the Lord, in granting the New Model Army its victory over King Charles, has spoken against kings and so does not wish him, Oliver – God's instrument – to go against His judgement. Parliament feels no such scruples, however, and so it is that, tipped off by John, I find myself slipping into the Banqueting House on the last day of March to watch as the members of the House of Commons, with great pomp and ritual, present Father with their new draft constitution engrossed in vellum.

I strain for a better view as Sir Thomas Widdrington, Councillor and Speaker of the House of Commons, steps forward with the offering.

'We beseech Your Highness,' he begins solemnly, 'to assume the name, style, title, dignity and office of King of England, Scotland and Ireland and the respective dominions and territories thereunto belonging; and to exercise the same according to the laws of these nations.'

I wait, my heart in my mouth, for Father's reply. Seconds stretch before us all – a bubble of silence in which the whole room could have heard if a pin slipped from my hair. Out of the corner of my eye I catch sight of the black head of Bulstrode Whitelocke as he shifts from one foot to the other. Somewhere, near the middle of the room, someone coughs. Rubens' divine King James watches in wonder from his heavenly cloud on the ceiling over our heads, waiting to see if the farmer who routed his son's army on the battlefield and signed his death warrant will now accept his crown.

At last, Father speaks, his face grave, his tense, strained voice bursting the bubble as if with a rapier.

'Gentlemen, I acknowledge the great importance of what is offered to me as it concerns the welfare, the peace, the settlement of three nations and all that rich treasure of the best people in the world.'

But it is time he then speaks of, all he asks for. Time to consider the proposals, though he promises a speedy answer. The atmosphere of the room breaks into a fever.

Is it done? Harry asks in his latest letter, which I find waiting for me in my room. *The little secretary, my Lord Broghill and Edward Montagu write highly of the new constitution but I cannot be so certain about Father accepting the crown: the return of kings would not be welcomed here across the Irish Sea . . .*

No, I scribble back hastily. *He stalls, he struggles. We have no choice but to wait. Though there can be few in all these three nations who have more riding on his decision than your little sister . . .*

Our escape to Hampton Court at the end of that week has perhaps never been so welcome, not least for Father, who has been suffering from debilitating headaches. In the febrile atmosphere that grips the nation, even greater care is taken over the security of our journey and Mary and I do not know until the very last moment the time we are to leave nor whether to dress for travel by barge or carriage. This time we go by carriage and I cannot help but shudder at the huge barriers erected on either side of the road for the last and most exposed mile of the journey through Hampton Wick to the palace. Secretary Thurloe has not been idle since he learned of the many assassination attempts by Sindercome and his fellow plotters. I am pleased that, on this journey, John's dog Badger has chosen to ride in our carriage rather than his master's, though the biscuits secreted in my purse may have swayed his choice. Seeking comfort, I bury my face in Badger's fur.

I hope too that I will see more of Robert in the relaxed environs of Hampton Court and my wish is granted on Saturday morning when he joins our party to go hawking. This, above all others, is Father's favourite pastime, and I can almost see the burden of his current deliberations slide from his shoulders as we set off at a trot into the deer park.

'Hawking represents a gentler, nobler time,' Father tells me as we ride together, the crisp morning air filling our lungs. 'The time of my grandparents and their parents before them, when England was settled and thriving in its old ways – before the first Scottish king came south and before his son brought in his French wife and her Catholic ways. A time when a gentleman had the leisure to walk abroad in the fields with a hawk on his fist. We had eighty years of peace before Charles Stuart raised his standard against us at Nottingham, did you know that? Was it any wonder none of us knew how to fight? We had forgotten, you see. We had to learn the art of war all over again.'

Father is flying his favourite bird today – his peregrine falcon, a bird reserved only for kings – and I see him glance back over his shoulder every hundred yards to check on the bird, perching hooded in its corner of the square-framed cage on the back of his falconer. The cadge man, as the falconer is called, walks carefully, picking his feet high to keep the birds on his back from swaying too violently. But still, they call softly to each other; the siren screech of Father's peregrine falcon, the goose honk of the lesser saker and lanner falcons which will be flown by the nobles among us, and the rapid squeaks of the small merlins reserved for Mary and me.

Traditionally, these hawking outings are sociable affairs and so, once Father has his falcon on his gloved arm and is suitably distracted, I see nothing amiss in edging my horse towards Robert's.

'Highness.' He bows over his reins.

'Sir.' I straighten up above mine. 'I trust you are well.'

'I am, my lady, though plagued by bad sleep and the most vivid dreams.' Robert smiles at me wickedly.

'Dreams, my lord?' I struggle to keep my tone light, directing my gaze away to where Father's falcon wings off from his arm in pursuit of prey; it really is a magnificent bird – a gift of rare value from the Prince of East Friesland. 'Does the same apparition come to you night after night or do you suffer a multitude of dreams?' I ask.

'Oh, the same,' Robert says airily. 'An angel comes to me in a garden and, at her voice and her touch, I find myself spinning into darkness.'

I blush with pleasure and relief, moving my mare a little closer to Mary's lest anyone should see my cheeks. 'How troubling for you,' I reply over my shoulder. 'I myself sleep like a baby.'

'I have spoken with grandfather.' He drops his voice to a whisper, edging his horse after mine. 'And he has raised my suit with your father.'

'Any luck?'

'Not yet,' he replies, his playful tone exchanged for one of concern. 'Your father is set fair against me and told Grandfather so in no uncertain terms. It does not look good. And I do not know what else to do. I have even written to Father, though I hate to ask anything of him. But I doubt anything will come of his interceding, were he to choose to help me; your father holds a low opinion of him too and made that quite plain to Grandfather.'

I am raised with hope and dashed with despair in the same instant: thrilled that Robert has formally asked for my hand, devastated that Father appears implacable.

'Grandfather will keep trying,' Robert attempts to reassure me as he sees the alarm in my face. 'But we must take care. Now that your father knows my intentions he will watch us like one of his hawks.'

I am turning back towards him to reply when Father's voice rings out over the group.

'Frances, Mary?' Father is looking for us over his shoulder. 'Come and join me.'

I glance at Robert who sets his lips as if to say *I told you so*. Leaving him behind, I weave my horse towards Father, hastily gathering my thoughts and quieting my feelings. As I approach, I incline my head to the strong-jawed, romantic figure of General John Lambert mounted beside Father. My nerves increase: of all Father's colleagues and friends, it is Lambert who leaves me the most tongue-tied. He is a living legend of the age: the hero of Parliament's victorious Scottish campaign and a passionate military genius beloved of his men; the sharp mind that drafted the Instrument of Government – the constitution which made Father Lord Protector; the most eminent politician at court and a powerful member of the Council; and, of all others, the nearest to Father in greatness. Is it any wonder that John Claypole raised Lambert's name when we discussed Father's possible heir the other evening?

Still, I am surprised to see Lambert so close to Father

when the whole court knows that it is he who leads the army's opposition to Father becoming king. He will certainly have his old friend's ear today.

As I draw level with them, I see that Father's falcon has returned to his glove, where it tears into the flesh of a wood pigeon pinioned between its talons. Mary appears on his other side, as elegant and natural in the saddle as ever.

'Tell me, upon what subject was young Robert Rich entertaining you?' Father asks, keeping his tone even and his eyes on his bird.

My mind races. 'On the subject of dreams, Father.'

'Ha!' he scoffs. 'I dare say he is a dreamer, that one. Not like you and I, eh, Johnny?' Father looks to Lambert for agreement and the general nods solemnly. 'No. We leave the dreaming to other men,' Father goes on, 'men like Thomas Rainsborough, who dreamed of a world where all men could vote and who paid for it by taking an assassin's bullet; Henry Ireton, who dreamed of a godly, prosperous Commonwealth where all men were equal under the law, and paid for it in fevered blood to leave your sister a widow.'

His eyes glaze over a little and I breathe again as I feel his attention wandering away from Robert. I glance across at Mary, who gives me a private smile of encouragement.

'It is the practical men who win wars.' Lambert takes up Father's theme. 'Men who can see straight. Men of action, of pupose.'

'Very true,' Father nods, 'though I do like to have a few dreamers about me. They tell me how the world should be and I work out how we can get there with

God's help. Their dreams and my realities; their thoughts and my deeds. That's how we won the war, that's how we will build the future. It is the destination that matters, not the route we take, yet someone has to bring a map.'

Father stops his horse suddenly and beckons to the falconer. 'Here, Sam, come and take the bird. Frances – take your turn with the merlin now and then we'll see what Mary can do. My dear John,' Father addresses Lambert affectionately, 'prepare for instruction; my daughters are fearless with the hawks and Mary, my second youngest here, is a natural.'

Lambert turns his gun-metal eyes first onto Mary and then onto me. Mary glows with pride and I feel a stab of envy: I have never been able to match her at outdoor pursuits. I really should practise more.

'Is it true that Harry is sourcing some more hawks for you, Father?' I ask. 'If so, perhaps he might send a bird for me? I might practise more with my own bird.'

'Aye,' Father replies, grinning at me. 'Harry tells me the best birds are to be found on the far west coast of Ireland and so I have told him to find me a goshawk. You write to him; ask him to track down a little ladies' bird for you too.'

'Ireland you say, Oliver?' Lambert interrupts us, his words flat in the accent of his native Yorkshire, his tone playfully challenging. 'I doubt you'll find a better bird there than you will in the western highlands of Scotland. George Monck is taking a little time out from commanding our army there to procure me some falcons. We have a nice little import business planned.'

Father draws himself up in his saddle, his eyes flashing. 'Do you now? I'll tell you what, John. When we get our hands on the birds, we'll fly them together. Have a little friendly competition before the court – what do you say?'

Lambert nods in agreement and his horse whinnies as the two most powerful men in the country square up against each other.

It is my turn to fly a bird and my pulse quickens with nervous excitement as Father's avenor laces the long padded glove to my left arm and hands me my merlin. As always I am surprised by her weight and mesmerised by her gaze as she swivels her small striped head left and right, pausing briefly on my face in the middle of each panoramic look. Carefully I unhook her string and raise my arm as a branch, feeling the instant aftershock as she launches herself powerfully into the air in the direction of the beech trees ahead.

I scan for her return, my eyes darting and roving the treeline before, on a high whistle from the falconer, she swoops back to me, a lark in her claws. When she is safely restored to my arm, I look away politely as if to afford her some privacy for her meal. But really, I have a weak stomach for these moments of the sport. Still, the joy I feel as time after time she wings away from me high into the air, always returning like a thunderbolt, recompenses me a thousand fold. I will write to Harry and see if he can find me a bird of my own.

'I compliment you, Your Highness,' Lambert says generously, pausing his horse while I return my bird to the avenor who takes it over to Mary. Continuing through the park, we watch as Mary flies the merlin over our heads to the trees.

'Thank you, General. Your own flying was most impressive.'

I glance sideways at his profile – the long, arched nose, the silver-grey tinges in his hair and sleek neck putting me in mind of a greyhound. Now Father has wandered a little away to talk to Dick, I wonder if Lambert will speak to me again.

'Your father and I used to enjoy hawking on campaign in Scotland,' he says at length. 'We saw a golden eagle once; an extraordinary creature.'

'How wonderful,' I reply, genuinely thrilled by the idea. 'And a most welcome respite I am sure from the hard fighting you saw there.'

'True,' he nods in rhythm with his horse's head. 'It was a gruelling time. But I had become accustomed to it by then; I had been in arms for nine years, as had your father.'

Nine years – at eighteen, that is half of my life that Lambert had spent in the saddle and at war. The scale of the conflict that raged while I was a child still has the power to shock me. We owe the men who triumphed lasting gratitude, I think, not for the first time. And who am I – and cosseted courtiers like me – to question the wisdom of such proven giants? 'Nine years,' I repeat. 'No wonder, General, that you, that Father and all who served with you, feel such loyalty to your army.'

He is pleased with my remark and rewards me with a thin smile.

'I do, Your Highness. When you have seen as much blood shed on English and Scottish soil as I have, you cannot help but believe as I do – will always do – that the men who won the war deserve a powerful voice in government. The army's interest must be protected against those who would betray it to further their own.'

It is clear that he refers to those Members of Parliament and his fellow Councillors who are pressing the new civilian constitution to replace his military Instrument of Government; the men like Bulstrode Whitelocke, Nathaniel Fiennes and his young brother-in-law Charles Wolseley, General-at-Sea Edward Montagu and Lord Broghill, whom Harry had mentioned in his last letter, my own brother-in-law John Claypole (and, I suspect, Secretary Thurloe) who seek to settle Father as king, presiding over a traditional government not in thrall to the army.

Is Lambert after his own power? Does he desire to become Lord Protector when Father dies, to lead a more martial government once the advocates of kingship have been defeated? If there is a void in power, I can think of none better placed to ride into it. Yet I am not sure. Lambert's heart is still on the battlefield, that much is clear to me. And looking at him now, his stern grey eyes fixed on the merlin soaring against the horizon, I cannot help but feel some sympathy.

We have just finished our midday meal in the Great Hall when a fierce commotion erupts in the passageway outside. Secretary Thurloe slides between the long tables to approach us, his manner apologetic.

'It is these Quakers again, Highness, come to complain about a new play which is being performed in London. I have summoned the playwright, imagining you would wish to hear both sides of the business.'

'You know me well indeed, John,' Father smiles. 'I'll hear them now – let them approach.'

A gaggle of wagging tongues presses forward towards our table, though they fall silent when they reach the dais. I watch the scene eagerly.

'Master Fox,' Father warmly addresses a young man in sombre clothes, 'and Mistress Fell, I believe. Welcome back to court.'

There are a few hissed intakes of breath around the room; I know many think Father too lenient towards these notorious radical trouble-makers. But Father has told me before that these new Quakers are men and women of God just as we are and that he will let them be as long as they live peaceably. 'If it was such a trial for King Charles to be Defender of the one Faith,' he said, 'remember I have a thousand faiths to protect.' I know that liberty of conscience and toleration of all faiths that cause no sedition are the foundations of his beliefs: he had admitted the Jews to England once more, after all. And I admire him for it. But I for one dislike the ranting disapproval of these Quakers and would give them less time than he does.

'I enjoyed our last debate,' Father is saying now, clearly relishing the fight to come. 'On what subject would you beg my ear today?'

George Fox thrusts himself forward, his broad hat fixed resolutely on his head as is the way of his people. 'On the subject of a disgraceful stage-play which is even now corrupting the good people of London and turning the city into a Sodom and Gomorrah,' the Quaker says.

'In contravention of Parliament's long-standing ban of the theatres,' Mistress Fell adds with a vigorous nodding, her large white collar bright against her black dress.

'Ah. And the playwright?'

'Here, Highness.' A pug-faced man of middle age dips into a bow, his feathered hat sweeping the floor. 'William Davenant at your service.'

'What say you, sir?'

'I say, Highness, that there is much of moral worth in what I have written . . .'

'Pah,' Mistress Fell interrupts. 'Poison! That is what it is, dripped into the ears of the weak and unknowing.'

I cannot help admiring her fortitude, however much I dislike her views. It is wonderful to see a fearless woman speak her mind so publicly.

'Have you been to see the performance, madam?' Master Davenant counters. 'It concerns the Siege of Rhodes and is a sober and worthy piece, not a bawdy farce.'

George Fox leans across his companion protectively, shaking as he gesticulates. 'She would not set foot in a theatre, sir, for fear of what she might tread in.'

'Peace, peace,' Father says, holding up his hands. He moistens his lips and sits back in his chair while we all await his words.

'On the question of entertainment, I will tell you what I believe,' he begins at length. 'I do not hold with music in church: it distracts from the true and honest word of God and smacks of popery. Neither do I hold with the playhouses – Parliament was right to close them, for lascivious plays often lead to sinful thoughts and the theatres had become centres of drunken, violent rabble-rousing and rebellious royalist assembly. That was the issue with horse races too, though I myself am fond of the turf. Gambling now I cannot abide for its corruption of good men. But, I am not a saint and nor do

I expect others to be: a man has appetites and must take his leisure and seek out beauty where he can. Moderation is the watchword. There is much to admire in the craftsmanship of fine paintings, tapestries and statues. The pursuit of sports gives men vigour and exercise. A little dancing, done with decorum, does no harm; neither do a few glasses of wine. And music in its proper place – out of the churches – performed with skill, elegance and virtuosity is for me the highest form of art.'

I smile. Even if I would wish a little more gaiety in life than my father and a few more opportunities for harmless transgression to teach me the ways of the world for myself, I cannot fault his moderate views or their mild expression. I look over to where the Major-Generals sit together – Lambert flanked by Charles and Uncle Desborough with some of the other officers about them – and wonder if they heard what I had in Father's speech: a subtle shift away from the hard Puritanism they had imposed when they ruled the counties. For with each passing day, I feel the regime softening and settling around me as the power drains from the army leaders and flows towards their civilian rivals. Surely Father would welcome the chance to return England to the 'gentler, nobler time' he spoke to me of earlier? And what would be the easiest way for him to turn back the clock? I think as I shift my gaze back to him. To become king and repair the line that had stretched unbroken back to Athelstan.

Master Davenant places a lace-cuffed hand over his heart. 'I agree, Highness, and that is precisely what I aim at . . . this is a new form of drama, an "opera" which is sung rather than acted.'

'Ha.' Again Mistress Fell snorts her derision but Father holds up a hand to stop her continuing.

'So it is a piece of stage music?' he asks. 'And the story then, the moral – is it a good one?'

'Yes indeed, sire. It is an account of the famous battle and aims to educate the listener as much as enthral him.'

I watch Father carefully, seeing his brain working as he nods his heavy head. 'And you would like to write more such "operas", Master Playwright? What is your next subject to be?'

'I plan an opera concerning the cruelty of the Spaniards in Peru, Highness.'

Father gives a great burst of laughter. 'Ha! You would like that, Charles.' He gestures along the table to my brother-in-law and his mirth has a lightening effect on the whole room. 'Well, that sounds like a fine subject for you, Master Davenant,' he continues. 'I wish you well. Parliament may go its own way of course and my friends here,' he nods politely to the Quaker pair, 'have spoken in good faith and shown you that there are many godlier than I who will disapprove of your works. But I for one will not stop you. Come.' Father rises to his feet then. 'Let me show you the great organ I had installed over there; I'll have Master Hingston and his boys sing for you and I'll challenge you not to think them the finest trebles in the country.'

Father puts an arm around William Davenant's shoulders and leads him away a few steps before looking back at the Quakers. 'And Master Fox, Mistress Fell, I hope you will stay a while too, share some of your beliefs with me. I am certain that if you and I were but an hour together we should come nearer one another.'

As I watch them go, I think that this is what I love most about Father: his charm, his kindness. His humour and tendency to see the fun in things. I love his ability to soothe and reconcile the irritated, his open mind and willingness to see other points of view and admit his own mistakes. His gift for seeing the best in people, for spotting talent wherever it grows, for reading minds and forgiving what he finds there. And so he goes on: always listening, always balancing. A king in waiting.

After this excitement, we spend the rest of the day closed up in our private apartments with Master Marvell, whom Father has engaged to instruct us in foreign tongues. While these lessons aim to brush up our Latin and Greek, they place much emphasis on our understanding of French which – as the language of diplomacy and of our new allies – Father now considers essential that we master. As deputy to the brilliant, blind John Milton in the Latin secretariat, tasked with translating the government's documents and correspondence and being his master's eyes, Andrew Marvell is a suitable choice to undertake our instruction. He is also the court's foremost poet and so a person of great romance and glamour to Mary and me. At our coming to the court three years ago, the darkly handsome Marvell was the first man whose name we whispered together at night and whose entrance into a room prompted a flurry of elbow poking. He no longer provokes such a girlish response in us, but the legacy of the first, chaste affection we felt for him lingers in us both in secret, smiling pleasure.

In my case, the pleasure of Master Marvell's company is matched by my love of the study itself and I pore over my scratched translations with relish, making tiny correcting marks in the margins. Mary – always of a less studious bent than me – keeps up but is never the one to set our pace. And so, when Mother comes in to us at the end of the lesson, it is me who thrusts my best work into her hands while Mary packs away her things and smooths her skirts, thinking, no doubt, of how soon she can escape out to the stables. It is a comfort somehow to feel myself slipping back into the simplicity of girlhood in this way, chewing my lip as I wait for Mother's verdict. But truly I exist in both worlds. For when Mother has given me all the praise I wanted and declares that her true reason for coming is to speak to Mary about a private matter, I feel myself dragged forward into adulthood once more.

For I know what this means. My glance at Mary prompts her to ask that I too be party to the conversation; we both know that we will be stronger together in any talks about our marriage prospects.

Turning to Master Marvell, Mother bids him withdraw with her thanks and, having laid down a book, our handsome tutor backs from the room. She turns to the pageboys next and motions for them to leave us too and we watch as they bob and bustle through the doors. She waits, perfectly still and grand, until we are entirely alone, and then sighs, relaxing her shoulders and gathering us to her with a loud kiss each. Slipping out of her embroidered shoes, Mother draws us down to sit either side of her, the many stiff silk layers of her skirts puffing over our laps and the pearl drops at her ears and corset wobbling as she sinks onto the couch.

'Now,' she begins, turning to Mary. 'Your father has

mentioned to me a prospective match for you, Mary, and asked me to raise the matter with you.'

Mary stiffens in anticipation. I keep my hands still in my lap and wait.

'Thomas Belasyse, Viscount Fauconberg.'

'But the Belasyses are royalists!' I cannot help exclaiming, snatching Mary's right of first reaction as I spring to my feet. 'The whole family fought for the king!'

'True,' Mother nods, her voice even. 'But Viscount Fauconberg himself was too young to fight and you've seen how your father never considers a royalist background insurmountable for a man of talent. Look how he has promoted Lord Broghill – he was all set to cross the Channel to the exiled court before your father personally persuaded him against it. And the young Sir Charles Wolseley, who now sits on the Council of State despite his father fighting for the king. Besides,' she looks from Mary to me and back again, 'your father desires to make peace with the noble royalist families of the realm for the good of his Protectorate. Think what a great gesture of reconciliation such a marriage could be, how much good it could do.'

I fall silent then though my mind is racing. My feet strain to match my thoughts and so I begin to pace around the room, stopping by the window seat to follow Mother's example and take off my shoes when I feel them rub. Although I struggle with the idea of Mary marrying into a royalist family, I cannot deny that a viscount is a higher class of husband than any that were offered to Bridget or Elizabeth – a reflection of our exalted status since they were on the marriage market – but Mary has never even met him. I glance upwards, almost expecting to see the crown that hovers over Father's head, hovering there above us all. What was it Master Marvell had written about Father in his ode on the first anniversary of his rule? He 'seems a king by long succession born'.

Mother is waiting for Mary to speak.

'Thomas,' she says quietly after a few moments, as if tasting the name of her proposed husband on her tongue. 'What do you know of him, Mother?'

'I know that he is of a noble house with a fair estate in Yorkshire,' Mother replies, smiling reassuringly, 'worth around five thousand pounds a year, I believe.'

I think of John Lambert and his flat Yorkshire vowels. It was he who governed that vast county as the regional Major-General until only a few months ago; I wonder what he will say when he hears of this proposed match with one of our enemies.

'Yorkshire,' Mary repeats dully, and I know she is thinking of the many hundreds of miles that lie between that rough part of the country and London; how very different its great hills and vales are said to be from the flat fenland pastures of our childhood; how fierce was the king's stronghold in that sympathetic county until Parliament's victory at the great battle of Marston Moor swept him from the north.

'But do you know anything about him? His character, his temperament,' I prompt, returning to the couch and dropping heavily onto the cushions.

Mother shifts a little beside me, the layers of her gown rustling.

'I know only that he lost his wife last year and has since sought comfort in travelling on the Continent.'

'A widower.' Mary whispers the word to herself and I reach across Mother's lap to take her hand.

'That is not always a bad thing, Mary,' I say, trying to convince myself as much as her. 'Such men know what it is to take a wife and, more, what it means to lose one. They can value their second wives even more highly – look at Charles with Biddy.'

'So he is not here at court.' Mary continues her chain of thought from Mother's words. 'How is this negotiation occurring in that event?'

'He is in Paris, I believe,' Mother says. 'Our ambassador, William Lockhart – your cousin Robina's husband – is talking to him on your father's behalf.'

'William,' Mary nods over his name.

'I like William,' I venture. 'He will not do wrong by you.'

'Your thoughts, my dear?' Mother leans into Mary, tucking a loose ringlet behind her ear.

Mary loops her arms around her in response, dropping her head onto Mother's shoulder. As I watch them, the relaxed intimacy of their gestures catapults me back to our ordinary life in our old home. It is so hard for us to live naturally and familiarly in our gilded cage, when every word of ours, every gesture is observed and examined for the proof it must be of our humble origins and lack of breeding. We are given no second chances – there is always someone waiting for us to fail, watching for us to slip and make fools of ourselves. And we do: I stoop to pick up something I have dropped when I should wait for a servant to do it; Mother slips into serving food and drink to others when she loses concentration; my brothers reach to open doors and bump into the guards whose job is to do it for them; Father draws disapproving stares when he bends down to build up a dying fire. It is even harder for us, I imagine, than the true-born royals who lived in these palaces before us, who were at least raised to know nothing else, who never encountered a door that was not opened for them, never fetched a toy or a book for themselves, never lit a fire or poured a drink, let alone cooked a meal. Who thought that being in a room full of servants was the same as being alone.

'I will think on it, Mother,' Mary replies. 'You cannot expect me to say more when I have not met him.'

Mary looks across Mother to me and I smile at her in support.

'Of course, darling, of course,' Mother replies quickly, her voice relieved. 'Think on it and I will try and find out more.'

We sit together, silent in our tableau, for the next few minutes while my mind spins off into its own orbit; I know it is only a matter of time before we have a mirrored conversation about me. And how will I answer? How can I answer while Robert Rich wants me for his own?

Returned to Whitehall, we find the atmosphere in the palace and the streets around it as tense as before. Spring has come upon us suddenly and the city bakes in a flush of unusual heat as blue tits nest in the topiary of the gardens and a pair of wrens raises a noisy brood in the ivy that climbs around my bedroom window. Mary and I long to escape into St James's Park to see the carpet of primroses and the ducklings and goslings on the pond, but Secretary Thurloe will not let us leave the palace and so we content ourselves with sitting under the blossom in the orchard along the edge of the bowling green, reading and talking away the hours.

But the next day brings an end to our relaxation and reveals the reason for Thurloe's restrictions. It is Dick who comes to find us in the orchard to deliver the news.

'The Fifth Monarchists have risen up in great swarms to the east of the City,' he says, his hands on his hips as he regains his breath before beckoning us to stand up. 'You must return with me to our rooms, quickly.'

'The Lord save us,' Mary whispers as we scramble upright.

'Is there any danger?' I ask, wondering frantically where Robert is.

'Not any more,' Richard replies as he helps us gather up our things. 'Thurloe knew what they had planned. His agents had infiltrated the rebels and so no sooner had they gathered on the green at Mile End at first light this morning than our troops arrested the ringleaders.'

'Mile End,' I repeat, thinking of an earlier time when men had massed on that green in protest – the peasants of Wat Tyler's rebellion who had brought their brave demands to King Richard II. That had been a just rebellion concerned with freedom, as all such rebellions are. But today's Fifth Monarchist rebels are no heroes, with their visions and violence and their frenzied calls for a government of the godly, elected by church congregations to rule by the strict text of the Bible alone, while awaiting the coming of Christ; I shiver at the thought of such a theocracy.

'Where's Father?' Mary asks, alarmed, as we hurry through the privy garden.

'Father wished to see the ringleaders – he has just finished with them. I was there, just before Mother found me and sent me looking for you.'

'And what did he say?' I ask.

'He heard them out of course and remonstrated with them. But you know what these madmen are like – theirs are the fixed convictions of zealots, set and unbreakable as mortar. They've gone to the Tower and Father has retreated to his study to brood.'

As soon as we reach the palace, I slip up the stairs into the stone gallery and go in search of Robert. I find him in the Great Court just outside the door to the wine cellar.

'I thought I'd better check we had adequate supplies if we're going to be besieged,' he calls to me as he sees me approach.

'I'm glad you find this amusing,' I reply, straining to sound nonchalant even as my heart pounds.

He draws towards me before checking himself as group of courtiers stroll past. 'It is only amusing so long as you are safe, my darling,' he says, keeping his voice low. 'Come, let me escort you back to your family's apartments.'

'So what do you think?' I ask him as he ushers me up the staircase, past a doubled brace of guards, our fingertips brushing whenever we have a moment out of their sight. 'Every time we face a threat, the government reacts in one of two ways. Will this uprising strengthen the army leaders' call to restore direct military rule? Or will it be grist to the mill for the MPs pressing for Father's kingship?'

'You're right,' he replies and stops me at an empty corner to plant a quick kiss on my mouth. 'This time, though, my money's on the politicians.'

Robert's wager is a sound one. Fired up with renewed fear about the stability of the realm, Parliament takes steps to break the deadlock over the issue of Father becoming king once and for all. And so it appoints a grand committee of one hundred MPs who, in turn, choose ten representatives to sit in conference with Father for as many days as it takes to hear and allay his reservations about taking the crown – Bulstrode Whitelocke, Lord Broghill and the brothers-in-law Councillors Nathaniel Fiennes and Charles Wolseley among their number.

John, who sits on the committee of one hundred, is equal parts hope and nerves each day that they sit; neither he nor Elizabeth makes any secret of their hope that the committee will persuade Father to become king.

'This is our last chance,' John says when he finds me with his wife in their rooms one afternoon picking out some of Betty's older gowns for me to wear, now she is too big to fit into them. Shedding his boots, John drops theatrically onto the bed, Badger springing up after him and licking his face. 'It's the last chance for those of us in Parliament who oppose the army's power to persuade your father in our direction. It will all hinge on the small committee's skill at advocacy. But we picked well.' He pushes past Badger's muzzle to wag a finger in the air above his face. 'We've packed it full of lawyers – the Lord Commissioners, Lord Chief Justice and Master of the Rolls – and Broghill is as smooth a politician as you'll ever hear.'

'You've done your best, John,' Elizabeth says, holding the last dress of pale green satin against her swelling stomach before tossing it to me with a tut. 'And I will try and speak to Father again.'

'I do not see how even you can change his mind, Betty,' I say, gathering the pile of dresses from the chair and pressing them into Katherine's hands for alteration. 'Did you not hear him at supper last night? He made it clear that the title of king is the stumbling block for him and said he didn't see how, if he rejects that, he can accept the rest of the proposed settlement, even though that was exactly what Charles was urging him to do. Though really that was just Charles trying to find a compromise, I thought. I doubt Lambert would tolerate any part of the new constitution when it is aimed so clearly at lessening the army's say in government.'

'If anyone can persuade Oliver, our men can,' John says, pushing Badger off him and sitting up on the bed just in time for his eldest son Cromwell to scurry into the room and hurl himself into his father's arms, his governess trailing in his wake. 'The lawyers especially. You should hear them when they're in full flow.' John opens Cromwell's clenched palm and counts on his chubby fingers as the boy squeals with delight. 'They argue that the name and office of king have been known in England for a thousand years; that it is bound inextricably into all of our laws and customs; that men know their rights under it and the limits of the king's prerogative too where the Lord Protector's power is unbridled. And so on and so on . . .'

Bridget, when she hears John give this same speech later at supper, scoffs at so many words spent on 'a bauble, a mere feather in the cap' as she dismisses the title of king. 'It is an unworthy obsession of men which God has smashed into the dust.'

'Why not let him accept it then?' Elizabeth counters, her tone as ever resembling a calm sea, whatever the rockiness of her words beneath. 'If it matters so little, sister, what then is the fuss?'

Hearing my two oldest sisters speak one after the other I notice the slight East Anglian burr of their accents: testament to the fact that when I moved to London at eight years old – still with time to lose my country vowels – they were already grown-up married women set fast in the ways of the fens. Bridget does not reply and, as I watch, I see the terrain of a much-fought battle mapped in the looks they exchange. Though they are as different in turn as their husbands are from each other, I know Biddy and Betty can read each other's minds as easily as Mary and I can.

'I know they love each other but I am so grateful we never argue like that,' I say later that night as I stand in my nightdress and gown combing Mary's hair. 'It must be so tiring. But what if Father makes you marry the royalist viscount? You'd disagree on everything.'

Mary frowns as I tackle a knot in her curls. 'I doubt it would be as bad as that,' she says, though I fancy more in hope than certainty. 'Besides, he may lose interest in the match if Father rejects the crown.'

'And if Father takes the crown, he may find a great royalist noble for me too. It's funny,' I muse, lulled by the rhythm of my brush strokes as Mary's hair begins to shine. 'A few years ago I would have been thrilled at the idea of becoming Princess Frances. But now, I wish nothing more than to lose all credit in the marriage market and marry the man I choose.'

Mary smiles at me in the mirror and I drop a kiss onto her head before placing the comb in her hand and absently picking up a bottle of scent to smell it. I expect her to relinquish the stool to me as it is my turn to be combed but she does not move. Instead, as I watch, her face contorts in pain and she clutches her stomach. Slowly she rises from the stool and I watch a tiny spot of blood appear at the back of her nightdress.

'Oooh.' I grimace in sympathy and put my arms gently about her, leading her towards the bed. 'Wait there, dearest. I'll find your rags and send Anne down to the kitchens for some hot peppermint water.'

Mary keeps to her bed for the next few days and so I wander about the palace trying to pick up news from the committee meetings to take back to her. If nothing else, it is clear to me that what flows underneath all of the MPs' arguments is their lingering distrust of the army. Father's loyalty to the soldiers is the sticking point.

The young Councillor and member of the MPs' committee Sir Charles Wolseley confides as much to me when I come across him outside the chapel after prayers one morning. Finding ourselves crossing the courtyard together, we fall into a companionable step and I seize the moment to ask him how the committee meetings progress.

'Not as well as I would hope, Highness,' he replies as he fixes his stylish peacock-feathered hat back on his head. 'For every time we press upon him that Parliament represents the will of the people on this matter your father, despite the nods of his head which show his appreciation of this fact, talks instead of the army; the honest and faithful men who took up arms with him against the king for the liberty of the people. He says they would struggle to accept any political settlement with the title of king in it.'

I know this a sore subject for Wolseley as he is not well loved by the army leaders. Wolseley's father fought for the king and Wolseley himself might have done too had he not been too young to take up arms. He only sits on Father's Council now because he made a shrewd marriage to the daughter of the parliamentarian grandee William Fiennes, Viscount Saye and Sele, and his new brother-in-law Nathaniel Fiennes smoothed the way for Wolseley to join him on the Council, seizing his chance to import another moderate ally who would strengthen his side against the Major-Generals. They, for their part, scoff and jeer at the young man for having done nothing to advance the Good Old Cause and earn his place at the table – 'that fool,' my brother-in-law Charles Fleetwood tuts whenever Wolseley's name is mentioned in our private family conversations, 'what does he know?'

'We see this as a matter of constitutional law and political sovereignty where the people's mandate is clear,' Wolseley continues, pausing to turn to me and search my face, 'but your father sees it as a question of conscience that only he and God can answer. It is impossible.'

I tilt my head in sympathy. 'Truly we all struggle with that side of my father, Sir Charles. When he is locked in conversation with God, none can get a word in between them.'

The young courtier gives me a weary smile in gratitude

before hurrying off to join his colleagues as they prepare for yet another committee session with Father. Watching him go, I wish not for the first time that I could join him in those meetings and see my future ebb and flow for myself.

Thinking of Robert, my nerves hovering somewhere at the edges of my body, I decide to go in search of him. Miraculously, I find him walking alone in the stone gallery as the rest of the court sleeps off a heavy dinner in the warm spring afternoon. Falling upon me, Robert pulls me into the darkened recess of a latticed window and kisses me, hardly pausing for breath as he covers my skin and lips with his.

'Has your father spoken to you?' Robert whispers into my hair as he catches his breath.

I cling onto him desperately, my eyes closed so as to feel every sensation of our embrace. 'Not yet. Though surely he must do soon now your grandfather has raised your suit with him? If he doesn't speak to me of it in the next few days I'll raise it with him. Perhaps with Mother first . . .' I add, suddenly baulking at the thought.

Robert nods and I breathe in the spiced leather smell of his hat as its brim presses into my forehead.

'My father is hopeless,' he says, 'but we have a new advocate. My grandmother, the dowager Countess of Devonshire, is made of finer stuff and she has also pledged her support to our cause. And I know your father respects her, whatever her past loyalties to the king.'

'Good. Speak to Secretary Thurloe too,' I urge. 'He is as deeply woven into my marriage negotiations as Father himself; perhaps he can help us.'

'I will.'

Robert leans back out into the gallery, looking each way. 'Someone is coming.' He wastes no more words but kisses me again, clasping my whole body to him, his arms pressed around me with such force that my heels rise from the floor. Breaking away from me he springs backwards, dropping into a deep bow. 'Keep faith with me, my darling,' he whispers, before hurrying along the gallery away from me.

Faith, I think, shivering despite the warm breeze that wafts from the open window over my flushed skin, as I am reminded painfully of the loss of Robert's body wrapped around mine; that is what all of this comes down to. Faith.

CHAPTER FIVE

I know that I am living on borrowed time and that the same interview that Mother had with Mary about Viscount Fauconberg awaits me. But I could hardly have guessed the form it would take the very next morning. Mother and I are sitting together on the long velvet couch in the withdrawing room, she sewing, while I read the latest edition of the government newspaper *Mercurius Politicus* which features a comment piece by its prolific editor Marchamont Nedham, advocating Father's kingship.

As I turn a page, Anthony Underwood, whom Robert had once suggested as a suitor for me, comes in from the outer presence chamber to usher in no less a person than Lord Broghill. Lowering my broadsheet, I watch as he bows grandly before us, a great feathered plum-coloured hat sweeping the carpet at his feet to reveal a powdered periwig on his head. I know him to spend profligately on the latest fashions and cannot help but admire the luxurious vermilion waistcoat and matching coat trimmed with lace and ribbon in which Lord Broghill, unashamed of his royalist pedigree, appears before us – Robert would turn the colour of his green coat with envy, I think with a smile.

Knowing him to be a favourite of Father's, Mother welcomes him warmly and invites him to take a glass of wine with us. As they exchange pleasantries I examine Lord Broghill closely, seeing in his wide smile and assured manner something of the commanding vigour I have heard he expended first as the powerful defender of Irish protestants against the Catholic rebellion before and during the war and then when he came over to Father's service and governed Scotland as president of the Scottish council in Edinburgh. Lately he has been one of the foremost MPs putting the case for Father's kingship. My brother Harry, I know from his letters to me, is a great admirer and friend of Lord Broghill's – both men natural coalition-builders working in parallel in the difficult realms of Ireland and Scotland – and Harry's judgement carries great weight with me. Nonetheless, I know the man before me to be a shrewd fixer and handler, second only to Secretary Thurloe in his manoeuvrings, and so I keep my wits about me.

'Your Parliament committee is not meeting with my husband this morning?' Mother is asking.

'No, Your Highness. We meet this afternoon. I, indeed, am one of those named to speak today, which is of course a great honour.'

'How exciting,' I cannot help saying. 'Are we permitted to know something of the thoughts you intend to voice, my lord?'

He turns his level gaze to me for the first time and offers me a charming smile. 'Certainly, Your Highness. I make no secret of my views on the question and would be delighted to share them with you. Many greater minds than mine have already spoken, particularly of the weighty legal arguments for the crown. Yet, as one former soldier to another, I wish to draw your father's attention to some of the more practical advantages of his coronation, two in particular.'

Languidly, Broghill sits back in his chair and crosses one ankle over the other. He is conceited, I have no doubt, but also shrewd.

'First, that this would be a selfless act offering far greater protection to those who serve His Highness. It is well known that after the last civil war that beset this nation, the new Tudor King Henry VII enacted an indemnity law safeguarding those who serve one claimant from the retribution of another should he become king. This law would apply once more if your father became king, protecting his subjects and, in so doing, strengthening his support from those otherwise too nervous to openly serve his regime.'

It is a neat point which appeals strongly to me with its evocation of historical precedent. I can see entirely how well this would play with Father's more cautious subjects, though, narrowing my eyes a little, I cannot help thinking how his foremost advisers, such as Lord Broghill, stood to benefit most from such legal protection.

My face must give away my thoughts, as Broghill continues quickly, after taking a sip of his claret:

'Lest you think me moved only by my own interest, Lady Frances, I would add my second argument: that taking the crown would also strengthen your father's hand against the exiled, pretended king, Charles. There are those among the army's leaders who argue that, conversely, crowning your father would reduce our late civil war from a conflict over the kind of government we have to nothing more than a clash between the rival houses of Cromwell and Stuart; just as the wars between York and Lancaster and all our conflicts before then had been before the new-found understandings and liberties of our own age. And that, furthermore, the House of Stuart is bound to come off better in the fight.'

He pauses there, to let us absorb that unnerving point of view. I glance at Mother for a clue to her thoughts but her face is impassive and she is sitting very still, the index finger she runs under the pearls of her bracelet the only sign of her racing mind. We wait in silence for one moment, then two before Lord Broghill seamlessly picks up his thread.

'Now I disagree with the army leaders on this. To *my* mind, were your father made king, it would be madness for the royalists to cast off the blessings of the monarchy restored just to change the occupant of the throne. A restoration of the monarchy vested in the House of Cromwell would take all the wind from their sails. As I plan to put it to your father: there is at the moment only a divorce between the pretending king Charles Stuart and the crown of these nations and we know that persons divorced may marry again. But if one person is remarried to another it cuts off all hope . . .'

I glance at Mother and see her quite transported by Lord Broghill's eloquence. I wonder if at last I see a glimpse of her own view on this mighty question, a view she has hitherto guarded jealously, even from her own children. She has told me before, when I have pressed her for her thoughts on Father's great decision, that she cannot be the support for Father that he needs if she is known to favour one path of the fork in the road before him: 'He must be able to lean on me whichever he chooses to take,' she had told me a few days ago as I kneeled beside her in prayer. 'The Lord will strengthen me to strengthen him.'

It is clear that Mother cannot speak and so I answer Lord Broghill in her stead. 'Those are fascinating ideas, my lord,' I say, my flattery genuine. 'The image you ended with of the marriage and divorce between a ruler and his crown is most striking.'

'Your Highness.' He nods in gratitude and I think my words have genuinely pleased him as the smile he offers me warms by the moment. 'But the fervour of my speech has blown me off course. The marriage I have come to speak to you and your mother about this morning is a different, though related, one.'

It is my turn to flounder and I look at him in alarm: I know he is married, so of whom is he speaking? Luckily Mother has regained herself.

'A marriage, my lord?'

'Yes. I do hope you will forgive my impertinence, but I have come to take a sounding from you both as to an idea I have for a marriage for Lady Frances that might do our nations a great deal of good.'

'Have you spoken yet to my husband?' Mother says, sitting a little straighter against the couch as she takes my hand.

'No, Your Highness. With the great pressures currently weighing on His Highness, I thought I would raise the matter first with you before adding to his burden. It is also somewhat dependent on the outcome of our negotiations with His Highness over the crown.'

'How so?' I find my voice, quailing at the thought of yet another thread binding my fate to that of this most intractable question of state.

'Well, Your Highness, as I have said, my greatest desire is for your father to accept the crown and to nominate his own successor, ideally your brother Richard, of whom I am a great admirer. However, I am a firm believer in having a second and indeed a third course opened before the first is decided on. If we cannot reach an agreement with your father on the new constitution, we are left with the vulnerable state of things as they are. And, in that case, I believe it would be in your power above all others to see off our enemies and set our fortunes in stone. In short, Lady Frances, there is one who, in that situation, would seek your hand above all the riches of the earth: the young king in exile, Charles Stuart.'

Charles Stuart, the son of the dead tyrant king. The prince who escaped our army's clutches to fly into exile. Our enemy who was crowned by the Scots and lurks now, across the Channel, plotting against Father to take back his throne. I am astonished.

Broghill sets down his glass and edges closer to us, leaning forward in an attempt at reassurance. 'It is an idea fit to blow cobwebs from the mind, Your Highnesses. A shock, indeed. But think for a moment about what it would mean. It is well known that the young king is desperate to escape his exile and regain his throne; your father and Parliament could set him any terms, any limitations they wished – terms which his father was too stubborn to accept. And, with you beside him, my lady, his heirs in your belly, your father and the rest of the Cromwell family would be untouchable and secured of a lasting legacy: a new and joint dynasty of Cromwell and Stuart, learned of the lessons of the war and uniting all three nations behind it.'

I hardly know how to order my thoughts. The power of Lord Broghill's vision overwhelms me. All thoughts of Robert are temporarily dazzled by an image of me sitting on the throne beside King Charles II. Me – the mother of all future kings. Me – the youngest of all Father's children – the one to secure his immortality.

But doubts immediately crowd my mind like steel-edged clouds. What of Richard, whom I would disinherit? What of our new alliance with France, a chief purpose of which was to stop the Stuarts from being able to invade us from their shores? What happens to that if we now simply invite the exiled 'king' in? And what of the man himself? How could he and I find any common ground after all the bloodshed of the past fifteen years? And, what is more, what kind of husband would he make when the whole world knows he trails a bevy of mistresses in his wake? I remember back to the previous year when one of his mistresses was captured by Thurloe's spies and testified to the fact that Charles had fathered children on her and paid her a pension; our whole court was shocked by the scandal, even the most loose-living among us. Could Father really consent to my marrying such a dissolute, godless man even if it did secure the nation's peace, when he objects so strongly to Robert whose sins are trifling by comparison?

Thinking of Robert leads me to more physical concerns. I summon to mind the portraits I have seen of the young prince, so tall and haughty, his black curls and matching black eyes almost menacing in the assured directness of their gaze, and try to imagine kissing his curling mouth. But my whole body rejects the sensation, sending my senses racing to Robert whose last kiss still burns on my lips. I feel tears pricking the inner corners of my eyes and, for the first time since I entered this palace as daughter to the ruler of England three years ago, I buckle inwardly under the weight of expectations. Somehow, I do not know how, I keep myself still, but Mother reads my wild thoughts and covers my hand with hers.

'You speak for Charles Stuart in this matter, my lord?' she asks.

I watch as he weighs his words, anxious no doubt not to blot his copybook with us by admitting to too close a relationship with our bitter enemy, yet needing to legitimise his proposal. 'I cannot say too much of my interactions with Charles Stuart and his court, Your Highness. But you can rely on his position as I put it to you. But be assured,' he adds hastily, 'that whatever I have said today, my foremost, my abiding loyalty is to His Highness and to your family. I will serve you and only you until the end.'

The end. His words ring in my head as I gaze away out of the window and onto the court below. What will the end be? And when?

Still I hear no word from Father. Indeed, I barely see him, as he oscillates from meeting the parliamentary committee to his state bedchamber, where he retreats into convalescence from a terribly sore throat for days on end, the Council forced to convene at his bedside. It is from John, rather than from him, that we learn of the outcome of the last meeting with the committee urging the crown, where Father reaffirmed his reservations about the title of king despite the monumental efforts of the nations' finest orators and advocates, who had paraded before him for ten days. The committee retreats to Parliament, tail between its legs, to consider Father's views; the kingship lobby has received a powerful blow but the battle for our constitutional future is not yet over.

And my own war has only just begun. In the coming days, I am assaulted by friends and rivals buzzing with the rumoured match between me and the exiled 'King' Charles. I do not know if the rumour-mongering is part of Lord Broghill's plan or what part his scheme might play in the larger campaign to persuade Father to become king, but I know that I am suddenly at the centre of every room I enter, however much I cling to the walls. The fight I imagined to secure the liberty to choose my own husband – to navigate my own future – is now terrifyingly real. And now that I face the battle, I do not know how to fight it nor see a way through to winning the war. I wonder if I should get word to Robert but I hardly know my own mind and prevaricate too long on what to write to him. As a result, he hears it first from another and Katherine brings me a hasty, agitated note in his familiar looping scrawl asking if it is true. 'If it is,' he writes, 'it is the worst nightmare I could imagine. How can I compete with a king?'

His pain stirs my heart and I go in immediate search of Mother, determined to tell her all. Finding her in the chapel, I wait until she has finished her discourse with Chaplain White and we are alone, before collapsing onto the pew beside her and pouring out my conflicted heart: my passion for Robert, my horror at the thought of marrying anyone else, but my lust for the lasting glory and chance for peace the match with Charles Stuart would grant to me and to us all. I feel my duty to Father and to the country battling with my search for my own happiness – what was the notion Robert had told me the ancient philosophers called true fulfilment? *Eudaimonia*. But then those philosophers were all men, I think angrily; men who could put fidelity to their own nature ahead of all else. What would they know of a woman being asked to leave the man she loves to marry another for the sake of her country? Words fall upon anguished words like swelling rain as the relief of revealing my feelings sweeps through me.

Mother wraps her arms around me, the layered silk of her wide sleeves bunching against mine, and takes deep rhythmic breaths to still my shudders. I press my face into her neck, sinking gratefully into the skin with its familiar scent of soap, lavender and pearls.

'I wish I could give you more comfort, my dearest,' she says, her voice soft and singing. 'But you know that this is how it has always been: we marry at the behest of our fathers. That is what I did, what my mother did and what your sisters have done. Though a kind father, like mine and like yours, chooses wisely and looks for the spark of liking between the bride and groom that promises to grow into a loving flame. But I assure you,' she continues more fervently as I wipe away tears, 'I will raise your feelings with your father and do my best for you. Keep faith, my darling, keep faith.'

I think of Robert urging me to do the same and

wonder again if this is all I can do. And it is such a vague, unhelpful notion. Where exactly am I supposed to place my faith: in my lover? In my mother? In the Protectorate? In God? I cast my eyes around the white-washed walls of the chapel, pressing my hands together in prayer, asking the Lord to help me. But though I feel his presence, I do not hear his voice the way Father does.

Frustrated with abdicating my faith to others, I decide to place a portion of it within myself and, burying my pride, set about an intense lobbying campaign. The subject is so delicate that there are few I can discuss it with safely, but that still leaves me a few powerful advocates. I go first, of course, to Elizabeth.

I find her in her rooms with Master Hornlock ordering clothes, bedding and blankets for the expected baby. Again, I wait for him to leave and ask her to dismiss her maids before I speak.

'Oh, Fanny,' she says when I have laid my head in her silken lap as I used to when I was a child. 'Can my little sister really be in love?' Betty seems almost more amazed by my feelings than Mother; and I think, as I have often done before, how much of a mother's love – and a mother's disapproval – lies within that of a much older sister. Is it unfair of me to think that Elizabeth feels a part of her own youth remains while I am still a child? Will I ever be able to catch up with her, to make up those magical nine years between us and match her womanly beauty with my own?

'My dear, sweet girl, in love for the first time,' she continues grandly. 'I remember what that was like; the intensity, the desperation! I was fifteen when John first kissed me, though I had been kissed once before . . .' She winks before floating away on her memories, and though I long to know more I force myself to pull her back to my predicament.

'But Father approved of John, he will not agree to Robert. And, worse still, the government is plotting to marry me off in a treaty. Perhaps to Charles Stuart! I confess I did not want Father to become king as you do but now the tables have turned on me. At least if he takes Charles Stuart's crown there can be no more talk of a marriage between us. You're always talking to Father about his dilemma – speak to him for me too, please.'

'Hush, hush,' Elizabeth coos softly as she strokes my hair. 'I will do my best for you, little one, I really will. And Father is kind and wants us to be happy. It may be all right yet.'

Under her soothing hands, I close my eyes in silent prayer that she can work her practised charms on Father.

I consider taking my anguish to Bridget next, but think better of it. She and I have never seen eye-to-eye in the matter of love and duty and she is bound to tell Charles, which would mortify me. But the choice is taken out of my hands when she drops Robert's name casually into our next conversation, revealing that Elizabeth has spilled my secret to her. I round on Betty in fury but am calmed by Mary: 'They too must have been confidantes once, dearest, just as we are, and you wouldn't keep anything from me for long . . .'

I write to Harry in my annoyance, finding it so much easier to confide in him on the page than I would to speak to Dick or my brothers-in-law in person. *You and Elizabeth Russell were the last among us to marry*, I write. *And you married in love, did you not? And has that not served you well these last four years? Can you not urge Father to allow me the same?* I will not have his reply for several weeks, but the mere act of sending these words across the sea to him calms me.

The last advocate I approach requires the most courage. I am crippled by embarrassment as I creep towards Secretary Thurloe's office one morning – the heavy slanting rain that thunders against the windows of the passageway helpfully drowning out my thoughts – but I know that nothing will happen to me, good or bad, without his say. Robert encouraged me to it the night before, reminding me in a furtive note secreted in Katherine's pocket that nothing I could ever reveal to the 'little secretary' would be a surprise, such is his proximity to power and strange ability to coax confidences from all men. I wonder, as I wait after knocking at his door, whether he will have the same effect on me.

The door is opened by a red-faced clerk and I see another two young men sitting on stools at high writing desks in the corner of the room, shirtsleeves bunched and hunched over their work like toads. Thurloe himself is sitting behind a large oak table which is covered in neat piles of paper, stacked and placed at exact right angles and weighted down with cubes of black stone. Coloured slips of dyed paper poke from each pile at random intervals betokening, I assume, some secret filing system of the secretary's invention. The air is thick with paper dust and a heady smell assaults me which, after a few moments' thought, I identify as a perfume of wax, ink and biscuits.

Thurloe leaps lightly to his feet and ushers me to the large round-backed comfortable armchair that waits at the visitor's side of his desk. It contrasts starkly, I note, with the uncomfortable, straight-backed spindled chair of his own. I make some brief remark to this effect and Thurloe smiles.

'I like my visitors to feel comfortable, Highness, at ease. To feel they are welcome as they share their thoughts with me. I, on the other hand, have far too much to do to recline in soporific comfort. My chair keeps me alert and safe from complacency: it is an old friend from the days when I was myself but a humble clerk in the fens.'

He makes a whisking gesture with his hands and the clerks scramble from the room, closing the door softly behind them. I wonder absently if he expects them to hover outside for the duration of our interview or if they are allowed to take a well-earned break in the kitchen.

When we are alone, Thurloe moves over to a small cabinet and returns to me with a glass of blackcurrant cordial. I settle myself in the cushioned chair and examine him closely as he perches on his seat, his fingertips pressed together. Can I trust him? For all his attentiveness, is he really my ally? But I have no alternative and so I plunge in.

He listens to me quietly and I find that under his still and sympathetic gaze, I pour out a larger measure of my private feelings than I had intended. Throughout my confession he gives little nods and shakes of his head, tuts and coos; as smooth and comforting as silk sheets heated by a copper warming pan. When I have, at length, said my piece, Thurloe unpeels his fingers and spreads them wide as if he would embrace me across the table.

'I will do my best for you, Your Highness,' he says,

'but you must understand that we are a new state – a fledgling Protectorate – beset by enemies at home and abroad. We are isolated and vulnerable, in need of all the allies and supporters we can muster. Your and your sister's hands in marriage may just provide us with the means to the lasting peace and security we long for.'

'I appreciate that, Master Thurloe.' I reply, placing my empty glass on the carefully positioned coaster at my edge of his table. 'I see too that my value on the marriage market depends a great deal on Father's becoming king, which is something I believe you above all others desire.'

Thurloe does not reply directly to my assertion but sits back in his chair, regarding me carefully. 'You understand a great deal, Highness,' he says with a measure of respect. 'I do indeed wish it. It would be a popular course: men took up arms in '42 not to effect a revolution in government but to restrain an overreaching king. Men say that in giving us victory, God testified against the *man*, but had he given witness against the *office* of king? Restoring the monarchy would bring swathes of the old political elite back into the fold; powerful families who baulked at the king's execution, but were otherwise aligned in all else with our government. With their backing, government would at last be placed on a stable, secure and lasting footing. And with your father king and able to name his successor, the peace and security of the nation will no longer rest only on keeping him safe from assassins – a task which keeps me from my bed night after night.'

I see the puffed bags under Thurloe's eyes and cannot deny his great efforts for our safety. I feel the moment of guilt that he no doubt intends: when others have sacrificed their lives for the welfare of the nation, is it too much to ask one ordinary girl to marry a prince? But he will not convince me that my happiness must be the price paid for this peaceful future. Would it not be ironic if we fought a war for our freedoms only for me to be forced to serve the Good Old Cause by relinquishing my own? I know such an argument will hold little sway with Thurloe, however; his is the mercantile world of facts and figures, of ledgers and testimonies, of backroom deals and unedifying compromises. He accepts that there will always be a price to pay.

'Robert belongs to a powerful family,' I say instead, 'a family who could be of use to us.'

'He does, Highness.' Thurloe picks up his own glass of cordial and swivels it between fine, thin fingers. 'But the Earl of Warwick is already our staunch supporter and the Countess of Devonshire as fair-weather a friend as she will ever be. We have need of new friends now.'

'Such as Charles Stuart,' I say, twisting the bracelet at my wrist. 'If Father does not agree to become king, you and Lord Broghill would restore the Stuart king with a new Cromwell bride in his bed to heal the breach.'

'It is but a rumoured proposal, Your Highness,' Thurloe says quickly, his tone soothing. 'I doubt it will come to anything.'

But I will not be soothed. 'What of my love? My happiness?' I blurt out the words driven by desperation even as I am aware of how selfish and childish I must sound.

'As I say, Highness,' Thurloe purrs in reply, 'I will do my best for you and for your interests, I give you my word.'

*

Speaking with Thurloe is all very well but it is Father I must persuade. Yet he remains elusive. I have a few sightings of him in chapel and at dinner in the Great Hall and a handful of snatched words with him when he sups privately with us in our apartments, but otherwise he spends many hours shut up with his closest advisers – Bulstrode Whitelocke, Lord Broghill and the ubiquitous Secretary Thurloe among them, I notice. His birthday on 25 April draws him out into the daylight to receive the usual pageant of presents from the court: fine clothes and jewels, books, plate and paintings.

He seems particularly pleased with the joint gift from Mary and me of a beautifully embroidered hawking glove of emerald green-dyed buckskin, which we urge him to use when, at last, Harry sends him his Irish goshawk. I seize the moment where none but Mary can hear us to slip Robert's name to Father, like casting a fly from a fishing line onto still water: 'May we speak of Robert Rich, Father?'

But Father bats it away brusquely. 'Not today, Fanny. Your mother had me up half the night pleading your case and we quite fell out over it. Run along now, I won't be moved.'

My cheeks smart as if he has struck me and I back away from him, almost stumbling down the step at the dais. Luckily, Mary has my elbow and we keep our dignity before the intense gaze of the court. But this is a very public day and so I have little privacy to nurse my hurt feelings. We celebrate Father's birthday with the court at a fine dinner in the Great Hall at midday and privately with a family supper in the evening. Mother fusses over the preparations for the meal, sending down her own recipe for Father's favourite eel pie to the kitchens, which she tells us mistily she has baked for him on every one of his birthdays since they were married – even sending it to him when he was away fighting.

'I hope they remember to rub nutmeg into the pastry,' she says nervously and I see her hands twitching for the feel of the dough. 'Perhaps I should go down and speak to them.'

'Heavens no, Mother!' Elizabeth exclaims. 'We are laughed at enough for our rustic domesticity. Do not add fuel to the fire by being seen below stairs.'

Mother sighs and it strikes me, not for the first time, that for all our luxury, she misses the simple pleasures of cooking; the immediate satisfaction of perfecting a recipe and watching the delight on the faces of her husband and children. In my childhood she was renowned among our neighbours for her skills in the kitchen and with the medicine chest. I see her even now standing on the chequered floor of our kitchen in Ely, pounding dough on the table and gossiping with the kitchen maid while I shelled a bowl of peas, the scent of honeysuckle and the sound of St Mary's bells drifting over the churchyard and through the low windows. If even I find the adjustment to our life as the foremost family of the nation hard at times, how must Mother find it after a half-century as an ordinary woman?

The pie is too bitter for me but Father, of course, loves it – each bite transporting him 'straight home to the fens and to our own hearth' – and is careful to credit Mother with the recipe and the kind thought.

I hear nothing further from him on the question of

my marriage that evening. Nor the next week, when we ride together in the carriage to Blackheath where Father is to inspect the troops we are sending to Flanders to fight with the French against the Spanish; his forehead instead pressed to the shutters, the bright May sunshine shut out. He turns from darkness to light for his men of course, riding along their lines calling out to them and speaking rousing words of the glory they go to, Major-General John Lambert watching from his grey horse. They, in turn, cheer and whistle, waving their hats and helmets and roaring his name, their massed ranks, bristling with silver pikes and the tips of muskets like a vast pin cushion, stretching as far as my eyes can see. I watch, transfixed as I always am when I am granted a glimpse of the battlefield father I hardly know.

Later that day, we travel down to Hampton Court and Father's mood deepens once more until the news that arrives after supper that Denmark has declared war against Sweden plunges him into a dark thunderstorm of flashing rage and sadness, his plans for a Protestant peace in the Baltic in tatters. Our new ambassador Meadowes, not yet sailed for Denmark, is summoned upriver in haste and sits up late with Father and Secretary Thurloe, the smell of pipe smoke and the strip of candlelight visible under Father's study door remaining until dawn. I wonder, as I pray with Mary, whether the news is an omen that Father will not be crowned the Protestant Charlemagne Thurloe and his allies wish him to become.

♛

I spend the next day trying to forget my worries with constant activity: a singing lesson with Master Hingston, some more language tuition from Master Marvell, a walk in the privy gardens with Mary. At supper I am forced to suffer the exquisite torture of watching Robert as he eats and talks on the far side of the Great Hall, his beautiful head turned away from me as we listen to the musicians sing for us after the meal. My feet, desperate in their desire to take me over to him, tap frantically under the table, only stilling when Mary moves her hand across from her lap to mine and presses firmly on my thigh. Out of the corner of my eye I notice Master Thurloe watching me and I bite my lip and lift my gaze away into the rafters above.

Later, my restlessness keeps me from sleep and, feeling the need to walk my way out of the maze of my thoughts, I take up a candle and shawl and slip from my room into the long gallery. It is a crisp, cool night, an alabaster moon throwing shafts of snow-coloured light through the shutters to form stepping stones down the length of the corridor. Leaving the ghostly figures of the guards behind me, my bare feet follow the stones to the end of the grand passage, my nightgown billowing about my ankles whenever I pass an open window. Reaching the end at the south-east corner of the wing, I turn into the shorter gallery that borders my parents' rooms and stop abruptly. Ahead, I see the flickering flame of another candle casting the heavy face beside it into the sharpest contrasts of light and shade.

Father.

He too is in his nightshirt and is standing motionless, holding his candle aloft as he peers at Mantegna's magnificent paintings that march down the length of the gallery.

I approach him slowly, anxious not to startle him from his reverie. 'Father?'

'You awake too, my little wench?' he asks, his voice hoarse with sleep as he keeps his eyes on the canvas.

I come to a stop beside him and turn to the paintings, letting my eyes travel from the start of the procession along the nine huge panels to its end; the earthy reds and browns golden where candlelight touches the paint. Looking at them now, in the still quietness of the night, I can almost hear the noises of ancient Rome on a hot day: trumpet fanfares blasting through the sun-filled sky, the rumble of carriages, the restless stamping of horses as they flick their tails at flies, the chatter and laughter of the crowd.

'They speak to me, these paintings,' Father says, his voice low and quiet as if we are in church. 'Of all the late king's collection, these are the finest. These were the ones I had to save from sale.'

It is plain to see why. Here – immortalised in the richest pigments by an Italian master – is Caesar: the greatest military leader of all, loved by his men and driven from the glories of the battlefield up to the heights of political power. A general, not a king; not invading but invited to pass through the gates of the Roman republic in triumph. He sits atop a chariot, captured in the moment a page crowns his head with a wreath of laurel – the same ring of leaves that encircles Father's head on his new coin.

'What message lies here for me?' Father asks, though it is not clear if he puts the question to himself, to me or to God.

I steal my smooth hand into his rough one just as I used to when I was little. I must speak to him in his own language. 'We have much to learn from the past deeds of men, Father,' I find myself saying. 'I know you urge the Lord's guidance and the Word of the Bible above all other teachers but I think that if we look carefully we may find His lessons written in our own history. For didn't God make Caesar and lay out his path even though Caesar did not know it? Was He not there on that day just as He is on this?'

I do not have much hope of persuading Father to my way of thinking; we have always been at odds in the set of our minds. For him, all strength, all guidance and support, all wisdom, sympathy and comfort is to be found in communion with God. But though I believe in God I do not find him of day-to-day help. Instead, if I seek such succour beyond the immediate love and kindness of my family, I look for it in the pages of the past. For what companionship is there greater than that of every man, woman and child who has trod the earth before us? What problem can we face that none has ever faced before? For me, history has the same capacity as faith to teach, to inspire, but also to tempt, to mislead. It produces in me the same sense of wonder that Father finds in the Word of the Lord, brings me the same comfort and greater perspective that comes when you see your own life merely as one stitch in a great tapestry of others.

'Perhaps.' Father nods then turns to me, his eyes wide as they search mine. I search his in turn, seeing not my sovereign but my father before me, battling, as he so often does, with himself. If he is truly lost then so are we all.

'You are my scholar, Fanny,' he says at last. 'You know my dilemmas, what should I think on?'

I bask in his warm regard even while I struggle to arrange my own thoughts under his gaze. How can I advise him when my own ideas and wants are as tangled as his? Do I wish him to refuse the crown whereby my chances now of being married to Charles Stuart must increase? Unless it happens, perhaps, that Father does not approve the scheme and then, with my marriage value reduced on his refusing the crown, he may in time come around to my marrying Robert. Or . . . do I want him to take the crown, a thing which would surely end any question of my marrying the exiled king, but which would make me a princess, destined perhaps to marry in the highest ranks of the nobility or even a foreign prince? Each choice forces uncertain outcomes upon me and I am as much at a loss as Father.

And so, all I can do is try to speak the truth as I see it in front of me.

'You can think on what happened to Caesar,' I say, directing our gazes back up to the canvas. 'Here he is at the height of his power and popularity: the conqueror of Gaul, the subduer of thousands. But you see the crown above his head – the shadow of his fate hangs over him. The people sought to make him king but there were those who thought him overmighty. And it was Caesar's own friends who pulled their daggers upon him and laid him down in the blood and dust of the Senate, all in the name of safeguarding the republic.'

'His own friends,' Father repeats, and I know he is thinking of his son-in-law Charles, of John Lambert and Uncle Desborough.

'But what end did their noble treachery serve?' I say, anxious not to cast my arguments too heavily on one side. 'Preventing Caesar from becoming king may have stopped his tyranny but it led to civil war and the emergence of an emperor who took even more power for himself than Caesar.' I shake my head in confusion: is this to be the fate of Charles Fleetwood and the other army generals if they move against Father? To be the fools of history who pave the way for another to abuse his power? A Major-General Fleetwood? A Lord Protector Lambert? Or even a King Charles II?

I am so lost in my own thoughts I am surprised when Father voices a reply.

'I see you play an advocate for the devil, my dear, laying choices and consequences before me, countering my thoughts whichever way they turn.' He smiles, his face drooping with tiredness. 'But that is good, that is what I need.' Letting go of my hand, he takes a few steps away from me then, pacing back and forth in front of the panorama, his gaze now dropped to the floor in thought.

I know to wait; he is forming his next thoughts.

Father comes to a halt beside me. 'Some have called me Caesar, did you know that? Others Brutus. Did I wield the knife? Or am I destined to fall beneath it?' He sighs and lifts his head once more to the scene. 'But there is a difference. It is the extent of the power itself which was at issue there,' he says, crossing his arms over his night-shirt in contemplation. 'Where, in our case, I believe the principal objection of the army – and indeed in my own heart – is to the title of king, not to its office. It is the word "king" that sticks so in our throats when we ourselves witnessed how God laid the title of king in the dust under our feet. I cannot build Jericho again when Jehovah himself has blown the walls down.'

As always, Father returns his thoughts from men to God, where I struggle to follow. I hate it when he turns from our family to God. Why can't we be the last layer of his skin, why can't I – here, now – be the lone voice of comfort in the night? But it is God, not us, whom Father clings to; it has always been. The Lord is his true soulmate and I envy God in that relationship, not Father. I know it is un-Christian, even sinful, but sometimes I resent God for all the torturing He does to Father: for the temper He stirs up, the dark moods He casts, the doubt He sows in the heart of His most loyal of all servants. I blame Him for the danger He has led my father into, the battles He has had him fight, the friends He has forced him to lose, the long dark nights of the soul like this one. Yes, God gives Father love, but so do we all and we don't ask for his suffering in return.

Here lies the greatest distance between us, the great darkness in his character which I fear above all others: the voice of God in his head. I fear both the decisions Father makes in haste and those he takes too long over at God's behest. The way God turns the pragmatist I know into the idealist I do not, forcing him into entrenched positions that cost him friendships; the brave decisions that turn him away from the easiest path and fuel his enemies' rage. And now that rage threatens us all – it points a musket from a crowd and plants a bomb in our home.

I can say none of this to Father of course; there is no answer I can give at all. But none is needed as Father continues his train of thought almost at once.

'Yet this is what Parliament would have me do. This is what most of my Council would have me do. This is what they tell me the people want, and I am fully persuaded of it; I myself have always believed a constitutionally limited monarchy to be the best form of government. They all tell me this is the only way to lasting peace and security, and who am I to deny that to these nations? Besides,' his voice drops to a whisper as if he speaks now only to himself, 'if I were king I could force Parliament to be more tolerant to many faiths; we would have no more martyrs, no more so-called heretics I could not save from punishment. You remember the case of James Nayler? Yes, vaguely? He was Lambert's quartermaster in the war, before he joined the Quakers. Anyway, I won't bore you with the details, but suffice to say, Parliament saw blasphemy in a man riding a horse into Bristol to re-enact Christ's entry into Jerusalem on Palm Sunday. The Presbyterian MPs used the case to say that my policy of toleration had opened the country to the Quaker threat. They convicted Nayler, lashed, bored and branded him, and I could do nothing about it.'

It is a disgusting image which plunges us both into silent darkness. But after a few moments, Father jolts as if started out of a reverie and pivots back towards me, uncrossing his arms and clasping his hands instead behind his back.

'And did Caesar have a daughter? What of her?'

I chuckle at that, recognising the new dance as he leads me into it. 'I don't know, I'm afraid, Father, we have reached the end of my knowledge of Plutarch. You'll have to ask Master Milton or Master Marvell.'

'I will,' he chuckles in mirrored reflection of me, 'I

will pay a visit to the Latin secretariat office first thing in the morning and ask them. Let's hope they're at their desks: that will put the cat among the pigeons otherwise!' But then his face shades once more with serious thought. 'And you, my dearest. What place for you in all this? A queen to young Charles Stuart perhaps?'

I catch my breath, held in his appraising look like a deer stunned by the approaching hounds. I try to wipe all thoughts from my head, aware of his uncanny power of mind-reading. Robert's name pushes on the tip of my tongue, bursting to escape, but Father sweeps it aside, smiling again as suddenly as the sun escaping a cloud on a drizzling, dappled day.

'I tease you, my dear, though I shouldn't. It is no laughing matter. It is only fair to tell you now, before events tumble away from us still further, that I do not look kindly on such a match. I hardly think it practicable, after all that passed between the dead king and us, for his son and I to unite our families. Even if I could countenance it, I cannot believe that he would. But, more than that, I could not paint myself such a hypocrite in your eyes.'

'A hypocrite, Father?' I cannot imagine what he means.

'Didn't I say you were not to marry young Robert Rich for his looseness of character?'

I swallow though my throat is dry. 'You did, Father, though you know my hopes that you will change your mind.'

He pretends not to hear me and continues his own train of thought. 'I could hardly say no to Robert Rich and then give you away to the most debauched man in Europe purely for my own political gain. It is not that

I am one of those fathers who thinks no men are good enough for his daughters – I took Henry Ireton, John and Charles into my heart. But I do set high standards for your happiness, and no prince, whatever his royal blood, may have my girl if he is not worthy of her.'

He leans forward and kisses my forehead. 'Off to bed now.'

Dazed, I turn and drag my feet away from him along the gallery under Caesar's eternal gaze, hardly knowing whether to laugh or cry.

I wonder thereafter if our midnight conversation has had any effect on Father. I certainly sense a change in the air when we return to Whitehall a few days later as the kingship party, cast so low only a week before, walk around the palace with renewed confidence. Secretary Thurloe has lost some of the grey circles under his eyes and John is positively beaming.

'It is won,' he whispers to Mary and me as he leads us into dinner on Wednesday. 'Your father has told Thurloe and some of the others privately that he intends to accept the constitution – the title of king and all. He has summoned Parliament to meet him tomorrow at Westminster where he will announce it!'

I must see Robert and so I prevail upon John, who has always had a soft spot for me, to invite him to join the three of us for a game of bowls in the afternoon. He raises a questioning eyebrow but doesn't refuse me – I suspect Betty has shared my feelings with him. And so, a few hours later I find myself standing on the bowling green concentrating every effort not to reach out and take Robert's hand. As we watch, Mary retakes a shot under John's interfering direction, his dog Badger worrying at his heels to get at the ball. It is Robert's turn next and I cannot help narrowing my eyes as he aims a perfect strike against my ball, shunting it far across the green to leave his own ball beautifully in line with the jack.

'Oh, really,' I exclaim in exasperation.

'My apologies, Lady Frances. But you would not have me do you the discourtesy of playing any less firmly against you as I do your brother-in-law.'

'Of course not,' I say quickly; as the youngest in the family, nothing infuriates me more than being allowed to win at any game. Has Robert already learned this about me?

He bows to me, winking under his hat. 'But neither would I do you the discourtesy of allowing you to retrieve your ball alone. Let me escort you to the far side of the green.'

I see his true game now and try to hide my smile as I take his proffered arm. As soon as we are out of earshot of the others he leans in to me as if to speak but really kisses my ear, the action needed hidden from their view by his hat.

'Darling,' he whispers, rubbing his shoulder against mine as we walk in step. 'How I long to be alone with you.'

My heart hammers in my chest and I replay each delicious word in my head to fix it there for later. 'I too, Robert, more than anything else.' I breathe in his spiced scent with its hints of oranges and tobacco leaves and feel my stomach drop down through my body, such is the strength of my desire for him. We reach the ball and

I turn to face him, willing my eyes to absorb every inch of him as soap onto a sponge.

He takes a step closer to me. 'I know exactly what I will do when I have you alone; where I would kiss you first. Where next. And after that . . .' His voice drops lower and lower as his eyes rake over me and my whole body hums like a bee before a bright flower.

Reluctantly I put up my hand to stop him. 'Listen, we don't have long. I must tell you Father is against the match with Charles Stuart.'

His face breaks open into a bright smile. 'Thank God. Well, I can count myself in good company then on your father's list of rejected suitors.'

I cannot help but laugh at that even though the sound that escapes my throat is tightened with pain.

Robert draws another step closer to me, his face serious again. 'You remember what we pledged to do that night in the Banqueting House when you stole my heart. We pledged to fight for our freedom, to put everything we had on the line. This is the moment to do it; we have no time to waste. We must work on your father, find a way to change his mind about me. It will not be long before he has lined up another husband for you.'

'And there's more,' I say, drawing him back towards Mary and John, conscious of how long we have been standing alone in full view. 'John says Father has made up his mind to take the crown.'

My eyes are ahead of me but I hear Robert take in a sharp breath.

'God's blood. So it is to be Princess Frances after all; first prize on the marriage market of Europe. Then we have even less time – we must change his mind about us now. Where is he?'

'He is walking in St James's Park, I believe,' I say.

'Then we must go and find him, tell him of our love – throw ourselves on his mercy.'

I shrink back from him, caught by a sudden fear. 'We can't!'

'We must. He loves you. If he saw how I feel about you, heard how I will work to make you happy. Learned what I have already done to mend my ways: abandoning the pleasure-seeking of my youth, taking on more responsibility for the family estates from Grandfather. Convincing my grandparents that I am worthy of you, that they will not lose their hard-earned credit with your father by pleading my case.'

I long simply to enjoy his words but I can't when they may turn out to be mere castles in the air. I look over to Mary, who is watching us anxiously, shielding her eyes from the afternoon sun, John talking idly beside her. Robert slips his arm behind me and squeezes my waist in reassurance. Joined together – just for a moment – I feel a shaft of steel within me. 'Very well. Mary!' I call to her as we approach. 'I tire of bowls and I am so far behind you all now. Why don't we walk over to the park? John, you'll join us?'

'Really?' John looks up at the sky where the sun has already dropped to graze the top of the tennis court building. 'But I simply can't waste all afternoon,' he says but then Badger, who heard nothing but the word 'walk', bounds after us. 'Oh, all right then.' John follows with unconvincing reluctance. 'Just a short walk.'

Leaving our bowling balls where they are, we cross

to the west end of the green and slip through the gate, past the guards and into King Street, our ladies-in-waiting trailing behind us. A short walk takes us past the tennis court building and around the Cockpit, where we lived for the last few years before Father became Lord Protector. Just beyond that, another gate brings us out into the lush green expanse of the park shimmering in the May sunshine. Almost immediately I see Father a little way ahead of us on the wide tree-lined gravel path, his guards fanned out behind him. He is standing quite still, his grey cloaked back towards us, head bowed, one elbow jutting out from it above a hand resting on the hilt of his sword. Two men are talking urgently to him and something in the scene makes me pause. I put out a hand to stop Robert from continuing further.

'John, Mary, wait.'

We stop and John curses under his breath.

'God's teeth. That's Desborough and Charles with him; they're talking him out of it!'

Glancing sideways, I see a flash of hope in Robert's eyes, in stark contrast to the despair written on John's face.

We watch, uncertain what to do, just out of earshot but not daring to approach any closer. Charles has seen us but carries on talking regardless and we hang back respectfully, each of us trying not to show how we strain to hear the words. But it is no use, Charles and Uncle Desborough are standing too close to Father for us to hear, though their frantic gestures and the way Father's head hangs, his eyes on the gravel, tell us all we need to know.

'We must stop it,' John says, straining forward from

us, glowering at Charles. 'They know how to work upon him and he's facing them alone, not even Thurloe with him.'

'No, John,' Robert says, gripping his arm. 'Leave them be. I'll take you back, my ladies,' he says softly, taking Mary and I on either arm and turning us back to the palace, a flock of startled pigeons fluttering up into the air from the path ahead.

On the following day, to everyone's shock Father cancels his meeting with Parliament at the last possible moment. Instead, once again he locks himself in with its committee all evening before the news filters out that he will meet the members of Parliament the next day, only now the venue is the Banqueting House, not Westminster. This time, no one dares to guess what he will answer and even Secretary Thurloe appears to be in the dark. Mother will not talk to us of it and she and Father retire to bed early with instructions not to be disturbed.

The next day dawns bright but clouded and a sudden shower of rain in the late morning hurries the MPs as they swarm along Whitehall and into the Banqueting House. Seeing their approach from our private gallery, I hurry along the passage to tell Mother, who instructs Anthony Underwood, who is waiting upon her to escort us all to the House. And so it is that Mother, Mary, Elizabeth and I enter the room grandly, taking our seats just to the side of the dais. Scanning the room, I see Bridget standing at the back. I wave to her, catching her eye and gesturing for her to come and sit beside me; but she gives the slightest shake of her head and turns instead to speak to our brother Richard, who is milling among his fellow MPs, clearly believing his place to be with them for this announcement rather than with us. I look for Robert's auburn head in the crowd before remembering that he – as neither an MP, nor a member of our family, Councillor or chief officer of the court – will not be there. I imagine him waiting in a passageway nearby with the broadsheet hacks, ready to spring upon the first person who leaves the room for the news.

At length, the door behind the dais opens and Father comes out, followed by the Council and Secretary Thurloe, John and the other foremost officers of the court. A great hush falls over the room as hundreds of heads turn from all directions to face him, as so many needles finding north. I expect Father to sit but he stays standing, rolling on the balls of his feet while he waits to speak. I hardly listen to his opening remarks – his apologies for wasting so much time and his customary circulatory preamble – and a glance at the upturned faces of his audience suggests that I am in the company of many others. All we want to know is his answer. And then, suddenly, it comes.

In a clear, ringing voice he tells us he considers the constitution proposed excellent in all but one thing: 'The title as to me. I cannot undertake this government with the title of king, and that is my answer to this great and weighty business.'

I taste metal in my mouth, my mind wiped blank. There is one collective noise of reaction, though the tone is confused with some men sighing, some muttering approval, some gasping with surprise, others groaning with disappointment. The quietest tut slips from Elizabeth, sitting next to me, though her smile never wavers. In contrast, I see Bridget nodding in approval, though her face remains set in a serious frown. How very different my two oldest sisters are, I think for the thousandth time. It is not hard for me to keep my face impassive as the choir of voices inside me seem to drown each other out into silence. My vain disappointment that I am not to become a princess shames me even as my heart gladdens at the sliver of hope this gives to my chances of marrying Robert. My relief that Father has listened to his conscience battles with my sadness that he has rejected the settlement I know he believes in his mind to be best.

Father meets straight away with his Council but the rest of my family hurry back to our private rooms, where, away from prying eyes, we pull and unpick his words and thoughts, naming the implications of his choice, counting the costs. Mother is impassive, John downcast, Elizabeth appalled, Bridget righteous. Mary wants to know if Father will be made safer while, privately, I long to know if he will be made more receptive to my marriage to Robert. We are at least spared Charles's pious gloating as he is in Council with Father, though John's reckoning with his fellow brother-in-law can only be postponed.

'It was their conversation in St James's Park, I know it,' he mutters darkly to me as he refills his wine glass for the third time.

Richard is the last to join us and we fall silent for his thoughts, aware that Father's answer may affect him more than any of us. Throughout the past weeks, he has been careful to keep his views to himself, cripplingly conscious, I suspect, that any opinion he gives could be twisted into an expression of self-interest as he is more likely than anyone to be nominated Father's heir to succeed him as Lord Protector. And now, though Father has rejected the crown, he has accepted the rest of the powers the new constitution grants him. This is not what Parliament wants but if it agrees to his suggestion he both has his cake and eats it and Father will be able to choose his successor after all.

Dick will not be drawn, even now, though the way he helps himself to a drink and slumps into a deep chair beside Bridget speaks volumes. Though he has never confirmed it, I guessed where his sympathies lie from the many hours he has spent talking, walking and playing billiards with his fellow MP advocates for kingship. At times, I have even wondered if the tight circle of Thurloe, Bulstrode Whitelocke, Lord Broghill, Edward Montagu, Nathaniel Fiennes, Charles Wolseley and the others proponents of Father's kingship is bound together as much by friendship and loyalty to my brothers Richard and Harry as by their collective hero-worship of my father. This seems especially true to me of the younger men among them – after all the glamorous nobleman Broghill, dashing General-at-Sea Edward Montagu and boyish brothers-in-law Charles Wolseley and Nathaniel Fiennes are much nearer Dick's age than Father's; it is on him that they pin their future hopes.

'It all depends on Parliament now' Richard says gloomily. 'The House began these negotiations by telling Father he could have all the new constitution – the title of king included – or none of it; a deal for it all or no deal at all. Now he has called their bluff, we must wait to see their response.'

Parliament capitulates. After all the bluff and bluster, on 19 May they give Father exactly what he has asked for: the new constitution but with the single word 'king' scratched out and the two words 'Lord Protector' inked in. Almost no one is happy with the compromise. The kingship party mourns the loss of the symbol they consider the key to a more secure future; while the army leaders frown at the small print of the new constitution which, clause by clause, siphons power away from them and towards Father and Parliament.

Yet the substitution of one word for another is not a simple change. Another committee is formed to consider exactly how the details of this are to be managed, how to transmit all that relates to the king in English common law and statute into this new constitution and this now permanent office of Lord Protector: the first of a dynasty of Lords Protector. More than this, the committee must consider how to circumscribe the title; how to constrain the powers of Father and his heirs with the same limiting effect that precedent has on the title of 'king' – the very feat the great orators and lawyers on the committee had said could not be done. As Bulstrode Whitelocke puts it to me in wry tones after chapel one morning: 'We went to war to keep a king within the ancient limits of the law – what would we have done with the tyrant King Charles without them? But perhaps that was the easy part, though it little felt so at the time. If this sorry business shows us anything, my lady, it is that it is far easier to pull something down than to set it up.'

'It is a fudge,' I say to Mary as we powder our faces,

taking the edge off the day's shine before supper, 'and everyone knows it. And where does it leave us?'

'I have no idea,' Mary sighs, as her lady-in-waiting Anne, standing behind her, slides a pin into her hair. 'Perhaps the viscount will give up on a match with me now I will not be a princess. We may find the pressure lifts from both of us.'

'I pray so,' I reply, staring at myself in the mirror and setting my mouth before reaching for my pot of pink lip stain. 'But I have no time to wait for my fate. Father has told me Charles Stuart is out of the frame, thank the Lord. And now, I hope, our continuing lack of royal status will put off other suitors. I have a window – a small one – before Thurloe unearths another suitor for me and I must find a way to fly through it to Robert.'

And that evening brings me encouragement from an unexpected source. We are joined for a private supper by Harry's wife Elizabeth Russell's family: her father Sir Francis Russell, his wife Catherine and eldest son John, now in his mid-twenties I would guess. Though the couple that unites us in kinship is far away in Ireland, still the Russells feel like part of our family now and we enjoy their visits. As Mary and I enter the antechamber to the dining room, John Russell breaks away from his parents and moves shyly over to us. He has a pleasant face, I think as he bows to us, and his greeting takes me home instantly with the East Anglian cadence of his voice. But his brown suit is a little big for him and at least two seasons out of fashion.

'I am glad to see you, Lady Frances,' John Russell

says, dropping a hand into his pocket, 'for I have something for you.'

He passes me a creased square of folded paper, the smudged handwriting bringing a wide smile to my face. 'Harry!'

John returns my smile. 'Yes, his letter to you was in our family's packet and, as we were coming to court, I thought I would deliver it personally.'

'Oh, thank you.' I press his hand in gratitude and return my fingers to the letter where they dance over it in anticipation. I look down at it greedily.

Mary, seeing my desire, reminds me of my manners. 'You can read it later, Fanny, we have guests to attend to now.'

'Oh no,' John says hastily, 'don't mind me. You must open it of course.'

I look between them. 'I will just skim it; see what it's about. I can read it properly later.' I break the seal and open the paper with just enough time to flick my eyes down the page before Sir Oliver Flemyng summons us in to dine. The last lines leap from the page and straight into my heart: *You ask me how marriage is for me, little wench? Well, my Eliza is the sun and moon to me, my daily companion and my nightly comfort. You must marry where you love, Fanny, if it is in any way possible. I have written to Father to say as much. PS. I have sent out inquiries for a little hawk for you – what a busy brother I have been!*

Beaming, I slip the letter into my purse and take John Russell's proffered arm into supper.

'Your brother's letter pleases you, Lady Frances?' he asks. 'Does it bear good news?'

'The best of news,' I reply happily, 'a brother's wisdom and support.'

'That is the best of news indeed,' he answers, as we take our seats together.

It is a lively meal, the tone, as always, defined by Father who is in excellent spirits, reliving the campaign he and Sir Francis Russell fought together in East Anglia in the early years of the war. They are not granted long to enjoy their war stories however, as midway through the meal, Thurloe sidles in with a whisper and a letter, and Father follows him from the room. I am sorry to see him leave his supper half finished but at least his absence allows the rest of the family to gossip about him.

'This must have been a difficult time for you, Lady Frances,' John Russell says quietly and I am taken aback by his kindness, that he should have thought of my uncertain position in all this.

'It has been,' I confide. 'At times it seems as if my future is suspended from a thread that dangles from the throne itself.'

'It has been a trying time for us all,' Bridget interrupts from John Russell's other side. 'With Father wrestling and wrangling with his conscience night and day.'

'There are some who doubt his sincerity though, Biddy,' Dick says. 'We watched his struggle, but others didn't. I have heard it said there are men who think that this compromise was actually the outcome Father always wanted: that he has, in fact, played a blinding hand, getting more power for himself without taking the crown and losing the army's support.

This statement is met with a nervous silence before Sir Francis Russell laughs heartily and the tension breaks. 'I have known your father these long years, my dear boy. And I can safely say that if that's true, he has turned more wise men into fools than ever before!'

Over the next few day and weeks, as the groundwork is laid for the enactment of the new constitution with its centrepiece ceremony of Father's new 'investiture' as Lord Protector, it becomes clear to all of us that Father is going to become king in everything but the name. As the realisation dawns on the court, reactions harden once more and any hope our new constitution might unify the warring voices on the Council dwindles. And if we can see the true nature of Father's new powers at court, the point is not lost on the people of London, where the streets are soon littered in pamphlets, newsbooks and sermons adding wildly opposing voices to the wall of sound that deafens us. I try not to take the hundreds of stamped inky pages to heart, try to rise above or below them, but it is hard to read both of Father's sainthood and of his black hypocrisy, and of my and my family's wanton greed and assumed airs and graces. Temperate voices are few when their sales are dwarfed by the extremist writers; and when the two most extraordinary examples of these publish within weeks of each other, I begin to wonder if we are living in a truly mad and dangerous time.

The first is a panegyric penned by an ecstatic Welshman who claims Father to be descended from the ancient princes of Britain. Our descent from the Williams family – the name my forebear replaced with Cromwell in honour of his uncle Thomas Cromwell – is known well enough but the elaborate genealogy drawn for us in these pages brings a blush even to Master Marvell's cheeks, he who writes odes to Father's greatness. Father, it claims, is Britain's long-prophesied conqueror and, once more, the image of Julius Caesar's triumph into Rome plays before my eyes. We dismiss it as foolishness of course, though after the horror of what followed it through the printing presses, I looked back on it to find comfort.

The second pamphlet was hidden from Mary and me for days. Even the pageboys, I later discovered, were paid off by Mother not to bring it to us. But still, news of it trickled through the court and into my earshot like the dirty stream that runs from the common jakes of the palace into the River Thames. When three hundred copies are seized in London on the same day that Father accepts Parliament's revised constitution, Mother can shield us from hearing of it no more and Richard, worn down by my insistence, brings me a copy. Titled 'Killing No Murder', the sheets I hold in trembling fingers urge the people of England to do no less than assassinate my father. This, it claims, would be 'no murder' but a lawfully sanctioned killing of a tyrant which God and man would forgive. I think immediately of the Pope's instruction, nearly a hundred years before, for good true English Catholics to kill Queen Elizabeth. Her spymaster Walsingham alone had saved her; would Master Thurloe keep Father as safe from this?

The text of the work is framed in such a way as to make sick rise into my mouth: it begins with a mocking preface addressed to Father himself and ends with a homily to the dead plotter Sindercome. 'To Your Highness justly belongs the honour of dying for the people', it opens, and Mary – always so frightened for Father's safety – hardly gets any further before collapsing in a storm of tears. I manage to read it through to the end, but only by pretending that the pages do not prick my fingers, and fling it away from me as soon as my eyes reach the last word as if it is written in poisoned ink. Immediately, I am taken back to the night of Sindercome's bomb and, trembling, I scuttle to my room and send Katherine at once in search of Robert, caring little for the rashness of this. He comes to me within a quarter of the hour, finding me hiding in an arrow-slit alcove half way up the back staircase to the stone gallery, which I know to be deserted at this hour and beyond the earshot of the nearest guards.

This time I have no words and I tear into him roughly as a starving man would into a banquet, slipping my hands under his shirt to the warm skin beneath and pushing my tongue into his mouth. I feel him stiffen with surprise under my fingers before his body relaxes and he matches my heat with his own. His arms are around my back now, up in my hair, then running down over my skirts to pull my hips fiercely to his. When Robert drops his lips onto my collarbone and down over the skin above my bodice, I feel my breasts leap and tingle under his breath. His hat falls and tumbles down the staircase as I thread my fingers into his hair and lean back until I feel the cool evening air from the narrow window on my face. He is lifting me backwards into the depth of the stone now, his hands moving under my skirts so quickly that I hardly realise they are there until I feel his fingers slipping into me.

I am in oblivion, my mind whisked out of my body and flying through the night air just as my skin and my bones push against his. I hear nothing, see nothing. Every thing, every sensation is deep inside me where warm waves wash through me as we kiss and kiss and kiss. And then, suddenly, I feel as if I am falling from the window and in the sheer terror of this I pull apart from him, pushing him back so his hands come away from me, even as my fingertips continue to cling to his shoulders.

'I'm sorry,' I gasp when I can speak.

'It is all right, my darling,' Robert says softly, his breath quick and shallow as he regains himself. 'I'm afraid I was rather carried away.'

'So was I.' I smile at him now, grinning in desperate relief that I have not upset him, have not done the wrong thing.

Robert matches my smile for an instant before it drops from his lips as he takes my face in his hands. 'Frances, we must, must marry.'

PART TWO

June–December 1657

CHAPTER SIX

Summer comes quickly and feverishly. Robert and I grasp every perspiring moment we can together while the heat dulls everyone's senses and Father and the government are distracted by the ratification of the new constitution. But then, to my despair, Robert is called home to his estate in Essex to help his father oversee the summer collection of rents and to amuse his half-sisters while his stepmother is in the final stage of another confinement. He is gone before we have a chance to say goodbye, but my disappointment turns to joy when I find a parcel in my room: an emerald ring, nestled in the pages of a copy of St Augustine's *City of God* – the passage on the search for *eudaimonia*, or true happiness and fulfilment, underlined in the faintest ink. I dare not display the ring in public, nor even take it outside my room, but hang it from a chain about my neck and wear it under my nightgown every night.

Like Robert's stepmother, Betty too has withdrawn into her confinement as she waits anxiously for the baby. Bored without Robert, I follow her, spending the hot afternoons in the cool darkness upon which the physicians insist, lying beside her on the bed reading and gossiping lazily. Beyond our sanctuary, the warm scented days are well matched to the almost unhinged carnival atmosphere of the court as everyone counts the days until the great ceremony of Father's investiture. No one voices the word 'coronation' – as after all there will be no crown placed upon Father's head – yet it is behind everyone's lips as the elaborate preparations are made. New coins are minted from last year's captured Spanish bullion and tensions are further released when the news reaches us that General-at-Sea Robert Blake has won a great victory against the Spanish by capturing their Plate Fleet off Santa Cruz. London and later the whole nation celebrate with a day of thanksgiving and Parliament votes the victorious Blake a jewel worth five hundred pounds as a reward. Father, almost bursting with pride, summons him to return to England in glory, though in part this is motivated too by reports of his ill health. Mary and I thrill at the news, conjuring as it does the ghosts of our childhood heroes Francis Drake and Walter Raleigh. I imagine receiving the General-at-Sea on his return just as Queen Elizabeth had her favourite adventurers and unearth a copy of Raleigh's great *History* to remind me of the rhythm of his voice.

There is one at court who does not join in the celebrations, however. General John Lambert and his supporters have always pressed friendship with Spain over France, as much from the commercial interests of the wool traders in his native Yorkshire as from any other motive. But now, the air of triumph Lambert carried after he persuaded Father away from the crown, and which has drooped a little week on week as the true civilian colours of Father's new parliamentary regime have appeared, falls entirely from his soldier's frame. Now he lives in a world where England is at war with Spain and the army has lost its influence, and he stalks the palace with a heavy frown, his grey eyes flashing beneath his brow like the new silver coins minted for Father's investiture. Mary and I add him to our prayer list and I find myself hoping that General Monck has sent him the Scottish falcons he wanted and that Harry will find my bird soon.

But if we are sorry to see Lambert's discomfort, John Claypole, Bulstrode and the other promoters of the crown are less charitable.

'I have little sympathy to spare for the great Major-General,' Bulstrode says haughtily. 'Not after the hours we spent in that committee with your father.'

And I can see his point, when the defeated MPs have been wandering the court like bedraggled hounds ever since Father refused the crown. Some of their number have even left London, retreating to lick their wounds in the seclusion of their country estates. Lord Broghill, Richard tells me quietly, even threatens to return to Ireland and quit public life entirely, such is his bitter disappointment at Father's betrayal.

Now that the dust has settled on the issue of Father becoming king, I resolve that it is time to question Mother on the latest plans for our marriages. Mary agrees and so, one morning when we are at Hampton Court, we swoop on Mother and steer her out into the courtyard where the heat is less oppressive and our ladies-in-waiting cannot listen so easily to our conversation. Mary and I take an arm of Mother's each and, linked together like a silver bracelet, we orbit the fountain, the water tinkling as above us swifts whirl around the square, dipping and diving into their nests in the eaves.

'What news of Viscount Fauconberg, Mother?' Mary begins. 'Does he still press his suit to William Lockhart in Paris?'

'I have little news, I'm afraid, dearest. Ambassador Lockhart writes to Secretary Thurloe that conversations with the viscount have stalled in recent weeks.'

Mary peers past Mother to me half in puzzlement, half in relief, while I cannot help a fishwife tut escaping my lips.

'He was waiting on Father's decision on the kingship, I imagine,' I say, irritation at the man's evidently calculating self-interest overriding my usual care with Mary's feelings. 'Not willing to commit himself to our family while the issue hung in the balance, before he knew if he was bargaining for a lady or a princess,' I continue, watching a swift looking quickly to left and right before it whips out and up away from its nest.

Mother nudges me in rebuke and I hang my head in silent apology.

'If that is the case, Mother,' Mary chooses her words carefully, 'ought we to look for another? A man nearer to home perhaps and more closely bound to Father and to the Good Old Cause?'

I cannot imagine Mother misses the hopeful edge to her voice. I examine Mary closely, wondering if she is thinking again of Nicholas Baxter, or if someone else has caught her eye while I was too busy looking at Robert to notice.

'I am sure that there is a perfectly reasonable explanation for the delay, darling. But I do also know that your father and Secretary Thurloe are considering some other prospective suitors, though I think they are set on a conciliatory marriage into a noble royalist family.'

'Do you know who?'

Mother slips her arm from mine and adjusts the pearls at her neck. 'I have heard the Duke of Buckingham and the Earl of Chesterfield mentioned.'

'The Duke of Buckingham,' Mary repeats in surprise.

'Surely not?' I counter, for he is the son of the notorious Buckingham who was assassinated for being too much the favourite of the young King Charles.

'Even he,' Mother nods.

'But he is at the exiled court with the young 'King' Charles, is he not? How could he marry Mary?'

'There has been a falling out between them, I believe, dearest, though I know no more than that. We must all wait and see,' she says, her soft eyes fixed on mine but power in her tone.

Mary stops walking, her eyes sunk to the flagstones. We all loose arms then and I turn to face Mother. 'As we speak of the exiled king, Mother, what of me?' I meet her gaze squarely. 'I know Father is against the royal match. Is it abandoned?'

'He tells me there are still a few voices in favour of it – Master Thurloe, Lord Broghill, as you know – but he himself sees no blessings in it.'

I nod, thinking back frantically to what Thurloe had said to me when I went to his office. Clearly, he still thinks to use me as a means to an alliance, however honeyed his words. I must be careful in my dealings with him. I lift my eyes to the swifts at their nests.

'And Robert?' I ask, my voice barely above a whisper. 'What of Robert?'

Mother pauses for a moment and I fancy, for the first time, that she may truly see the depth of my love for him.

'I understand, dearest, that the Earl of Warwick has offered a substantial sum in support of his grandson's offer for your hand . . .'

I turn back to her in an instant, my face alight with hope.

'But, but . . .' She holds a hand up to stop my thoughts. 'I am afraid your father remains immovable on the idea.'

'How can he?' I shake my head in frustration. 'The earl is his great friend. Robert has a noble name and a true heart and, by your account, there is even now a substantial offer of money. And, more than all this, I love him! Does that count for so little with Father?'

'Hush, dearest,' Mother says quickly, her eyes darting to the colonnades where knots of our ladies hover.

But I feel the anger working up inside me until it sends me to pace around the fountain alone, Mother and Mary's eyes following me as I circle the water ordering my thoughts. 'How can Father choose to be the author of all my unhappiness?' I ask plaintively when I return to them.

'I know, my darling, I know,' Mother says, her words catching in her throat. 'And I am more sorry than I can say. But your father has never been wrong about a match before and I know, I *know* that he has your best interests at heart. You must try to distance yourself from Robert; try to open your heart to the idea of another.'

'Frances . . .' Mary reaches out to me but I can listen to no more and shaking my head, wordless with anger, I whisk away from them as swiftly as the swifts.

*

I nurse my feelings for the rest of the day and insist on a supper tray in my room. As the evening wears on, I wait anxiously for Mary to return from supper so we can discuss our conversation with Mother. But we never have the chance as around ten o'clock Elizabeth goes into labour. Though this is her fourth pregnancy, it is a long and complicated birth and more than once my brother-in-law John lets tears fall on my shoulder as he clings to us in his fear. But the terrifying night passes and the next day too and at the end of that all I can feel is relief that my beautiful sister has survived and that her baby boy – Oliver – appears to have done so as well.

The bells ring out across London and Father, who had been almost as frantic with worry as John, grins from ear to ear. Gifts and messages flow into the Claypoles' rooms, visitors too once Elizabeth can bear them. Bridget comes with flowers and soothing ointments and, as we four sisters sit together in our two pairs, she and Betty swap horror stories of their childbeds while Mary and I can only listen, shut out of the conversation in an insurmountable way. Once or twice, I catch Biddy wiping away a tear and I remember that, for all their differences, before Mary and I were born and the events of the war drove them apart, my older sisters would have been all in all to each other.

Mary herself is utterly besotted with the infant and spends every possible moment at Elizabeth's bedside, cradling little Oliver and helping the midwives to clean and change him. She has endless opinions on his looks, his movements and gestures: so like John in this way, so like Elizabeth and even his namesake grandfather in others. While I – I confess only to myself – see little to distinguish him from any other baby and cannot help an uncharitable annoyance that Elizabeth should have honoured Father with his name, particularly when she called her firstborn Cromwell; both gestures bound to make her even more his favourite daughter as I have always secretly feared she is.

Faced with Mary's almost audible ache for a child of her own in a refracted mirror of my own indifference, I wonder as so often before how she and I can have been moulded so differently from the same clay. While her heart is filled with the longing for a baby, my body craves only the means to the end as the darkly carnal, rumpled-sheets atmosphere of the childbirth rooms stirs my passion for Robert. Leaving them later that week for a dress fitting for Father's grand investiture, I am fired as never before by my love. And as Master Hornlock moves his hands lightly over me, a measure of tape in one hand, his lips pressed taut over dress pins, my body burns with the furious conviction that none will prevent Robert and me from reaching our marriage bed. If I must, I will take my future in my own hands.

The day of Father's great ceremony on 26 June dawns bright and beautiful as if God is indeed happy with the outcome of the long weeks He and Father spent wrestling with the issue of kingship together. The mid-summer sunlight sparkles on the river as we come by barge from Whitehall and, leaving Father at Parliament Steps, process straight to the Great Hall in the Palace of

Westminster while he goes to meet the Speaker of the Commons and MPs in the Painted Chamber.

The great hammer-beamed hall before us is breath-taking. Huge banners and ribbons – twenty, thirty feet high in red, white, blue and black, the colours of our Cromwell coat of arms – hang from the five-hundred-year-old rafters with the rampant lion seeming to scale each one, its red claws and tongue like spots of blood. At the far end, beneath the huge window, a beautiful gold canopy has been erected over a raised platform with banks of covered seating on each side. I am so overwhelmed I have stopped quite still. But Sir Oliver Flemyng ushers me and the other women of our family forward – first Mother, then Bridget, Mary and me, Aunt Liz and cousin Lavinia, our ladies trailing in our wake. Carefully, we climb into the stands. When we have each reached our appointed place, we settle together like nesting birds, our vivid satin skirts folding and rustling into one great multicoloured sea of shining fabric. Around us the hall is buzzing with voices and, as I glance upwards, a white dove flaps between the hammer beams where the streamers flutter in the breeze.

Mary's hand steals softly into mine and I take a deep breath as I survey the scene. As I watch, MPs, judges and civic officials follow our lead and climb into the stands, pushing past knees and greeting each other with handshakes and tipped hats. The ambassadors are there too and I see Signor Giavarina taking his seat, arranging his velvet cloak neatly around him and granting me a little wave when he catches my eye. Watching him, I wonder absently if he is still waiting for his promised audience with Father.

Now that I am here in the room, I have lost any lingering doubt that we are to witness a ceremony as splendid as any of the coronations that have come before it. There is no crown on the pink and gold cloth-covered table that stands close by on the platform, but all the other symbols of a monarch's investiture are there: the robe of purple ermine-lined velvet, the shining sword and heavy gold sceptre and the great gilded Bible. And the chair of state waiting under the canopy, Mary whispers to me and Bridget, is none other than the ancient coronation chair carved for Edward I to accommodate the Stone of Scone on which kings had been crowned since time immemorial: the same stone on which Jacob had laid his head to dream of the angels climbing up and down the ladder to heaven.

Gazing at it now, as we wait for Father to make his entrance, I can almost feel the kings and queens of the past hovering in the hall. Though, wondrous as I find this, I cannot escape the chill of the last king's presence; he who had been sentenced to death in this very room. This is in my mind, and in no doubt many others', when the procession enters the hall, though the rich sight before me soon drives away the melancholy thoughts.

Every man of any standing or office in the court walks with Father: all of his household officers, the Council and Secretary Thurloe, ranks of the nobility and the Mayor of London carrying the sword of the City. Dick is there, self-conscious under his soft smile; John has a prominent place of course, sparkling and smiling in his brilliant livery; and Charles too, serious and stately as he walks beside Uncle Desborough. But it is not they, nor even Father who brings the wide smile to my lips. It is

Robert, who I had feared would not return from Essex in time, whose every step, every turn of his head, every smile stops my heart and whose inclusion in Father's entourage fills me with hope. He is wearing a new coat in his favourite green, gold buttons flashing as they catch the sunlight streaming through the high windows. My heart calls to his so loudly that I think the whole room will hear, but he does not catch my eye. Nonetheless I am content with the rare pleasure of being able to watch Robert without him, or anyone else, seeing how I feast my eyes.

My hopes are boosted still further when I see the special honour accorded to his grandfather, the Earl of Warwick. Tall and graceful, it is he who bears the sword of state before Father – the same part played by Major-General John Lambert three years ago in Father's first, more muted, investiture as Lord Protector under the Instrument of Government constitution he had drafted. Lambert himself is there, walking with his fellow members of the Council, but the message is clear: notwithstanding Father's rejection of the crown, this is a new Protectorate based on a traditional civilian footing with the whole of the legislature, judiciary and nobility of these nations – at least in appearances – behind it.

No one, I think with a degree of comfort, could see this array of power and influence, of old families and new, of Parliament and army, and deny that Father – that our family – is now supported by the whole establishment. Scanning the crowd, I hope that the agents of Charles Stuart, who are no doubt among us, report that same view back to him. Surely none would suggest I marry him now?

The ceremony itself is a sober affair with the Speaker of the Commons, Sir Thomas Widdrington, proclaiming Father's title as Lord Protector, now settled by the full and unanimous consent of the people of the three nations assembled in Parliament. Distracted by Robert's three-quarters profile on the far side of the hall and remembering the feel of the sharp angle of his jaw under my hands as we kissed, I do not follow all the speaker's words, though I regain my concentration when Robert's grandfather and Bulstrode Whitelocke together lift the ermine robe onto Father's shoulders. Once he has this, the great Bible, sword and sceptre, Father swears his oath of government, is blessed by the chaplain and then moves to lower himself onto the great coronation chair.

'They say if it groans then the ruler is royal,' Mary whispers to Bridget and me. 'If the chair stays silent, then he is a usurper.'

I stare at her. 'But Father's neither!' She shrugs and we all strain forward to hear. It is hard with so many hundreds in the room to make out the exact noise as Father sits but I think I hear a creak. 'It groaned!' I whisper.

'I heard nothing,' Bridget counters and I look at her in horror.

But the ceremony continues regardless and I soon forget the legend when a trumpet fanfare heralds the loud proclamation of Father as 'His Highness Lord Protector' with great shouts of 'God save the Lord Protector' ringing around the hall with echoing cheers. I glance back at Father, wishing I could read his thoughts in this moment, but his face is an inscrutable mask. Those about him smile with relief, however, and I notice Bulstrode

Whitelocke and Edward Montagu glance at each other as they stand before Father's chair with their swords held aloft. The Dutch and French ambassadors who sit either side of Father nod and clap; the symbolism of the endorsement of the great Catholic and Protestant powers for Father's elevation lost on no one.

And then my heart leaps into my mouth as Father rises and bows to the ambassadors and dignitaries who surround him, and Robert moves forward with a couple of other young nobles to take up the corners of Father's train. As Father steps off the dais and begins to move through the crowds I catch Robert's eye for the briefest moment and he twitches the corner of his mouth before his face settles into solemnity for the procession. Watching Robert and Father sweep past me together I lift a fan to my face to shield the two tears that carve down my cheeks to meet the smile beneath.

The ceremony at Westminster Hall is followed by a magnificent procession along Whitehall. Father travels in his state coach with Richard, the Earl of Warwick, John Lisle, Edward Montagu and Bulstrode Whitelocke, with John riding immediately behind them leading the pride of Father's stables. All through the cities of London and Westminster bells ring and later bonfires blaze while cakes are handed out and French wine flows through the streets like the great River Thames itself.

We girls do not take part in the procession but make our way quietly back to the palace by river to change into our evening gowns. When Father and his procession return the feasting and celebrations begin and our family takes centre stage. The atmosphere in the palace is heady, with all sides of the recent disputes feeling a measure of tension relieved at the temporary resolution of their quarrels. The army generals who have little taste for such opulent display nonetheless bring themselves to drink Father's health and break bread with the politicians of the kingship party, who smile in spite of the hollowness they see in the day's compromise; past and future both brushed under the wine-splattered carpet for now as we celebrate today for its own sake.

Such is the merriment and the crush of people that I feel sure Robert and I would not be missed if – somehow – I can find a way to escape with him. But though I am always aware of where Robert stands in the room, as if he is picked out in flames in the corner of my eye, I am never alone to go to him, always surrounded by my parents or siblings. Eventually and miraculously, I find myself momentarily overlooked as John and Dick share some gentleman's joke behind gloved hands. Immediately I feel Robert as he brushes past me, smell the orange spice of his neck as he leans in to whisper.

'Outside. The stairs behind the pantry in the corner of the Great Court.'

I do not have time to reply before he is gone, his green back swallowed into the crowd. Hastily, I look around me. Katherine is speaking to her husband, Richard and John have quite forgotten me in their joke. Only Mary catches my eye as she looks my way while a servant hands her a glass of wine. Quickly I move over to her.

'I'm going outside for some air,' I whisper as I pass her. 'Please cover my absence if anyone asks for me. Tell them you were just with me and that I have gone to fetch my fan, or to wash my hands. Whatever comes to your mind first.'

'Frances . . .' Mary calls after me, her eyes wide, but I do not pause for an instant.

I hardly notice how heavily I am breathing until I emerge into the summer evening air. There is still some light in the sky as the last of the birds share the twilight with swooping bats. Picking up my skirts I weave in and out of doorways and around walls, hiding my face from the servants who duck in and out of the pantry, until I find myself at the bottom of the staircase. Immediately a hand reaches out and pulls me into the doorway.

'We can still be seen!' I whisper urgently before we lose ourselves in kisses. 'It is not yet dark.'

'This way,' Robert says and quickly he leads me up the stairs and along a passageway. As we go the sounds of the servants banging and crashing around in the pantry and the larders beneath us recede until, passing around a corner and into another corridor, we find ourselves in complete quiet. I have never been in this part of the palace and look around me with a mixture of nervousness and excitement until Robert stops at a door. Glancing to left and right along the deserted landing he opens it and pushes me inside before turning to lock it behind him.

We are in a small chamber overlooking the court of Scotland Yard, an unmade bed in the centre of the room, a desk and chair beneath the window with a tankard and bowl of apples. Looking around breathlessly I see the familiar clothes, the piles of books, the evergreen coat. I turn back to him.

'This is your room?'

Robert looks at me and I see for the first time an uncertain, almost embarrassed frown on his beautiful face. I expect him to come forward to me, to take me in his arms, but he stays where he is, leaning against the door as if his back is fastened to it with paste.

'Yes. Presumptuous, I know. But I had to be alone with you just for a few minutes, and this was the safest place I could think of.'

I continue to look at him while I think quickly; we may never have another chance to be together like this.

He continues to examine me. 'I am sorry, Frances, did I do wrong?'

In that instant Robert looks so young and nervous, so unlike the swaggering courtier that I first knew, that I burst with love for him.

'Thank you for my presents. The ring . . .'

'It was my mother's,' Robert says quietly. 'I wanted to show you, I wanted you to know that in my heart you are already my wife.'

Slowly I step forward until I am a few inches from him and reach up to pull the hat from his head. Keeping my eyes on his, I move my hands to his coat and inch it up over his shoulders where it falls to the floor. My fingers find the gold buttons at his waistcoat next and slide them from their fastenings – his chest rising and falling heavily under my hands – until I see the shirt beneath. I slide the waistcoat over his shoulders too and, rising on my tiptoes, thread my hands around his neck to untie his collar. As my lips near his, he takes my face in his hands and pulls me to him for one gentle kiss. Releasing me again, he drops his hands to my bare shoulders and, finding the ribbons at the back of my dress, slides it down until it sinks onto the floor into a stiff pool at my ankles.

Robert takes a moment to stare at me as I stand before him in my underclothes, my skin prickling under his eyes as my breasts swell above my corset, the thundering of my heart almost bursting my stays. Then the gentle hesitation is gone as he sweeps me up in his arms, his hands moving all over me as if he would feel every single inch of my skin. Shaking, I fumble with his shirt until it loosens and he pulls it over his head to reveal acres of bare flesh. I cannot believe the size of his chest, the breadth of his shoulders. Overwhelmed by longing I reach up for them and Robert stoops to pick me up and carries me to the bed. The sheets smell of him and I turn my face into them, closing my eyes to inhale his scent while I feel his hands at my skirts. Then, suddenly, it is the scent of his neck as his great shoulders rise above me, his hair falling onto my forehead as he kisses me, my hands running up and along the arms that carry his weight, tensed at either side of my head.

The heavy gathered pearls which normally hang from my neck down into the hollow between my breasts slide to one side of my neck and onto the bed just as I feel Robert's hand between my legs. I close my eyes and my mind goes blank as he rubs and kisses me so I hardly realise he is slipping inside me until he does it, slowly and smoothly while he presses his forehead against mine, one hand cupping my face. I stiffen in sudden pain and gasp but he covers my mouth with his – half kissing, half breathing in and out in the space between our lips. He moves inside me, gently at first then with more purpose, and though I remain rigid with fear that he will break me, after a time I find myself relaxing with each of his movements as if my body is swelling in welcome to him. With each breath I feel him deeper inside me until he is at the centre of myself. And then I am lost.

Afterwards, we lie together, sprawled and tangled, staring up at the canopy over the bed. I cannot speak, can barely think. Have we been there for minutes or hours? I look at Robert's limbs as they lie beside mine and cannot get over the marvel of him. Cannot stop thinking that all the times I have seen him before – have talked with him, danced with him, kissed him – this body, these muscles, hairs and freckles lay beneath his fine clothes, waiting for me to touch them.

How odd it is, I find myself thinking, that I live among all these men in the palace and I only ever see their faces, their necks, perhaps their hands, uncovered. I had seen my brothers in their undershirts before, and Father too of course, though I was much younger when we last lived together in the intimacy of an ordinary house. So I know that a man's body differs from a woman's. But I had never touched one before; never felt the muscle so hard just beneath the skin, the long bones and the coarse hairs, the lump at a man's throat and the strength in his hands.

Dazed and overwhelmed I might have lain there all night had Robert not brought us to our senses.

'Darling. We must go back, you will be missed.'

I know he is right but I cannot bear to get up from this bed, to part my skin from his. A sudden fear floods me like a summer storm: will he still want to marry me now I have given myself to him as all the whores of Surrey must have done before? And how could I compare to them? I close my eyes and turn my face away from him in case he reads my thoughts.

But he does.

'Frances, my love.' Robert turns my face back towards him and kisses my eyes. 'We will find a way to be together again soon, I swear it to you on God's blood. You will be my wife and I will be your husband.'

It is exactly what I need to hear and I seize him roughly, pressing him to me as the tears flow freely now. His desire was my only doubt, not any longer the objections of my father. Now I have lain with Robert I have the ultimate weapon in this fight. Though I shrink with horror at the thought of telling my father what we have done – at the damage I would do to my relationship with him – if he leaves me no other choice then I know that I can. He would have to let us marry then.

Ten minutes later, I slip into the Great Hall to find Master Hingston and his musicians playing a suite of folk songs. Though many faces are turned to the music, the bustle in the room remains and I scan the hall looking for any sign that I had been missed. Seeing Mary sitting with Bridget and Mother in the far corner, I weave through the court towards her, my cheeks burning as I feel as if I am walking naked among them. Surely they can see the change in me? How could I be doing what I was doing only minutes ago and yet no one see it in me now? But I attract nothing bar a nod of the head from Master Thurloe and, as I take a seat beside Mary, I exhale slowly and quietly in relief. She turns her knowing grey eyes on me and raises an eyebrow in question. But I cannot tell even her what has happened, not yet. A volley of laughter takes my eyes across to

Father standing with Elizabeth and holding little Oliver and, as I look at him resplendent in his kingly robes, my skin still tingling from Robert's touch, I feel a rush of hope for the future – a future of my own making.

♛

The next few weeks pass me by in a blur of excitement as hot as the July sun. Robert and I meet whenever we can but we have few chances to be alone as we were on the day of Father's investiture. Still I keep my own counsel though I know I will break and tell Mary soon: I cannot bear to hide my life from her sight. I know she will scold me though and for now, I wish nothing to spoil the dream I am living. And there is something thrilling about the secret that Robert and I share, the knowledge we hold about one another, the meaning behind our locked gazes which no one else can guess. I do not believe we have been discovered yet; though, even blinded by my desire, I am not so foolish as to think that we can hide for ever from all of Secretary Thurloe's eyes and ears. If he can know what is said at the very dinner table of the 'exiled king' Charles – as rumour has it he does – then what chance have we to hide ourselves from his sight living in the same buildings?

It is possible that our subterfuge is helped by the feverish atmosphere at court where strong feelings match the hot weather. With the parliamentary session ended, all focus returns to government by the Council which meets for the first time under the new constitution in the first week of July. Parliament has required all Councillors to swear an oath of allegiance to the new constitution, or 'the Humble Petition and Advice' as it has become known, and this causes great difficulties for General

Lambert, who storms and rages and cannot bring himself to swear. It is a bitter pill for Father to swallow from his second-in-command and the architect of the whole Protectorate. I fear our bubble of happiness from Father's investiture has been pricked for good.

My brother-in-law Charles Fleetwood explains Lambert's dilemma to us one evening when he joins us for supper at Hampton Court following a late meeting of the Council.

'Lambert cannot go along with the new constitution,' he says, his chin drooping low onto his chest above folded arms. 'He was relieved your father did not take the crown, as I was . . .'

John glances at Charles with irritation but Charles appears not to notice and continues.

'. . . But unlike me, his love for your father and for our family is not sufficient for him to accept the new powers this constitution grants to Parliament and the kingship party over the army.'

I think back to our conversation out hawking and the distance in Lambert's voice when he spoke of the war.

'And I suppose you have some sympathy for that argument, Charles?' I ask. 'Being so close to your men and the other generals.'

Charles sighs and runs his thin hands through his fine fair hair. He looks conflicted himself, his arms tense, his tone uncertain. 'Some sympathy, yes, Frances,' he says at length, 'but I would never act against your father or any of your family; you are my own family now.'

I smile at his words. I am quite fond of Charles in his own prickly way. I know too the great love he bears for

Bridget and for Father above all others, though he is not the loving brother-in-law to me that dear John is.

'There are those who say Lambert is ambitious for himself,' John says, bringing my eyes back to him. 'That he only stood in His Highness's way to further his own career.'

'There are others who say Oliver is forcing him out of the Council because he is afraid of what he can do, of his popularity,' Charles counters, his dark blue eyes – so unusual against his fair colouring – lifted to John in challenge. 'So you cannot credit what men will say.'

I shift uneasily as I listen to them for I, a woman outside the two warring camps of the court to which my brothers-in-law belong, can see that any rift between the army, Parliament and Father – whatever the merits on any one side – weakens the Protectorate and endangers us all. Lambert is a powerful friend to Father and would make an even more powerful enemy and I pray that Father can draw on his usual skills at diplomacy to keep him on the Council.

But my prayers go unanswered. In only a few days Lambert has refused the oath, left the Council and taken himself off to his palatial home in Wimbledon where he claims he will garden and paint and reacquaint himself with his wife and ten children – 'Only Whitelocke has so many,' Dick comments wryly. The rift with Father is complete and Father asks Lambert to resign his commission as Major-General in the army: a crushing blow to them both, I am sure, after so many years' comradeship in adversity. But a man of Lambert's stature does not quit public life without leaving substantial holes behind him which other men are quick to fill. In the army, this falls to Charles and Uncle Desborough who now, between them, lead and speak for the troops and their officers. And on the Council, to the astonishment of many though not to me, Lambert's boots are filled by the soft shoes of John Thurloe: 'the little secretary' no longer as he is promoted to full Councillor.

I cannot help but see much of what I have learned of the character of our famous forebear Thomas Cromwell in Thurloe's incredible ascent: the man of humble birth always working behind the scenes, always the first to know anything, and giving the last word of counsel to Father as Thomas Cromwell had to King Henry VIII. An administrator, a fixer. A secretary. Now a member of the Council in his own right. And this only a matter of weeks after the great ruin of all his plans to make Father king; for I have come to believe more and more that the events that led to Parliament's offer of the crown to Father were somehow shaped by the little secretary. 'If this is how Thurloe emerges from disappointment,' I say to Mary as we take turns in the bath, 'I would love to see how he handles victory.'

Then, barely as Thurloe has assumed his new position, he pulls off one of the greatest coups of his other role as the head of Father's intelligence network. The notorious Edward Sexby – the Leveller former friend of Father's who was the brain behind Sindercome's assassination attempt in January – is arrested. Sexby is taken as he boards a boat for Flanders, disguised, or so the press report, as a roughened native of the Low Countries. Though Mother and Mary are pleased at the news, Father feels mostly sadness.

But it is impossible for Father to remain in low spirits

when he has the means to cause so much pleasure. Almost as soon as he had been invested as the new 'Royal Protector', as some at court have taken to describing him, Father uses one of the most ancient kingly rights to create hereditary peers to fill the benches of the new House of Lords due to be established later in the year. John is among the first to be ennobled and he and Elizabeth can barely contain their pleasure at this, for all Bridget frowns and pleads for humility. Mary and I tease them of course, calling them Lord and Lady Claypole and dipping curtseys to them, but they take our jests in good humour, especially since Betty is recovering from another bout of the illness that seems to strike her every few years. It had been a trying few months for them, with Elizabeth pale and feverish, but now with her health regained once more, baby Oliver thriving and the older children happy, I do not think I have ever seen the Claypole family in such good spirits.

Richard too has benefited from Father's elevation as he is chosen to take his place as Chancellor of Oxford University. Again, we are all bidden to an elaborate ceremony in the Banqueting House where Dick is conferred Chancellor with almost as much regal pomp as Father's recent investiture. He is pleased in his own quiet way, though admits to me how the post renders him embarrassed for the first time in his life at his own lack of university education. I believe him sincere in his desire to prove himself in the role and know him to be an able administrator. Nonetheless, watching him robed and blessed, I cannot help a stab of jealousy that he who, according to my other older siblings, never loved his books and his lessons the way I have, should be invited to spend his time and efforts in this highest seat of learning. 'What of us, Mary?' I ask her that night as we lie together on her bed reading the fortunes in each other's palms. 'What do we receive in this embarrassment of riches?'

♛

With Parliament dissolved, the new Council established and the summer fighting season upon us, Father's focus turns to matters of foreign policy. It amuses me to hear him mispronounce the names of far-off places and I reflect with renewed amazement on how this ordinary Englishman, unschooled as princes are in other languages and the finer points of international diplomacy – a man who has never stepped foot on the continent of Europe – now duels and dances with foreign kings across our great vellum maps of the world.

The handsome General-at-Sea Edward Montagu explains our position to me at supper on the eve of his leaving to rejoin his flagship *Naseby*. As Father has held this small family supper in his honour, I am thrilled to have been placed next to the gallant sailor who shines in his buffed uniform and sports a continental periwig to rival Lord Broghill's.

'Your father has tasked me with keeping up pressure on the Spanish in the Channel, Highness,' he says and the title *Highness*, light on his tongue as butter, reminds me that Edward Montagu was one of the key members of Father's Council who had wished him to become king. 'Our offensive alliance with France against Spain is gathering pace now. On land, our brave Ironsides are showing their mettle to their French counterparts with whom they besiege Spanish-held towns across the Netherlands. While at sea,' he pauses to beckon forward the servant hovering behind my chair with a treacle tart, 'my fellow General-at-Sea Robert Blake continues his blockade at Cadiz, where his fleet are ransacking Dutch ships for Spanish bullion and supplies.'

'But has Father not summoned Blake home, General, to collect his reward for his great victory at Santa Cruz?'

'Yes indeed,' Montagu smiles, showing a set of teeth far better, I imagine, than those of his crew, 'and his last letter to me signalled his intention to return forthwith. Speaking of letters, I received one from your dear brother this morning.'

'Harry?' I beam. 'He has mentioned before how often you correspond.'

'Ah, well, we are great friends, Lord Henry and I,' Montagu replies and again I notice the almost royal way in which he refers to us Cromwell children. 'He is doing a fine job in Ireland, much as Lord Broghill did in Scotland. And with Henry in post, General Monck commanding our army in Scotland and me with the fleet in the Channel, we are well placed to repel all our enemies. You can be assured, Highness, that your father has the best of men guarding the edges of his realm.'

He is so charming and confident, a little of his optimism rubs off his polished gold buttons and onto me and, gazing at his fine profile as he attacks his piece of treacle tart, I wonder briefly whether Father's Protectorate may endure after all.

From then on, General Blake is watched for daily on the south coast and when news comes a few days later that his ships have been sighted off Cornwall, all the officers of the court busy themselves with preparations for his welcome: a great feast and reception ceremony where

Blake is to be given Parliament's jewel is planned, and Mary and I hastily send our best gowns to be steamed. But Providence is a cruel mistress for sailors and, barely a matter of hours later, a tearful messenger arrives in the night with the news that brave General Blake, veteran of our war with the Dutch, hero of our campaigns against the Spanish, died aboard his ship within sight of Plymouth Sound.

It is a devastating blow for the whole country and I feel it particularly keenly, though I barely knew the man. I cannot help but see some portent in the sudden death of one of the Commonwealth's greatest heroes. As if it is a bad omen for the Protectorate as a whole, sent to shake me free from the fleeting confidence I had felt dining with General Montagu. Besides, there is something so unfair, so wantonly cruel about Blake dying when he was almost home that I can think of little else for days. Thoughts of death send me to seek happiness, just as they did in the days after Sindercome's plot, and I go in rash search of Robert. With our desperation to be together briefly overcoming our terror at being caught, we manage to hide ourselves among the orange trees in the palace privy gardens for long enough one night to lie together again. It is hot and humid in the darkness and with a cricket in the hedge, the scent of orange blossom on the breeze and the stars bright overhead, I can almost imagine I am drifting with the ghost of General Blake off the coast of Spain, the waves lapping against the hull of the ship as the desire swells through me.

Sir Oliver Flemyng, who as our Master of Ceremonies had taken charge of preparations for the celebrations of Blake's return, is forced to transform his plans into a state funeral at Westminster Abbey instead and spends the next few weeks working on this with the admiralty commissioners. The timing is especially poignant for Father, as we all spend the day before the funeral marking the date he finds most stupendous and miraculous in all the year – the third of September – which saw two of his greatest victories in battle: alongside John Lambert against the royalists and their Scots allies at Dunbar in '50 and, in the final battle of the wars, at Worcester in '51. The day is celebrated with a repeat performance of the six-part verse anthem which Master Hingston composed for last year's anniversary. His music, twinned with the words of the poet Payne Fisher, brings the court to its feet in applause when the six singers and six instrumentalists take their bows. And none is more moved than Father, who speaks repeatedly of God's purpose for each of us as he prepares to bid his greatest sea-faring general farewell.

This mood of mournful self-reflection has a profound effect on me and I retreat early to my room that evening to contemplate the fate of my own soul. I think of lying with Robert among the orange trees in the moonlight, and of how I felt that God was there too, drifting on the night breeze. But conflicting thoughts crowd in upon each other. It was a sin, the Bible tells us this, and Father would never forgive me if he knew. A hasty note delivered from Robert plunges me into further despair: *I went to see your father myself today but found him in a dark mood. He still refuses us. Oh my darling, I don't know what else to do . . .*

Mary, coming to find me later with a comb in her hand and her prayers for General Blake composed, finds me sitting in the window seat, tears trickling down my flushed face.

'Dear heart.' She crosses to me at once and pushes the hair out of my eyes, her own eyes wide with concern, the pale moonlight turning her dark hair silver. 'Is it Robert?' she prompts at last.

I nod wordlessly, knowing that now is the time to tell her all; I have slipped too far and am floundering without her help.

'We have gone further than you know,' I say quietly. 'Beyond all turning back.'

'You don't mean . . .'

I sink my eyes into my nightgowned lap. 'I couldn't help myself, Mary, I love him too strongly. And this may be the only way to force Father's hand.'

She gasps at that. 'No! You cannot possibly tell him, nor Mother. It would change everything; they would never look at you the same way again.'

A fresh spring of tears blinds me. 'I know, I know! But what choice have they given me? I cannot marry another man, it is impossible.'

Mary turns to look out of the window and her hand slips from mine. I try and read her face like a map through my tears and feel a sudden horror that she will not look at me the same way again either. Does she feel I have betrayed her by making the greatest leap of our lives without her? Not just before her but without her even knowing? Does she think I have crossed into womanhood and left her behind alone? Worst still, does she judge what I have done in the sight of God? For once, Mary's thoughts are hidden from me and I feel a sadness even deeper than that which had engulfed me before.

'Mary?' I creep my hand onto her lap. 'Please forgive me.'

'It is not for me to forgive.'

'It is. I care for no other's forgiveness more than yours.'

She turns her face back to mine then and I see the question playing on her lips before she asks it.

'What was it like?' she whispers eventually, as if the curiosity itself is shaming to her.

'Oh, darling!' I seize both her hands then, such is my relief. 'It was . . .' How, how to possibly put it into words? 'It was the only true thing I have ever done, the one great act of my life that has cast all others into oblivion; a true heaven.'

'But a heaven without God.'

'No! I felt him there with us. Indeed, I have never felt closer to Him than I did in those moments, and you know how I have sometimes struggled to see Him.'

It is Mary's turn to cry and I watch a single tear swell in her eye and burst over the lid onto the pale cheek below. 'But Frances, what of the dangers? What if . . .'

I watch her lips struggling to form the words.

'What if you were to bear a child? That is unthinkable . . . What of Father? His position? All we have would be snatched from us in an instant.'

I have no answer to any of this, either for her or for myself. Somehow the prospect of a baby has never felt real to me, though I know it could not be more so to her. All I can do is clasp her hands more tightly. Mary slides from the seat and I grasp at her nightdress, bright in the moonlight.

'Don't leave me.'

'I must, dearest, I must think. Hush now and get some sleep.' And with silent steps Mary is gone from my room like a barn owl flitting noiselessly from a moonlit field into a dark thicket.

I do not know what to make of Mary's words. What can she have to think about? She knows what I have done, what risks there are for me; knows too what I plan to do if Father will not move in his opposition to my marriage. What can she possibly do to help me? I find little sleep that night and, as a result, drift through the next day as if in a dream. At least we have come now to Hampton Court and so it is easier than it is at Whitehall to escape alone into the gardens and sink my turbulent thoughts into the cream pages of a book, even if I have to keep rereading the same page time and again. I cannot quibble with the subtitle of the newly translated French romance I am reading – *Love's Masterpiece* – but I find little comfort in my new knowledge of the subject.

My tears and sleeplessness seem to have brought on a sore throat and so I am excused my singing lesson with Master Hingston and sent to my room early in the evening with a tray of hot lemon water and honeyed porridge. Leaving Mary with Mother in the withdrawing room, I cannot help the uneasy sense that they plan to talk about me as soon as I am gone; something I so often find myself doing with Mother or my other sisters when one has left a room. So, despite my coughing, I do not undress and keep from my bed, pacing around the edges of the carpets in my room, tracing the patterns of the woven borders with my toes. It is with an odd sense of foretelling therefore that I hear the tap on my door a little later and let Mary into my room.

'Are you well enough to come with me to speak to Mother and Father, Frances?'

Nerves prickle my back like a hedgehog's spines. 'What for?'

'I have been thinking about you and Robert and talking with Mother – don't worry,' Mary adds hastily, 'I have not told her your secret, of course.'

'Of course,' I repeat in unthinking echo.

'Listen, dearest, place your trust in me for the next few minutes. I have an idea.'

I have no choice but to do as she says and I let Mary lead me from the room. It is an odd sensation; not since I was very young have I let Mary treat me as an older sister would. We have been equals, partners, peers; a pair of playing cards, two sides of a coin. But something has shifted between us. It is almost as if my transgression with Robert has, far from advancing me into womanhood ahead of Mary, cast me as a vulnerable child in need of her protection. Or perhaps it is only in taking me into her care that Mary can reassert herself in both her own sight and mine. I, the youngest of my parents' children, know all too well how it feels to be left behind and so I cannot begrudge Mary's reaction.

We find Mother and Father in their private bedroom: a room much smaller and simpler than the state bedchamber in which Father gives audiences. There is a bed of course with bedside tables and a damask-covered couch and stools arranged around the fireplace, but few other objects. The main – in fact the only – striking feature is the set of exquisite tapestries hung around the walls, which seem to weave the whole room in a haze of reds and blues. Indeed the remarkable depth of perspective in the fabric – the Italianate towers just visible through receding colonnades, the ruined temple on the distant hill – draws the eye into the very walls themselves as if this room were but one chamber in an open, expanding villa. The tapestries depict the story of the lovers, the gods Venus and Mars and their discovery by Venus's blacksmith husband Vulcan. Before anyone speaks, my eyes sweep over the sequence with familiarity, though I cannot help but see something new in the clandestine lovers' embrace now that I have felt such a thing for myself.

Returning my gaze to the room, I see Mother sitting on the couch, her maid combing out her hair while Father emerges from the dressing room next door at the sound of our voices, drying his hands on a towel as he walks.

'Girls?'

'May we speak with you, Mother, Father?' Mary says.

'Of course, my dears.' Mother takes the comb and nods to her lady-in-waiting to leave her and Father calls after her retreating back: 'You can tell Anthony I will not need him again tonight.'

'Certainly, Your Highness, thank you.' The lady backs out of the door with a bow and we are alone again; a normal family once more. I hear the sigh escape from each of us as we breathe easily again.

Mother holds out her hands to us and we go to her, sinking our wide skirts awkwardly onto the narrow chairs facing her. Father dries his face and lays down the towel before wandering across to join us, dropping heavily onto the couch beside Mother with a creaking of joints. He massages his right thigh before putting his stockinged feet up on a stool and crossing his ankles. Mother still has the comb in her hand and she gestures to me with it: 'Shall I comb your hair, Fanny, as I used to do?'

In that moment I can think of nothing nicer and so I go and sit on the floor in front of her skirts, my back to her and Father, my eyes on Mary. Mother begins to pull the pins from my hair, one by one, her ringed hands soft on my neck. Instantly I am returned to our house in Ely where she would do this for me by the parlour fire after supper while Bridget read to us from the psalms and my brothers banged in and out of the room. We lived on top of one another then in just a few rooms, with no fine attendants and ladies-in-waiting, just a girl to help in the kitchen, a spotty apprentice in Father's tax office and an old groom from the town. The sharp tang of polished leather from Father's boots kicked off on the floor beside me brings me back from my memory, and I hear his heavy breathing behind me; he is not the young man he once was.

'Father, we wish to speak to you about Frances and Robert Rich.'

Mary speaks softly but with assured purpose. I, however, feel no such calm and my pulse thunders in my wrists as I knot my hands together in my lap like a penitent. I have no idea what Mary will say but I decide in that moment that I will not leave this room without Father's permission for my marriage, even if that means I must reveal our carnal acts and debase myself for ever in his sight. I feel curiously light-headed at the resolution, almost excited by my bravery, the images of Venus and Mars caught in the moment of their illicit lust swirling around my vision. A small sigh escapes behind me, although I am too distracted to notice if it comes from Father or Mother; I know how vexed they have both been over this match these last months. I watch Mary prepare her next words, summoning them as if from deep within her body; she, among us, is most conscious of Father's health and happiness and always shies away from causing him distress.

'Father, I will say what Frances will not. She and Robert have a deep and abiding love and I must tell you that she will never be happy if they are not allowed to wed. I know you have objected to his character but I can assure you that, from what I have seen of him, he is far steadier and more constant than you assume. He comes from a noble house, one which has become closely aligned to ours, and you know how deeply his family desires this match.'

I feel Father get to his feet behind me and hear his steps as he strides back and forth behind the couch.

Mother speaks next, though she does not pause in her attentions to my hair. 'What Mary says is true, my dear; it is not so unsuitable a match.'

But still Father does not concede. 'I understand all of what you say, my dears, but after what I have heard of his dissolute behaviour, how can I be assured this young man will prove a worthy husband for Frances? How can I be sure of his nearness to God?'

Mary looks at me and I know the time has come for me to reveal my trump card. It will be easier at least with my back turned to my parents. I open my mouth to speak but hear Mary's voice instead.

'Father, I implore you. I love my sister beyond anything else and so I tell you now that if you will let her marry the man she loves, I will gladly accept any husband you choose for me. Any at all; whoever will be most advantageous to you.'

I stare at her in disbelief. Behind me, Mother's hands pause over my hair as Father's pacing stops abruptly.

'Mary!' I can find no other words.

Mary holds our gazes firmly, the low light of the fire flickering on the pearls at her neck.

'Oh, sweetheart,' are the only words Mother manages and we three wait then, knowing that it is only Father's words that actually matter.

'Daughter.' Father moves around the couch to Mary and lifts a hand from her lap. 'Dear child.' He kisses her slight hand and clasps it to his chest in both of his large ones. 'You move me by your gesture Mall, by the strength of your love. And you, Fanny,' he turns his broad face back to me, 'you move me by the force of your love for young Rich; by your constancy. If I have harboured doubts about his steadfastness, I can have none about yours.' Father shakes his head then, his tired face carved in shadows in the firelight. 'I grant your wish, my dears. How can I deny you all now?'

Tears stream down my face and I clamber forward, not to Father but to Mary whom I clasp from the floor, laying my head in her lap in thanks. Turning my blurred eyes sideways onto Father, I reach one hand up to him and he grasps it so that the three of us are linked together as one for a moment. But it is for a moment only as Father, squeezing my hand in ending to our discussion, retreats to his dressing room and disappears from sight. Watching him go, I swivel my gaze onto Mother who is beaming at us, tears in her eyes and the comb still poised in mid-air.

*

When, later, I can find the words, I pour my love and thanks and my outrage on Mary in a whirlpool of emotions. 'You shouldn't have done it for me, Mary . . . I would never have let you if I'd known what you intended. But I am so glad you did, I am so happy! But what of your happiness? What if Father makes you marry the widowed royalist viscount or the notorious Duke of Buckingham?'

Mary says little in response, though I can see from her shining eyes that she is sharing in my joy just as I am sharing in her sacrifice. 'I ask only one thing of you in return, Frances,' she says seriously when we have calmed ourselves. 'That you do not lie with Robert again until you are married. You owe it to me to be careful now that you will have what you want.'

'Of course, my dearest, anything you ask of me is yours.' I gaze at her in wonder before dissolving into giggles. 'Though I hope that Father lets us marry quickly!'

CHAPTER SEVEN

Robert sweeps me into his arms at the news, even though we are just outside the chapel, in full view of half the court. But it is Mary to whom he directs his joy, falling to one knee before her and kissing her hand in gratitude. He offers an arm to each of us then and guides us out of the palace into the deer park for a long walk among the first fallen leaves golden against the grass, our arms linked and heads bent together in collusion. Later he goes with his grandfather to see Father and then meets with Secretary Thurloe and two members of the Privy Council to set the dowry and agree a tentative date for November.

The autumn weeks ahead promise to be the longest of my life and yet, knowing what joy awaits me at their end, the widest smile hardly leaves my face throughout. I am true too to the word I gave to Mary, and Robert and I kiss and sigh but no more, keeping ourselves always within sight of Mother, Mary or Katherine, never tempting ourselves too harshly. Immediately that the bargain is struck, I write to my brother Harry in Ireland with the news and Mother, Elizabeth, Mary and I set about the wedding plans and preparations. The finest tailors of the City come to show us their latest silks, lace and taffetas, some of the fabrics travelled from as far as the end of the Silk Road.

Robert too is to have a new wedding suit of uncut velvet and he even threatens to wear a periwig of the sort now so fashionable on the Continent and which I have seen modelled on the roguishly stylish Lord Broghill and General Montagu. Though I tease Robert for a dandy, secretly I love the modern way he dresses.

We discuss the music with Master Hingston, the ceremony and the feast with Sir Oliver Flemyng, and my jewellery with Father's jeweller Master Riddell. The wedding will be at Whitehall and Elizabeth promises it will be even grander and more lavish than my cousin Lavinia's which I had so admired. I remember how Robert danced with me that day, how he hurt me with his jests about my family, how he later teased me in the stables about my own wedding, and all I can do is wonder at the workings of Providence.

But around our busy excitement, government continues. Our position against Spain in Europe still looks precarious as our alliance with France falters. Rumours swirl around London that the Spanish are preparing an invasion force, a new Armada. Faced with this, Father is persuaded to agree to the allied army marching on the town of Mardyke where – we learn to universal great amazement – the opportunistic 'exiled King' Charles and his brother, the so-called Duke of York, fight alongside the Spanish against our troops: 'Our civil war is not ended,' Father says wearily, his eyes blank over his cup of dark wine. Meanwhile, on the other side of the world, our Spanish enemies try to recapture Jamaica but the new governor resists the attack, winning great praise at court. It is a source of wonder to me, and to all, that we should have defeated the mighty Spanish who own most of the New World; that there is a small island somewhere in the far-off Caribbean that is ours. The English are pirates no longer.

In the midst of this a letter arrives from Richard's house at Hursley in Hampshire to say that he has broken his leg hunting in the New Forest; a piece of news which sends Mother into a frenzy of worry and bundled into a coach out of London on the road to Winchester, her bags packed with letters and cakes from us, and Father's own physician to accompany her. She returns within the fortnight, comforted that the wound is clean and her eldest boy is not in any danger of his life, though I cannot help but worry that he may not be fit enough to travel up for my wedding.

Dick has been greatly cheered, Mother tells us, by the news she was able to take him that Father has appointed him a member of the new second chamber of Parliament which will sit at its next session. And indeed, the other nominations for this new House of Lords provide Father with his greatest day-to-day preoccupation as he weighs and selects candidates from among the slowly widening circle of public men who will work with his Protectorate. With Dick and John chosen, and with most of the other nominees among those we know, we talk of little else at our family meals in those weeks.

While I am alight with excitement as our wedding day approaches, my darling Mary frets about her own future, though she is too kind to show it to me and too proud to reveal it to anyone else. I know she remains fearful at the prospect of marrying a former royalist and I urge her to approach Father on the subject but she will not, believing herself bound into silent acceptance by her promise for my sake to marry any man of his choice. In the end, she does not have long to wait for a definite answer, as Father reveals to her only a few days later that he has invited the royalist widower Viscount Fauconberg to sail back to England to claim her hand.

Though the match has not yet been announced, the court is buzzing with the rumour. For the Protector to give his daughter away to the heir to such a prominent royalist family – a family which has fought against his own for over a decade – is nothing less than astounding. Father and Master Thurloe maintain that it will be a great gesture of unification that will do much to heal and settle the country, but whispered doubts continue on all sides. As the Venetian ambassador puts it to me: 'Is the viscount truly reconciled to your side, *Principessa*? Or is this a royalist plot to place one of the exiled king's most loyal friends at the centre of the ruling family of his enemy?'

Even Robert is uncertain: 'It will hardly be a large wedding party on the groom's side,' he comments to me when we cannot be overheard. 'His uncles fought in the uprising against your father only two years ago: one is under arrest and the other is at the exiled court. And Fauconberg's only relative who fought for Parliament, Black Tom Fairfax, has fallen out with your father, so I hardly think he will come.'

All of this renders me deeply uneasy and I cannot help the dark currents of guilt that pulse through me as I look at Mary's pinched and nervous face as we wait for the viscount's arrival. She is too kind, too mindful of my guilt to voice her fears to me. But she does not need to, I know them all: what if her bridegroom is a royalist spy? Worse still, what if she does not like him? What if he is unkind or irritating or horribly unattractive? Or drinks too much, or gambles? Could she ever love him as I love Robert?

♛

Thomas, Viscount Fauconberg, arrives into this storm of conjecture on what, in the time of superstition, used to be called All Hallows' Eve, only eleven days before my wedding. Rooms are found for him in the Palace of Whitehall and the scene is set for his introduction to Mary in our private family rooms before we sup in the Great Hall. Mary is beside herself with nerves, trying on this dress and that; the blue silk with her set of pearls or the pink taffeta with her ruby necklace? Her maid Anne, Katherine and I try to calm her but there is nothing truly helpful that we can say. Desperate for the first moment of meeting to be over, we hurry to Father's presence chamber where we find the rest of the family assembled with Master Thurloe hovering by the door. Mother arranges us so that Mary is shown to her best advantage, sitting between herself and Father, the firelight catching her jewels and the line of her collarbone.

We have hardly settled when the door opens and the Yeomen of the Guard announce the viscount, along with Lord Broghill. I inspect the viscount closely: he is young – not above thirty, I would guess – which is a great relief. And his face and figure are not displeasing, though his nose is a little too large for his face, long and hooked above a small mouth. But the eyes are a pleasant brown and the hair deepest black, which is striking against his grey-blue coat and high white collar. It is a fine suit too, with silver brocade and matching buttons, though any man suffers when he stands beside Lord Broghill, who is arrayed in the most expensive vermilion velvet.

'Your Highnesses.' The viscount addresses us in a light tenor, going on to exchange pleasantries with my parents and Broghill. His words are polite and his delicate Yorkshire accent noble, though his tone is reserved and I notice that he hardly looks at Mary. She, I see, is blushing furiously while attempting to hold a glass of wine to her lips without her hand shaking. They only come to speak to each other when Father directs us to go in to supper and offers Mary's arm for the viscount. He accepts her graciously enough, though keeps his head high and his eyes directed ahead as they walk from the room together. He is not a tall man and, I notice as I fall into step behind them, appears to have block heels on his silver shoes. But he is just taller than Mary at least, so I am grateful for that.

I am not seated near them at supper and the viscount makes his excuses soon after the meal, claiming the fatigue of his journey. And so, it is only when Mary and I are next able to speak alone later in the evening that I hear anything of their conversation. Mary does her best to relate it to me behind her hands while we watch Father and Mother play a duet on the virginal with Father's teacher Master Farmulo hovering behind.

'I cannot say a word against him,' Mary says, speaking quickly in her relief to share her thoughts with me. 'He was perfectly polite. Told me of the sights of Paris he had seen and a little of his native Yorkshire. But . . . I don't know. He was very reserved in the manner of his speech. Careful, almost reluctant at times. It fell to me to draw him out and not the other way round. In fact I don't believe he asked me anything much about myself. Perhaps he is not interested? Perhaps I bored him?'

'Oh no, I'm sure not, dearest.' I try to reassure her though I have little to go on. 'Perhaps he was nervous. And tired, he was certainly tired.'

'Yes,' she says with a little sigh of relief. 'Yes, perhaps that's it.'

'I thought him quite handsome,' I say next, horribly conscious of my own evident self-interest in promoting the man whom I alone am responsible for my sister marrying. 'And I did like his suit a great deal.'

'Yes,' she concedes. 'But it is so hard to believe that I am to be the wife of this stranger. That we are to spend our lives together, each day and each night . . .' She tails off and I know of what she is thinking.

'It will be quite all right, Mary, I know it,' I say with more confidence than I feel. 'Look at the intimacy between John and Elizabeth; look at Mother and Father. Even Charles and Bridget came to closeness eventually. You will find that too as soon as you get to know each other.'

Mary attempts a smile before moving her gaze onto Mother and Father, now laughing together as Father's rough hands make a mistake in their duet.

I examine her profile anxiously and resolve to do all I can to further Mary and the viscount's acquaintance over the next few weeks, beginning the very next day. 'We are going riding tomorrow,' I remember and whisper to her above the music. 'I hear your betrothed is a fine horseman and that will be a marvellous thing for you to have in common. Just you wait and see.'

Though I try my best to bring Mary and the viscount together over the coming days, arrangements for my wedding take up a great deal of my time and any spare moments are snatched with Robert. My chief concern in these last days is to rehearse with Master Hingston as the great poet Edmund Waller has composed a masque for my wedding in which I have been asked to take a starring role; something neither I nor any other ladies of my father's court have ever done before. Indeed, this will be the first masque performed at the palace since before the war. Father takes some persuading to reintroduce an event so symbolic of the Catholic decadence of the Stuart court but he has high regard for the skills of Master Waller who has, after a long period in exile, reinvented himself as a staunch supporter of the Protectorate. Masters Waller and Hingston assure him the piece will be virtuous both in its morals and musical skill and bring him the manuscript, which Father peers at for a full half hour scribbling notes in the margins, before finally, cautiously, he consents. I had half hoped he would refuse as the prospect holds equal parts of terror and excitement for me, my nerves about the performance almost dwarfing those I have for the wedding ceremony itself. Robert teases me for a little girl but, secretly, I think he is as excited to see me sing and dance as I am to be seen, and I take pains to reveal no details of the masque to him so it will be a surprise.

Mary's engagement to the viscount has still not been formally announced and so I am amazed when she herself suggests they marry at Hampton Court only a week after Robert and me – on 18 November.

'So soon?' I ask her. 'Are you sure?'

'I am,' she nods, her face setting in the determined features of Father's. 'If it is to be, I would rather it were done quickly. And it will be a smaller affair than yours, it won't need such preparations. Besides,' the corners of her lips twitch into the smallest smile, 'I don't want you to leave me behind. This way we will begin our new lives together.'

With two weddings now looming, we fall into a frenzy of activity. Mother sends our Master of Ceremonies Sir Oliver Flemyng downriver to Hampton Court to begin planning for Mary's wedding and he leaves his deputy there to oversee preparations while he hurries back to Whitehall to continue his work on mine. Several of the rooms next door to my own are cleared and prepared for Robert and me to share, and a similar set prepared for Mary and the viscount, and I delight in choosing the furnishings in consultation with the Surveyor of Works, little Master Embree, and the imposing Colonel Philip Jones, the Controller of the Household. We are to have striped wallpaper in our withdrawing room with a pair of velvet armchairs and a full closet of fitted shelves in our dressing room. It all still seems a game of make-believe to me; like preparing a house for dolls.

I only begin to believe it real when the guests start to arrive. Richard manages to make it up to London from Hampshire, his leg still in bandages and his wife Dorothy fussing over him and their small children. Bridget too comes to stay at the palace for the few nights before the wedding, her severe disapproval of our luxuries seemingly softened by the thought of her baby sisters becoming wives. Of my siblings, only Harry is missing as it is decided that he and his family will not undertake the troublesome journey from Ireland for our weddings; his in-laws, Sir Francis Russell, his wife Catherine and son John Russell will represent them instead. The news pains me greatly. Harry has been gone for over two years now and it is hard to believe that the next time we will see our big brother, Mary and I shall both be married women.

A great many of the old nobility also come to court for the wedding: faces who have not been seen in Whitehall since the old king was killed find that the time has come to lay aside their wartime differences and embrace this fresh royal order. With each arrival, I am more and more aware of the greater significance of my wedding than the mere union of my sweetheart and myself. But though this causes me a larger share of nerves than many brides, the truth is that I take great honour in it; delighted at last to play some part in our nation's history. It will be my day, my contribution.

And finally the day comes. The day which defines the lives of women above all others, and which so many have foisted upon them, but which I have chosen for myself; the beginning of the rest of my life.

The morning dawns blustery with bronze leaves whipped through a pewter sky and I wake with the thought that it will be the last time I do so without Robert. The realisation brings a wide grin to my face which hardly leaves it at any point during the next few days. Staring at the canopy over my head, smelling the smoke from the hundreds of fires throughout the palace that have been lit earlier than usual, I resolve to treasure the happiness that I have fought so hard for and been so lucky to win; to commit each moment to memory. And yet, later, when I come to look back on the days of feasting and nights of joy, I can barely remember a thing: not who I spoke to or what I ate or the words of love we exchanged on our pillows. The whole week passes in a blur as if I am watching another's life through a latticed window pane.

Katherine brings a breakfast tray to my room and Mary and I share it in bed: rolls still hot from the oven, butter, honey and hot apple juice. Then we bathe and beautify ourselves, laughing and pinning each other's hair until the arrival of Mother and Elizabeth, fully dressed and commanding, brings a new industry to our endeavours and they paw and preen me, fussing and fluttering until, between them, they lace me into my wedding dress. Katherine brings the full-length looking glass and I gaze at myself in wonder, seeing another woman – a princess, not Fanny Cromwell – swathed in the lightest silver organza which caresses my skin, a bodice of silk brocade studded with pearls glimmering in the morning light. Mother fastens her own pearls around my neck and smiles at me in the mirror. And that is that.

Sliding Robert's mother's emerald ring onto my little finger and pausing for Elizabeth to dab her favourite rosewater perfume over me, I leave the room and am ushered along to Father's outer presence chamber in a daze. I barely notice the courtiers who bow and clap as I pass, nor the garlands of winter evergreens that thread through the rooms like a river, leading me to my beloved. I see nothing until Father, waiting for me in fine grey velvet and silk stockings, gold-laced garters glinting at his knees, and then, when the doors to the inner presence chamber are opened for us, Robert. Gift-wrapped in a suit of red velvet edged with gold, the threatened brown periwig nestled on his head, he is pacing around the centre of the room, his whole body limber like a racehorse. He stops when he sees me and we grin foolishly at each other.

The wedding ceremony itself is quick and sober, only our promises to be loving and faithful to each other and then the signing of the register in the presence of selected friends and family and before the Justice of the Peace, Master Scobell, Clerk to the Privy Council. Weddings did not use to be secular affairs of course. Ten years before, when Elizabeth and Bridget had married, marriage services were still performed by clergymen in church. But in the intervening years the Puritan Parliament had come increasingly to the view that marriage was not an elaborate sacrament belonging to the church but a simple experience common to mankind and open to all. Often before when we imagined our weddings, Mary and I would bemoan our luck to be the first generation of brides not to sweep up aisles to sweet singing or to pledge our love bathed in the dappled sunlight of a great east window. And of course anything that our older sisters had done or had which we could not was a source of vexation. But here, on my wedding day, I find I do not care one jot for the ceremony as soon as I see Robert's handsome face turn to me as Father passes my trembling hand into his.

But if I embrace the new secular style of ceremony, Robert surprises me with his traditionalism, requesting a prayer of blessing on us from one of Father's chaplains;

an indulgence which Father grants. When Jeremiah takes his place before us, his restless limbs swaying as he speaks to God, I have to lower my eyes to avoid meeting his, conscious of the courtship scene we had once played together – something which Robert of course knows nothing of. But I have little time to reflect on the irony of this as the wedding is over seconds later and we are pronounced man and wife. The news is carried from the room and spreads through the court and out into the streets of London where church follows church to peal its bells for us. I do not notice at first with all the windows fastened against the November chill, but as we are ushered out of the Presence Chambers and along to the Great Hall, I catch the sounds and ask Robert to pause and open one of the windows of the gallery so I can hear the peals. We stand together in the window just for a few moments and I close my eyes against the almost painful beauty of the sound of the ancient cities of London and Westminster rejoicing in my happiness.

'Happy?' Robert whispers into my hair and I can only smile up at him in reply, tears welling in my eyes.

We are swept along then by the throng of guests until we spill into the hall where liveried servants wait for us with great trays of wine glasses and plates of sweetmeats. Looking around me I see a sea of faces both new and familiar: the new – formerly estranged members of the old nobility, friends and connections of Robert's powerful family; the familiar – Uncle Desborough, my aunts, cousin Lavinia and her handsome husband, the Captain of the Life Guard Richard Beke, the Russell family, Bulstrode Whitelocke and Master Thurloe, Lord Broghill, Sir Philip Jones and Sir Oliver

Flemyng, Masters Marvell, Milton and Hingston and the ambassadors, Signor Giavarina among them, who winks at me and grins. Surveying them, my whole body tingles with the thrill of entering the room hand in hand with Robert just as my mind swells to contain the knowledge that we are now husband and wife. Every sense is heightened and I smell the wedding feast and later hear Master Hingston's sublime music as never before though, curiously, all appetite deserts me and I am too distracted to eat a thing all day. Yet this hardly matters as there are to be at least three more days of celebrations to follow before we move on to Robert's grandfather the Earl of Warwick's splendid house on the Strand for yet more revels.

I glide among my friends talking and laughing, touching everyone as if I long to pass on my joy. Father makes a speech and after toasting our health, announces that Mary and Viscount Fauconberg are to be married next week, news that, even though it had been expected by the court, still sends ripples and murmurs around the room on the heels of the round of applause. Over a shoulder I see the black-coated figure of Marchamont Nedham, editor of our government newsletter *Mercurius Politicus*, circulating notebook in hand, and realise with a thrill that he will report on the wedding. If so, the details will be read across the three nations and even at the exiled court itself, perhaps even by the young 'king' who once sought my hand. Brides up and down the country will pore over the account and I take a vain and guilty pleasure in the thought that my wedding may influence others.

I am proud too of my family, every one of whom

shines in their spectacular new clothes. I wonder how Master Nedham will describe them: Father in his costly new suit of uncut grey velvet made in the Spanish fashion; Mother in a new dress of deep green silk, her second-favourite pearls at her neck while her favourite set adorns mine; Elizabeth in a pale blue gown edged with silver, her children about her skirts in delicate white lace; and Mary in rustling layers of pink taffeta with a pearl trim – a masterpiece of a dress which I hope her betrothed appreciates. Truly Master Hornlock has excelled himself. Even Bridget is dressed finely in a simply cut deep blue dress, with Charles beside her fresh and cleanly scented with the brightest white collar above his suit, their assortment of children a rainbow of colours. John is in his full courtly regalia, of course, and Richard and Dorothy have taken trouble with their clothes too, though Dick is forced to spend much of the day with his broken leg propped on a chair.

It is he who beckons me over and demands the gift-giving begin. Robert joins us eagerly and we sit like a king and queen as our friends and family bring us their presents. Robert's grandmother, the Countess of Devonshire, gives us a set of plate worth a rumoured two thousand pounds – a sum which astonishes me. John and Elizabeth giggle like newlyweds as they give us a pair of huge silver sconces which can hold twelve candles apiece; though I hardly know where we are to put them until Robert inherits his family house of Leighs Priory and we have a Great Hall of our own to decorate. Still, they are a fine gift.

My favourite present of all, however, has travelled across the sea from the west coast of Ireland. It is John

Russell who brings the cage to me, its contents hidden by velvet curtains. 'I am entrusted to deliver this gift to you from Harry with his love,' he says, before whisking off the drapes to reveal a small silver-blue bird, its breast speckled white beneath the hood that covers its eyes.

'A merlin,' I say, clasping Robert's hand in excitement. 'My own bird. Thank you, John, thank you!'

Robert kisses the back of my hand before dropping it so that he can lead an applause. Smiling shyly, John Russell moves away, re-covering the cage as he goes.

We have almost reached the end of the gifts and Dick and Doll are the last to approach, presenting us with a great quantity of Canary wine. It is Robert's turn now to be delighted and there is much back-slapping between him and my brother and promises of many a late night sunk in wine to come. I notice Father's brow crease into a frown at this and nudge Robert to remember his promise to mend the recklessness of his youth.

Yet, in truth, Father's disapproval is short-lived and, as the evening dances on, it becomes evident that he is the merrier for wine more than almost anyone else. Before the night is done indeed, he is running around the hall like a schoolboy, flicking his drinks on ladies' dresses and hiding pastries and jellies on chairs, dissolving into fits of laughter with Uncle Desborough and his other army friends when unsuspecting guests sit upon them. His jesting reaches its apogee when he whips off Robert's wig and sits on it, causing my new husband to colour momentarily with annoyance. 'It's a sign of favour,' I whisper quickly. 'He only plays practical jokes on those he likes.' And, as if to prove me right, Father is up on his feet again in a trice, the wig returned to his new son-in-law with a slap on the back and a bow of apology. Mother watches Father with a wry smile and raises an eyebrow to me as if to say: 'You have a husband now, you will see.'

And my husband, oh my husband. We dance and dance until almost five in the morning before our desire to be alone sweeps us quietly from the hall in a whispering, giggling run to our new rooms. Drink and exhaustion almost get the better of us and Robert falls asleep in my arms for half an hour before waking reinvigorated, just as I am sliding into sleep, and covering me with kisses. There is no sleep for me then.

We wake entangled in mid-morning to a great booming sound as guns fire from the Tower of London to mark our wedding. Robert laces his fingers through mine as we listen.

'Did you know, wife, that the last time the Tower fired its guns to salute a marriage was when the old King Charles wed his French bride?'

I shake my head in wonder. 'And to think that they then lived here in the same rooms my parents now have.'

'Extraordinary,' Robert agrees and we lie there in silence for some time gazing up at the canopy over our marriage bed, each cowed suddenly by the enormity of who we now are.

'And yet that is the fate of the family to which you now belong, my darling,' I say at last, twisting a curl of hair around my finger. 'How does it feel to become a Cromwell?'

He chuckles at that. 'And I may ask Your Highness how it feels to become a Rich? But yes, I cannot pretend it to be a small matter to join the ruling house of England. I will have to work hard to accustom myself to it and not least to overcome my nervousness of your father.'

I smile to myself, still the cherished daughter of a playful, affectionate father, struggling to imagine how others see the same man from a distance. 'You will, dearest, you will. Once you come to know him better. And, however strange it may seem, his joke with your periwig was his way of showing favour.'

Robert raises a doubting eyebrow. 'I thought it rather his way of putting me in my place.'

'No, no.' I laugh. 'It was his way of showing that you will be friends. He was making the first move, after his own bizarre fashion.'

Even this little talking utterly exhausts me and the thought of rising from the bed for the next day of our wedding celebrations is almost too much for me to contemplate.

'Do we have to get up?' I turn to Robert and bury my face in the hot skin of his neck. 'Can't we just stay here?'

'Mmmm. I think that would be entirely reasonable.'

He runs his hands through my hair, pushing the loose, damp curls off my face before pulling it up to kiss. For all my tiredness and growing hunger, I feel myself draw into him and we are a tangle of limbs and sheets once more when the poor servant who knocks discreetly at the door with our breakfast receives Robert's fierce shout to go away.

The wedding masque is planned for that evening and so after supper, at a sign from Master Hingston, I slip away with Mary and Katherine, who help me change into my costume behind the raised platform at the end of the Banqueting House which is to be the stage. I am to play the goddess Venus who is born from the sea and Master Hornlock has made a gown of silver-blue satin which winds around me in waves of sea spray edged with pearls, looping over my shoulder like a Roman toga. It is too much trouble to change my hair and so we simply slide hairpins topped with seashells into my ringlets, which we can remove again easily after the performance.

I climb up onto the stage, which is hidden from the audience by a rich pair of curtains hung beneath a huge proscenium arch. Behind me, the stage hands test the painted wooden waves with their hidden pivots, which they turn from the wings so that they form a rolling sea. Above our heads, a blue sheet is the sky, tiny star-shaped holes pricking the deep blue. Master Waller is bustling about speaking last-minute instructions and Master Hingston's singers are gathered now on either side of the stage whispering excitedly, the boy trebles giggling and poking each other. Peeping around the edge of the curtain, I watch as the wedding guests take their seats, Father and Mother on large gilded chairs in the centre of the front row of the special tiered seating, Robert smiling on one side of them; Master Waller, as the author of the masque, now taking his place on the other. I swallow to ease my dry throat and try to think of my last rehearsal, repeating one of the harder lines of my song under my breath, picking my notes from the orchestra as it tunes up.

And before I know it, the strings have started the great swell of the opening music and I rush back to crouch behind the waves before the curtains are slowly drawn apart to reveal our timeless ocean scene, which is greeted with a pleasing gasp and applause from the audience. Master Hingston then brings in the singers and the voices of the little trebles soar over the waves like the calls of sirens. I know my cue at the end of the first verse and try and slow my breath so I can hear it above my thumping heart. 'Peace,' the singers call to the violins. 'Peace when the bride begins to charm us with her voice.' The orchestra falls silent and there is a heartbeat, a hair's-breadth pause when I think I cannot do it, and then instinct takes over and I begin to sing.

Slowly, I rise from behind the waves and uncurl my new bridal body like a water nymph as I send my song forward, my voice wavering at first but growing more confident as I see the smiling faces arranged before me. I dare not look at Robert in case I lose concentration and so I lift my gaze over his head to the last row of chairs. I sing of the sea that gave me life and of the love to whom I go and as I do I feel a surge of power run through me; the power to hold the entranced gaze of all the court, to have won the love of the handsomest and best man in the room; and perhaps most of all, as I let my eyes meet the moistened eyes of the Lord Protector for just a second, the power to please my father.

My verse is over before I know it and I freeze in echo of the privy garden statues while the singers take up the song, joyfully bidding the orchestra to play once more so the bride can dance. I unfurl each arm to instruct the waves to part before me and, as if by magic, they roll back to let me through to the front of the stage. There I glide and twirl while the choir sing of Venus outshining the stars around her. I almost gasp indeed when turning around I see real stars glowing in the sky as the stage hands standing on ladders behind the sheet sky hold candles to the star-shaped holes. This is greeted with another sigh from the audience who burst into applause when a fleet of model ships then sails through the moving waves in honour of Father's naval victories. It is with him and me that the song ends, the singers contrasting his military glory with my beauty and grace. I stop dancing and gesture forward to Father, bowing my head to him just as Master Waller instructed me. The choir and orchestra fall away to leave a single violin dueting with the sweet treble of the smallest boy who sings the closing couplet: 'So honey from the lion came, and sweetness from the strong.' It is an allusion to the Bible story of Samson where bees are found making honey in the body of a dead lion, which I know Master Waller will have chosen to please Father: I am the honey and Father the lion and Providence smiles on us both.

My gaze is on the floorboards and all I can hear is the thundering in my chest as I wait for the applause. And then it comes, crashing over me like a flood, and I splutter and laugh with relief. Standing I curtsey to the room and gesture for the singers and Master Hingston's orchestra to receive applause. Only then, at last I allow myself a look at Robert, who is standing to clap an ovation and beaming at me. When Father rises to his feet alongside him, the rest of the audience stands and the applause peters out as each face turns to Father for his response. I watch with the rest as he beckons a servant forward with a tray of wine. Taking a cup and raising it high, he turns away from me to the audience behind him and toasts: 'My beautiful daughter, the goddess Venus!' Great cheers and echoes of 'Venus, Venus!' follow as he strides forward to the platform and offers his hand to help me down the steps. With a kiss on the top of my head as I reach him, Father leads me over to Robert and places my hand in his, calling for the chairs to be moved so there can be dancing.

'I must change,' I whisper to Robert, suddenly conscious of my godly attire now that I have come back down to earth.

'Oh no, you don't,' he says, tightening his grip on my waist. 'I want to dance with my goddess bride.'

And so we do. I dance with Robert, with Father and John before I am claimed by a succession of my new relations and their grand friends from the old nobility. The most exciting of these is Mountjoy Blount, the Earl of Newport, a handsome, sprightly man in his late fifties whom I know to have been a great favourite and ladies' man at the courts of the dead King Charles and his father the Scottish King James as far back as the early '20s.

'It was my perfectly pointed beard,' he sighs to me as he relives those days while we dance. 'That was what earned me the admiration of the court. Van Dyck called it a work of art and it was the envy of Prince Charles himself, who took a great interest in fashion. But that must seem horribly old-fashioned to you, my dear; there is hardly a moustache at your father's court, where I can see the clean-shaving of the Ironsides reigns supreme. Look there – even Sir Thomas Billingsey, who was a courtier even before my time, has shaved off his beard to match the new fashions here. And his beard was almost as fine as mine!'

I cannot help laughing at this; the earl is quite right. None of the young men would be seen dead with a beard nowadays, though I have no wish to say so and hurt his feelings. Instead I say: 'You put the young men here in the shade, my lord, even now. Saving of course my husband.'

'Haha! Thank you, my lady. And may I compliment you on your gracious performance. It was quite the equal of the great masques we used to have at court before the war. Indeed, I saw the young Queen Henrietta Maria sing and dance once as you did, though you quite outshone the memory of her performance today. Isn't it quite something?' the earl continues, his eyes drifting away from me into the distance, his voice dropping as if he speaks only to himself. 'Here I am today – after so many years and so much fighting – dancing once again with a princess; but a princess from among our own people, not born to a royal house of Europe. A new era indeed.'

I blush at his words, even as I know Father would chide me for vanity if he were to hear my thoughts. I excuse myself when the dance ends, desperate suddenly to rest my feet. Finding a glass of wine I sink into a chair and have barely taken a sip before Signor Giavarina appears before me, his dark eyes shining with humour as he rises from an elaborate bow.

'You have made another conquest, *Principessa*.' He nods to the earl. 'Or should it be *la divinissima*?'

I laugh. 'You tease me, Ambassador.'

'Indeed I do not.' He affects mock offence as he takes the seat beside me. 'I was most affected by your portrayal of Venus, for you know our city of Venice is closely associated with her. Venice has been married to the sea for over six hundred years and we celebrate their wedding every spring.'

'How wonderful! I would love to see that.'

'I hope you will one day, *Principessa*. You could reprise your role as Venus and delight my master the Doge and the Senate just as you have me.'

I incline my head at his ambassadorial flattery and wait for him to say what he has really come to tell me. Giavarina leans closer.

'But beyond your obvious beauty and grace, *Principessa*, there was a serious message in your performance which I and every other ambassador here will this night be scribbling back to our masters.'

I stiffen at little, anxious to hear what analysis my Italian friend has of Master Waller's masque, for I know such allegories are open to multiple interpretations; that they always convey messages of politics as much as love. 'Ambassador?'

Giavarina pauses briefly for effect. 'It is a message of hope, *Principessa* – of hope and of reassurance to those at court who despair of your father's closeness to the army; the closeness that stopped him becoming king as perhaps he should have done. The song tells them to be patient. That though your father, his most serene Highness, God protect him, may be a brave soldier set in his ways, he will eventually . . .' He struggles for the right words in English. '. . . give way to a new generation of graceful, courtly Cromwells more palatable to the old nobility and the Parliament. Sometimes you need the view of an outsider, as I have told you before.'

He turns his dark eyes to survey the room, and, as ever, I follow his gaze, now seeing signs of the hesitant reconciliation he speaks of everywhere. There is Secretary Thurloe standing with Bulstrode Whitelocke and the fashionably attired trio of Lord Broghill, Councillors Nathaniel Fiennes and his brother-in-law Charles Wolseley, talking with Viscount Fauconberg. There my brother Richard, who has hobbled over to share a glass of wine with the Earl of Warwick and a group of Robert's other noble relations. And there, the Earl of Newport and Robert's father Lord Rich, who are now dancing with their swords and cloaks in the old Jacobean style to the whoops and cheers of their friends. Father, perhaps a little the worse for the previous day's excesses, I fancy, sits on his great chair and watches them, his brows knitted in thought while two of Elizabeth's children play on the floor at his feet.

'I hope you are right, Ambassador,' I say, but as he bows and makes to leave me, I reach forward quickly for his hand. 'And I hope too that you will always be my friend, whatever the future may hold. Go write your report for the Doge and make sure you tell him what a fine wedding it has been.'

'Of course, my lady.'

Robert comes to claim me soon afterwards, determined to carry off his goddess at last, and I go with him happily, leaving a trail of seashell hairpins all the way into our bed.

♛

The court spends the rest of the week in holiday mood, the celebrations of my wedding gradually blending into the preparations for Mary's, especially once we have all travelled out to Hampton Court where she is to be wed. Father and the Council enjoy a brief respite from the concerns of foreign policy, though the newest Councillor John Thurloe continues to burn his candle at both ends and I can see that his thoughts never stray far from the latest intelligence report or dispatch from the Continent. Father is in an expansive mood and takes a moment from the festivities to bestow a knighthood on my brother Harry in Ireland, finally persuading the Council to confirm him governor now that Charles's term of office has lapsed; formalising the work he already does governing that fractious and divided country on behalf of Father's Protectorate and releasing him, at last, from Charles's arm's-length interference.

The future glitters for all of us Cromwell sons and daughters. Yet as the day of Mary's wedding approaches, the questions about her betrothed, his true motives and the political fallout of their marriage gather pace as they scamper about the palace. It is Bridget with her characteristic candour who voices them to me most clearly as we sit in our private balcony room sewing ribbons for Mary's wedding bouquet.

'The news of Mary's marriage has not been well received by the army,' Bridget says, keeping her eyes on her stitching. 'Charles tells me the other army leaders aren't happy at all.'

I sigh at this, for all the newlywed smile that will not leave my face. 'When are they ever happy though, Biddy? If we could never do anything but that which pleased *them*, life would be dull indeed.'

She tuts. 'Frances, this is not a game.'

'Indeed it isn't, not for Mary certainly.'

'There is no need to be defensive. I know you feel responsible for this match.'

Bridget has me there, her finger precisely on the point of my conscience as only an older sister's can be – it is the one hole in my joy: my fear that Mary's happiness may be the price of my own. Seeing this, Bridget presses home her advantage.

'You would feel a greater sympathy with the soldiery if you had ever lived among them as I have, with Henry and then with Charles. While you were a child I was on campaign with the army, enduring the men's privations, seeing the war at first hand. It is their suffering that has led to our luxury, their blood that has bought our liberty and peace.'

'I cannot help the cosseted life I have led, Bridget, any more than you can help the trials you have suffered,' I say. 'It is not my fault that Father's great elevation came while I was still almost a child. I know you think I have enjoyed our status more than I should but that is only because I believe I have been extraordinarily blessed.' The great happiness I feel keeps my tone conciliatory even though I always hate it when Bridget uses the fourteen years between us to belittle my views, fearing nothing so much than that she thinks me a vain, spoilt girl.

'That is true, dearest.' Bridget relents a little. 'But to return to this Fauconberg. What do we really know of him? Who's to say he will not turn out to be a viper in our bosom, sent to spy on us for Charles Stuart? And yet Father, in his wisdom, gives him Mary's hand, a dowry of fifteen thousand pounds and Lambert's former regiment in the north. You can imagine what Charles and Uncle Desborough think of that, what John Lambert himself thinks of that.'

I try not to drop a stitch as I order my thoughts. 'But I can see the wisdom in it, Biddy. Father means to make the marriage a moment of reconciliation with former royalists who, after all, make up half the nation – there would be little point to it if he didn't give Thomas some power and positions of his own.'

'But this stranger will hold the balance of power in the north. Is that not rash? And you have seen how he now advises Father on foreign affairs and sits at his side when he receives ambassadors.'

'We must trust to Father's judgement,' I say with more hope than confidence.

'And Mary?'

I lay my sewing down in my lap and look at Bridget but she keeps her grey eyes on her needle. 'I suppose she must learn to trust her new husband,' I reply eventually, the guilt swirling within me once more. 'Thanks to her I have had a choice but she, in her kindness, has surrendered hers. What choice does she now have?'

'Very little.' Bridget shakes her head. 'Just as I had.'

Disquieting thoughts about the viscount continue to swell in my mind and send me stealing into Mary's chamber late the night before the marriage, leaving the beloved husband, whom I alone among my sisters chose completely for myself, asleep in our bed.

'Mall?' I tiptoe into her room, my bare feet seeking the warm carpets as stepping stones over the cool tiles.

'Come in, Fanny.'

Mary is sitting up in bed, a book absently in her lap which she places to one side as I approach. As I look at her moonlit in her nightgown, waiting as she always has for my embraces and my secrets, my teasing and my tears, I feel a sudden swell of grief.

'After tomorrow, I will not be able to do this,' I say, a lump in my throat.

'I know.' She pats the bed beside her and I hitch my dress to clamber up. 'Several times in the last few days I have thought of slipping into your room to talk of some moment of the day and stopped myself, once already half along the landing, when I remembered that your new husband would be with you.'

'And what shall we do when we are not even in the same house?' I ask, my mind reeling at the idea of our separation; the first of our lives. 'Thomas plans to take you into Yorkshire soon after the wedding, does he not? And Robert promises he will take me to visit his grandfather's estate in Essex at Christmastide; he wants me to see the house which will one day be ours.'

Mary sighs and puts her arm around my shoulder. 'Truly I do not know how I will bear it. At least you will remain here for the time being, close to Mother. And . . .' She tails off but I know what she would go on to say if she were less kind: *And you have a husband who you love and who you know already to be your best friend whereas I go into unfamiliar country with a man I hardly know . . .*

I choose to answer the words she has not said. 'Mary, my love, I will never be able to thank you for what you have done for me and for Robert. And I know – I *know* – that God would not be so cruel as to punish such great kindness with unhappiness. I believe you will find love with Thomas, I truly do.'

'And if he has ulterior motives?' Mary interrupts me. 'If he is marrying me to further the cause of our enemies?'

I shake my head, truly at a loss for a reply. 'We can only trust Father and Master Thurloe in this. And why should Thomas not wish to ally himself with our house? Besides, I like his face. It is an honest face. He has a warm smile and gentle eyes, whatever the awkwardness of his conversation, and he couldn't take those eyes off you when you wore the pink taffeta. When he sees you tomorrow . . .'

She smiles at that though I feel her tense a little too and I know she is thinking of the wedding night to come; an experience I struggle to imagine with a man I knew so little.

'You will be worried about your first night together.' Again, I choose to address her thoughts rather than her words. 'But it will be easier and less frightening than you imagine. I know.' I put my hand up to her gaze – a gaze which says I can hardly know how it will feel in the same circumstances. 'I know that he will be kind. And you will find it becomes easier once you have kissed for a time and your limbs have relaxed. Have plenty of wine and try and encourage him into conversation first. Take his hands in yours – he is shy, I think. Speak gently, let him kiss you. Try and be soft however much your body stiffens against him. You know where to find me if you need me; Robert be damned.'

Mary pulls me to her roughly and for a few minutes we cling to each as other if no one else but us exists. And then, with no words left to say between us, we clasp our hands and close our eyes for our last prayers together: prayers for a safe future, prayers for our new husbands, prayers for happiness and for love.

♛

For all her resemblance to Father, Mary is a vision on her wedding day and I am gratified to see a spark of enthusiasm in Thomas's eyes and the hint of pleasure about his mouth as he takes her hand before the Justice.

In the prayer led by the Reverend Dr Hewitt I squeeze my eyes shut, praying desperately for them to be happy; indeed I do not believe I have ever longed for something so much with the exception of my wish to marry Robert and, despite the brave words I had for Mary last night, my deepest fear remains that the one will be the price for the other.

The wedding is a smaller, more private affair than mine, the date not even revealed to the public beforehand. Much of Thomas's family stays away, yet Father spares no expense and the Great Hall at Hampton Court glimmers over the wedding feast as the haze from the candlelight layers over the tapestries along the walls so the figures woven within them seem to move shimmering around us. I take a few moments to look around my family and friends and count my blessings, grateful for the chance to relive a day so close to my own wedding and yet one which will pass at a normal pace and allow me to form the memories I have barely managed to retain of my own. All eyes are on Mary and not me and I find myself surprised to enjoy the change, letting my hand slip into Robert's beneath the table, my head resting happily on his shoulder as if no one is there but us two.

It is in this same pose later in the evening that we sit to watch the masque that Master Marvell has written for Mary's wedding to match that composed by Master Waller for ours. It is Father himself who has commissioned it, having so much enjoyed the performance at our wedding. And if the audience retains any doubts whether this revival of the royal masque will last at the Cromwell court, the Lord Protector banishes these in a single instant. For when the masque begins, the curtains are drawn back to reveal Father himself, swathed in a toga and breastplate and atop a throne as Jove, the benevolent king of the gods, who rules the imaginary world of the stage and watches the play unfold beneath him. It is a non-speaking part, and Father shifts a little uncomfortably in his seat, but the impact on us all is enormous. Never before, I think looking up at him, has our court been closer to the ones that came before.

But I am soon caught up in the story. Where my masque was a seascape, this is a pastoral scene with mythical shepherds and shepherdesses evoking an ancient English idyll. Unlike me, Mary has no desire to perform, hindered she told me not only by her own shyness but by the awkwardness she feels as bride to a little-known and politically contentious husband. Yet Master Marvell has no such reserve and the songs he has composed cast the young couple in every bit as heroic and romantic a light as that which shone upon us. This time, the bride is portrayed as the mythical Cynthia to her new husband's Endymion and the songs tell the story of their courtship as hired dancers play it out beneath the benevolent gaze of the almighty Jove.

Mary struggles with embarrassment as the singers heap praises onto her and Thomas, though none but I could tell what she feels behind her serene bridal expression.

I cannot help but whisper my suspicions to Robert:

'Mary should take it in good humour. It does no good to shy away from the absurd position we East Anglian farmers now find ourselves in. We can only rise to the challenge and surprise our enemies with the nobility of our charm, else they have more weapons against us.'

I would go on but Robert hushes me, his eyes lifted to the stage, 'Shhh. I think they sing now about us.'

I focus once more on the singing, just in time to catch the chorus in the guise of shepherds instruct the bridegroom on his courtship of Cynthia:

Courage Endymion, boldly woo
Anchises was a Shepheard too;
Yet is her younger sister laid
Sporting with him in Ida's shade.

I gasp, my composure momentarily deserting me as a few glances both knowing and unknowing turn from the stage towards us. The reference, to my mind at least, is as clear as Venetian glass: I am the younger sister who sported with my lover before our marriage – a Venus indeed in my ungovernable passion. Have I imagined it or has Master Marvell broadcast Robert's and my premarital indiscretions to the entire assembly and immortalised my unwedded loss of virginity in verse? But surely it can't be. How could he know? Did everyone know all this time? I glance at Mother but she is smiling at Mary while, from the stage, Father continues to impersonate godlike impassivity.

I am numb for many moments before I feel the pinch of Robert's hand on my thigh.

'Smile, darling. You were saying something about taking it in good humour?'

♛

The new Viscount and Lady Fauconberg leave court for the long journey north into Yorkshire only a few days later, Thomas eager to travel before the Wolds are blanketed in the first snow. I lend Mary my fox fur stole and matching gloves, though otherwise we have barely a moment alone before she is gone.

From that moment of separation I never cease fretting about her, missing her like a part of my own self. Adrift, I look for companionship elsewhere and find myself spending more time with my cousin Lavinia, who knows almost as many of my secrets as Mary from when she used to live with us when we were younger. With her I enjoy the knowing conversation of young wives, which I used to watch with fascinated envy, and we spend many hours sitting together exchanging our discoveries about married life behind our hands.

Although the thrill of being a bride does not leave me for months, around me the court gradually settles down after the excitement of our weddings to resume normal life. Yet my family has scarcely known such a thing as normal life and, once more, frightening events beyond our walls disrupt any domestic peace. Again Councillor Thurloe's spies earn their pay when they reveal a planned royalist uprising intended to coincide with a Spanish invasion to restore the exiled 'king' Charles Stuart. Rumours flow along the streets of London like dirty rainwater in the gutters and the Council of State orders the guards doubled at the Tower and all other strongholds, summons more men in to the defend the city and dispatches weapons and munitions all across the country. Beyond the palace privy gardens, the streets ring with the clink of breastplates and the shouts and stamps of soldiers.

In private the family huddles and whispers its fears, though Bridget chides us for nervous fools and Charles, who is a passionate hater of Spain, rails and rants and prays to God as he oversees the mustering of the army. 'I wish Lambert were with us, for all his love of the Spanish papists,' he admits to me one evening. 'The men need him.'

Father distracts himself with his nominations for the new House of Lords, or 'Other House' as everyone awkwardly refers to it, remembering the hasty abolition of its predecessor after the old king's execution. There are sixty-three names when he finally finishes the list, among them not only Richard, but also my other brother Harry and each of my three brothers-in-law: Charles, John and the newest, Thomas, Viscount Fauconberg. My grandfather-in-law the Earl of Warwick is asked to sit alongside them; Uncle Desborough, Lord Broghill, Bulstrode Whitelocke, Edward Montagu – who, since he has returned from the sea, has also joined the Council of State – and many others of the erstwhile kingship party too. Robert tries to hide his disappointment that he alone is overlooked and I seek every opportunity to explain how Father could hardly raise him up to the level of his grandfather, the great parliamentary war hero. This of course is true but I see how Robert champs at the bit like one of Father's new Arabian stallions.

'How would you like to go and see my family estate in Essex?' he asks me one evening while I watch him take a bath before the fire in our bedroom, the water itself seeming to blaze with the reflected flames against his chest and knees. 'It's an old priory, you know – quite beautiful. I long for the fresh air there and to have something more substantial to do.'

'Do you mean to tell me, my dear husband, that Robert

Rich wishes to give up his life of carousing around court for some more gainful employment?' I tease him because I know he enjoys it even though I am secretly pleased at this new application of his.

'Aye, wife. I am a husband now with a princess to keep in the style to which she is accustomed. No more free and easy bachelor life for me.'

'Very funny,' I laugh, tossing a towel into his outstretched hand.

He grabs my hand then and pulls me in for a wet kiss, my sleeves dragging in the water until I yelp in protest.

'Besides, my grandfather has work for me to do there – building works to supervise, tenants to manage, gentlemen of the county to interview for new civic appointments. My father is hopeless in his management and Grandfather would have me take on my share. What's more, it would please me for you to spend time with my father and my little half-sisters and to see my home where we will live in years to come. The mistletoe on the great oak will be in flower soon; it's quite a sight.'

'I should like to have known your mother,' I say, reminded of her absence by his mentioning his half-sisters.

'I hardly remember her. She died in '38, when I was four.'

'The year I was born,' I say.

'Hmm.' Robert gives a wry smile. 'The Lord giveth and the Lord taketh away.' But in another moment he has regained his excitement. 'Well?'

I grin widely at the prospect of the adventure and plant a kiss on his lips. 'When?'

'After this threat of invasion has passed. I would not take you out of the palace before then.'

Indeed, we are all but confined to the palace in the face of this new danger – incarcerated under the strict orders of Secretary Thurloe. Restless, I take my new merlin out and into the edge of St James's Park, which is the furthest my guards will allow me. 'Venus', Robert had suggested I call her as his hands were undressing me for what felt like the hundredth time, and I warm myself with the memory as I watch her soar divinely through the chilled December air.

It is the oddest of seasons, with my wedded bliss in sharp contrast to the cold climate of fear at court and with the hopeful strengthening of our position I had felt since Father's investiture – with our reconciling weddings, the new House of Lords and the Protectorate's slowly broadening base of support – contradicted by my creeping sense of our enemies circling once more. While within the court, the new compromise constitution is still but a sticking plaster over the divisions between the army and the politicians. And Father is not the young man he was.

A crash in the bushes nearby brings the guards' hands to their muskets and I whistle Venus back to my glove before hurrying back to the palace.

PART THREE

December 1657–September 1658

CHAPTER EIGHT

As winter steals over the city I wait and pray for Secretary Thurloe to tell us the royalist plot has been foiled so that we can make our journey to Essex. I am excited at this first opportunity in my life to travel as a married woman, to move about as I choose, emerged from the vast and eclipsing shadow of my family. December passes into January, though there are no celebrations of Christmas at court of course. I only have the dimmest memories of the holy day of Christ's mass, as it is more than a decade since the wartime Parliament outlawed the festival. Yet still there are many who cling to the old customs and I find signs of them everywhere: a sprig of holly in a flower arrangement, a carolling tune on the lips of a sentry, the smell of warm cinnamon and nutmeg through the open door of the palace kitchens. And though Parliament orders the Lord Mayor of London to ensure the city remains open for business on 25 December, when I look out of the palace windows onto Whitehall that day, the street is empty and eerily silent.

The chaplains preach against the popish festival, asking us to search our Bibles for instruction to celebrate Christ's nativity in this way which, of course, we will not find as Christmas is a creation of the Catholic Church. Yet Father, who doesn't observe Christmas himself, takes little interest in whether other men choose to or not, hoping rather to get through the season without offending one side of the argument or the other; I can almost feel his relief once the old year gives way to the new.

I receive my first proper letter from Mary as the year turns. It is odd to see my name addressed in her spidery hand, so familiar from the schoolroom, as we have never before been separated and forced to exchange our most intimate thoughts on paper. I sense Mary's echoing frustration even in the inked words on the page: how can she tell me about her married life with Thomas in the black and white testimony of pen and paper? How can she tell me about their wedding night? Still, she does her best and I find some comfort in what I can read between the lines: that they are getting along well; that Thomas's estates are very fine and his family kind; that she likes the country house Newburgh Priory, which will be their primary residence. But the single sheet leaves me restless and dissatisfied and I long to see Mary so much that my chest aches.

January is blisteringly cold and everyone catches a chill. My cousin Lavinia sickens, to universal alarm, and the cold carries off the conspirator Edward Sexby – a pleasanter end than a traitor's death at Tyburn, as I hear many at court remark. Parts of the Thames freeze over, delaying the busy river traffic as boats stick in the ice and crash into each other and the frequent angry shouts of the watermen carry over the palace walls. The politicians summoned to the new session of Parliament scurry around Whitehall and Westminster bundled up in heavy cloaks and scarves and I watch them through frosted windows. It is too cold to fly Venus or even venture into the gardens for the briefest walk and so I curl up by the fire instead, nursing my cold. I spend time at cousin Lavinia's sickbed, disturbed to see my friend, who had been so beautiful on her wedding day, now so pale and thin.

With the MPs assembled, all talk is of the first meeting of the new Other House. The House of Commons itself is suspicious of its new partner and many hours and days are wasted on debating the arrangement and legitimacy of the new upper chamber, until Father presses the Members to concentrate on more substantive issues. My brother Richard, now sitting in the Other House and appointed too to the Council of State itself, becomes my primary source of intelligence. Now he is spending more time at court, Doll and their children usually left behind in Hampshire, Dick often finds his way to our rooms after supper, where he takes a glass of wine with us and shares the news and gossip. How we laugh at his account of his first attendance at Council when Father had his granddaughter, Bridget and Henry Ireton's oldest little girl, sitting on his lap for the whole meeting. Apparently one of the other Councillors had objected to her presence and Father had replied stoutly that there was not a thing he would choose to say to his Council that he would not say before his granddaughter.

Through these evenings, Dick and Robert become even closer friends and it delights me to listen to them chew over affairs of state, their shoes kicked off at the end of a long day, while I bob up and down to wait on them, summoning sweetmeats and wine, pretending I am mistress of my own home. I love to play house in this way and, wrapped up in my husband, our sets of rooms at Whitehall and at Hampton Court become my world. I still find it thrilling to retreat to them hand in hand each evening, to fall asleep together to the calls of the nightwatchmen, to hear Robert breathing, feel him turn over in his sleep and to wake beside him to the bustling noises of a palace morning. And, when we do venture out to mingle with the other courtiers and dine with my family, I am surprised anew every time someone speaks to me of my 'husband' or my 'lord' and I thank God that the man they allude to is my darling sweetheart and not some crusty courtier or foreign prince. I pray daily that Mary will find such happiness.

I am growing eager for our visit to Essex and fret that Secretary Thurloe can give me no comfort that the threat of the Spanish invasion has passed. Indeed our enemies mass on all fronts: not only are cavaliers and papists stirring against us, but those other equal and opposite opponents of the Protectorate – the republican MPs led by Sir Arthur Haselrig, religious radicals and disillusioned officers – choose this time to unite their efforts behind a petition to abolish the Protectorate and restore the Commonwealth. The ranting Fifth Monarchists rail against us too and the streets of London simmer with a witch's potion of poison. When it seems the pot will boil over into the fire, Father surprises us all by dissolving Parliament and summoning the army officers to put their grievances with the government before him instead. Many of the men speak fairly but six of those from Father's own regiment of horse are so violent in their opposition to the Protectorate that he has no choice but to dismiss them from their posts; an act which plunges him into a foul, despondent mood for days afterwards, where I can almost hear all the demons of the kingship debates chattering once more in his head.

Everywhere it seems the news is of war. Ambassador Meadowes writes from Denmark to say that the Danes have suffered a mighty defeat at the hands of the Swedes and to suggest that England and France try to mediate a treaty between the two nations once more. Talk begins again of assembling a Protestant League against the Catholic powers of Spain and Austria, and the idea restores the spring to Father's step as he and Councillor Thurloe sit up late into the night planning the future of Europe. Richard is all for it – Charles and the rest of the Council too, he reports to us over his customary late-night cup of wine. But though the King of Sweden accepts our negotiations, he refuses to end hostilities until these are concluded. Instead he leads his army on a daring march across the frozen Belts towards Copenhagen. And so men continue to die in the ice.

Surrounded by all this tension, I begin to wonder if we should go into Essex regardless of the continued threat; if we may indeed be safer, and certainly happier, outside the capital. But though I am now fully recovered from my sore throat, Robert has caught it now, making a winter journey, even a short one, unwise. Still I long to go, and find myself impatiently counting the days that he is laid low: three, four, a week. But then two weeks have gone by with no improvement and his head and palms begin to warm despite the frost at our windows. Robert protests that he is feeling stronger and makes a great show of riding out in St James's Park with Richard and John, but he returns exhausted and as I help him into bed I notice a slur in his speech and dullness in his eyes. Alarmed, I summon the court physicians at once.

'We thought it only a cold,' I say again and again to the clustered backs of the black-frocked doctors who move around our bed, examining every inch of Robert's body, his blood and the contents of the chamber pot. I tell myself that it will be nothing, that there is no cause for alarm. But they are at their examination for such a long time – hatted heads bowed, low whispers under solemn glances – that I send Katherine to fetch Mother; if there is bad news, I will need someone to keep calm, to concentrate on the doctors' diagnosis and suggested treatment while all capacity to listen or think drains from me.

She comes quickly, Elizabeth sweeping in behind her, and without speaking they move either side of me to wait for the physicians' verdict.

Finally they come towards us, Dr Bate, the most senior doctor, gently taking my arm to guide us out of Robert's earshot. I drag my feet after him like a condemned prisoner. Stumbling, I try to place one foot securely in front of the other.

'Tell us.' It is Mother who speaks.

'Your Highness.' Dr Bate nods. 'I am grieved to tell you that it looks like a fever of the brain.'

My head begins to swim and I hear the doctor's next words dimly as if through a thick evening fog low on the river:

'The young lord is very weak, his temperature high, his pulse low, his senses slipping. Of course he may make a full recovery, with adequate bleeding and purging to draw the fever from him. But on the other hand . . .' He leaves this sentence hanging like a loose thread dangling from a piece of needlework.

'He may die.' They all turn to look at me as I finish the doctor's sentence without thinking, my words sounding in my ears like they have been spoken by someone else. In the silence that follows, an icicle suspended from the overhang above the window breaks loose and falls, splintering onto the ledge.

I spend the next few days in utter denial of the words I had spoken. I simply cannot accept that I could lose my love, who has always been so strong and vital, and after all we have surmounted to be together. Yet the bright, sinewed body that I watched bathing in the firelight only a few weeks before seems to waste before my eyes. Nevertheless, I will not allow myself to countenance the worst even for a second, as if by one careless negative thought I might break the magic that keeps Robert here tied to this world. And so I busy myself with his care, buzzing around our bed like a bee, wiping away sweat and blood, feeding him and changing his clothes and sheets as any ordinary housewife would. But I also call on all the help that only a princess can: summoning physicians from the city to offer second and third opinions, dispatching Katherine to every apothecary in London asking for remedies and sending every healing recipe I can find in the conduct books and medical textbooks of the palace library down to the kitchens at all hours of the day and night. I send, too, for the Earl of Warwick and write to Robert's father and scarce half an hour goes by without either Robert's grandfather or one of my sisters or parents joining me at his bedside.

Robert himself remains cheerful when he is lucid, chiding me for fussing and wanting nothing but for me to sit by his side and chatter to him of trivial nonsense. He calls me his Venus, tells me he loves me and talks of our trip into Essex and his plans for the future as if nothing is amiss. Thus, for the most part, he joins me in my campaign of denial and we sit in shared stubbornness that all will be well; the only reality that either of us can imagine. I tell myself God is testing us, that we will emerge stronger than before but humbler too, conscious of the fragility of a happiness that rests so wholly on another person, grateful for our second chance.

And then, as if by Providence, Robert begins to strengthen again on the fourth day after he took to our bed. He eats chicken soup laced with herbs, tells a couple of jokes and summons Dick for a hand of piquet, the playing cards sliding over the blankets as he shifts his weight beneath them. I watch them from the shadows by the fireplace and feel myself breathe deeply, as if I have been holding my breath for days. My lungs crave fresh air and so I take the opportunity to walk in the garden with Betty, the cold air healing on my sallow, indoor skin.

When I return, Robert is asleep, the fresh bandage on his arm where he has been bled and scent of lavender on his lips evidence of the doctors' visit. He sleeps for hours and when I put my hand to his forehead late in the evening I find a film of sweat. I place a cooling flannel on his brow and he wakes at my touch. But it is not the same Robert who fell asleep who wakes; the humour of earlier replaced now with anger and tears. Seeing me he closes his eyes and turns his face away, the flannel sliding wetly onto the pillow.

'I wish we had never met,' he says, tears rolling down his flushed cheeks.

I cannot help bridling in shock but recover myself quickly. 'Darling.' I reach for his shoulder but he flinches away.

'Don't, I can't bear it. I was quite happy before; no thought for the future, no one to think of but myself. No hopes or plans. No desire to become something better than myself. Nothing to live for but pleasure, nothing to lose. But now I have you, could lose you . . .'

I don't know what to say in comfort so I climb into bed beside him and gently, slowly wrap myself around his back, which radiates heat through his damp nightshirt. I bury my face in his neck, loving nothing so much before in my life as to feel his skin under my lips, hot and alive, his pulse beating time against my cheek.

'You will never lose me, sweetheart, there is nothing to regret,' I say softly. 'Besides, you will be well again, I know it, you have been growing stronger today.'

He does not reply but grips my hand, lacing his fingers through mine. I feel some of the tension drain from his shoulders as he relaxes under my touch until a minute or so later I can tell he has returned to sleep. I close my eyes, hoping that I reassured him, praying that he wakes next to his usual good humour. Exhaustion hits me then with all the force of a twenty-oared barge and I too sink into a dreamless sleep.

When I wake, stiff and aching with cold in my clothes, I cannot tell the hour nor how long I have slept. Someone has been in to stoke the fire and replace the candle on the nightstand, else I would not be able to see as dawn has not yet reached around the edge of the curtains. I lie quite still, listening as I slip in and out of wakefulness until I hear the clock in the court chime four. It will be another three hours at least before day breaks. I contemplate getting out of bed to undress properly but I could not unlace my stays without Katherine and the chill outside the bed covers is enough to banish the thought. Sighing, I turn over towards Robert and, closing my eyes for sleep, slide under the sheet towards him, seeking the warmth of his body.

He has moved in his sleep and now lies on his back so I find his arm and shoulder first. They are cold and so I snake my arm across his body to find the heat of his chest. But it is as still and cool as a marble figure upon a tomb. Still I do not dare to open my eyes but clench them shut over welling tears as I move my hand under his shirt and through the coiled hair at his chest to lie over his heart.

It is only then that I know.

Pain stabs and slices through me, tearing at my flesh as if I am on the executioner's slab at Tyburn. A scream builds inside me, sending my knuckles rammed into my mouth to stifle it.

If I scream, someone will come. If they come, they will take him away. As long as the night lasts, we are together and nothing has happened.

I nestle my head against Robert's shoulder and breathe in the musty smell of his neck – the heady mix of spiced orange, tobacco and the scent of his sweat that still weakens my knees. How can he still smell of himself when he has gone? Can I keep his scent somehow? If I pressed my handkerchief there for the next few hours and never washed it could the smell of him linger there? My mind reels further, spiralling away like a child's spinning top. How can Robert have left me when his body lies here under my hands? Has he divided himself into two, or three, or into an infinity? I move my hands over his body, mapping it in my mind, stroking his skin at first then pinching and pulling at him, bewildered that he cannot feel what I do, urging him to spring to life under my assault. But he does not move. A sob escapes me and I kiss him in apology, taking deep exaggerated breaths in horrible mockery of his own stillness, desperately trying to take his scent deep within me where I can keep it safe.

Some time later I find myself talking to Robert. As time passes, we play a game where every hour more that we have to ourselves is a decade of our life together – the future he was so desperate not to lose. I tell him the story of our life as it happens: the mistletoe we find on the great oak at Leighs Priory; the summers we spend there with his family, the autumns at court, riding and hunting and dancing just as we had on our wedding day; the schemes Robert invents to improve the running of his family estates; his ennoblement to the Other House and work on various committees for foreign affairs – the golden future of the Cromwell family just as Giavarina had painted it. I tell him of the children we have – four boys and two girls; of their names, looks and habits, as clear as crystal in my mind's eye. How the oldest boy Robert (though we call him Robin) is the spit of my father and how his school friends christen him 'Old Noll' in tribute. Of our littlest girl, named Anne after Robert's dead mother, who is quite the match for her brothers and how her father calls her his 'little scholar' just as mine used to call me.

I tell him how, when he is much admired in silvered middle age, my brother Richard, now Lord Protector, sends him on various embassies abroad, how he holds the fate of nations in his hands and is showered with honours for his shrewd diplomacy; how I join him at the courts of Europe, where poets write of our great romance and still handsome good looks. And I tell him how we grow old and cross together, bickering happily as our grandchildren grow up around us . . .

A servant knocks, interrupting my thoughts, and I shout for them to go away, just as Robert did on the morning after our wedding: if that was our wedding, this is our marriage. I pull the covers up even higher over us both, clinging to Robert even as his body chills mine. But however hard I try I cannot stop the sky lightening outside nor the morning noises of the palace occupants, who rise unthinking from their beds to another innocuous day. The third time there is a knock at our door, my shouts have no effect and the door opens.

I hear footsteps, feel Mother's ringed hands on me, but I will not move, will not give him up: 'No! No! Leave us!'

When they eventually prise me from Robert and my fingertips leave his skin I scream and beat against them with my fists, swinging my arms around, knocking the water jug to smash on the floor. They carry me somewhere and a warm liquid is trickled into my mouth until everything vanishes into black silence.

I am blind. Blind with pain. Blind with rage. I do not know the day nor the time of day. I am moved from room to room, into and out of beds. Katherine changes me from nightgowns into dresses and back again. I eat a bowl of soup but taste nothing. Now a glass of strong wine, glinting in the firelight. People come and go. Faces peer at me and lips move. Mother is there. Later Father, reading from his Bible. Elizabeth and John bring me a puppy that licks my hand. Someone says that cousin Lavinia died the same night as Robert but I cannot remember who she is. I lie down, I sit up, I walk. I breathe. I talk even, though I cannot hear my own words.

I do all this and yet I am dead.

Though I feel utterly and completely alone in my grief, it seems everyone else wishes for a portion and the whole court sinks into the deep, formal mourning customary for a royal death. Father clothes himself in purple, the imperial colour of mourning allowed only to princes; bells are silenced, all singing and dancing cease. I do not see all this for myself but hear it from Elizabeth who tells me of everyone's sadness at Robert's loss, of the kind words whispered with shaking heads, of the grand gestures, the letters of condolence and get-well gifts, of the tears Robert's grandfather the Earl of Warwick sheds on Father's shoulder. But I can feel no empathy for any other's pain but my own and can find no solace in the actions of others when my beloved will never stir his hand again. I do not want anyone to come between us even now.

They tell me that Robert's body had lain in state at

Warwick House like a prince before being taken home to Leighs Priory in Essex for burial but I do not understand. I panic that they will take his things too, and rush blindly into my rooms, howling like a wolf at the servants who are even then packing away his clothes. With startled, staring eyes they melt away before me and I snatch an armful of Robert's shirts and drag them into the bed with me as a vixen would take her kill back to her den. Burying my face in his linen, I slide towards sleep both yearning for it and fighting it; longing for the oblivion where I can live with Robert in the half-light while knowing that I will wake each time only to die of grief all over again. But the temptation to see him is too much and I drop into a heavy sleep, the smell of his laundry seeping into every pore of my face. My body relaxes as Robert comes to me in my dreams. I hear his low voice on the pillow beside me, feel his breath on my cheek, watch him come in and out of rooms, his laughter vanishing around doorframes with his shadow.

Now that I am once more in my own rooms, I refuse to leave them. I am convinced that something of Robert lingers here with me, some spirit, some presence, and that if I once leave our rooms he will not be there when I return. And so well-wishers come to me and sit holding hopeless conversations with the space where I should be while I barely mask my desire to be left alone. Mother, Elizabeth and Bridget are there most often, their visits timed so well I suspect them of having drawn up a rota. Once Mother brings Signor Giavarina with her, hoping, I imagine, that my Italian pet will be able to coax a smile from me. But the ambassador is solemn, telling me first that the Turks have retaken the Dardanelles as he feared, before talking to me of Dante's love for Beatrice and how it transcended her death to inspire his work: 'We Italians understand love and death, *Principessa*. I know how you suffer.'

In this way, my visitors bring their own experiences and understanding of grief to lay as trophies at my feet as if, by listening to their survival stories, I can learn how to return to my life. Katherine speaks to me of losing her husband William at Marston Moor. As she dresses me and brushes my hair she tells me how she coped as a widow and how she has found new life with Jeremiah. Her personal account barely registers with me; indeed I hardly hear her voice above the roar in my ears. But there is one whose words somehow reach me, stirring my bitterness.

'I too know what it is to lose a beloved husband, dearest,' Bridget whispers over a bowl of porridge, breaking off her words to blow on the steaming oats before she offers me a spoon. 'Nothing can take away the pain but I promise its sting will begin to ease in time; everything is God's will.'

'What God? Besides, how can you know?' I lash out, blind to any pain but mine. 'Robert was all my own – I chose him, we had to fight to be together. Father arranged your marriage to Henry and you married Charles quickly enough when he died.'

Even in my angry haze I see her wince as she touches a spoon of porridge with her tongue to see if it has cooled. 'Hush, dearest,' she says after a few moments, offering me the spoon again. 'You were too young to understand.'

'I can feed myself.'

'Of course, here.' Bridget passes me the bowl and sits back in her chair, folding her thin hands in her lap and twisting her mourning ring absently between her thumb and forefinger.

I am still glaring at her when a soft knock brings a tall young man into the room. He approaches us slowly and it takes me a good length of time to fight through the fog to remember who he is: John Russell, Harry's brother-in-law, who I last saw on my wedding day when he brought me my beautiful bird. I feel Robert's kiss on my hand, hear him applauding.

'Lady Frances, I – I am so very sad, so very, very sorry for your loss. Here.' He reaches into his pocket. 'I have a letter for you from your brother. It came in the post bag from Ireland with his letters to my family and I thought you would like it straight away.'

I take the square of folded paper from him, the action stirring the memory of when I took a letter from his hands once before – the page on which Harry had urged me to marry the man I loved. I think I manage a small smile in thanks, though I cannot tell as my cheeks are numb; my face no longer feels part of my body. I begin to open the letter, then change my mind and lay it on the counterpane beside me. I do not think I can handle any more condolence for the moment, especially not the guesswork of my adored big brother who never witnessed my love for my husband, never saw me wed and now never will.

'He won't know his little sister when he comes home,' I say, neither to John Russell nor Bridget but to the room at large. 'She no longer exists.'

Time stretches before me like a twisted rope. It snaps and coils, flattens and kinks so that I cannot tell if days, weeks or mere hours pass me by. Occasionally I hear sounds or news of the wider world – a world without Robert – and it pins me to a calendar. The church bells that ring across Westminster tell me it is Sunday. Dick apologises for having been away for a week in Hampshire. My brother-in-law John brings me a vase of budding daffodils and tells me of the great triumph of Father's mediation between Sweden and Denmark with a peace treaty signed at Roskilde. Yet John says there is little outward celebration as the court continues to mourn Robert. I think of my first argument with Robert at Ambassador Meadowes' appointment ceremony when he doubted we could secure peace in the Baltic. All I want to do is tell him *I told you so*.

Giavarina tries to cheer me with news that the details of the royalist plot for the Spanish invasion have been uncovered: 'A triumph for Signor Thurloe's spies,' the Italian says, his eyes glimmering over his wine glass with the delight of an ambassador with superior information about his host nation. But I cannot summon any enthusiasm for this news; it is too late for Robert to take me home to Leighs Priory, so what do I care?

Though time passes in a blur, there is one marker I do notice, or rather I notice the absence of it. I realise that I have not bled since Robert died and I begin nervously and then desperately to wonder if I might be with child. I have no idea how long it has been but I know that it has been too long. The thought swells within me until I can think of nothing else and pin all my hopes on a miracle; on the tiny chance that I could be carrying a fragment of Robert within me, that a part of him might still live. I tell no one of my hopes but start to take more care of myself; to rest and to eat properly. I can see the joy in Mother's face that I am no longer refusing food and I know she thinks, falsely, that it is a sign that I am coming back to the light. The thought of Robert's baby restores some purpose to me and replaces my memory of his death as my first thought on waking. Each time I slip my fingers below my nightdress and bring them gingerly to my eyes, praying not to find blood.

But my prayers go unanswered. Any shred of faith in God's Providence that had survived Robert's death drains out of me with the blood when it eventually comes. It is a cruel blow, tearing open the bandaged wound of my grief once more as Robert dies before my eyes all over again. I turn my face to the wall and send all food away while Mother cries in the corner of my room.

I sink beneath the waves once more, seeing nothing, hearing no one but Robert's voice in my head and an emptiness in my belly. I hover on the edge of consciousness, the days and nights measured only by the burning down and replacement of the candle I can see on my nightstand. I speak to no one. Indeed I have quite made peace with my own death when a solitary voice reaches deep within me and turns me from the wall.

Mary. Mary has come back to me.

CHAPTER NINE

Mary is all mine. She sits by my bed by day and sleeps in it with me at night, just as she did when we were children. I cling to her greedily and somehow, as the days pass, I find my senses returning to me like pins and needles.

'Thomas?' I ask her eventually as we lie side by side in the darkness, the firelight, now flickering low in the grate, occasionally catching the gold thread that criss-crosses the deep green velvet canopy above us. 'Tell me.'

I hear her breathe a few deep breaths and know she is choosing her words.

'He is a good man, kind, considerate. He gave me a beautiful pair of grey mares as a wedding present. He rises early but if I am tired bids me stay in bed and sends the maid up with hot apple juice and toast. He travels a good deal. But if he is at home then in the evenings he reads the news-sheets while I play the virginal for him.' She takes my hand, her fingers small and cold in mine, not like Robert's. 'He brought me back to you when I asked.'

It is a thin list of kindnesses, spare and lean. I listen, examining Mary's words as if I could see them hovering above our heads, searching within them for a fraction of the love I have for my husband. Robert flashes before my eyes like a passing reflection in a window. I see him talking and teasing me as he sits in the bath, his wet pruning fingers laced through mine; hear him laugh at a joke across the supper table before catching my eye, his wink assuring me he will repeat the jest for me later; feel a rustle beside me in the bed as he turns in his sleep and folds himself around me, his sleepy lips creeping up my back as he rouses himself. The hopeless irony of our position floods me once again, welling up inside me until it overflows in tears.

'You accepted Thomas so I could be with Robert,' I say, the words choking out of my mouth like bubbles. 'But now you could have been free to have anyone you wanted. God is cruel: he will give you and Thomas the long life of marriage he denied to us in penance for our bargain. I know that now.'

'No, no, no.' Mary shakes her head, rubbing the pillow beside mine, her voice urgent, fierce. 'You must not regret the choices we made. And who is to say my husband and I will not love each other in time, or that you may one day love again? God has purpose still for all of us, I know it.'

She is wrong but I say nothing. I cannot take her faith from her, not after everything she has already given me.

Robert comes to me in my waking hours when I receive a parcel from his father. Mary reads me the letter from Lord Rich but I scarcely hear his words as I unfold the layers of paper to find a miniature portrait of my beloved. A younger Robert smiles up at me from where he nestles in my palm and I grip the tips of my fingers around the tiny gilded frame, pressing him into my flesh. He lives in my hand from then on, sometimes displayed in the open, at others held under a fold of my skirt, in a pocket or beneath my pillow. I find myself growing stronger.

Lord Rich's letter is followed soon afterwards by a visit from his own father, Robert's grandfather, the Earl of Warwick. He slopes into my rooms, his once tall frame, which had been as rigid as the masts on the ships he commanded to the far side of the world, now bent over, all the air gone from his sails. He sinks into a chair opposite me and stretches out a large bony hand to take mine. He says nothing but lets his eyes rest on my stomach for so long I begin to worry he is looking for a sign of a child; a boy to pick up his line where Robert, his sole heir, has dropped it. I try very hard to swallow the bile that rises into my throat.

'My dear,' he says at last, dragging his eyes back up to meet mine. 'I am sorry to disturb you but I come on a commission from my son.'

I nod my understanding, running my thumb along the smooth edge of Robert's oval frame.

'Robert's father wishes to ask a great kindness of you. I imagine it is the very last thing that you would want to do at the moment, Frances, but my son wonders, hopes that you would consent to sit for a portrait.'

I stare at him blankly.

'You see,' he presses on, 'the whole family was greatly looking forward to Robert bringing you home to us in Essex. My little granddaughters – Robert's half-sisters – had talked of little else for months. They adored Robert you see . . .'

The earl pauses then, pretending to search for something in his pocket while I watch him fight his tears.

'You will always be one of the family, Frances, of course. But the girls and their father would like a permanent reminder of your marriage to Robert, of your love. We have a fine portrait of him – painted when he reached his maturity – and it is our dearest wish to have a matching likeness of you to hang beside it at Leighs Priory.'

I am quite overcome by the request. Though the earl is right that the idea of reassembling and prettifying myself sufficiently to sit for one of the court painters is unimaginable in my current state, I love the idea of Robert and I spending eternity together, watching other lives unfold beneath us side by side on the wall.

'I will,' I say, though no other words form to follow them.

'Bless you,' the earl says.

Father commissions John Michael Wright, the famed Italianate portrait artist, to paint his grieving daughter. Lord Rich had wanted to pay but Father insists the painting will be his gift to the Rich family; an act of penance for the dead bridegroom he never wanted. Master Wright is a puffed-up peacock who takes every chance to flaunt the years he spent learning his craft in Rome at the temple of the old masters. But he is kind and gentle with me, instructing and soothing me as if I am a frightened doe; I imagine he has experienced all shades of humanity from behind his outstretched paintbrush. And, strangely, there is something calming in the way I must sit in still silence for hours at a time, nothing more expected of me than immobility.

In any circumstances but these I would have been thrilled by this honour, fussing over my dress and hair, equal parts nerves and excitement. But my new self spends not one thought on how I look, indeed I have not even asked for a mirror to see how my sisters and Katherine have put me back together. Gently they bathed me, and Katherine dried my hair, curled and pinned it while Mary and Elizabeth chose my clothes and jewels, whispering their consultations as they ran their fingers over my things like housewives at a haberdasher: 'The silver-blue gown with the lavender trim.' 'Really, not the green?' 'The pearls, she loves those.' 'But will they complement the brooch? Robert gave that to her, I know she will want to wear it.' I barely feel the expensive silks and pearls as they are layered onto me, as if they are being laid on another body, a porcelain doll's. It is as if all of my vanity died with Robert. The young woman who danced as the goddess Venus, soaking up the admiration of the court, has gone. Who cares what I look like now? Robert will not be able to look on me as I hang beside him, but he will have what I believe he loved of me most: my conversation, my companionship.

Master Wright is remarkably quick and has my likeness after only three sittings. He tells me he will paint an autumn evening scene behind me – some wispy trees and a moonlit sky – the whole effect one of wistful reflection at the end of life. Resting under my fingers will be a white turtle dove; that common staple of widows, symbolising the constancy of my love for my dead husband. I cannot object, though I fear it will seem trite. If only I could have posed with a real bird, I think, imagining the softness of downy feathers under my fingertips, feeling the buttery lightness of the creature in my hands before I lift them to the sky and set it free.

When it is finished, Master Wright's portrait is displayed in the Banqueting House for all the court and London society to admire his skill and my grief. I do not go but keep to my rooms where, eventually, the painting is delivered to my care, wrapped in cloth. I do not even look at it before the Earl of Warwick comes to take it back to his family. Mary, seated beside me, offers the earl a glass of claret and, taking it, he lowers himself slowly into a chair by the fire. He takes a sip of wine and once again his eyes shift onto my stomach. I can bear it no longer.

'I am not with child, my lord,' I say, the words tumbling out of me, 'much though I wish I were.'

Mary glances quickly at me, her expression half in sympathy, half reproof. I realise I have spoken bluntly and for the first time since Robert's death I recognise the pain of another mourner in the sudden crumpling of the earl's face.

'I am sorry,' I rush on. 'I did not mean to speak so bluntly, but I could not have you continuing to hope now all my hope has gone.'

With a great effort, the earl brings his disintegrating face under control. He meets my eyes then, his own glazed and shining. 'I understand, my dear, you have no need to apologise.'

Within a few minutes he has gone, his manservant carrying the portrait behind his shuffling steps. A week later I receive another letter from Lord Rich who thanks me for the painting and reports that his father, the legendary Earl of Warwick, parliamentarian and privateer, died in his sleep on the night he brought my picture home.

Weeks pass and bit by bit I venture a little further from the womb of my rooms, first into the family's private apartments and then, when we travel down to my beloved Hampton Court again, drawn out into the gardens by the slipping of spring into summer. Beyond unavoidable travel where I have kept myself huddled into the corner of the carriage or barge, I have not been out of doors properly since February and the gardens embrace me like a long-lost friend, the warm May sunlight beating against my closed eyes soothing me as I listen to Robert's voice on the wind. I keep to the private parts of the gardens and in the palace I hug the edges of rooms. The sound of laughter makes me wince and so I avoid crowds, will not dine in public nor attend chapel; the company of one of my sisters and the little puppy Elizabeth and John have given me is all I want and I have no desire to speak to God who, if He even exists, is proved the cruel God of the Old Testament, not the loving Lord of the New.

And so it is that I pay little attention to what is passing at court, only noticing those incidents that preoccupy my family. For Dick they are the final preparations for his and Dorothy's forthcoming tour of the West Country: something I gather Father has had Thurloe plan to raise Dick's profile among the people over whom he may one day rule. It is to be an extravagant affair, Doll tells me when she comes to bid me farewell, and I shudder to think of the many miles of smiling and waving that await them. Father, meanwhile, is consumed by the ruination of his plan for Protestant peace in Europe as the Swedish king abandons the treaty to resume his war against Denmark. Father kicks the logs in the grate when he hears the news, leaning his broad shoulders against the mantel, head bowed low so only the flames can see his face.

While he broods, my sisters are preoccupied with the trials and executions of the men who plotted the Spanish invasion, as one of them, Dr John Hewitt, is none other than the clergyman who officiated at Mary's wedding. He had been a great favourite of Mary and Elizabeth, who had often gone to hear him preach in the City, and Hewitt's fate grieves them both bitterly. Night after night I listen as they plead for him with Father. But there is nothing to be done, even by Betty whom Father dotes on above all and who has so often shaped his thoughts towards the forgiveness of others. 'I cannot save him,' he tells them as his hands thread through Betty's chestnut curls. 'There can be only one end for those who conspire with a foreign power.'

Though I now reside in perpetual gloom, my only ambition for each day simply to survive it, I am sorry that my family must face such disappointments. So it brings me a detached pleasure when Father shares the brighter news with us that our allied Anglo-French army has defeated the Spanish to liberate the great coastal fortress of Dunkirk. This 'Battle of the Dunes', as the men at court begin to call it, is a great triumph for Father's government: King Louis XIV himself handing the keys of the city to our ambassador, Sir William Lockhart. It is the glittering prize England has longed for; once again we have a foothold on the Continent. I cannot share the joy that radiates from the faces of Thurloe and the other Councillors and pours out of the printing presses but I do feel the slightest pinprick of pride in my slumbering heart as I think of the honour we have finally regained from Bloody Mary Tudor's catastrophic loss of the port of Calais almost exactly a century ago – although, of course, our enemy then was the French rather than the Spanish. What a jig we have danced between those two great powers all these years.

I mention this to my own Mary, who smiles and takes up a conversation designed to interest me more than her – happy, I can tell, to see me begin to engage again with the wider world. I manage a thin smile in return, thankful beyond words that Mary is still with me and grateful to her new husband for loaning her to me. Mary herself does not seem to miss him as she lives and sleeps by my side. Nevertheless, I still catch the questioning look that flits across her face when others speak of Thomas's political affairs. Has he really abandoned his former loyalty to the exiled Charles Stuart? Will he be in touch with him again once he travels to the Continent as Father's newly appointed Ambassador Extraordinary to Paris? I wonder how Mary will fare then if Thomas leaves her alone with his recalcitrant royalist family in Yorkshire. Mary does not speak of her new family but has instead slipped quietly into her old life as a puritan princess. I am thankful for it, even as I know it cannot last.

And then, just as the summer days are lengthening and Father's government basks in the sunshine of a rebellion quashed, an invasion thwarted and an enemy defeated, God strikes at us again for the sin of pride. Once more

Mary's strength is needed, and now by more than me, for little Oliver, Elizabeth and John Claypole's baby, falls into a fever and dies – snatched from his parents so quickly it is as if a demon is at work. He was a year old and transforming into a little boy before our eyes, crawling busily around the palace, panting and pulling himself up into our laps like a restless puppy. Betty is stricken, John too. And Mary, who had doted on Ollie, as she does on all babies, pushes her grief deep down inside to take their care upon herself, just as she has been doing with me. For myself, I am shocked, stirred from my foggy inertia into practical tasks, chief among them looking after my other nieces and nephews while Elizabeth and John howl their pain out of earshot. Mother moves between the nursery and Elizabeth's bedside and Father – himself ill and weakened of late – retreats into his work, his great faith as well as his body shaken by God's taking his namesake grandson.

'I am reminded of little James,' he says to me as we sit together late one night once the Claypole children are asleep, the candles guttering around us, the air thick with summer heat. 'Your older brother died in my arms, did you know that? Just a babe he was. His hand fitted around my thumb like this.' He shows me how their hands held each other for that brief time and I think how strange it is that he calls a baby my older brother. 'But we must remember that children belong to God,' Father says quietly. 'He only entrusts them to us to steward on His behalf. If He wishes to call them home, we must accept it, however much it grieves us.'

I search Father's face for evidence of this acceptance but find instead the deep lines etched there from the deaths of the three sons he lost: first James as a baby and then, even more cruelly, his oldest boy Robert from illness when he was on the cusp of manhood, and his second son Oliver during the war. How I would love to have my three lost brothers here with us today. I lean my head on Father's bulky shoulder and sigh for all the children taken and for those who will never be.

It is a devastating blow for Elizabeth, of course, but both Mother and Bridget reassure me that Betty will recover her spirits in time; *not like you, Frances*, their words imply, and I understand their meaning – most women lose at least one child in infancy, few lose a young husband of their heart when they are still honeymooning. I chide myself for these unworthy thoughts, competing with my big sister even in our different griefs. How can I know the unspeakable pain of losing a child? I grieved deeply even for the loss of a phantom baby. But I console myself with these thoughts too, hoping that Elizabeth will come back to us and resume her life much as before, just as my parents managed to do after the loss of baby James. Bridget had done so too, in time, after the death of her and Charles's little girl Anne, now buried in Westminster Abbey.

In the weeks that follow, John emerges from his grief, coming to dine with the family, moving around the court in his fine clothes, albeit with a stooping gait and a few days' growth on his chin that he did not have before. But Betty keeps to her bed. I sit with her frequently, and on the national day of thanksgiving for our victory at the Dunes, spend the whole day at her side – my puppy on her bed – grateful to hide away with her, our parallel sadness safe from the gaiety of the court. And it is on that day, as I sit beside Betty, my fingers tracing the frame of Robert's portrait in my lap, that her grief for baby Oliver turns to sickness. She stops talking, beads of sweat appearing on her forehead before she vomits the glass of watered ale I have just given her. I send for the physicians – my heart pounding as my body travels back in time to Robert's own illness five months before. Mother is there in a few minutes, her ceremonial duties for the public holiday abandoned with her high-heeled shoes. John arrives next, breathless and wide-eyed, his dog Badger snapping at his offspring puppy, who scampers off the bed with a yelp.

Father comes a few hours later, breathing heavily from the effort of rushing, and from then on, he hardly leaves Elizabeth's bedside, often indeed sitting with her all night long. Slowly, as the days pass, government business grinds to a halt, though Master Thurloe still creeps into the room at intervals to place a paper before Father for signing or to whisper him a message. The court respects our private crisis, shares in it even – for Elizabeth Claypole is widely loved. Even our state visitors show restraint: the Dutch ambassador, Master Thurloe tells me one evening as we meet outside the door to Betty's chamber, has kindly refused the usual pomp of a state visit, knowing Father and his family to be in such distress. A personal meeting with him is one of the only responsibilities Father cannot avoid, however, but he travels up to Whitehall to see the ambassador as quickly as possible, rushing back to Hampton Court only a few hours later; his best carriage horses steaming with the effort in the August heat. In all this, I watch Elizabeth and Father closely, observing the duelling kindness between them – her trying to hide her pain, him his grief. Elizabeth rises to the occasion as she does always, however: a model of graceful, feminine stoicism, beauty in her every movement.

Day after day the physicians bicker at the end of Betty's bed, but they all agree she has been struck by the same illness she has suffered at intervals before. She has always recovered in the past and the roses that return to her cheeks every few days bring hope that she will do so again. But I know what is to come. I alone recognise the descent into hell, having travelled it so recently. As I watch, the Claypoles' rooms become the stage for Southwark theatrics: Mary's false cheerfulness as she plays with the children; John's borrowed bravado as he refuses to accept that he could lose the woman who is so much his partner in all things; Father's all-consuming despair that shuts everyone out. Mother subsumes herself once more in the practical, conferring with Bridget, dispatching her and Charles on errands and dispensing instructions while Richard, now thankfully returned from his regal progress into the West Country, takes on what he can of the burden of official business. In all this activity, I flit between them like a moth among lanterns, floating above the scenes as they play them out.

It is perhaps this detachment, this clarity that comes from my own raw loss of Robert, that is the reason I know I am about to lose my big sister too. The old Frances – the girl that danced as Venus – would have fought for my beloved Betty, struggled tooth and nail to wrench her from the reaper. But instead I lay my cheek against hers and let my memories and my love pass through our skin from my mind to hers. I tell her how

I have worshipped her since I was a small child. How I grew up emulating her glamour and easy style, envying her small waist and watching and copying her manners; how she flirted with the officers who were always in and out of our house, how she wrapped Father around her little finger. How I loved her in a wholly different way from my other sisters – Bridget, so much the eldest, whose stern ways used to frighten me a little; and Mary, so close to me in age and so gentle I always felt the older, protective sister in our pair.

Running my finger along the lace neckline of Elizabeth's nightgown, breathing in her rosewater scent, I acknowledge to us both how I have envied her closeness to Father and longed for him to talk to me with the same adult intimacy they shared. But it was ever out of reach – I would always be nine years and five months younger than Betty. And it seemed to me there was some mystery, some magic in those nine years of our family life that she had lived before me. In those years she had witnessed Father's darkest time and watched his extraordinary flight into greatness through the war, where Mary and I had just caught the tailwinds. This seemed to matter, as if Father valued her love all the more because she had been his companion in his frustrated obscurity and loved him nonetheless.

But I was always the baby. Would always be the baby; even baby James who died before I was born is counted my older brother. It is horrible, perverse the way death can muddle us all out of order with our siblings. And now Betty. I have spent my life running to catch up with her and now I will. Slowly, day on day, year upon year, I will grow towards her until there comes a day in nine years and five months' time when I will overtake my older sister in age. I hate this thought more than any other because I am finally being granted what I always wanted but at such a terrible cost. And who will I model myself on with Betty gone? Who will show me how to grow into full womanhood with grace and beauty, how to raise children without losing myself, how to navigate the middle years of life with dignity? Who will show me how to do these things?

Lying there listening to Betty's shallow breaths, I realise that I have always measured my life against hers even to this last moment. Perhaps I always will. I close my eyes to remember her as she was and cherish her vivacity, her lively wit and deep store of kindness.

I ask her not to leave me behind, not to die when she is at her most perfect.

And I say goodbye.

♛

Elizabeth dies in the early hours of that night, the sixth of August, her departure from our midst cracking us apart like a thunderbolt cleaving through an ancient oak.

♛

This is a new grief; a sadness not centred within me but shared by us all. A public loss. The whole court indeed seems to have lost its sheen: if any one woman could have laid claim to being the darling of the court, its beating heart, it was Elizabeth. She and John were always the shining, smiling centre of palace life, and without them, our painted world fades to printers' grey.

I accept the pain with a heart already opened to sorrow. But it is not so easy for the rest of the family. Betty's older boys cry into their pillows and little Martha frowns in confusion. John goes into shock much as I believe I did after Robert died. Mother and Mary seek comfort in the arms of one another and in prayer while Bridget is devastated, her usual strength and stoicism melted away. 'We were always so different,' she sobs to me, a sodden handkerchief pressed to her eyes. 'But she was my only sister for so long. My bedfellow, my companion. It was she I talked to of my feelings for Henry Ireton, she I laced into her wedding gown, she I held each night when our brothers died. And now she is gone. Gone to God before me when it was always I who longed for Him, not her. Betty would see the irony in that.'

But though we are all heartsore, there is one among us who is wrenched apart at the seams, who disintegrates in body and mind before our eyes: Father, poor Father, crawls away into the darkness, half-crazed with grief for his most darling girl. The effect of Betty's death upon him is so immediate, so profound that even Mother, even John who has lost his beloved wife, make room in their grief to tend to his. He shuts himself in his privy bedchamber and will see no one save ourselves. Even Thurloe, Father's shadow and confidant in all things, is barred from his presence and forced to turn to Richard as Father's eldest son and member of the council.

Elizabeth is to be accorded the royal honour of being buried among the old kings and queens in Westminster Abbey: a resting place of such grandeur that it is only she of my family who seems to me glorious enough for it, though it may yet come to us all. She will join our brother-in-law Henry Ireton and the two extreme ends of our family – Bridget and Charles's baby Anne who lived but a few weeks and our grandmother who lived into her ninth decade – who are waiting for her there. I cannot help but wonder morbidly who among us will be the next to be laid beneath the marble, before dismissing the thoughts angrily: there can be no more death, for I would break beneath its weight.

For now, all focus is on the arrangements for Elizabeth's funeral, due to take place in a few days' time on Tuesday, 10 August. Father will not speak of it, John neither. And so we are all grateful for the combined talents of Colonel Philip Jones, the Controller of Father's Household, and Sir Oliver Flemyng, the Master of Ceremonies, who between them see to all of the details. They do this out of our sight, only occasionally sliding into our rooms with the softest feet to collect a simple nod or shake of Mother's head over a proffered piece of paper, a list or diagram and a whispered question. And through all this, Father remains stricken in bed, with Mother and Mary fussing over him anxiously. He has lost his fenland yeoman's ruddy colour, his face pale above the ruby-red counterpane of his bed, looking so much older than his fifty-nine years.

The day of the funeral comes and the last preparations are made for Betty's final journey. In the afternoon, Mother gently raises the question of his attendance with Father as I hover at the end of their bed. But he merely shakes his head, sinking even further below the covers even as he reaches for Mother's hand, his eyes pools of tears, his brow beaded by sweat. A few minutes later he has fallen into a ragged sleep, drugged out of his pain by a sleeping draught. Mother lays his hand down carefully before drawing me across to the window.

'I hardly know what to do, Fanny,' she says, gathering

me to her like a rag doll. 'I cannot leave him, not like this. But I should be with Betty. I should be there when she is lowered into the ground.' A small sob escapes her and I hug her fiercely, aware as never before in my former childishness of how Mother looks after us all and has no one to take care of her.

'Hush.' I stroke her hair as she has done mine so many hundreds, thousands of times, the grey strands fine among the brown. 'Keep Mary here to help you. I will go to the funeral with Bridget, Charles and Dick. I will help John to bear it and I will take yours and Father's love with me to give to Betty. Remember, she has gone to God already,' I find myself saying, even though I no longer know if He even exists.

Mother nods over my shoulder. 'You are right, dearest. I was brought up to pay little heed to the church rituals, your father too. There will be nothing of Betty there for the priest to pray over. Her soul ascended straight to heaven when she died and she lives there now and in here.' She pulls my hand onto her chest and I feel her heart beating fast beneath the black brocade of her corset. 'God knows the content of my heart and so does Betty.' I squeeze her hand and kiss her wet cheek before slipping from the room.

As Elizabeth died at Hampton Court, her body is to be taken downriver to Westminster by barge. The funeral will take place at night as is the custom and so it is not until the early evening that I make my way, with the other straggling members of my family, to the palace river steps. There we board the Protectoral barge, its bright colours and gilt smothered in black, the liveried boatmen arrayed in mourning, their eyes cast low.

Behind us, a mass of noble figures of the court queue along the bank waiting to board the flotilla of other vessels waiting upstream. Despite the throng of people there is a hushed quiet and I hear little but the soft murmured instructions of the officials and the gentle lapping of the river against the pier.

Betty lies in the centre of the barge, her coffin topped with a beautiful effigy, raised on a platform covered with a fine canopy and torches lit at each corner. It is only once we are underway and have travelled a few miles that I appreciate the purpose of this as I see hundreds of faces crowding the banks of the Thames, straining for a sight of the young dead princess floating through the August twilight. Looking behind our boat, I am awestruck by the sight of the procession of boats following slowly and silently in our wake, each lit by flaming torches which seem to set the very river on fire. Bridget takes my cold hand in her gloved one and we share a sad smile at the sight. John, for his part, barely takes his eyes off the coffin, oblivious to all but his wife who will, in a few hours' time, be taken away from him for ever.

The crowds swell as we reach London so that by the time we moor at Westminster steps at eleven o'clock, there must be thousands of people waiting for us. Elizabeth's coffin is carried onto the land by the liveried boatmen before the bargemaster helps us onto the landing steps. Peering through the torchlit gloom I am relieved to see Sir Oliver Flemyng, Master Thurloe and others from the Council and Parliament emerging to guide us into the Palace of Westminster. For the rest of the eerie night, I follow Richard, John and the other members of my family from one place to another. First to the Painted

Hall of the palace where Elizabeth lies in state on a great hearse until midnight, whereupon we process silently through the maze of the palace to the abbey, whose vast facade soars overhead until it is lost in the night sky.

The funeral ceremony itself is stately but swift and Elizabeth is being lowered beneath the floor of the chapel of the first Tudor king, Henry VII, before we know it. I find it harder somehow to leave her behind in this great, cold place with its vaunting ceiling and royal ghosts. Though I knew the beautiful Elizabeth Claypole to be grand and gracious enough for the honour – perhaps the most regal of us all – my thoughts keep returning to my big sister Betty Cromwell, who grew up a gentleman farmer's daughter in the fens and who never lost the traces of the East Anglian accent from her voice; the glamorous young woman whom I, even as a child, could see half the young men of Ely were in love with. How has it come to pass that she will spend eternity in the cold company of the Tudor kings and queens? Betty Cromwell for ever lying alongside her icy namesake, the mighty Elizabeth, the Virgin Queen.

We return to Hampton Court and continue in crisis for the next few weeks, layering our grief for Elizabeth with our concern for Father's worsening health; both, in my case, built upon the shattered foundations of my widowhood. The strain tells on us all while around us the court watches and waits. I find I am missing Robert more than ever and I wonder often how differently I would bear these griefs if I were Venus still, my beloved husband by my side. Thinking of him takes me often to John whom I comfort as best I can for the loss I, more than anyone, can understand. Together we sit for hours at a time, his dog Badger and the puppy he sired, that John gave me to cheer me in my grief, in a temporary truce at our feet. 'You really should name that dog,' John says absently. But I cannot bring myself to make even this small choice for the future.

Where John is numb, my other brother-in-law Charles Fleetwood is as lively as dry kindling, marching through rooms and pacing around beds. He is everywhere at once: conferring with Mother and the physicians in whispers at the door to Father's room; meeting in quiet corners with knots of his fellow Councillors; opening letters and dispatching messengers; travelling up and down from the army in London to our apartments at Hampton Court. Once I catch a rare unguarded look on Master Thurloe's face as he watches Charles bustle from a room and I wonder, not for the first time, of the relations between them. A mass of questions throng in my mind. Does Thurloe suspect Charles of angling to succeed Father? Could Charles bring himself to do that to Richard? And if he did, would Thurloe fall into line behind Charles or press for Richard's claim? What would any of us do?

My fears are shown to be well founded when Bulstrode Whitelocke appears at my elbow outside the hall after breakfast one morning, and asks if I know any more about what Charles is up to. He is all politeness of course and I take care not to speak badly of Charles, but our shared concern is clear. 'We must keep an eye on your brother-in-law,' the lawyer says quietly, his peat-black eyes shifting from me across the courtyard. 'He has summoned the army officers to meet, just as he did in the spring. Then it was to proclaim loyalty to your father in the wake of the uprisings. But now?' Whitelocke shakes his head, his curls shifting black against his white collar. 'Now he is sending a signal to those of us on the civilian side of the government, telling us the army will keep its dominance in the state, whatever becomes of your father. Your brother Richard will need to watch his footing should the worst happen. Fleetwood would make a powerful enemy. Lambert too of course, and what is to stop his return to government in that case? We are all hoping that your father will make his intentions clear and formally nominate your brother his successor before it is too late.'

I tell him that I know nothing further of Charles's intentions, nor can I believe that Charles should ever betray our family. But a small voice inside me questions my certainty even as I voice the words: I know the streak of wildness that runs in Charles, his godly fervour and devotion to the army. It is what Father so loves in him, Biddy too. When Charles's blood is up . . . I squeeze Bulstrode's arm and tell him to come to me if he learns any more and fancy, in the deep bow with which he leaves me, that he understands my position.

The weather echoes our mood; just as government and the court is at a standstill, so the heavy August heat hangs, always on the edge of a thunderstorm, a taste of rain on the air. We have returned now from Hampton Court to Whitehall, Father's doctors hoping the change of air will aid his recovery, but the summer heat is just as oppressive in London, more so perhaps. Wandering to and from Father's rooms, I sweat in my mourning dresses, wishing I had a version in a lighter fabric. Briefly I contemplate placing an order with Master Hornlock but I would hate to appear vain or frivolous at such a time of crisis. And so I sweat on, Katherine doing her best to freshen my gown with steam. It is muggy in Father's room, where open windows can do little to counter the decaying smell of illness. Sometimes he lies, fatigued after another fit, sleeping away his pain. At others, he sits up and listens as Mother or one of his chaplains reads to him, his speech quite lucid and some colour restored to his cheeks.

There is one such time when, for a few short minutes, Father and I are almost alone, only two of his attendants clearing away the remains of a supper tray. It is early evening, the last blackbird singing even as the first bats begin to swoop outside the latticed windows.

'What will the histories say of me, Fanny?' he asks, his eyes fixed on the massive muscled figure of the god Vulcan who half hangs out of the tapestry opposite the end of his bed.

'Father, no,' I say, reaching for his large hand. 'You will be well again.'

'I might,' he nods, his eyes far away. 'But if God calls me to Him?'

I swallow, seeking the words. 'They will say you have been a great prince.'

'A prince,' he repeats, the word sticking slightly in his throat.

'A great ruler then,' I readjust. 'A good and kind ruler. A humble man who loved God and who fought for liberty against a tyrant. Who brought peace, stability and religious freedom to the people.'

Father turns and smiles at me then, sadness twitching

the corners of his mouth. 'My little scholar. Whatever anyone else says about me, if you give that account to your children, I will be well pleased.' He must see the blankness in my face at the unthinkable prospect of my now having children, for he grips my hand tightly. 'You will be happy again, Fanny, I promise you. Yes,' he answers my unspoken protests, 'and have your own babes too. I want to think of you living to be an old lady, taking me with you well into the century after this. Without Betty . . .' Tears creep once again to the lower lids of his eyes and he pauses for a few moments, bringing his feelings under control. 'Without Betty, you must have strength. Be a support for your mother. Support Richard. He will need you all beside him when I am gone. Listen to God. Look to Thurloe, he will help.'

'You will nominate Dick your successor then?' I ask him, fear driving me to plain speaking even as I choke with tears.

'I will, he is ready.'

Relief floods through me as Father squeezes my hand. The next moment brings Jeremiah White into the room, a well-thumbed Bible in the crook of his arm.

'Ah.' Father is pleased to see him and beckons him to an armchair on the other side of his bed. 'Read me Paul's letter to the Philippians, Jerry.'

Jeremiah begins to read and I sit back a little in my chair, still holding Father's hand though his attention has shifted away from me. I watch him as he nods along to the reading, his lips occasionally mouthing a phrase as the familiar beloved words soak into him. His heavy brow furrows a little and I have the sense that he is waiting for some passage or other that he knows is to come.

'There,' he says suddenly, his whole body tensing as he leaps after Jeremiah's words. '*I can do all things through Christ, which strengtheneth me*,' he repeats, his tone wondrous. 'That's it. Those are the words I love, the words I clung to when my sons died. First James as a baby in '32,' he is telling Jeremiah as if he does not already know. 'Then Robert when he was away at school. In '39 that was. And then my own young Oliver, God bless him, in the war.' He turns back to me, eyes shining with joyful sorrow: 'You remember, Fanny?'

I smile and nod, feigning understanding and encouragement to smooth over his confusion. Baby James died six years before I was born and I was only a baby myself when Robert died at the age of seventeen. I can remember my elder brother Oliver, just: can see him now pulling me up to sit on his horse while he checked the saddlebags, the last time he left home to join Father on campaign. Where are they all now?

'I can do all things through Christ, which strengtheneth me,' Father says again. 'All things. All things.'

The next day is the third of September, Father's most sacred day: the day the nation celebrates his army's great victories at Dunbar and Worcester and gives thanks for Parliament's triumph over tyranny; the day that Providence marked out for him. As if at a cue in one of Master Marvell's masques, the great summer storm we have waited for finally comes, the sky splitting with lightning as fierce rain hisses through the hot air. We go to the windows, glass cool on our cheeks, faces upturned to heaven and hardly notice amid the clamour when God Himself reaches down and plucks Father from among us.

♛

I have no more grief to give, no more of my heart to break. And so I drift, numb and cold, watching history happen through a blur of unfelt tears. Mary is inconsolable, weeping in her husband's uncertain arms as Mother and Bridget pray at Father's bedside and Dick stares blankly ahead. I take in the scene with a strange calm, observing how from the end of the bed, quietly, politely, John Thurloe steps into the void that has yawned wide in time and space. Satisfied the Lord Protector has departed this life, even as his bulky body is still warm, Thurloe murmurs something to Henry Lawrence, President of the Council, who stirs himself. His voice hoarse, Lawrence calls to the other Councillors pressed around the bed to reassemble in the Council chamber. I watch them leave, my heart thumping in my chest. Had Father nominated Richard to succeed him in the end? He told me he intended to but had he actually done it? My whole life has been so dependent on Father, I think anxiously, more so than any daughter's could ever have been; will all I have taken for granted crumble to dust now he is gone? Will the sun even rise again tomorrow?

The Council is gone a few hours, by which time Richard, his wife Dorothy, John, Mary, Thomas and I have retreated to the dining room, leaving Mother to have her final hours alone with Father. Bridget is with us too, upright and armoured in godly grief; Charles, of course, off with the rest of the Council. We are sitting forlornly around an untouched supper table when the guards at the door announce the Council into our presence. My gaze flies to Charles as he strides in and for one fleeting moment I imagine that he is to be presented to us as our new Lord Protector. But relief floods away my anxiety in another instant when the Lord President of the Council steps forward and kneels before Richard.

'Your Highness,' the elderly Henry Lawrence says, his voice grave and trembling. 'We the Council are satisfied that before his death your most gracious father the Lord Protector nominated you, Lord Richard Cromwell, his eldest son, to succeed him in this office in accordance with the written provisions of our constitution, the Humble Petition and Advice. And so, we come to you to place the government of these nations in your hands. My fellow Councillor Lord Fleetwood is to convey this news to the army and tomorrow you are to be proclaimed our new Lord Protector throughout the land. We are drafting the proclamation now, to be signed by our Council, the Lord Mayor of London and the Council of Officers of the army.' He pauses for a few moments before a tentative question follows: 'What says Your Highness?'

My whole body courses with shuddering relief. I look at Charles and, seeing tears of grief in his eyes, think in that moment how his love for Father, birthed on the battlefield, was as fierce as any of ours. My gaze shifts from him to Dick, who has risen from his chair and is standing with his head bowed, his hands clasped before him. Even though at thirty-one my brother is twelve years older than me, I think how very young he looks in this heavy moment. It seems an age before he speaks his reply and I hear nothing but the slight rustle of Doll's skirts as she rises to stand beside her husband.

'I thank the Council for this great honour,' Dick says at last, his voice hovering on the edge of tears. 'And I thank them for the support they always gave to my father, who was ever mindful of their good counsel, which I hope they will continue to provide to me. I am inexperienced in the matter of governance – in the great affairs of nations – with all still to prove where my father had none. I recognise the enormous task ahead of me . . .' He falters, glancing to left and right as if looking to us for reassurance. I catch his eye, hold it for a moment with mine and force my lips into a smile. In that instant I know that this is the purpose Father set for me when we last spoke: to support Richard, to help him to continue Father's work and keep our family safe. I feel something stir within me – a determination I have not felt since Robert's death.

I have lost my husband, and with him my future. Now Father too, and with him my past. But Dick is still here having to play the hand he has been dealt.

And so am I.

PART FOUR

October 1658–July 1659

CHAPTER TEN

Life now seems to consist of the twinned and mirrored acts of birth and death. A new person, Richard, Lord Protector (or King Richard IV as I ever hear the pageboys call him between themselves), is fashioned before my eyes just as the old Protector, my dear father, is stripped back to his mortal remains: his body embalmed, a death mask taken, a painted wooden effigy built to take his place among us. Chaplain Hugh Peter preaches to us at Whitehall on the text *'Moses my servant is dead'* and the cleric Samuel Slater replies from his pulpit that though this is true, we must rejoice to have a Joshua to succeed him: 'What the other happily began, may this more happily finish.' This is a new succession, he suggests – by appointment and merit, not by royal blood.

Yet I dream of violence and can hardly bear to look from the palace windows in case an angry mob appears before me. It had always seemed to me that Father alone held up the world like the Titan Atlas and, without him, every moment I expect it to come crashing down about my ears. But, to my amazement, the transition from a world ruled by my father to a world ruled by my brother is seamless – or at least seems that way. The monarchs of Europe forget that we are rebel-born and stir themselves, their ambassadors crowding the great presence chamber, pressing their masters' continued friendship upon the new young Protector. Richard is proclaimed by trumpet fanfare and herald in London, Edinburgh and Dublin and, from every corner of these nations, cities and corporations dispatch their loyal addresses to him in the saddlebags of their fastest riders. The army and the navy pledge their loyalty and all the Protectoral officers away from court, the ambassadors, governors and commanders, send their condolences and assurances – Harry's letters blurred with tears.

As the town criers pace the marketplaces and Richard's proclamation is nailed to town hall and church door throughout the land, new histories of our own time pour from the presses, swirling into the gutters on the first autumn winds. Each day, in their inky pages, I see my father stare back at me. I find him too looking out at me from familiar portraits on the walls of the palace and nestled in my coin purse where, in time, he will be replaced by the new coinage bearing Richard's profile that Master Simon of the Mint is even now working on alongside Father's ceremonial death medals.

Only, the man captured in oils, carved into metal or stamped in ink is never the father I knew. He is a colossus, an emperor, a new prophet; a traitor, a usurper, a devil. Moses on one page, Lucifer on another. I see at first hand how when a great person dies, they multiply like the Hydra, taking myriad forms they could never have imagined and meaning a thousand things to a thousand people. With each new version of my father, I find myself more and more determined to do what I can to preserve his legacy and protect our family name. I cling to the knowledge that I am one of a precious few who truly knew him, even as I begin to doubt if I ever really did. It seems no one can fathom that Father is dead and gone: those that hated him as much as those who loved him. Instead life itself turns upside down as if the world Oliver Cromwell did so much to fashion is simply unimaginable without him in it; without the great force of him driving events, an ear always cocked to catch God's whispered commands that he alone could hear.

As my shrunken family hunkers together in grief, we feel the fight for Father's image rage around us. 'We must wrest control of it from the masses, Your Highnesses,' Thurloe explains to us as Mother, Mary and I walk solemnly through the privy gardens, our mourning clothes reflected in a thunderous sky, a straggle of ladies whispering behind us.

'And how do you propose we do that, Councillor Thurloe?' Mother asks wearily, her eyes never wavering from the horizon.

'By planning a lying-in-state and funeral fit for a king,' Thurloe replies gently. 'I have discussed it with Sir Oliver Flemyng, the Lord Chamberlain and the Council, and we are all in agreement.'

'But what will you take as your precedent?' I ask him, thinking of how the last king was buried quietly at Windsor Castle once they had sewn his head back onto his body.

'A good question, Lady Frances. We intend to follow the ceremony accorded to the late king's father, King James. That was over thirty years ago, of course, but we have found the accounts of it in the archives and can update it as appropriate.'

So Father is finally and irrevocably to be presented as the king he never was, I think, and I cannot help a bitter smile at the irony.

A few weeks later, Father is taken to lie on a great black velvet-draped bed of state at Somerset House, as King James was before him, his embalmed body safe within a lead coffin enclosed in turn in a wooden coffin topped with his lifelike effigy: a body of wood, a face of wax and eyes of glass. I cannot bring myself to look upon this idol, particularly when word reaches me that, beneath the robes of purple velvet and ermine, the figure has been dressed in the grey velvet suit Father wore to my wedding – known to us all to be his favourite outfit. Most of the family stays away, preferring to remember Father as he was to us, but Charles goes to see him and describes the scene to us at supper.

'They have placed a crown above the effigy, and the orb and sceptre in its hands,' he begins, the word 'crown' sticking in his mouth.

Bridget tuts besides him but says nothing and, with Mary on the edge of tears, I am grateful to her for that.

Charles swallows and lifts his chin. 'Around the bed are symbols of Oliver's rule: a suit of armour, a crest, a plaque inscribed with his lineage, achievements and all of your names.' He takes a moment to look around the table at his wife's family and I wonder if my name will be buried with Father when the time comes.

'The bed itself is supported by great pillars carved with crowns and shields,' Charles continues. 'And after it has lain on the bed for a few weeks, the effigy will be stood up, its eyes opened, as if the Lord Protector lives once more among us.'

'Idolatry,' Bridget hisses suddenly, and at the head of the table Dick squirms in his chair.

Though we stay away from the grotesque scene, the great and the good and a multitude of Father's ordinary subjects flock to gawp at him and poor Father lies there, dead and yet above the ground, for weeks on end until Mother can bear it no longer. The date set for his state funeral is still several weeks away but all any of us can think of is returning Father to God as he would wish. The pomp and circus of his public journey to burial means nothing to us and neither, Dick explains privately to the Council, would it have meant anything to Father. He would want only for his family, his closest friends and his God to witness the interment of his earthly remains in an honest square of soil. And so the Council agrees to let us bury Father's body quickly and quietly near Betty's in the vault of Henry VII's chapel at Westminster Abbey on 10 November. He has a beautiful plot, in the curve of the east end of the chapel, itself the very easternmost point of the abbey, so that the sun will lie first upon him each morning. Rows of carved stone angels watch over him from the walls on either side, crowns held between their linked hands: if Father was not a king in life, he is in death.

With Father himself interred, the honours of the state funeral a few weeks later fall on his wooden substitute, staring unseeing in everlasting life from above the empty coffin. We women stay away as is traditional, though in truth we are grateful to do so. It takes seven hours for the funeral procession to make the short journey from Somerset House to Westminster Abbey, an exhausted

John tells me later when I have gone to his family's rooms to read bedtime stories to my motherless niece and nephews. John collapses onto a chair in the nursery and begins to unbuckle his shoes.

'Seven hours,' he repeats, rubbing the soles of his feet. 'And all in front of a crowd of thousands. The people paid for places on great viewing scaffolds erected around Westminster and they thronged along the route. The army had to station men one arm's length apart to control the crowds and keep the peace.'

Little Cromwell's head droops against my breast, heavy with sleep, and I close my eyes and picture the scene as John paints it. There are pedlars and salesmen doing a roaring trade in food, beer and souvenirs among the throng. Father's effigy travels in a chariot drawn by six horses with nobles and peers, the Council of State, dignitaries of the court, Yeomen of the Guard, soldiers and MPs riding or walking in the pageant. Every servant of the Protectoral household accompanies the coffin resplendent in livery, from Father's life guard and bargemen down to the falconers, grooms, cooks, bottle-washers and kitchen boys. Even the arts that Father patronised are represented with his court musicians and the poets and scholars Masters Marvell, Milton and Dryden marching together, doubtless forming lines of verse in their minds as they walk.

Richard cannot attend, observing the ancient custom that the new ruler does not publicly mourn the old. Harry is absent too – commanded to stay at his post in Ireland, though Dick has sent Anthony Underwood to him to give a first-hand account of Father's final illness. So, with neither of Oliver's sons present, his sons-in-law command the stage: the role of chief mourner at the funeral falls to Charles in flowing state robes, whose train is borne by assistants including Thomas, Viscount Fauconberg. Behind him comes John himself as Master of Horse leading Father's favourite stallion, riderless and decked in elaborate plumes; a visual reminder of the empty place where Father should be and an echo of all of the hundreds of times that Father rode into battle on behalf of Parliament in all corners of these nations. In this way all of our living husbands mourn their father-in-law together, while the dead – Henry Ireton and my darling Robert – welcome him into heaven.

'I've got to hand it to the Council, the whole scene was magisterial,' John concludes. 'Apart from one moment,' he chuckles, 'when a pig broke through the crowd to wander among the chief mourners – that wasn't part of Thurloe's plan!'

I chuckle too at this, despite my sadness, thinking it the one moment in all the long day that Father would have enjoyed.

For the next few days we Cromwell women remain hidden away in the palace with Dick: none of the ritual matters to us. Instead, it is the remembrances of Father we share around the fire, our hugs and prayers alone that count. Master Marvell's poem on Father's death – a funeral ode he performs privately for us after supper the night following Father's burial – is worth a thousand state funerals in my eyes and I listen transported as he weaves together myths and legends of Father's heroic life. It is his words of Elizabeth that bring tears to Mother's eyes, however, as Marvell speaks of her virtues and tells us that Father died not in battle but of love and grief for her. The father he restores to us with the images he paints in the air is the only one in all these weeks that I recognise as ours: the private man, father to his family before his country:

'Straight does a slow and languishing disease
Eliza, Nature's and his darling, seize.
Her when an infant, taken with her charms,
He oft would flourish in his mighty arms,
And, lest their force the tender burden wrong,
Slacken the vigour of his muscles strong . . .

Nature, it seemed with him would Nature vie;
He with Eliza. It with him would die,
He without noise still travelled to his end,
As silent suns to meet the night descend.
The stars that for him fought had only power
Left to determine now his final hour,
Which, since they might not hinder, yet they cast
To choose it worthy of his glories past . . .

If he Eliza loved to that degree,
(Though who more worthy to be loved than she?)
If so indulgent to his own, how dear
To him the children of the highest were?
For her he once did Nature's tribute pay:
For these his life adventured every day:
And 'twould be found, could we his thoughts have cast,
Their griefs struck deepest, if Eliza's last . . .'

As Marvell goes on, his black curls fringed with firelight, I feel the tears I have been waiting to shed for Father come springing to my eyes to mingle with those that always hover there for Betty; their cool dampness almost a relief on my flushed cheeks.

We struggle on together, each of us knowing we have lost the two brightest stars from our night sky while I, in Robert, have lost the very air itself. Throughout these terrible weeks, Mother is a wonder to me, seeming to grow in stoicism and steadfastness, as always pouring the balm of herself into the gaps and cracks in us all, even though it is she now who has lost the other half of her very self. It is she who picks up the pieces of our family and tries to fit us back together as a restorer does a fractured pane of glass. I spend much of my time helping her to sort through Father's personal possessions and to pack her things for her forthcoming move into St James's Palace, leaving her private apartments at Whitehall Palace free for the new Lord Protector and his family. Dorothy, the new Lady Protectoress, and her children will spend most of their time in the palaces now, leaving behind the quieter, quaint life in their Hampshire estate to assume their position as the first family in the land.

Richard himself is reluctant to put Mother to the trouble but the Council insists on the move: it was customary for Father, and the kings who came before him, to conduct certain audiences in the state bedchamber and Richard's previous set of rooms will not do, having no suitable set of antechambers in which guests could wait to be received into his presence. Mother herself is happy to move, feeling the change will do her good. Her one concern is that the arrangement will take her further away from John and the children who, more than anyone else, have come to rely on Mother's care.

'But I will be with them as much as I can,' Mother tells me as we wrap her furs in layers of paper. 'It is all I can do for dear Betty now. The little ones deserve to have her here to care for them but, as she cannot be, I will do my best in her stead.'

And what of me? I want to ask her. Don't I deserve my mother to care for me? But I know it a selfish thought; their need is far greater than mine. She can do so much good in Betty's family, for the children dote on her and, of late, I have noticed John too seek her out, drifting absently into her company in his new solitary state. And Mother bends towards him in turn, taking the place next to him at the supper table, sharing a parent's quiet observation about one or other of the children as they pass in and out of eyesight. In this way, it is as if Mother and John have been bound by their care for the children into an ill-assorted marriage of their own where each mourns the place beside them: a living mirror image of Elizabeth and Father's devoted closeness which has extended now even into death, where they lie together in Westminster Abbey.

Mother's effective absorption into the Claypole household is just one part of her gradual withdrawal from her public role. She provides us all with what she has always done: with love, with gentle guidance when asked, with a place to bring our grief. But she is careful to watch Dick's rule from afar, to smile in encouragement, not whisper in his ear. Not for her a dowager role, a brittle queen ruling by proxy as widow and mother. She was born to run a merchant household, not to command a room, still less a kingdom – she is no Queen Marie of Medici, no Eleanor of Aquitaine. The mantle has been well and truly passed on to our generation, just as Signor

Giavarina predicted on my wedding day, though so much sooner and more sadly than I had expected, and without Robert to take his portion by my side. His loss always finds new ways to pain me: what good could my darling have done working alongside Richard, his close friend? How many golden opportunities would there now have been for him in this youthful second age of the House of Cromwell?

But if Mother expends her energy on the Claypoles, I am determined to use mine to support Richard, now the custodian of Father's legacy and our good name. I find some new meaning in bolstering his confidence and safeguarding his interests as my husband would have done and as my father bade me do; and Dick certainly has the weight of the world on his shoulders. While the rest of us can lose ourselves in mourning if we choose, Richard has to enter into the day-to-day business of government – though it is several weeks after Father's distressing death before he can bring himself to attend Council meetings and apply himself fully to his new office.

Often after the Council has risen, he comes to see me just as he used to when Robert and I were newly married. Comfortable together, we share a glass of wine and discuss the business set before him that day: the despatches from our generals on the front lines of our war with Spain; the regime's accumulated debts and annual deficit. 'Two million pounds,' he tells me one evening, his eyes wide in the firelight, 'and the army owed nine hundred thousand pounds' wages.'

I sip my mulled wine to cover my shock. 'Can it really be that much?'

'I'm afraid so. It seems Father just ignored the numbers

in his final months, and there are a hundred decisions of diplomacy he ignored too.'

'Then they are decisions you must make,' I counsel, remembering what Signor Giavarina had said to me of the importance of a king making firm choices on foreign affairs. 'Listen to Thurloe, he will guide you. And Edward Montagu – he has returned from the fleet now, has he not? He has a sure grasp of our position in the world.'

'I have,' Dick says softly, draining his glass and placing it on the table beside him. 'I am sending Montagu with the fleet to mediate once more between Sweden and Denmark. Father's peace-making policy in the Baltic was one of his best and I will cleave to it.'

This both delights and surprises me and I lean back in my velvet armchair to consider my big brother anew. What keen understanding he shows me, what quiet resolve. I would have loved him but dismissed him once as a quiet country squire, better suited to a day's hunting than the politics and paperwork of government. But he has sharpened, has learned to listen more than he speaks and to weigh his words fully when he does. And as I see the change in my brother, I think he sees a comparable alteration in me: appreciates how, since Father's death, I can stomach the practicalities of politics now better than I can digest the intensity of personal feelings; understands that I would rather discuss the preservation of our Baltic trade with him over a glass of claret than cry with Mary over our broken hearts. Whatever my youth and sex, he values my advice now – he must do. Why else would he be here night after night?

Certainly the all-seeing, omniscient Thurloe observes these changes and the closeness that has grown between

Dick and me in recent weeks. So it is that he approaches me one morning as I stand at the back of the outer presence chamber watching Richard receive petitions. Our chief spymaster's steps are light yet I see the telltale dark circles under his eyes and know that he has faced his own private mountain of grief for Father's loss. But Thurloe has proved himself as steadfast to Dick as Father told me he would be; the preservation of Richard's rule, it seems to me, providing him with the only means to overcome the loss of the great man around whom he shaped his life. It is clear to me that the fanatic loyalty Thurloe once showed to Father has transferred, seamlessly, to his son, though I must concede the true balance of service and self-interest in Thurloe's work for either can be known to none but himself.

'I love him as you do,' the once 'little secretary' purrs in my ear after taking his position beside me and turning his placid gaze back onto Richard. 'He will need you, Highness, and the rest of your family behind him in what lies ahead. We must show strength and stability. Solidarity. Continuity.'

I do not turn towards him but keep my eyes fixed on Dick as he beckons a petitioner forward to give some more detailed explanation of his case. 'His succession has been remarkably smooth, Master Thurloe,' I comment truthfully. 'All interests have pledged their allegiance to him and the people are quiet; they are giving him time to find his feet.'

'Indeed, Highness, your observations are as accurate as ever. It has been a peaceful transition. But still,' he rises slightly in his soft shoes, his gaze sweeping over the room, 'there are those in the army, in your own family even, who do not share our staunch belief in the young Protector's abilities, who question his commitment to the parliamentary and godly cause. Those who resent his elevation without his father's military experience; who think perhaps that command of the army should be placed in another's hands. Some of the officers have petitioned for Lord Charles Fleetwood to be appointed Commander-in-Chief in your brother's stead.'

'But Charles himself does not say so,' I answer quickly. 'He has ordered his men to stand down, declares himself loyal to Richard. And Richard has reassured the officers himself that he will be their staunch and godly defender and will consult Charles as Lieutenant-General of the army in all things, so long as he remains Commander-in-Chief above him.'

In former times I would have pleaded ignorance to Thurloe's meaning, would have danced around his words as around a maypole, but I am more straightforward, more plain-speaking now than as the young princess I used to be. Thurloe knows this too; why else would he lay his thoughts so openly before me – someone he would have considered a mere frivolous girl before the terrible events of this last year refashioned me from soft dough to oven-hardened clay?

Thurloe inclines his head in concession if not assent. 'It is true that your brother-in-law Lord Fleetwood stands by him, for now. But there are many who question His Highness's ability to command the loyalty of men the way your father could.'

'And yet there are others,' I counter, 'who think it is the very absence of Richard's historic relationships that will stand him in good stead; that he is fresh, untainted, capable of bringing together a wider coalition of support than Father was, precisely because he has not provoked strong feelings in others – either of love or loathing. I may have adored my father, Master Thurloe, but I am under no illusions that he did not inspire the fiercest enmity.'

'You are wise, Highness, beyond your years, and I agree with much of what you say. Nevertheless, speaking as one whose wish for the success of your brother's rule is as strong as yours, I hope that you will counsel him wisely and come to me if you sense that matters are coming to a head within your family.'

He does not wait for my agreement but merely bows before sliding away into the crowd of courtiers, leaving the bitter taste of his words on my tongue.

In truth, I know Thurloe's concerns about Charles to be well founded, and only that very evening see the bubbling tension between my brother and brothers-in-law spill into the fire. Without Father's commanding presence and Elizabeth's winning charm keeping our own family peace, I suppose it was only a matter of time before the cracks would begin to show. Though I do not expect the argument, when it comes, to be about money.

'It is a large sum,' John is telling us, running an anxious hand through his hair as around the table the servants clear away our supper dishes. 'The physicians demanded immediate payment and, as I could not raise the cash straight away, they have brought a lawsuit against me.'

I take his hand in sympathy. 'We must help John to pay.' I look around the supper table for agreement. 'The debts demanded of him are for the medicines given to Betty.'

'Little good they did her,' John mutters into his wine glass.

'Of course we will help,' Richard agrees.

'Is that wise, Your Highness?' Charles grates his teeth as he speaks, so the final word seems to emerge with a sneer. 'When only today the Council was wringing its hands over the size of the government's debts?'

John shoots Charles a look of loathing and I squeeze his hand in a bid to prevent any angry words following hot on its heels. In the past he always had Elizabeth to support him in his verbal duels with Charles, ever ready to finish his sentence with a choice adjective and a smile.

'She was my sister, Charles, as I have no need to tell you.' Richard's voice is stern, experimenting with his new commanding role.

'Of course,' Charles rows back a little, 'and none was fonder of her than I. But you owe my soldiers months of pay.'

'My soldiers, surely,' Richard counters smoothly and I have to admire his quick, needling riposte.

Charles bristles but holds his tongue.

A brief silence then Thomas speaks in his polite, aristocratic drawl. 'John, I would be glad to help with the bill.'

I look from him to Mary and see her smile at her husband in gratitude; a smile that gladdens my heart. I have sensed a growing affection between Mary and Thomas lately and indeed, my one consolation in the dark days after Father's death was seeing how tenderly Thomas comforted his wife. She in turn seemed to move towards him in the fragility of her deep grief and as I watched I could almost see the inches close between them as the days passed.

'Well, of course you are wealthy enough to do so, Viscount,' Charles barks across the table. 'And it is a fine way to ingratiate yourself with our Lord Protector and with John and his Parliament friends too.'

'Charles!' It is Mary who exclaims and she reaches instinctively for Thomas but even her urgent hand cannot prevent Thomas from rising from his chair and walking proudly out of the room.

I watch helplessly as my family disintegrates and turn to Charles in amazement. 'I don't understand,' I say, shaking my head against my bewilderment. 'Charles, why attack Thomas?'

Mary cuts in before Charles can answer, though she throws her words towards Bridget now rather than me: 'Do you want to tell Frances, Bridget, or shall I?'

I have never seen Mary so angry and I look at her as if on an entirely new person. Is this fierceness further proof of her growing love for Thomas? 'Tell me what?'

Bridget is staring at Mary in equal astonishment, a knife hovering in mid-air.

'No? Very well.' Mary looks at Bridget before returning her level gaze to me. 'Charles has voted against Thomas joining the Council. Dick wants to nominate him and Lord Broghill to become Councillors but Charles and Uncle Desborough won't have it.'

'Charles!' It is my turn now to exclaim his name in reprimand.

Charles looks from Mary to me, his eyes flashing

angrily like a cornered stag at the end of one of Richard's Hampshire hunts. 'This has nothing to do with you girls.'

'My sisters are entitled to their opinion, Charles,' Richard says, and we all fall silent under his words, now that his every utterance is imbued with a ruler's significance. 'They may not attend my Council but they have to live with those of you who do. I, for one, would have appreciated your support for the nominees of my own choosing.'

'How could I support you in choosing dandying royalists to join your Council?' Charles replies. 'Men who would bring back the exiled Charles Stuart at the first sign of your weakness, whose every word would work against the interests of your loyal army? They are not true believers in the parliamentary cause – not like me, not like your father who fought alongside me. He would never have appointed such men.'

'Men who, in the viscount's case, your father-in-law brought into our family,' John reminds Charles, his words somewhat slurred over the edge of his glass.

'The family is one thing,' Charles replies with a meaningful glance at John; 'there are always compromises to make in the marriage market. But the Lord Protector's Council is another thing altogether.'

I have a sudden memory of Lord Broghill standing before me in his brilliant plum-coloured suit offering me the hand of the young king in exile; and another of the dapper lord leading Viscount Fauconberg in to meet us all for the first time shortly before his marriage to Mary. They were as far apart from Charles and his fellow army officers as men could be within my father's court, and yet could they really work to bring us down? Did they really wish to replace my brother with the young Charles Stuart? Wasn't it Lord Broghill who had worked so hard to place the crown upon Father's head?

Looking at the shocked faces around the glimmering table, I can't help but wonder: if Richard was ever weakened, would it be these former royalists who challenge him and restored the exiled king? Or would it be Charles himself reinstating the republic at the head of his godly army? I meet Richard's pained gaze and know he is wondering the same thing.

'And still they are not satisfied,' Mary complains to me when I go to find her later in her rooms, my puppy, grown larger now, bounding onto her bed. 'Thomas tells me that not only have Charles and Uncle Desborough blocked his appointment, but that they are agitating still further for the Council to be stripped of their opponents – demanding Thurloe's resignation and even claiming that Edward Montagu and Dick's other staunchest supporters on the Council are plotting to kidnap them! Uncle stormed out of the Council chamber, apparently.'

'I cannot believe it,' I say, rising from the end of her bed, where I had been perching, to pace the room. The glamorous, courtly General-at-Sea Montagu whom I had dined with in the summer, who shone with confidence and certainty; how could Charles expect anyone to believe that that same man now plotted such a low deed? 'It is absurd. Surely Charles goes too far. He has overreached himself at last.'

'But what can Dick do?' Mary asks, her face pale. 'Charles is too powerful, too beloved by his soldiers. Dick must bear his agitating and overcome it somehow.'

'Well, he will never agree to lose Thurloe,' I say, a measure of confidence returning to me. 'And as long as Thurloe is on the Council, he won't let Richard be bullied.'

Mary twists her hair out of its pins. 'But poor Thomas, caught in the middle of it all.'

I examine her closely. 'So you do care for him then, dear heart? I thought you must do when you defended him so fiercely at supper, but I would prefer to hear it from your own lips.'

She blushes then, a shy pink faint as rosewater appearing on her pale cheeks. 'I do care for him, yes. Perhaps not yet in the way you . . .' Mary checks herself but she knows me well enough to know I would so much rather that Robert's name was spoken than that it had died alongside his body. '. . . The way you and Robert loved each other. But he is a good man, kind, generous. Charming once you have earned his trust. I know Charles and Bridget still distrust his motives, think he stays in touch with the exiled court, scheming and placing his bets on all sides. I have heard the rumours about him. But what I can say to that? I know nothing of his affairs and must be a loyal wife to the husband I have been given. And besides, I think that perhaps – at least I hope – that I am with child.'

'Oh, my darling!' I spring towards her then, almost unbalanced by a happiness I had forgotten.

'It is early still.' Mary holds up a cautioning hand. 'I may be mistaken. But I am praying for it day and night and surely God will grant us some good fortune at the end of this terrible year.'

'Come,' I say happily. 'Let us pray for it together.'

CHAPTER ELEVEN

None of us is sorry to see the new year come to replace the one that took Lavinia, Robert, baby Oliver, Elizabeth and Father from us, the numbers '1658' carved into so many plaques and headstones. It is 1659 and we must look to the uncertain future – to Richard's future as Lord Protector and those of the rest of us which hang so delicately by threads suspended from his. The army temporarily quieted, all talk now is of the new Parliament – both Lords and Commons – which Richard has summoned to sit at the end of January. This will constitute a newly elected set of MPs and appointed lords – as each Parliament convened by my father during his Protectorate had been.

Richard is to open the new Parliament and he and Thurloe write his opening speech together. It is a delicate task: under the new constitution, Parliament has gained more control over its own membership and so a greater number of MPs hostile to Richard and the Protectorate have been returned. Dick brings the draft to me and we sit for many hours in the evenings rehearsing it as Doll sits and sews by my side, interrupting her husband every now and then with a suggested word. He will pay tribute to Father of course; seek proper pay for the army – 'the best army in the world', Thurloe has drafted in his neat, spidery hand – and emphasise the necessity of continuing the war with Spain, supporting the Protestant cause abroad and protecting our liberties and justice at home. Dick will end with a sincere plea for Parliament to show wisdom and peace and a hope that they all work together to make this 'a happy Parliament'; words which, though I am but his much younger sister, fill me with pride in him.

But it is a false hope, just as Mary's imagined pregnancy turns out to be. Although Richard's address is warmly received, within a few weeks it is clear that this will not be a happy but a warring Parliament. The new Parliament is unhappy with that done by its predecessor: unhappy with the unclear limits of Richard's powers; unhappy with the make-up of the newly appointed second chamber, the 'Other House' of Lords; unhappy with the sixty Scottish and Irish MPs now sitting in the House of Commons. Richard leaves Parliament to itself but his supporters from the old kingship party work hard to secure majorities in support of his government, the MPs voting with them volubly hostile to the army. Nevertheless, a republican minority asserts itself in opposition, led by the grand Sir Arthur Haselrig – himself a relic from the earliest years of Parliament's struggle with the dead King Charles. Though fewer in number, they grow in influence when they find alliance with Charles Fleetwood and the other Major-Generals on Richard's Council.

Once again, Richard is forced to go in person to address the army officers, this time in no less significant a venue than Charles and Bridget's home, Wallingford House, just outside the palace. But Dick holds his ground in spite of them all, refusing to give up his position as Commander-in-Chief of the army and commanding the officers not to go behind his back to lobby Parliament to work against the government. Once again, we all hold our breath, but the rebellion is stifled for now.

It is an anxious time, made worse by my loneliness. Following his snub by the Council, Thomas retreats to Yorkshire, taking Mary with him, her eyes above her fur wrap puffy from the disappointment of her failed pregnancy. She is nervous to leave me, though this time her anxiety is more for the sister she leaves behind than for herself.

'Will you be all right?' she asks as we cling to each other in the January cold. 'Things feel so precarious here at present and with Mother away such a lot . . .'

'I will be fine,' I reassure her with false confidence. 'But I will miss you, my dearest, more than I can say. Write to me, please. Often. Every day!'

With Mary gone, I face the anniversary of Robert's death alone. I miss Mother too; even though she is only a few minutes' walk away at St James's Palace and is often to be found with the Claypole children in their rooms, it is not the same now I cannot slip into her bed at night and whisper my fears to her. With Bridget living just beyond the palace boundary, and visiting us less and less each week, it is only Richard and I left as the husk of our family struggling to find our way in the dark. Dorothy is often with us too, though she takes the children back to Hampshire from time to time at Dick's insistence: he wants them to retain something of the normal childhood he had, he says often, his eyes straying from the paperwork before him and out of the window. Without Doll, Dick and I fall into an unlikely marriage, observing the rituals of the palace day together in our own rhythm: prayers, meals, business, relaxation. And though we mould to each other curiously well, I cannot but reflect on how odd it is that it should be our relationship left standing after the storm.

Harry is much on my mind as I wander the corridors of the palace alone, and I pounce on his letters as a starving man on food whenever they arrive. *You do fine work there, Fanny*, he tells me. *Dick writes he could not manage without you*. John Russell brings this last to me, again from within the packet sent to his family, and I welcome him with the nearest I can now feel to warmth, so relieved am I to see the friendly face of one I can trust. I take him out to the avenor's hut beside the stables and show him Venus, who nibbles the scraps of bacon I offer, her sleek head twitching from side to side.

'Will you not fly her?' John Russell asks gently after a few minutes.

'No,' I reply, keeping my eyes on my bird. 'I have not since Robert died. I cannot bring myself to. But she is happy and well looked after.' I stroke her silver feathers as she preens herself on my glove and wonder if I will ever again say the same about myself.

As the weather warms with spring's tentative approach, one of my sisters returns to me, or at least a version of her. Master John Michael Wright, who painted my grieving portrait last year, has completed his latest commission: a posthumous painting of Elizabeth, which he unveils to us with much solemnity. It is a good likeness of Betty to be sure, though lacking her vitality and vivid spirit, showing that these can perhaps only be truly painted from life. But the image is so much more than a portrait of Elizabeth – rather it is a visual ode to Father's rule. For Betty is portrayed as Minerva, daughter of the Roman god Jupiter: swathed in bright blue and red silks, her favourite pearls around her throat, a cameo of Father at her breastplate, a plinth depicting the muscled god under her elbow, a crown and olive tree behind her (an allusion to Father's name, Master Wright points out smugly) and a sea battle in the background, darkened by a thunderous sky. The whole effect is dolorous and I glance nervously at John who frowns at the canvas beside me.

'She is beautiful,' I whisper to him, ignoring my misgivings. 'Regal, eternal.'

'Gone,' he adds.

'And yet here,' I reply, slipping one hand into his and the other into my pocket to find Robert's miniature.

Charles and Bridget do not join us to see the painting unveiled, neither have they dined with us since the argument over John's payment of poor Betty's medical bills. I see Charles often as he comes and goes from the Council, but each time he whisks away from me quickly, keeping his thoughts to himself. The Council meetings themselves are strained and when Dick emerges from them late in the evenings he is long-faced and weary and complains to me that he feels caught between Parliament and the army, who seem to have slipped into the comfort of their old conflicts; battles Father spent years fighting but which are new to Richard.

I am hardly surprised then when Master Thurloe takes the seat beside me at dinner in the Great Hall and moves his head close to mine as he waves away the wine.

'The time has come, Highness, when I must ask for your help,' he says, his voice low and melodic.

'With Charles?' I keep my eyes on the room.

'My informers among the soldiery tell me the army is stirring itself to move against your brother.'

I cannot help a gasp, though I cover my shock quickly, smiling at Uncle Desborough who is glowering opposite me, and helping myself to a powdered sweetmeat.

'They are fools,' Thurloe replies. 'Short-sighted idealists, gambling real coin in the purse for the dream of a fortune; cutting off the nose to spite the face. They do not see what I can see.'

I know Thurloe is not talking about his view from the high table in the Great Hall of Whitehall, but his place at the centre of the most sophisticated network of spies Europe has perhaps ever seen. The image of the spider twitching the threads of its web comes to me as I glance sideways at my black-suited companion, who is applying himself with great concentration to buttering a piece of bread. He waits until the coverage is completely smooth and even before laying down the knife and going on.

'What my agents at the exiled court write to me is that the pretended king Charles and his advisers are hoping that the army does precisely that; that it brings down our Protectorate . . .'

'. . . And with it, opens the door for Charles Stuart himself to return.'

He is gracious enough to grant me a small smile in appreciation of my understanding. 'Precisely. We have had five years of peace and stable government thanks to your father and brother but if the regime falls then the floodgates open once more and who knows upon which new rock England will be shipwrecked. If these late years of trouble have taught us anything, it is how easily one change can lead to another.'

His words fill me with foreboding and as I look around the hall with frightened eyes I see the laughing courtiers vanish in clouds of smoke, the rampant lion of Father's coat of arms stripped down from the walls, his and Elizabeth's portraits cast onto a bonfire and their bodies into a pit; Richard's blond head on a spike. My mind travels back to Bulstrode Whitelocke's words of frustration when Father refused the crown: 'It is far easier to pull something down than to set it up.' The memory sends me looking for my friend and I see Bulstrode sitting at the end of one of the long tables running at an angle from ours, watching us as he sips his wine.

I turn back to Thurloe.

'What can I do?'

The next evening, after supper, I wrap myself in my warmest cloak and slip out of the palace, making my way along the noisy street. Though Bridget's home at Wallingford House is only a few hundred yards away, I take the precaution of having Katherine and two of the palace guards accompany me; with soldiers clustered on corners and spilling out of taverns, the streets of Westminster are no longer a place for Cromwell's daughter to walk alone at night. I am admitted into the grand building by the steward who tells me that Mrs Fleetwood is in the withdrawing room, having lately emerged from seeing the children to bed. He ushers me quickly up the stairs, but not before I have seen the array of hats and cloaks on the hall table and spotted the figures of two soldiers leaning in a gloomy doorway, their muskets glinting in the candlelight. We pass a door behind which I can hear the low murmurs of men's voices, before the steward shows me into the withdrawing room.

Bridget springs to her feet as I enter, surprise evident in her pinched face.

'Frances, I was not expecting you.'

'Biddy.' I cross to her and kiss her warmly. 'You have been neglecting us of late so I thought I would come to you. I judged this a good time with the children lately gone to bed. You are well?'

'Yes, perfectly well.' Bridget steers me to a couch and fusses around the room before finding a bowl of sugared almonds to offer me. Her movements are jolting and I realise that she is nervous; a state in which I do not believe I have ever seen my sensible older sister before.

We talk of the children for a few minutes. She is saying something about the difficulties of forging a new family from two fractured ones – how her boy from her first marriage to Henry has been fighting with Charles's son from his first marriage – but really I am listening to the muffled noises from the corridor outside. It is clear that some clandestine meeting is happening in the house and I am desperate to know who Charles is doing business with so late in the evening. When the sounds of men's voices grow louder I make an instant decision, knowing what Thurloe would want me to do.

'Excuse me, Biddy,' I interrupt her before jumping up and hurrying to fling open the door.

And there they are. Furrowed faces caught in the sharp candlelight like one of Master Rembrandt's pictures, hands catching sleeves, necks craned to make an anxious point in another's ear: Charles, Uncle Desborough and a clutch of other leading officers of the army including, tall and imperious, hair moonlit silver, Major-General John Lambert himself.

They are an imposing sight and I shrink back into the doorway, fixing a polite smile on my lips as if nothing is amiss. 'Gentlemen,' I manage, and incline my head as, after a moment's hesitation, they bow to me in a wave; Lambert the first to do so, the others following him in a ripple. I wait for them to speak but they merely shuffle down the stairs, Charles casting an anxious glance over my head to Bridget before going to show them out. There is no time to make pretence of some errand which drew me from the room; I only have a few minutes before I expect Charles to join us. I move back into the room and close the door behind me.

'Biddy – you must do something!'

'What do you mean?' she asks, returning to the couch and pausing to pick a protruding feather from the cushion beside her. I have to admire her control; she has found her cool, older sister self once more.

'You must do something about Charles! I know you do not approve of the Protectorate – never have – but don't you see the danger in what Charles is doing?'

'He is my husband, sister.'

'Christ's blood!' I cannot help the expletive and Bridget startles at my blasphemy, causing me to thrill a little at shocking her. 'I know that. But you are a Cromwell first – you owe it to Mother, to Dick, to me, to Father above all, not to help to bring us in harm's way and cast out everything he achieved.'

'But I have two husbands to whom I owe loyalty, one dead and one living – husbands who showed me how the world truly is and how it could be. This is what my first husband would have wanted too.'

'Henry?' I look at her is disbelief. 'I may have been but a girl when he died but I know he was devoted to Father, none more so. Do you really think he would want our family ruined, even if it is in pursuit of his precious godly republic? The peace and stability we have built shattered and the cracks appearing for Charles Stuart to crawl through?'

'Oh, it is easy for you to say!' Bridget is back on her feet now, pacing the room, her pretence at cool indifference abandoned. 'You think only of remaining a princess, of keeping our family in power. You have always loved the attention, frolicking with Robert before you wed, dancing before the court as a pagan goddess with seashells in your hair.'

Her words slice through me like a hail of arrows. I feel tears come but they will not stop my words. 'How can you say that after what I have suffered this last year? Do you think I would not swap all of my fine clothes, my position, my life at the palace, for one more hour with Robert? I would have lived with him in a haystack!'

Bridget has the grace to pause at that and I know she regrets the strength of her words. But her blood is up.

'Perhaps that was unfair, but what I mean is that you have never been pulled in two, in three directions as I have! Your husband one way, your family another. Father betrayed Parliament's godly cause! The cause I loved as dearly as any man. He should never have agreed to rule: no one man should, however virtuous he is. Charles knows that just as Lambert does. It was only his great love for Father that stopped him speaking out against the increasingly regal Protectorate as Lambert did, that kept him loyal. But now Father has gone . . .'

'And Dick is left the sacrificial lamb?'

Bridget sighs, some of the fight leaking out of her. 'Charles is a good man and so are the soldiers he leads. They know Dick will not defend them against a Parliament that loathes and mistrusts them. They have only ever fought for our freedoms and what will happen? Dick and his Parliament will dismantle the army, break any power and rightful influence they have earned and whittle away the religious freedoms they fought for. If it comes to that, we would be no better than under the Stuart king.'

'You can't mean that!'

'No.' Bridget slumps on the couch as if her feet will no longer bear her weight. 'No, I don't mean that.'

'But that is the risk!' I run on, pressing my advantage as I crouch down before her, my hands on her knees, skirts puffed up around me. 'What the exiled king fears most is for Richard to continue in power, for he knows this the most stable form of government we have found without him. If the army brings Dick down, restores the republic, it opens the door to all of the arguments we lived through before and the clamour of voices – royalists as loud as republicans – will deafen us. Charles will pave the way for the return of the king and never, in all our history, would there be a greater example of unintended consequences. Charles will see us all hanged before he is done: himself the first in line! Please, Biddy, please. For me.'

She takes my hands then, clasps them in hers, and I can feel the caps of her knees under the stiff silk of her dark green skirt. We look at each other for a long time, one pair of Cromwell eyes staring into another, before she speaks again.

'Very well, I will talk to Charles, warn him of the risks. But I cannot promise anything, Fanny; events will unfold as God means them to.'

I return to the palace and go at once to Thurloe's rooms. Again he flushes the clerks from the room and I take the comfortable armchair – feeling about a decade older and sadder than the last time I sat there. I tell him everything, while he, perched on his own spindled chair, nods gravely and stares into his glass of cordial, as if my report is no great surprise to him. I wonder suddenly if he has a spy in Charles's household. Still, my mention of Lambert brings his eyes up to mine.

'Lambert was there?'

'Yes.'

His eyes return to his drink and we sit for some minutes, lost in thought, before Thurloe seems to remember I am still there. 'Thank you, Highness, I am most grateful.' He rises to his feet and I realise he means for me to leave; it is nearly midnight and we are both tired.

I pause at the door to look back at him. 'Can you stop them?' I ask while I still have the chance, the thought of what will happen to me if he cannot creeping through my veins like spreading ice.

Thurloe unfolds his hands in a gesture which I cannot

read: it may indicate that the situation is hopeless or equally that he has it entirely within his control.

'I will do my best, Lady Frances, but that may not be enough.'

It is not enough.

The first that I know anything is wrong is when a flushed footman brings me a hastily written note from Mother saying that large numbers of troops are massing around St James's Palace. Dropping my book open on the couch behind me, I hurry down the privy gallery to Richard's rooms, where I find him pacing around his inner presence chamber; Thurloe, Bulstrode Whitelocke, Lord Broghill and a number of his other closest advisers are huddled around him in whispering knots. Glancing at them, I slip across the room and fall into step beside Richard, my puppy trotting alongside us to keep up.

'Dick, what's happened? Mother writes that the army is gathering outside her windows.'

He does not answer at first, shaking his head, his hands clasped tightly behind his back as he paces. Walking alongside him I notice the slightest limp in his right leg and wonder absently if the bone he broke hunting shortly before my wedding set completely straight. How carefree he had seemed on my wedding day, I remember – his leg propped on a chair, laughing over his glass as he gifted us the case of Canary wine. The memory sends me chasing after other thoughts of the lost life Robert and I had begun to furnish for ourselves: what became of that case of wine and our other wedding gifts? When would I ever now use the huge silver candelabra

Elizabeth and John gave us? And Betty – I catch the lump in my throat before it can escape.

Richard is speaking now, bringing my attention back to the present.

'It is over.' A short laugh escapes him, a strange, unnatural sound so unlike his usual laughter I have to check that it came from him. 'And how did we get here, you ask? I'll retrace my steps for you, Fanny. You know that, as a gesture of good faith, I agreed to Charles calling together the leading officers of the army. Thurloe told me the troublemakers were meeting with cloak and dagger at Wallingford House and I thought it better it were all out in the light of day. I met with them, brokered a peace between them and Parliament – the officers would agree only to assemble with the consent of myself and Parliament, and Parliament in turn would pay the soldiers' arrears and move against the lingering royalists, as the army wishes it to. Well, so much for that: the Lords of the Other House – Charles and Uncle Desborough included – saw fit to reject the Commons' resolutions . . .'

We have reached the end of the room now and Richard wheels around so we retread our footsteps, every eye in the room following our promenade. Dick continues speaking, oblivious to them.

'. . . And so, on the advice of my Council of State, I ordered the army officers to disband. They agreed at first, pledged their loyalty to my face. But now the Commons is pressing on with its plans to reorganise the army, some of the MPs even saying they want to bring it back under their own control and . . . well, it's the end. And here is Uncle Desborough to tell me so.'

I turn in shock to see our uncle bearing across the

room towards us like a battleship, ignoring Thurloe and the other members of the Council of State as he barges past them. 'Richard,' he says, a note of warning in his gruff voice, and I am struck by his addressing the Lord Protector by his first name, even if he is family. Dick does not pull him up on it and that, more than anything, tells me he has lost his authority already.

'Uncle,' Dick replies coolly.

He is going to go down with dignity and I admire him for it. I move closer to my brother in support and nod my own greeting, though Desborough ignores me as he always does. Out of the corner of my eye I sense Richard's advisers creeping towards us so that they can hear the final exchange now it has come.

'Major-General Fleetwood not with you?' Richard asks, pointedly taking the opposite approach to our uncle and giving his brother-in-law the frostiness of his full title. 'I have summoned him to the palace and yet still he does not come.'

Uncle Desborough clasps his hands behind his back as if to stop them from doing something else. 'Will you agree to dissolve Parliament,' he asks bluntly, 'and entrust yourself to the army? We have no desire to pull you from your throne but you must choose to support us in this fight.'

'And if I do not agree?'

I watch them helplessly, my heart in my mouth.

'Then it is all over. Even now Charles is mustering the regiments at St James's. You can summon the men to rendezvous here instead but they won't come. They will choose Charles.'

Dick bites his lower lip and drops his gaze to the carpet.

I must do something, anything, to help.

'Will you give His Highness a few moments, Uncle, to consult with his advisers?' I ask, keeping my voice level and my delivery smooth.

Desborough looks at me then, his eyes locking onto mine like one of the crack-shot musketeers in his regiment fastening on a target. Still he will not dignify me with a direct address but he gives a short, stiff bow and blunders away to the other side of the room where he installs himself sentry-like by a window with his back to us.

'So what now?' I whisper, my pulse racing.

Seeing Desborough's removal, Thurloe, Bulstrode Whitelocke and Lord Broghill flock around us while Nathaniel Fiennes and Charles Wolseley hasten to join us, their boyish faces unusually grim.

'Gentlemen?' Richard turns to them, keeping his voice low. 'You are my advisers. My sister asks what now?'

'I am afraid you must dissolve Parliament, Highness,' Thurloe says carefully, glancing at Broghill who nods in agreement. 'We cannot have civil unrest, we cannot allow the army to rise in rebellion. It will buy us some more time to negotiate with the officers – they have more love for you than many in Parliament who secretly wish the king to return.'

His answer surprises me and I find myself wading into the debate as the old – or rather the young – Frances never would have done: 'But surely there must come a time when we take a stand against the army's power?' I look from one man's face to another. 'Father knew it needed to be done but could never bring himself to do it when they had been through so much together. But Richard, you need feel no such scruples. You owe them no personal loyalty as Father did. You have a majority in Parliament; they will back you in bringing the army to heel.'

There is a pause long enough for me to fear I have stepped out of my place too far.

'I agree with Her Highness,' Bulstrode says at length, his black eyes moving from mine to my brother's, and I smile at him with a young woman's gratitude. 'If you give way now you will be lost. You will be naught but the army's puppet. The Parliament is your only bulwark against the officers' power. Maintaining the Parliament is our best hope.'

Richard walks away from us then, his legs taking him across to the fireplace where he stands for some minutes as Father used to do, his face cast down into the flames. Softly I inch towards him, the better to hear his answer as I know that he will not turn around before he speaks.

'Charles and my uncle are family,' he says at last, keeping his eyes on the fire. 'I can reason with them. Besides, they have told me that if I will not dissolve the Parliament, then the army will do so by force, just as they did in '48 and '53. If they do that, the country will be under martial law and we will be left to shift for ourselves. I have to do it, I have no choice.'

My thoughts fly to the family I have left: to Mother and the Claypoles across Whitehall, to Bridget awaiting Charles's return from his troops, to Mary hundreds of miles away deep in a royalist county and traitorous family, and to Harry, frighteningly exposed in his command in Ireland. Will we all survive what comes?

But Richard's must be the last word and so we stand in silence watching as a flaming log disintegrates and falls glowing into the ash.

♛

After this, power slips through our fingers like water. In the coming days, no one officially tells me that the Protectorate of the House of Cromwell is being abolished, that Richard is fallen from his throne whatever Uncle Desborough's promises to keep him upon it, that our time as the first family of the nation is at an end. There are no uprisings, no battles, no arrests nor show trials and executions, as there would have been in the brutal time of our Tudor forebears. We are not taken to the Tower through Traitor's Gate or turned out of the palace, the fine clothes torn from our backs. In fact, my daily life continues much as ever: I dress, wash and sleep in the same rooms at Whitehall, am addressed with the same courtesy by staff and courtiers, sit at Richard's left hand at dinner.

Were it not for the restlessness of my still-nameless puppy, I might have barely noticed our wholly altered state. Plagued by his boundless yapping at my heels I decide to take him out for a walk in St James's Park one morning and persuade Dick – so upset and pale now, his rough humour forgotten – to come with me. But we only get as far as the staircase by the Chairhouse when a huddle of soldiers blocks our way. I look about me for our own Protectoral guard in Father's grey-and-black livery but they are nowhere to be seen. Richard regains enough vigour to demand of them what they think they are doing but they merely shrug and cross their halberds. 'Orders, Your Highness,' the sergeant says gruffly. 'I'm afraid you're not to leave the palace.'

'And my sister?'

Another shrug.

'And so we are under house arrest,' Richard says, taking my arm and steering me back along the privy gallery, the puppy worrying at our feet. 'I am still Lord Protector – or at least I was when I last checked – and yet I cannot walk in my own gardens. What would my father say to that?'

I am shocked and suddenly deeply afraid. I look at Richard for reassurance but find a broken man beside me, and my pounding heart aches for him; whatever befalls us, I know Dick will carry Father's imagined disappointment in him across his shoulders like a pilgrim's pack for the rest of his life.

Confined to the palace, any lingering ability Dick has to shape events is severely hampered. He spends his time frantically scribbling and, whenever he is not being closely observed by the soldiers, tries to get letters out to his deputies and officers away from court – the men Edward Montagu once confidently called *the best of men guarding the edges of the realm*. He writes to Montagu himself, who is brokering the Protector's peace from his flagship *Naseby* on the Baltic Sea, unaware of what is happening at home. To Harry in Ireland, to General Monck who commands the army in Scotland when he is not sourcing falcons for John Lambert, and to our cousin Robina's husband, General-at-Sea William Lockhart, who negotiated Mary's marriage in Paris and now leads our army at Dunkirk.

Dick shows me the letters: he writes cautiously, his words loaded and coded for we know not who will read them. Thurloe uses some of his best and most discreet couriers to carry the messages past the soldiers but nevertheless many days pass and no response returns from any but Monck who says he will not intervene on Richard's behalf. I don't know what to feel at Harry's silence: despair that it may mean the most powerful Cromwell left in the game can do nothing for us; or relief that it may mean my beloved brother will not risk his dear life for the lost cause we have become.

While Dick writes and waits, the senior officers of the army seize complete control in London. They discuss the future with the leading republican MPs and within days decide to bring back the 'Long' Parliament – the assembly that fought the civil war and the 'rump' of which condemned the king to death and continued to sit until Father expelled them in '53. The MPs elected to serve in Richard's Parliament are deselected and those elected before them reassembled, though the army is careful to allow in only those MPs who swore to uphold the Commonwealth in '49 after the king's execution, not those excluded before the king's trial in Colonel Pride's purge.

This is the first step towards Richard's removal and Thurloe brings us the news with a long face. Events tumble away from us after that. Petitions pour into London from the provinces demanding the abolition of the Protectorate and the return of the Commonwealth, and the senior officers of the army vote to do it. Quickly, they assemble an interim government to rule until a new Council of State can be appointed: a Committee of Safety, its very name a throwback to the civil war, enhancing the climate of fear. Charles is a member of course, with Uncle Desborough and Lambert added to its number a few days later.

When the Council of State is created two weeks later and the Committee of Safety disbanded, I am surprised to hear Bulstrode Whitelocke named to its ranks, and reflect on my friend's uncanny ability to keep his head above the water whatever flood engulfs us.

'Government must continue,' he explains to me, doing me the courtesy of at least looking a little sheepish. 'This may not be a legitimate government, *de jure* if you will; but it is nevertheless the government we have, *de facto* in other words. Better that I am there to help see the rule of law is observed by the others than that no one is.'

I think I understand what he means. Government of one kind or other must always continue or else man would fall into Master Hobbes' warring state of nature and life would be nasty, brutish and short. The world beyond England's shores cannot wait for her to prevaricate, of course; an odd realisation that comes to me when I hear that a truce has been declared between France and Spain and a treaty signed at the Hague for us to mediate for peace between Denmark and Sweden. It may be that the Cromwell family is being expunged from public life, but Father's foreign policy continues nonetheless.

And yet, no sooner am I reassured by one piece of news than I am disturbed by another. The orders dispatched from the Council chamber in the first few days of its sitting are restrained in tone, yet John brings me the news that the newly returned Rump Parliament rants and rages: the MPs smashing Richard's Protectoral seal and stripping the Protectoral arms from buildings, just as I imagined they would when Thurloe and I had dined together a few weeks ago. I shiver at the images that float before my eyes and search John's face for reassurance as he leans in the doorway of my room.

But he can only offer me a widower's sad smile. 'All we can do now is wait to know what will become of us. Take care of yourself, Fanny, I must get back to the children.'

I close the door and dissolve into a rage of tears, beating my fists against the oak. Once again I am cast as a helpless pawn in the political game, such a bitter, poisonous pill after all I have done to try and shape my own future. I think of that future, the one which shone clearly in brilliant colours, and the future that now clouds before me in a dull, suffocating haze.

Though the situation seems hopeless, I know Thurloe and Richard's other close advisers continue to scheme, playing the cards left to them while Dick is still formally in office, while there is still time. I see the French ambassador, Monsieur Bordeaux, slip into Thurloe's room late one night, when I myself have come to talk to him. I hover outside the door, desperate to invent an excuse to go in, but turn back to my own room instead, contenting myself with wishful thinking: was the ambassador offering his master Cardinal Mazarin's help to Richard? Could our French allies secure him in office? But, however much I long for his continuation as Lord Protector and for the guaranteed safety of my family this would ensure, I cannot reconcile myself to the thought of using foreign troops to keep us in power. If he did this, would Dick not be just as bad as the tyrant King Charles when he looked to the Irish for help at the very start of our late wars?

Furthermore, I do not believe Dick has the stomach for a fight. Though he retains his dignity and, for the most part, his good temper, each day he is a little more depleted, a little sadder and wiser, his heart heavy and his tread laboured. He does not resist what comes, but neither does he fall shrinking under the fire of his former friends. He shows his frustration and the deep well of sadness within him only to Dorothy, to Thurloe and to me. Before all others, he is equable and restrained: he questions, he negotiates, he accepts. And so, when at last they come to him and demand his resignation, Dick answers his officers and his subjects calmly and politely, emerging at the end with at least a form of settlement: he will abdicate as Lord Protector and take no future share in government but, in return, he will be treated generously. His official debts – which now, he tells me nervously, amount to some twenty-nine thousand pounds – paid, his removal expenses met, a London house and annuity provided. He will be a private gentleman once again, pensioned into an obscure old age at thirty-two, carrying Father's legacy and the Cromwell family name with him.

And what of me? What do I become? What do I live for now?

Nobody tells me.

Without instruction, I simply linger in the palace with Richard, waiting for the servants to come and box up our things for removal. As we wait, our life is dismantled around us. Carpenters clamber on scaffolding to remove our coat of arms from the buildings, wood chippings and dust falling like rain beneath them as they saw away at the symbols of my family. Our banners are lowered from the rafters in the Great Hall, servants folding them neatly and taking them away, though I have no idea where.

John and the children leave for the relative safety of his manor house at Northborough and Mother writes to tell me she is going with them: her transformation from Cromwell to Claypole in her dead daughter's stead complete. Richard, meanwhile, has already sent Dorothy and their children ahead of him to their estate in Hampshire. Mary and Thomas have remained in Yorkshire and she writes urging me to come to live with them. Harry also sends word to say that he has resigned his post as Lord Lieutenant of Ireland and is, at last, returning to us and to his in-laws' home at Chippenham near Cambridge; any latent hope of Richard's that his younger brother would launch a rebellion on his behalf is dashed in the neat folds of Harry's letter.

Once more, the note is delivered by Harry's brother-in-law John Russell and, almost without deciding it between us, we drift down to the bird hut to visit Venus. This time I don't even have the energy to send Katherine to the kitchen for scraps, but John pulls a small bag of raw minced meat from his pocket and opens it for me to feed her.

I smile at him gratefully and my face cracks with the effort.

'Will you be all right, my lady?' he asks softly and I remember Mary putting the same words to me when we last parted. 'What of you in all this?'

No one else has thought of me in months and I hardly

know how to answer such kindness when I have none of my own left to summon.

'I am at a loss,' I reply, absently tilting my head to mirror Venus as she gazes at me with burning marble eyes. 'I have lived here in the palace as daughter, wife and now sister. Where, if not here, am I to call home?'

'Lady Frances.' John Russell dips his head in concern and edges closer to me, keeping his voice low. 'You know your family is as dear to me as my own. We are kin. You are welcome to come and stay with us at any time, especially once your brother Harry and my sister have returned to us from Ireland. Could we not be merry again at Chippenham?'

'Merry,' I repeat in confusion as if the word is unknown to me. 'I cannot imagine such a thing. I cannot see a future at all.'

He flinches beside me as if I have rebuked him and I know I sound peevish and bitter. Yet I hardly care. The young Frances would have wanted to make a good impression, especially on a young bachelor like John Russell, a man of distant kinship to me who only means to be kind. But I do not. I turn to look at him now, at his pale blue eyes and concerned expression, at the shape of his shoulders shifting under his ill-fitting brown jacket, and see nothing at all.

He seems to sense my mood and I think he will say no more, but then he speaks gently: 'You will have a future, Lady Frances, I promise you.'

I watch Venus as she shakes her head and fluffs her feathers in pleasure, feeling the weight of her on my fist. They are kind words but hollow of any meaning to me.

*

At last, the servants come to pack Richard's things and he directs a few of them to my rooms to help Katherine, who has already begun to lay out my clothes in readiness. She cries as she does this for she is to stay at Whitehall with her husband Chaplain White, at least for now. Without her beside me and reluctant to make any journey alone, I have decided to go with Dick to his house in Hampshire and to stay there to support him, at least for a time. After that I do not know.

Our day of departure is set for tomorrow and, with no one else of our family left behind, Bridget comes to bid us farewell. We are having a funereal breakfast when she is shown in to us. We three remaining siblings stare at each other for the first moments before Bridget approaches and allows the footman to draw out a chair for her. I glance at Richard but his face is set hard, his napkin clenched in his fists.

'Dick,' she begins, leaning towards him, but Richard cuts her off immediately.

'No. I cannot . . .' He rises from his chair and, throwing the napkin on the table, strides out of the room.

Bridget shrivels back into herself and looks at me, her face lined with a curious blend of sadness and righteousness.

'Can you blame him?' I stare at her, longing for a sister's comforting hug even as, in this moment, I loathe her. If only it was Mary sitting where she is, or Betty. 'He is bitter against Charles, against him above all others.'

Bridget shakes her head and looks at me with Father's level gaze. 'I came to tell him it was not his downfall that Charles sought. He and Uncle Desborough fought to keep

Richard as Protector with reduced powers but the more radical officers wouldn't have it and they were outvoted.'

It is my turn to shake my head. 'You cannot undo what Charles has done to Dick, to us all.'

'Fanny . . .'

'Our lives are over. And for what? Can you tell me this new republic will last? Can you promise me the army and the Rump Parliament will work together happily as they have never before been able to do?' I laugh then, thinking bitterly of Charles and the hundreds of times he has sat around this very table with us. 'Charles has got what he wanted – he's Commander-in-Chief of the army now, isn't he? He has won. But the Rump says he must answer to Parliament and Lambert says it won't wash. And so here we go again . . .'

'It will work,' Bridget says, the usual fierce edge returned to her voice after only the briefest moments of supplication. 'It must.' Her cheeks are burning now though I cannot tell if it is from shame or determination.

I don't want to hear any more. I rise to my feet and move to follow Dick from the room, though I cannot resist a parting shot: 'It will not last, Biddy. The pretended king will return and God help you and Charles then. God help us all. You have ruined everything – for us and for England. All Father fought for, all of our hopes and dreams will end in devastation, you mark my words.'

Richard spends the remainder of the day with Thurloe receiving visitors and well-wishers while I spend my last day as a princess wandering around the palace, saying goodbye to friends and to rooms alike. My journey must serve a double purpose: bidding farewell to my other home, my beloved Hampton Court, which I will never now see again. After a tearful plea to the guards, they let me out into the privy gardens where I walk for the last time through the box hedges and around the sundial. I think of Robert standing there in the moonlight, scuffing the toe of his shoe in the gravel as he waited for my maid to meet him, and plant a kiss from my fingers onto the stone of the sundial.

I go next to the stables and then the kitchens, bidding farewell to Father's horses and hounds, to the grooms and the servants. Some avoid my eye; a few of the friendlier ones bob curtseys and bows in my direction before going about their business. I go to the chapel, the Great Hall and the offices of the secretariats, finding Master Hingston and Master Marvell, who are even now compiling their *curricula vitae* and assembling references as they look for new employment. I wish them both luck and kiss their cheeks. Thinking of my friends, I wish I had seen Signor Giavarina again but the ambassadors have melted away from the palace in recent weeks and I do not see how I could send for him in my newly reduced state. Perhaps I will write to him, I think, though as ever, without a sense of where and what I will be, I struggle to pin down any thought of my future self and what I might do.

Passing now into the Banqueting House, I am startled to see men removing sconces and tapestries and packing them into boxes. I think for a mad moment that they mean to send them with us but of course this cannot be the case: they belong to the nation, not to us. I approach a man holding a board with papers clipped to it who seems to be directing the operation, and ask him why they are removing everything.

'To be sold,' he answers shortly. 'It's all to be sold; the palace and everything in it, sold to pay the wages owed the army.'

'What? The palace itself?'

'Whitehall and Somerset House both, I believe. What's the need of them now we have no king or Lord Protector neither? What need has a republic of great palaces with no Stuarts or Cromwells to live in them?'

I am stunned into silence, baulking at his cheek before realising with a start that he probably has no idea who I am. I look around the room where I danced as a goddess before the court and my new husband, and breathe it in one last time before stepping quietly out through the door.

Lying in bed that night, I look at the beautiful tapestries that cloak the walls of my room and watch their story unfold for the last time. They tell of an ancient Greek prince who was fated to die when the fire he nursed dwindled into nothingness. I wonder if I am fated in the same way. Does our God play with our lives in the way the pagan gods did? I think now that the answer must be yes, that God's Providence – the light Father had us all live our lives by – is no more than a parlour game.

I try and banish these bleak thoughts by thinking instead of where I have been happiest: the Fridays I spent snuggling against Mary in our barge as we waited for the forest of red-bricked chimneys of Hampton Court to appear around the bend in the river; at Father's investiture, watching him laughing with Elizabeth and her baby in his ermine robes; in the Banqueting House dancing in Robert's arms with seashell pins in my hair before we fell into bed together. Thinking of Robert lying beside me, I summon him to come to me once more, and keep the candles in my room alight all night so I can see him clearly. He comes and I watch as he perches on the end of the bed unbuckling his shoes, as he soaks in the bath before the fire, as he plays cards at the table. He comes and goes before my eyes, opening and closing doors, laughing, talking to me over his shoulder, sometimes pausing to drop a kiss on my upturned mouth. I watch in agony and as the dawn light creeps around the curtains I bury my face in my pillow and cry as I did the day he died. It is fear that grips me; fear that he will not come to me again once I leave our rooms today, fear that for the rest of my life hereafter I will not be able to see Robert again so clearly. Surely my memories of him are so much stronger when they are attached to the real floor and furniture he touched, when I can remember scenes I have already seen, not have to create new ones in my imagination.

That morning, Richard and I leave together; the last of the Cromwells to go. Two of our household servants accompany us and, as they climb up next to the coachman, I settle beside my brother in the carriage with my puppy on my lap and Venus in a cage at my feet, listening to the City bells as they ring in the distance. I take little else with me, just some clothes and a few jewels, my books and papers, the copy of Augustine Robert gave me and his mother's emerald ring: I will not be accused of stealing government property. I take Richard's hand in mine and with the other pull Robert's miniature out of my bag, cradling it in my palm as the carriage lurches off from the palace gate and makes for the road south to Hampshire.

PART FIVE

August 1659–January 1661

CHAPTER TWELVE

How strange it is to be in an ordinary house in the proper countryside again. Before I came to Richard's house at Hursley, Hampton Court was the furthest out of London I had been since we moved down to the capital from Ely when I was eight. It is so quiet, so remote; the only noise I can hear from my bedroom window is the birds in the garden, occasionally a distant pheasant calling from the farmland beyond. There are no guards outside my room, no nightwatchman marking the passage of time, no bells to wake me in the morning. In this eerie stillness, I might almost believe the last twelve years of my life had been a dream turned to nightmare.

But it is not so simple to return to an ordinary life you hardly remember, in a house you do not know with a family that is not your own. How am I to conduct myself now? How do I speak to others of what has happened to my family? I do not even have our name to cling to any more, but am called by that of the husband I no longer have: I am Lady Rich now, not Frances Cromwell. Not Your Highness. Never again *Principessa*. If I wanted, could I shed my Cromwell self like an old skin, now it has been shamed? But I do not want to when it still means the world to me. I must think of the great Queen Elizabeth, I tell myself in moments of weakness: of how she went from princess to bastard to prisoner to queen, never once losing her sense of herself or her dignity.

If I struggle to remember who I am, it is far worse for Dick. He has been shaken clean out of himself by the extraordinary events of his recent life. No one knows how to treat him: not the servants, not his neighbours or local friends. Men bow then look uncomfortable, women keep their eyes lowered. Even his position within the household itself is an anomaly: the house belongs to his father-in-law, yet Doll's father calls him 'Highness' and defers to him, ceding his rightful place at the head of the table. And Dick in turn is at a loss. Each movement is a struggle for him: a need to unlearn the behaviour of a monarch which he had only lately begun to master. I watch as he forgets to stand when a woman enters the room or waits by a door for a few moments, expecting it to be opened for him by a footman who is not there. He still receives petitions of support and letters from those who would see him restored to power and he seems to exist in a half-life, not certain whether to move forward or back or even which is which. He has a haunted look, twitching with every knock on the front door or fresh packet of post, though I know his fear is as much of his creditors as of any opponents or assassins.

'If Parliament does not honour its promise to pay my debts, I will be ruined,' he says to me over and over again. 'I am receiving invoices for the salaries of the palace servants, bills for official entertainments for foreign ambassadors – how am I, now a private citizen, possibly expected to meet what were formal expenses of government?'

I have little comfort to offer him. Though I am treated as an honoured guest at Hursley, I feel entirely helpless without position or money of my own.

We are all in a muddle.

♛

I do not linger long. My brother Harry is now safely returned from Ireland and living with his in-laws the Russells at Chippenham in Cambridgeshire and I am desperate to see him. He sends his brother-in-law John Russell to fetch me, wary of my attempting the substantial journey with only servants to accompany me so soon after the latest royalist uprising, when the roads are still dangerous. Though I know that Lambert – sent to quash the rebellion by a Parliament as nervous of him as of any royalists – has prevailed, still I am grateful for Mr Russell's protection. He is a countryman of mine, I remember, as he hands me up into the carriage, and no one can match a fenlander for steady strength.

I pay little attention to the journey until John Russell comments that we are skirting the border of Essex and I feel my pulse quicken.

'Essex? Will we pass Felsted, do you know?'

John examines me carefully. 'Not closely; we'll come within a half day's ride of it, I should guess.'

'Could we make the diversion? Would you mind? It would mean so much . . .' Words pour out of me urgently. 'Felsted village is close to my husband's family home at Leighs Priory. And the church at Felsted . . .' The words stop as quickly as they began.

'. . . Is where he is buried.' John finishes the sentence I

cannot and I smile at him in hopeless thanks. 'Of course we can go there, Lady Frances, if you wish it.'

We reach the church of Holy Cross, Felsted, in the twilight of the early evening. A lone blackbird calls from the pitched top of the lychgate as we enter the churchyard but I struggle to hear his song above the pounding in my chest. I walk as if asleep, threading through the ancient graves of the long-dead towards the church. Inside an old man is lighting candles and he and John exchange a few words. The man gestures as if to direct us, but I do not need his help to find Robert, I can feel where he is. I hurry over to the south-eastern corner of the church and, passing through a stone arch, find myself in the Rich family chapel. And there along the near side is the stone that bears his name. With no thought in my head but a great yearning, I lie down on the floor and press my cheek onto the cold marble, spreading my arm across the space above where his body must lie.

'Hello, my darling.'

I have no more words, neither to say nor to think. Instead I close my eyes and sink myself into the stone, willing my love and my vitality to travel downwards and into him. I smile even as my cheeks dampen with tears; I can feel him close by.

I do not know how long I lie there but darkness presses against my eyelids by the time I hear a soft voice calling my name and a light hand on my shoulder. For a moment I think it is Robert come back to me and I almost cry out, but I open my eyes to find John Russell crouching over me with a candle.

'Frances. Lady Frances, it grows late; we should go.'

I do not move but stare at him, confusion pinching the place between my brows.

'Come.' He offers his hand but I close my eyes, wishing him to disappear. A moment later I feel gentle arms under my neck and around my waist and then I am lifted, vanishing into the air itself.

'Thank you,' I say, coming to in the carriage. 'I am so sorry for my unladylike behaviour.'

'Tush.' John Russell smiles gently at me. 'You could never be unladylike; you will always seem a princess to me.'

It is my turn to smile, warmed by the forgotten feel of a compliment. 'Nevertheless,' I continue, 'I can only plead a great love for my husband as my excuse.' I look out of the window then, embarrassed by my admission and fully expecting it to halt our conversation.

'That I could see clearly on your wedding day, Lady Frances, and I understand. Lord Robert was a good man.'

My head snaps back. 'You knew him? I did not realise.'

'I did.' John Russell nods. 'We were at school together.'

'What?' I am astonished. 'I had no idea! Do you mean here in Felsted?'

'Indeed. At the school founded by Robert's own family.'

'Then you were at the same school as my brothers too! How extraordinary.'

'Yes. They were a fair bit older than me so I knew them less well. I was a new boy, seven and in my first term, when your oldest brother died so unexpectedly in the school infirmary. I still remember the shock that ran around the school – he was such a bright lad, so sure of himself at seventeen.'

'I was but a baby then,' I reply, thinking of how poor Father had talked about his dead sons when he himself was dying. 'Though Bridget and Betty remembered it well and often spoke of him. But tell me about Robert.'

'No other boy could match him at football,' John says, smiling shyly with his schoolboy memoires. 'Or at word games, I remember that. How he loved puns and tricks: always trying them out on us. He was the golden boy – son of the school's chief benefactor. A couple of years younger than me. But we became good friends nonetheless, kept in touch after we left.'

My heart thrills at the discovery – as if I have found another path back to Robert, discovered another chapter of his life.

'What was he like as a boy?' I lean forward urgently, intent on gorging on this new information. 'Who were his friends? What did he enjoy at school? Tell me everything!'

John Russell leans slowly back against the seat, twists his old-fashioned hat in his large hands and begins.

♛

My reunion with my big brother Harry is joyful. With so much passed since we were last in each other's arms, we laugh and cry in equal measure. I think he looks older, more like Father. He thinks I have suffered. It has been four years since we were last together: I was a girl then and he a young man setting out on an adventure. We are both wiser now.

I find a happier atmosphere at Chippenham than at Hursley; the Russell family are warm and I feel a strong sense of home to be back in the fens so close to where I was born. From the house which sits grandly at the top of a three-mile rise, I can even see the towers of Ely Cathedral rising above the flat plains to the north – the same ageless cathedral in whose shadow I spent my childhood. The same fenland mist creeps around the house in the early morning and the servants speak with the familiar cadences I remember from childhood. Harry is by turns cheerful and despondent, his natural good humour in constant conflict with the incontrovertible fall of our family. Though he had not so far to fall as Richard, still Harry is cast low; his promising career also cut short.

'If only Dick had recalled me from Ireland,' he muses again and again, pacing up and down as Father used to do, 'I could have helped to stop Charles and Uncle Desborough. But they were too clever – kept me away deliberately. Every time I asked to return to London, the Council found a way to block it. And so I could do nothing.' Harry's words catch in his throat and I wonder, as I feast my eyes on his strange yet familiar face in the firelight, at the peculiar sadness he has had to bear: would it have been worse to be so far away when Betty and Father died? Never to have seen them again nor been able to say goodbye? Worse to receive the fateful news of each death so many days later in the pages of a letter long after their souls had flown?

'And not to be able to help Dick in the end,' Harry adds to my unspoken thoughts. 'I could have done – even after the generals had seized power – had he taken a stand, sent orders to me, to Montagu, Monck and Lockhart to rally our troops and the fleet behind him.

But once he had capitulated, what choice did I have but to fall in line?'

'You think you could have done better than Dick?' I watch him closely, thinking back to the time when dear John Claypole speculated that Father might make him his heir instead of Richard and I had protested that Harry would never betray his brother for his own power. How very long ago that seems now.

'No, no. Well . . .' Harry shifts in his chair, uncrosses his legs then crosses them again. 'This was how Father left things. Dick did his best and I was always staunch for his interest. But we must shift for ourselves now.'

The weeks and months pass at Chippenham with little to distinguish each day from the next. I write to Mary and Mother often, regularly to Richard and very occasionally to Bridget, though I hardly know what to say to her. One day a letter arrives for me from Signor Giavarina, its scribbled and scratched out addresses revealing the journey it has taken following me from house to house to finally reach me here. It is but a few lines addressed not to *Principessa* but to *bella Francesca* and wishing me well; I know he can write nothing more revealing for fear of embarrassing his Venetian masters, who must even now be paying court to the new government. But the gesture moves me deeply and I repeat his last line over and over to myself with its glimpse of future escape: *'If Venus should ever wish to see Venice, she will find a friend there . . .'*

We learn of the growing crisis in government as the days shorten, curling into autumnal sleep. In October the tension between the army and Parliament comes to a head, as I warned Bridget it would, when Lambert leads a coup against the Rump Parliament, his soldiers preventing the Speaker and other MPs from entering the House. I write to Bridget demanding to know what has happened but she merely replies that Lambert is driving events now, Charles and Uncle Desborough trailing in his wake – Charles trying his best to conciliate. She tells me that the Rump has tried to assert control over Charles as Commander-in-Chief of the army and that the senior officers have responded by dissolving the Council of State and once again resurrecting the Committee of Safety; a bad sign which all of us at Chippenham shake our heads to hear. Bulstrode Whitelocke is once more a member and I smile to myself amid my concern at my friend's diplomatic skills, even as I pray that he can be a force for good in government. Again and again I return to Bridget's letter, looking for the worry in her words – for the embarrassment or apology – but she writes as cleanly and dispassionately as ever, her loyalty to Charles ceaseless.

The news of Lambert's coup plunges Harry into an agony of incapacity. 'Monck cannot let this stand,' he declaims, pacing around the library. 'I can do nothing; I have lost my command in Ireland. Montagu has lost the fleet and Lockhart is in Dunkirk. But Monck can still act. He has five thousand foot and two thousand horse under him in Scotland, loyal to him above all others. He is the only one who can stop Lambert and Charles now.'

In the midst of all this, my concern for Mary grows. Harry's friends in London report that there is a rumour Mary's husband Thomas is to be arrested for working to help restore the exiled king and I write to her, careful to say nothing that would incriminate any of us should a government agent read my letter, but urging her and Thomas to stay safe and watch the road from London. I wait anxiously for her reply and when it finally comes, read it even as I run to find Harry who is playing with his son in the garden.

'Thomas is safe,' I say, the words tumbling out of me as I breathe deeply. 'He is safe because Monck has declared his support for the dissolved Parliament and is on the march, as far now as Yorkshire: he brings his army south to face Lambert, just as you hoped.' Perhaps Monck will bring Lambert his Scottish falcons too, I almost add, hardly knowing whether to laugh or cry.

Harry grins, his face almost splitting in two, before a frown replaces the smile as quickly as it came. 'It's what I wanted but even so.' He pulls his little boy close to him and he grips his father's leg.

'What?'

'It is civil war again. And even if Monck prevails and can restore the Parliament and break the power of the senior officers, what then? The Parliament he returns may demand the king returns in kind.'

I look at him in horror but have no words to offer in response. All I can do is shrug hopelessly. The great wheel of events has turned so many times in my short life; I can no longer keep up. Besides, what can the Cromwell family do about any of this now? How can I reclaim control of my own life, let alone anything else?

♛

Each day after that we wait for news of a great battle but it never comes. Though the interim Committee of Safety dispatches Lambert in command of an army to meet Monck in the battlefield and although he has the larger force, Lambert delays and prevaricates throughout November. I read between the lines of Bridget's letters that Charles and Uncle Desborough, left behind in London, swiftly lose control of events as first the port of Portsmouth, then the fleet, declare for Parliament and the troops in London allow the Rump Parliament to reassemble on the day that used to be Christmas Eve. Charles is removed as Commander-in-Chief of the army and withdraws into Wallingford House like an injured fox.

Yet Lambert and his troops remain at large, skulking around the country, waiting for their chance. 'Surely they'll give battle?' I ask Harry, but we hear nothing until we receive a most unexpected visitor late one evening.

I almost sense the little secretary before I see him, as if I feel his shrewd, silent gaze before I enter the parlour, where I find him standing with Harry warming himself by the fire.

'Lady Frances.' Thurloe bows, smiling kindly as he takes my hand to kiss it. It is months since anyone has done this and the back of my hand tingles strangely. 'I have been visiting family in these parts and thought I would call in and bring you the news myself before I return to London.'

'News?' Harry asks as he motions Thurloe into a chair I know to be far too comfortable for his liking.

Thurloe removes his travelling cloak before sitting, gingerly, in the deep armchair. 'News, Lord Henry, that Major-General Lambert and his version of the Good Old Cause is finished.'

It is such a powerful statement that I gasp. 'What do you mean? What has happened?'

Thurloe considers me carefully. 'Nothing and everything. Lambert made a stand but when the great parliamentary commander 'Black Tom' Fairfax, who won the civil war with your father, marched out of his long retirement to lead the Yorkshire gentry in support of Parliament – your brother-in-law Thomas, Viscount Fauconberg, newly created colonel by General Monck, among them I might add – it was all over.'

I think of John Lambert as Thurloe's familiar waterfall of clauses washes over me, of his pride and his skill, his ten children and his Scottish falcons, and in that moment I feel pity for him even though I count his downfall – and ours before it – in large part of his own making.

'God's teeth.' Harry stands up and runs his hands through his hair. 'Well, it is good news and bad, is it not?' He looks to Thurloe for guidance as if we were back at Whitehall with Father alive and Thurloe still his chief minister.

'You are correct, Highness,' Thurloe says and I note the title that no one else now dares to use to address us. 'Good news to have Parliament returned and the army's power broken once and for good . . .'

'But bad news if the MPs choose to bring back Charles Stuart,' I finish, and my old ally nods at me approvingly. 'And which outweighs the other?'

Thurloe spreads his hands in the familiar gesture and smiles. 'The good news,' he says with quiet confidence. 'General Monck trusts me and I can work with him and the new Parliament. I will have some influence again and I will devote it – as will my allies – entirely to restoring your brother and the Protectorate.'

At this Harry springs forward and clasps Thurloe

by the hand, but I do not move. Great though I know Thurloe's skills to be and much as I long to take heart from him, I cannot believe it. Too much has happened; we have fallen too far and too hard and, in Dick's case as well as mine I would guess, broken too many bones to ever get up again.

♛

At last 1659 comes to an end and with the year turned to 1660, I fall into a strange philosophical mood as if I have finally accepted that the world goes on without me. Harry watches for letters from Thurloe but I have no more stomach for politics. I wish rather for quiet companionship and find myself drifting into John Russell's company as neither of us has a spouse of our own to turn to. He joins forces with Harry to persuade me, finally, to fly Venus again and we take her out into the fields together, though the limp enjoyment this gives me pales against the memory of the joy I had felt when I first flew her in St James's Park, with the beautiful husband who named her waiting for me in our bed. I ask John often of his schooldays at Felsted, urging him to tell me stories of Robert. He in turn asks me of life at court, and I tell him of my days in the sun, of my courtship by the exiled 'king' and my friendship with Signor Giavarina. Of Father and how the world seemed to mould itself around him.

'You must find it a dull life here after all of that,' John says rather sweetly as we return with Venus from one of our walks.

'Some days I do,' I reply, always surprised and relieved by the open and artless way I feel I can talk to him; free to be my adult self, liberated by any need to impress or desire to flirt. 'I did love the attention, I can confess it now, but it was the excitement of being so close to great affairs that intoxicated me as much as the fine clothes, the music and dancing. But I do not miss the pain, the pressure; the great grief I faced. It was never the same after Robert died. Now it is balm to my soul to be out in the open countryside of the fens again, to wander as I please and have space to think.'

'Really?' He seems pleased by my answer, for all its frankness. 'You are fond then of Chippenham and of our family?'

I look around the orchard as we pass through the gnarled, sleeping apple trees, which will spring into unimagined life in only a few months. 'Yes. I love it and your family. I would stay here for ever.'

John does not speak again for a few moments and my attention wanders away from him and into the past as it usually does.

'You could stay here for ever,' he says at length, his voice soft and low.

I hardly hear him and only notice the words after he stops walking. I take a few steps before realising his steps aren't continuing beside mine and so I stop and turn back towards him. He takes off his hat then, twisting it in his hands as he does when he is nervous.

'You will always be welcome here of course, as Henry's sister and a member of the family. But I meant . . . I meant that you could make a life here with me; it will all be mine one day.'

It takes me a few moments to grasp his meaning.

'Marry you?' I shake my head in bewilderment and Venus gives a little cry from my hand. I place her down on a fence post while I struggle to think. 'But John, I have never thought . . . I could not marry anyone. You and me? I . . .' My head keeps shaking even as the words dry up.

John sighs then smiles, though the smile does not reach his eyes. 'I knew it was too soon to speak but I could not help myself. Forgive me,' he hurries on in sudden embarrassment, 'do not trouble yourself about it, I hardly expected an answer.' Replacing his hat, he moves away from me towards the house, cutting a path through the long, frosted grass. I turn to my bird and we stare at each other in confusion.

It is time to move on again. Although John is kind and endeavours to regain something of our carefree friendship, I cannot help my embarrassment at his unsolicited proposal. I had so enjoyed speaking to him without forethought, without the need to weigh and measure my words and with that lost to me, I feel my loneliness return, just in time for the next anniversary of Robert's death in February – a painful reminder of how impossible it would be for me to ever marry again. I cannot even comprehend the notion, let alone consider a flesh-and-blood candidate. I think of visiting his tomb again, perhaps calling on his family at Leighs Priory, but I am crippled by embarrassment: I cannot face the visit so soon after my family's disgrace. And besides, I have heard that Robert's father too has died so I would only find his stepmother and half-sisters there. All the Rich men have gone.

It is Harry who makes up my mind for me. 'It would be a good time to go to Mary at Newburgh,' he says, folding a news broadsheet after breakfast one morning.

'There was a great revelry in London last week: the people roasted haunches of meat on every street corner, crying out that they were roasting the "Rump". The MPs who sat throughout the civil war, including all those who objected to the king's trial and execution, are to be reinstated. And if Thurloe's efforts come to nothing, I fear the young exiled 'king' won't be far behind it. Viscount Fauconberg is the only royalist in the family and we all know Charles Stuart has a fondness for him. If King Charles is restored, Newburgh would be the safest place for you.'

♛

I break my journey north at John Claypole's manor house at Northborough. I cry with relief to see Mother again and am delighted to see dear John himself and my nephews and niece, who have each grown into quite different children in the months we have been apart. Their home is a medieval fortified manor house in the centre of the village, older and more modest than the estates my brothers married into at Hursley and Chippenham. Still, it is grander than our old timbered house at Ely and I think how the young Elizabeth would have thrilled to be brought back here a bride, leaving her childhood behind in Mary's and my small hands. Mother is clearly at home here, managing the servants and slipping back into running a prominent market-town household, her former life as *de facto* queen fading in her wake.

'Are you happy here?' I ask her, our arms around each other on the couch, my cheek resting on her neck, breathing in her familiar scent of soap, lavender and pearls.

'As happy as I could be anywhere without your father,' she replies, twirling a ringlet of my hair around her finger. 'I have the children to take care of, and John and I have always been close.'

'And the locals? Poor Richard does not know who he is down at Hursley and no one knows how to treat him.'

'Oh, poor Dick.' I feel Mother's thoughts fly to her eldest boy in his sorrow. 'I will visit him before long. But here, we keep ourselves to ourselves. I do find people staring in at the windows sometimes, knocking at the door to catch a glimpse of me in my scandalous wretchedness: "the Lady Protectoress as was" they call me, or "the Housewife Joan", which they used to call me in London when they ridiculed me for a country bumpkin.' She sighs and kisses my forehead. 'But I manage, darling, I always have.'

John comes in then and flops into a chair by the fire, a glass of claret in his hand and the hound Badger collapsed across his boots. Just for a few precious moments it feels like old times.

I stay but a few days; the latest letters John receives from London are full of the restored Long Parliament's clamouring for the exiled king's return and Lambert has been captured and imprisoned in the Tower – Charles too for all we know. I have the sense once more of history tumbling away from me and I am determined to fly ahead of it: if the pretended king is to come over the Channel, I want to be as far away from him as I can.

And so, to Yorkshire. I depart in the rain, leaving my nameless puppy behind with his father Badger: there is a joyful life there for him, settled in his own home and among children, which I cannot give him.

Venus, though, comes north with me.

♛

Mary, Mary, Mary.

There she is, standing in the great doorway of Newburgh Priory, her hand shielding her eyes from the sun as my carriage sweeps around the drive; her figure so small against the vast, grand canvas of the stately home. My heart aches for her and I leap out of the door almost before the horses have stopped, flying into her arms. We are as lovers reunited and cover each other's faces with kisses as tears stream down our cheeks.

'My darling.'

'My own.'

Mary gives me time to recover some composure before taking me in to Thomas, who rises from his desk in one smooth, courtly action.

'My dear sister-in-law, what a great pleasure to have you come to us at last.'

I take his proffered hand and smile, determined to get to know him better on this visit; to unpeel the many layers to him to get at the truth, whatever I learn of his real loyalties in the process. Without Robert beside me, I see how central my brothers-in-law, like my own brothers, are to my life. They are the pillars around which our households exist, the arbiters often of our fortunes and the gatekeepers to my sisters. John Claypole is as dear to me as Charles Fleetwood is lost to me. But I will make a friend out of Mary's Thomas, I decide, if it the last thing I do.

'How have you managed with the family?' I ask Mary as she fusses around my room, tweaking it into perfection. 'Do they accept us – as Father said – warts and all? Are you allowed to remain a Cromwell in any way among these royalists?'

She smiles, turning from the vase of freshly picked daffodils on the nightstand. 'They are not so bad, once you get used to them. And while, I admit, I do not express myself as staunchly as I might in the company of the Fleetwoods, the Claypoles or the Russells, I keep faith with Father's memory and I think they respect me for it. No one dares to speak ill of him before me.'

'Hmmm. So – keep to family loyalty rather than political fervour.'

'Quite.'

'Well, I'll do my best,' I say. 'But if the "king" does return, what then? Will Newburgh Priory hang out the royal banners in welcome? You know what they used to say of Thomas at court – that he had never fully crossed over to our side. That he was selling information to the French in return for jewels for you and Barbary horses for himself.'

Mary's hand flies to the ruby at her throat and her face creases with pain. I regret my words immediately and remember in that instant what Bridget had said to me once: how I did not know what it was to be torn in loyalty between my family and my husband. She was talking of Charles's treachery, of course, but was Mary facing the same challenges at the opposite end of our great conflict?

Mary sighs. 'You cannot know what it is like here in Yorkshire, Fanny. Everyone in these parts was for the old king – it is not like how it is where we grew up in the eastern counties. At Ely, at Chippenham and Northborough you can be sure you are surrounded by those loyal to Parliament. But up here . . .'

'. . . It is different, I see that; most people are still royalist – you have to adapt accordingly.'

Mary sits down on the bed beside me. 'Exactly. And Thomas's family is so important here – you should have seen the crowds who greeted us when we first journeyed into the county after our wedding. Hundreds of them lined the streets and we went from town to town to be welcomed like a royal couple.'

'I wish I could have seen it', I smile, though with a greater measure of sadness than pleasure. 'And Thomas?'

'We both knew Father had matched us in an attempt to reconcile his Protectorate with the old royalist nobility.' Mary goes on. 'It took us many months of marriage before we faced this: as if Thomas couldn't really talk to me about the gulf between us – reveal his whole self to me – before we really knew each other as man and wife, before we truly loved each other.'

'And you do love each other now?' I delight at her words, for all the unsettling context. 'You trust each other?'

'We do. Perhaps Father could see that we would.'

'Then I couldn't be happier, my dearest Mall; to see you find love in the marriage that I caused . . .'

'Hush,' she says, taking my hand. 'I am happy with him, although . . .'

The unconscious glance Mary drops to her flat stomach tells me all I need to know. I can almost hear the longing inside her; she has wanted a baby of her own since she was four years old. I prepare a gentle question but she pulls the conversation back.

'Thomas will tell you himself that he never betrayed Father nor Dick, never worked against the Protectorate.'

I look at her with eyebrows raised; there is no need for me to say 'But . . .'

'But since the army brought Richard down, I believe Thomas has been corresponding with the exiled court once more; he may have sent the young king money.'

I stiffen and a bitter taste creeps into my mouth. Is there nowhere I can be at peace?

Mary hurries on urgently. 'It's best if Thomas explains himself directly to you; I want you to be friends, more than anything in the world. And I know you both too well to imagine you will begin that friendship until you have had this out between you.'

I take Mary at her word and seek Thomas in his study after supper the following evening; if we are to talk freely, it must be alone.

He is reading papers at his desk, a pair of spectacles perched on his nose which he hastily removes at my arrival. I am surprised to see a young man wearing glasses but I forgive his vanity and pretend I do not notice as he guides me to the fire, which has an armchair on either side. While Thomas fetches me a glass of wine, I look around the room, impressed and not a little intimidated by the fine portraits of his ancestors reclining on each wall. His truly is an aristocratic house, and with his movements as much as his speech, Thomas wears his nobility easily, like a comfortable robe shrugged on at the end of a hard day.

We talk for a few minutes of inconsequential things but the spectre of the young 'king' hangs between us, listening to our conversation in a blur of dark curls and haughty lips.

'Do you think he will come?' I ask Thomas at length. 'I had the frightening sensation on my journey here that Charles Stuart was chasing me all the way up the great north road.'

Thomas takes a sip of wine and regards me closely over the rim of his glass. 'I believe he will come now, yes.'

'And this is something you welcome, even as it fills my heart with horror?'

'I neither welcome nor fear it; I await events.'

It is a diplomat's answer and I press further. 'I know you to be a royalist and I know you have kept in favour with the exiled "king". You are my brother-in-law now: do you not think it time we understood each other truly? For Mary's sake if for no other. I am a princess no longer, but a widow alone and adrift; a guest in your own house, dependent on your hospitality. You can speak freely.'

'I apologise, Lady Frances,' Thomas says after a pause, drawing a little straighter in his chair. 'You are right of course, and I owe you more of my confidence. If it does not hurt you to hear my views then, yes, I welcome the king's return.'

'But why? You wish to crawl under the thumb of a tyrant once more?'

He swivels the glass in his hand. 'Let me put the question back to you: why not? You are not against monarchy itself – Mary has told me you both wondered at the time if your father should have become king. And he himself spoke often of the benefits of monarchy.'

'Yes, but Father was chosen to rule,' I reply. 'He rose to his eminence by his own merit not by an accident of birth.'

'And Richard?' Thomas counters. 'What were his qualifications?'

He has me there and I take a sip of wine while I construct a response.

'All right. But what is to prevent the young King Charles becoming the tyrant his father was?'

'I would choose a different word than "tyrant" for the old king; he was . . . misguided.'

'Very well – I will rephrase the question. What is to stop another monarch waging war against his people if a Parliament does not do what he wants?'

Thomas regards me carefully before answering. 'I seem to remember that when Parliament didn't do what your father wanted in '53, he marched his soldiers into the chamber and dissolved it. And Lambert did the same thing last autumn. Is that what you want?' His words are as smooth and cool as milk.

'That was not Father's finest hour, I concede it. But if the king returns then what would have been the point of all the struggle and death of the last two decades? Why did Parliament win the war against the father if only to reinstate the son?'

Thomas gets up and glides across to the wine decanter, returning with it to fill our glasses.

'The point of it all will be that this king will not be the same kind of king as his father was. He will be restored under terms set by Parliament with checks on his power. We will never again treat our king like a divine being; we will see his flaws, challenge him, hold him to account. That will be the legacy of your father's time as Head of State, if nothing else.'

I shake my head at his naivety even as I wonder how

it has come to be that I, a mere girl, see the world in more shades of grey than this seasoned politician. 'That is wishful thinking, Viscount. Once the Stuart king is back on his throne he will do whatever he likes. You won't be able to control him. England will slip back into its old ways and we will lose all the freedoms we fought for. He'll muzzle the press, abolish religious freedoms, abandon our hard-earned role as Protestant peace-broker abroad, perhaps even sell Dunkirk to his French friends!' I count off my prophecies on my fingers. 'And we'll have to fight all over again if we ever want our freedoms back.'

Thomas stands again and I wonder if he needs to move around to order his thoughts, as Father used to do. This time he goes to the fire and, picking up the poker, prods the glowing logs until flames appear.

'Let's try looking at this another way,' he says at length, staring into the hearth. 'What is the alternative? I was fully behind the Protectorate, whatever you may think of my motives. Lord!' Thomas turns back to face me, spreading his hands as if to reveal himself fully. 'Do you imagine I would have married into your family, for ever linking my name with that of Cromwell, if I didn't support your father? Many of my relations counted me a traitor but I thought your father our best chance of a return to stable, traditional government. If your father had lived . . . If your own family hadn't betrayed Richard and brought him down . . . But martial rule? That is what we're left with – government by a cabal of army officers, ranting about God and dissolving Parliaments whenever they want at the point of the sword? That is no England I recognise.'

It is quite some speech and my mind races after its

loose ends: if only Father hadn't died so suddenly. If only Richard had been given more time. If only Charles hadn't betrayed us. Perhaps if Father had accepted the crown . . . would that have made a difference? I feel tears of frustration pricking behind my eyes and shake my head against them.

Thomas watches me for a few moments before continuing his argument, a little more gently.

'Think of it this way. It was king against Parliament at the beginning, was it not? At the start of the civil war. Then it was king against Parliament against Parliament's own army. But then, once the king was executed and your father's army finally defeated us royalists in Ireland and Scotland, then it became the army against Parliament – and who should we support in that fight? I'm with Monck – a free Parliament was what your father's side fought the war for and if a free Parliament votes to bring back the king . . . how can that be wrong?'

It is a wild circle of logic and my head spins.

Thomas sits down then, leaning towards me intently. 'What it comes down to, Lady Frances, is this: do you believe in Parliament's sovereignty or not? You think this is about the king but it isn't; it is always – has always been – about Parliament.'

'And what of us?' I know I should rise above self-interest and meet him on the field of constitutional theory but my family is what matters to me above all else. 'What of my family?'

He leans back in his chair then, allowing himself a gulp of his wine. 'The king will be forgiving.'

'Ha!' I snort. 'I do not want his forgiveness, I want his fairness.'

'I believe he will be fair,' Thomas answers quickly, holding a hand up against me. 'He is no fool. He does not want to regain his kingdom only to see it run red again with blood. He must build consensus. Young Charles Stuart is a man of honour, his advisers are pragmatists, men whom only a hair's breadth separated from their friends and colleagues on your side. There will be no retribution.'

I remember what Father had said when he refused the idea of my marrying Charles – not only that he was debauched and unworthy of me but that the young man would never forgive those who killed his father. I cannot believe in the peaceful future Thomas paints. 'Even for Cromwells?' I ask. 'Even for our friends who supported us and our Protectorate?'

'Yes!' he replies with sudden passion. 'If you present yourself in the right way. Think about it: your family and supporters – many of whom, like me and like Lord Broghill, always kept some friendship with the royalist cause – you could be the new king's most natural allies. You all believe as I do that the best government is by a single person and two houses of Parliament. You are all naturally conservative. That is why you sought to make Cromwell king. Present yourselves to the new king as lovers of monarchy and you will find him more accepting of you than the millenarian republicans and iron-clad godly generals like Charles. Perhaps you'll even find you have more in common with the moderate royalists than you ever did with Fleetwood and Lambert.'

My scepticism must be written on my face, for Thomas leans forward then to take my hand with surprising tenderness.

'Frances, I respected your father above almost any other man. And I think he saw that with our generation there was a chance at reconciliation. Why else did he have me marry Mary? Why else did he even for a moment countenance your marrying the exiled king – Mary told me about it,' he confesses in answer to my raised eyebrow.

'You will let Mary be a Cromwell,' I say firmly, 'whatever happens. She and I will never renounce our father's name. He is who we are.'

'I know and I would never ask you to, nor speak ill of him myself, you have my word.'

I squeeze his hand but rise from my seat; I do not want to argue any more.

'So I haven't convinced you?' Thomas looks up at me, his features relaxing into a knowing smile.

'You have spoken fairly, brother-in-law. You have put forward a good case.'

'But you are not persuaded?'

I shake my head, bewildered at the enormity of what he asks of me. 'I am a Cromwell, raised from a child at the heart of Parliament's struggle against the king – can you really expect me to overturn all the teaching of my life in one conversation?'

Thomas bows his head in gracious acknowledgement. 'It is your turn to speak fairly, sister; I stand,' and he does, 'rebuked.'

His charm breaks through to me and I cannot help a smile returning to my lips, for all my anxiety. 'You have persuaded me of one thing though,' I say, turning back from the door.

He looks at me questioningly.

'I believe we shall be friends after all.' I do not wait for an answer but leave the room quickly, climbing the grand staircase to my room. Even if I could come to trust Thomas in time, what if he is proved wrong, as I fear he will be? What would he do if his royal master demanded vengeance on my family?

♛

But the future belongs to Thomas and not me. Within a few weeks, the worst, the very worst, most unimaginable thing happens. Parliament votes to invite Charles Stuart home to take his throne; Thurloe and his allies have failed. Lambert escapes from the Tower and makes a last desperate bid to stop it: staging a rendezvous at Edgehill, site of the first great battle of the civil war. But not enough rally to him and he is captured again. They take him to Tyburn where he is forced to stand under the gallows imagining his death before he is dragged back once more to the Tower. The new king, meanwhile, issues declarations of love for his people and sails joyfully over the Channel. Father's former Councillor General-at-Sea Edward Montagu, who I had once thought so honourable and glamorous, himself escorts the king to our shores on Father's best warship the *Naseby*, which is rechristened the *Royal Charles* the moment the king places his stockinged, buckled foot on the gangplank.

There is polite celebration at Newburgh Priory and raucous revelling across the country but I only feel sick as the kind world I have always lived in crumbles to dust around me. It is so final, I think: as absolute an end to our great wars of words and blood as could be imagined. How can we ever come back from this? Thomas travels down to his London house ready to bend the knee and

Mary wishes him every success before retreating with me to her room to hide her shame. We spend much of our time closed up together; it is only on our own that we can grieve openly and enter fully into the new state of mourning we feel for a death every bit as real as Father's. I may be safe here at Newburgh but how I wish I were at Chippenham with Harry or with Mother and John. We write to each other but none of us knows what to say. John Russell writes to me to assure me that I am in his thoughts and to wish for my return to Chippenham, but I do not reply; his kindness now is almost more than I can bear.

Left to my brooding thoughts I think of the arrogant young king riding into London in mocking triumph; his procession as loud and grand as Caesar's marching along the golden gallery at Hampton Court. I think of Father's upturned face, candlelit below Mantegna's beautiful canvases, as he mused on the heavy responsibility of power. I think of my old homes and imagine Charles Stuart cavorting through the palaces, laughing at us all and bedding his many mistresses in the very rooms Mother and Father slept in; the very bed Father died in, the words of St Paul on his lips: *'I can do all things through Christ, which strengtheneth me.'* I do not know Christ any more and so I try and summon Father's strength to come to me instead. I try and bear this heartbreak as he would have done – as he would want me to do.

But my blood boils with too much rage. I think angrily of the simpering courtiers rushing to welcome the new king; I read the pamphlets my old friends Bulstrode Whitelocke and John Thurloe hastily publish, explaining their past mistakes and declaring their ardent new loyalty to this puffed-up popinjay. If the surface of the 'Restoration' – as they are calling it – shines and gleams with hope and happiness, it is skin-deep, a veneer hiding a rotten underbelly of fear and violence. Master Milton's books are burned by the public hangman at the Old Bailey, effigies of my father hang from windows and Parliament itself clamours for indictments and arrests as old scores are settled.

Whatever his honeyed words and promises of indemnities, the new king is out for blood and we wait anxiously for him to make his move against us while our friends in London try and wheedle their way out of arrest and imprisonment. Despite his efforts at apologising in print, I learn that Bulstrode Whitelocke avoids prison only with the help of consummate bribes paid to his former friends and clients. A rumour reaches us that Thurloe has escaped punishment only by brandishing a little black book full of secrets that would embarrass the new government; his insurance policy collected over his many years as England's chief spymaster. It is Charles Fleetwood I fear for most, whatever my anger at his betrayal, and there is an anxious time when his name is on the draft list of those who are to be exceptions to the indemnity promised to all. It is only thanks to the intercession of his friends in the House of Lords that at the last moment, his name is removed from the list. He is not to be punished but his public life is over as he is disabled for life from holding any office of trust.

And Dick? His is the saddest, most painful loss of all. As he feared, Parliament does not honour its promise to pay his official debts and he is hounded by creditors. Faced with an angry mob of merchants already banging at his door and the prospect of the king's men not far behind, Dick leaves in the middle of the night for the Continent. He goes into the unknown, into a solitary exile, leaving his children and his wife Dorothy, even now heavy with another child. He goes where we cannot follow and I fear I will never see him again.

♛

I am truly off the stage now. The princess who once danced as Venus is not even in the wings or watching the performance from the cheapest seats in the theatre. I am outside in the cold with no prospect of a ticket. I wonder sometimes if the new king ever thinks of me: the puritan princess he once sought for his bride, now living as just another one of his forgotten subjects. I long for the meaning my life once had and cannot help searching desperately for a new one, even as I feel myself slipping into obscurity. The more I am buried, the more I scramble for connections, living within the lines of the letters from my family and the pages of books, searching for answers in the distant past. Where Father used to look to God's Providence for guidance, I look for man's past choices: his triumphs, his mistakes, his ability to survive and to prosper against all odds.

With no power of my own, I do not want to know what terrible things are happening in London. Yet snippets of news reach me when I cannot avoid them: in the conversation of Thomas's family at breakfast or whispered by the servants who clean my room. And so, come autumn, I hear of the trials and grisly executions of the brave men whom the new king accuses of killing his father – the men who had known they took their lives in their hands when they signed King Charles I's death warrant over ten years ago. Where they had sent the king to a solemn, respectful death, they in their turn die in the carnival atmosphere of a bear-baiting.

To the gutter press they are 'regicides' deserving of the hideous death of hanging, drawing and quartering. But to me they are heroes – the bravest men I could imagine. And they wear their bravery to the end: owning their actions honourably at their trials despite the court placing the executioner nearby to unsettle them; explaining that as they had acted truly for God and their country, they are not ashamed to be punished now as their enemies see fit; always believing that the Good Old Cause would live again. When the millenarian Major-General Thomas Harrison is dragged to his death on the hurdle, even the most hostile journalists report his cheerfulness, steadiness of mind, contempt of death and magnanimity. I am as proud of these men – these brothers-in-arms of my father – as if I were daughter to each of them. For the first time in my life I am relieved that Father is dead and beyond the hangman's reach.

Or so I think. One evening an unexpected letter arrives from Bridget. I am surprised to see her familiar hand scratched across the outside of the letter, for we have barely corresponded since our last meeting on the morning Dick and I left Whitehall. I tear it open quickly and a pamphlet falls from within the handwritten page: a single sheet of bold type. I scan it first before sinking to the floor in a pool of skirts, the paper clutched and smudging in my fist. Mary comes into my room and I hear her voice from far away asking me what has happened. I look up at her, my eyes burning with tears.

'It is a Bill of Attainder.'

'What's that?' She lowers herself onto the floor beside me.

'It is where Parliament passes judicial sentence on an accused person as if it were a court of law.'

'What does it say?'

'It says that the remaining fugitive regicides – the men they are hunting down across Europe and the New World – are convicted of high treason . . .'

'And?'

'So are those regicides who are already dead: John Bradshaw, Thomas Pride, Henry Ireton . . . and Father.'

Mary shakes her head at me, pulling the sheet from my hand to examine it for herself. 'But how can they judge men who are dead? What does it mean?'

I grasp around on the floor for Bridget's letter. It is brief, written in just the clear and decisive way that my big sister speaks. I read it quickly before a sudden wave of nausea sends me to my feet, scrambling for the chamber pot. I reach it just in time and gasp, my chest heaving painfully as I stare at the sick glistening yellow in the bottom of the china bowl.

'They are to dig up Father's body from the Abbey, hang it on the gallows at Tyburn and then cut off his head.' I say the words into the bowl before I am sick again.

♛

Mary and I are on the road to London the very next day. We do not know what we will do when we get there or who we can ask to help us. But we know we cannot let this butchery happen to Father; we will throw our own bodies across his to stop it.

CHAPTER THIRTEEN

When we arrive at last at Thomas's London townhouse late at night, he is sitting up in the library reading. Mary flings herself straight into his arms before he can remove his glasses, succumbing to a wave of tears. I watch with hopeless longing, clutching Robert's miniature in my pocket so hard I fear it will break.

Thomas looks over Mary's shoulder to me and I snarl at him in return.

'You said the king would be forgiving, that there would be no lust for blood!'

'I know.'

'You said there would be no vengeance against my family.'

'I know. It is horrible, a disgrace. I am disgusted, as are a good many others.'

'We must do something!'

'Here, sit,' he says, trying to soothe me as if I am a yapping dog.

'I need pen and paper,' I say, moving past him to the writing desk without even removing my travelling cloak. 'I must tell Bridget we have come.'

We are at supper the following evening when Bridget

is shown in and my eyes widen to see the tall military figure of her husband Charles behind her. Thomas rises from his chair and goes over to them, his gentle breeding and diplomatic nature taking over. He kisses Bridget on the cheek and shows her to the table before returning to Charles. I watch in silence as my brothers-in-law lock eyes before shaking hands slowly, with no great enthusiasm visible on either side. My memory flicks back to the disastrous dinner at Whitehall almost two years ago when Charles had blocked Thomas's election to Richard's Council of State and baited Thomas so far he walked out of the room. Would things have turned out differently with Thomas and Lord Broghill on the Council as Dick had wished?

Mary and I stay seated and, though I have a sudden yearning to embrace my older sister, neither of us makes a move to greet her. Instead I nod an acknowledgement and Mary signals to a servant to fill their cups. As the servants circle, I watch Bridget and Charles. If I had expected them to look shamefaced, I should have known better: it has never been in their natures. But still, I fancy I see some depletion in their great stores of confidence and conviction, for all that they hold their heads up high, and Charles looks like he has aged ten years, his blond hair now ash grey. When the guests have drinks, Thomas motions for the servants to leave us: what we have to discuss cannot be overheard by anyone.

'You look well, girls.' It is Bridget who begins with unexpected softness. 'I have missed you both.'

I contemplate an answer but have no idea how I can begin to tell them both of the great anger I feel towards them, of the blame for all our misfortune that I lay at their feet. Perhaps they will tell me that I am unfair – that there were many other actors in this tragedy – but how can I think of others when I am blinded by the betrayal within my own family?

'We have come to London in answer to your letter, Biddy,' Mary says at length. 'We have come to see what can be done about Father.'

'It is a disgrace,' Charles says, his eyes glaring at Thomas in challenge even as he speaks sadly. 'To perform such an act on a corpse – on your father's body.'

'And on Henry's,' Bridget adds quietly and my heart stirs a little at the reminder that it is her first husband – her great love Henry – who is to be strung up beside our father.

Charles glances sideways at his wife and reaches for her hand. I am touched by his care for her, particularly when it is his predecessor in her affections who prompts her sorrow.

'And if they disinter them from the Abbey,' Bridget continues, looking now at Charles with wide eyes, 'will they dig up our baby Anne and Betty and Grandmother too?' Tears are forming in Bridget's eyes; a sight so rare that I stare at her, quite at a loss.

'We had more respect for the dead than they do,' Charles says bitterly and I recollect how he doted on the baby he had buried in the abbey above all his others. 'The king was given a respectful burial in the chapel at Windsor Castle after his execution,' he goes on, 'for all that he was a tyrant and a traitor.'

I expect Thomas to blanch at these words but instead he nods. 'I agree,' he says calmly. 'You will not find me defending such barbarity.'

Charles's head snaps back towards him, his grey curls shaking. 'Then we can speak freely about it before you? We can trust you for all your love of the pretended king?'

Thomas regards him coolly. 'I can promise you one thing, Fleetwood, that I will never betray my wife and her family for any cause.'

How odd it is to hear those words from him: the last addition to our family, the unknown royalist whom we all, Charles chief among us, suspected for so long. And yet it was Charles – whom Father loved above almost any other – who brought us down. I expect Charles to bridle at the barb but the fight has gone out of him as quickly as it came. He turns to look at Mary and then at me; a lifetime of pain and sadness in his eyes.

'Enough of the past,' I blurt out, surprising myself with my outburst. 'What of Father's desecration? Do we know when it will be? Can we stop it?'

'I believe it is planned to take place on the anniversary of the old king's execution – on 30 January,' Thomas says.

'How symbolic,' Mary says bitterly.

'That is still a few months away,' I say, looking around the familiar faces. 'We will have time to think of something, won't we?'

We sit in silence for a few moments before Charles gives a little cough.

'I have the beginnings of a plan,' he says quietly. 'It is dangerous and will in all likelihood fail, but we may have a chance of pulling it off if I can grease the right palms and call on some old loyalties. I can do it alone – I have nothing now to lose and I owe it to your father.'

'No, Charles, we will help,' I say quickly, looking to Mary, who looks in turn to Thomas.

All heads around the table are turned to the viscount. He rises to his feet, walks around his chair once with his chin dropped on his chest, then sits back down and reaches for Mary's hand.

'And so will I,' he says.

♛

It is nine o'clock in the evening when I slip out of the house by the back door. I pull my plain hood tightly around me against the cold rain that pitters and patters on this bleak January night. We have had several months to plan this evening and everything has gone smoothly so far: Thomas, Mary and I dined together at seven before I made my excuses and retired early to bed. Mary had laid out the stolen servant's clothes ready for me and, hidden in these, I creep from the Fauconbergs' fine townhouse unnoticed. Rounding the corner of the building I see Charles standing in the shadows of the high buildings opposite, watching for me under a broad hat. When he sees me he pulls his shabby scarf and cloak tightly around his face and climbs the stairs up to the house. I can just hear his muffled words in reply to the steward who opens the door; hear him say he has an urgent letter from Yorkshire to deliver to Viscount Fauconberg.

I carry on walking, bending my head low until I am around another corner, out of sight of the house. I wait for a minute for Charles to join me and without a word he takes my arm and leads me along the street and down an alleyway to a small courtyard behind the row of fine houses. There is a cart there, the rounded ends of some barrels just visible beneath a tarpaulin. A rough-looking man is waiting beside it, chewing his fingernails.

'Don't ask who he is,' Charles whispers before helping me up onto the driver's seat and climbing up beside me. I crane around and see the scruffy man lift the tarpaulin and clamber into the back of the cart just before Charles taps the horse and it lurches forward.

We drive through the back streets of London, the rain flicking into our faces.

'It's good,' Charles comments as I wipe my face with my glove. 'Means there are fewer people on the streets. As long as we can keep the sacks dry.'

We journey a long way: several miles across London. We pass so close to Whitehall that I can almost smell my old home, but Charles keeps us to the side streets so that I only glimpse the palace between buildings and down passages. At last we emerge into a field and he pulls into a brewer's yard behind an inn close to where we used to live in Drury Lane. There are other carts in the yard and some horses tethered in the stable but no sign of life in the buildings around; the only sound a creaking from the inn's sign painted with a rampant red lion – like Father's emblem – which swings lightly in the rain.

Charles waits a few minutes before slipping lightly down from the cart. 'Shhh.' He looks back up at me. 'You must stay here and keep watch.'

I nod and watch as Charles moves off to the back door of the inn, the man who rode with us slipping into step behind him. He taps lightly and a candle appears at the window before the door is opened quietly from within. The men go in and I pull my hood more tightly around my face. They are gone only a few minutes before the door opens again and Charles and his accomplice appear, struggling to carry a heavily shrouded object between them. Despite the weight they hurry quickly round to the back of the cart and I feel it creaking behind me as they heave the object inside. There is a shuffling noise before I see them again, hurrying back into the inn with what appears to be a large sack of flour hoisted between them.

All is silent once more and I think we are almost safe when I hear footsteps. Two men appear around the edge of the yard and walk unsteadily towards me. They pass under the lantern hanging over the entrance and I see that they are soldiers. My heart stops beating. I watch their approach, trying to think quickly. One of them stumbles and leans on the other for support. They are drunk, I think – thank God. Perhaps they will not notice anything amiss.

'Evening, mistress,' the stumbler says, grinning up at me from beneath his hat. 'You're a pretty girl; what are you doing out here all alone?'

'I am waiting for my master, sir,' I reply, doing my best to mimic the soft burr of a country servant.

'What's in the cart?' The other man peers at the tarpaulin behind me.

I think quickly. 'Some flour, sir, and barrels of ale. We were meant to deliver them earlier today but we lost our way.'

'Ale?' His companion grins.

'Yes, sir, though I can't let you have any; not without the landlord's say-so.' I force myself to smile even as I try to think what I should do if the men inspect the cart.

The man who is more alert cocks his head to one side

and examines me closely. After a few moments, he moves around the cart to the back. I have just closed my eyes in despair when I hear a retching sound.

'Eugh! God's teeth, man, you've covered my boots. Oh no! Again? Come here, quickly,' and with that the man hurries his drunk companion to the other side of the yard, where they disappear up a staircase.

A moment later, Charles and his helper slip quietly out of the back door. 'All right?' he asks me.

I nod, still shaking.

'Right.' Charles tips his hat to the other man, who hurries away, disappearing into the street. With a last check of the cart and tightening of the tarpaulin, Charles leaps onto the cart and we are away.

He drives more quickly now, glancing from left to right as we speed across the field and through the streets, heading north through the City. It is not until we have been gone for some minutes that I think it is safe to speak: 'Father?'

'Yes, he's in the back.'

I catch my breath, thrilled at the idea even as it repulses me. 'Is he . . . all right?'

'He's wrapped up well in many layers of sacking. He's all right.'

Tears well in my eyes; I do not know what I feel.

'And Henry? I thought we would bring both of them.'

Charles shifts against me on the seat. 'It was no good. I paid handsomely but, though the student physician could find a body to match your father's from among the criminals he dissects, he couldn't find one to match Henry Ireton. Henry died too long ago; the physicians don't handle corpses that old. Your father only died a couple of years ago and he was embalmed so a newer body of the right build, knocked about enough, could pass for his at a pinch.'

I swallow to rid my mouth of the taste of sick. 'Did you tell Biddy?' I ask when I can speak again.

'I had to. Poor darling, she cried horribly. But she understands, says it is probably safer this way anyway; the swapping of one body is less likely to be detected than two.'

'That is just like Biddy,' I say, admiring her generosity. 'She never puts herself first.'

'She wanted to come instead of you tonight,' Charles goes on, 'but I persuaded her to stay at home; she will need to be my alibi if it comes to it.'

'You were right. And Mary will do the same for me. But how did you make sure the bodies lay above ground tonight? They are not to be executed for another day.'

'Our brother-in-law Viscount Fauconberg has great influence at court. He planted the idea in a few minds that they disinter the bodies early so they could charge people sixpence to see Old Noll's coffin one last time.' Charles smiles grimly in the moonlight.

I shudder at the indignity of it. 'And the soldier guarding the bodies at the Red Lion? How did you buy him off?'

Charles smiles properly then; the first time I have seen his full smile for longer than I can remember. 'I didn't have to. He's a veteran of our army; served under Oliver in one of his old regiments of Ironsides. The old fellow told me he would do anything for the great Cromwell who he had loved so dearly; told me he would have followed your father to the very gates of hell.'

A few minutes more brings us to Clerkenwell Green at the north edge of the City. Charles pulls the cart down a narrow lane in the shadow of an old priory from where I can see the flickering lanterns of the Fauconberg carriage waiting just ahead of us. Charles looks around hastily; it is a secluded spot, not overlooked by any windows, and the streets are empty. He takes the lantern and holds it above his head. The lantern on the carriage ahead moves in answer.

Charles leaps down from the cart and then helps me to climb down after him. We stand there in silence until two figures appear out of the gloom: Thomas and his manservant. They hurry over to us and Charles clasps Thomas by the shoulder.

'Good man!' he says with a soldier's rough warmth.

Thomas manages a nervous smile in return. 'All well?'

'So far. Come, quickly.'

I watch, rooted to the spot as the three men move to huddle around the back of the cart. They bend and heave and then shuffle over to the carriage, carrying my father between them. They are just wedging him into the space under the carriage seat when I regain my senses.

'Wait!' I run over to them. 'I must say goodbye.'

'Quickly, Frances,' Thomas urges. 'I must get him out of London and on the road north as soon as possible. The servants think I left for Newburgh hours ago in answer to the letter Charles brought; I must make up the time.'

'A moment only.' They stand aside and I place my hand on the sack-covered bulk of my father's body. He is wrapped in so many layers I do not know what part of him I touch but I lift my fingers to my lips, kiss them and replace them on him, pressing into his soft form so that he can feel my touch. 'Goodbye, Father. God speed.'

I stand back and Thomas climbs in, arranging himself on the seat above Father. His servant places a large blanket over his lap and closes the door before climbing up on the driver's seat. He flicks his whip and with a last smile from Thomas they are gone.

I watch them go as Charles puts his arm around me. 'They will be all right,' he says, squeezing my shoulder. 'No one will think to question Viscount Fauconberg – a great favourite of the king – travelling up to his own estate.'

I laugh through my tears. 'Thank you, Charles,' I say, as I put my arm around his waist.

♛

We stand together, shoulder to shoulder, skirt to skirt, like a chain of paper dolls, come to see our father's execution. Our hoods are pulled low over our faces and a frosted blast of wind whips around my cloak to send the three nooses hanging from the gallows before me swinging.

When men come to write of this they will say how the people cheered to see Old Noll, the great usurper, strung up and cut down to size; how justice was done and how God smiled on this day.

But we will know the truth. We are here too.

I put my arms around my sisters, my tears now of triumph rather than grief. 'We did it,' I whisper. 'We cheated them of their revenge.'

Bridget nods then looks at me, her eyes bright and shining. 'Henry would have wanted us to save Father. He is looking down on us now and he understands.'

I hope so. I clutch her to me and feel a great surge of energy at our victory; a sense of release too. 'We have taken Father back,' I say. 'Our lives are our own once more. Charles Stuart tried to steal my future from me but he won't have it.'

'And what of my future?' Mary asks quietly. 'I can't have children, I am sure of it. More than three years have passed . . . and nothing.'

I kiss Mary's head, a tear trickling down my cheek and onto her forehead. 'You may yet, dearest, you may yet.'

My mind travels back to Mother and Father's great bedchamber at Whitehall and I hear Mary offer to marry any man Father chose if he would allow me to have Robert. Something inside me softens and I know in that instant what lies ahead for me.

'Listen to me, Mary,' I say. 'You married for me once. Now it is my turn to marry for you. If you cannot have children, I will have them for us and they will be yours and mine, I promise.'

EPILOGUE

It takes many minutes for us to climb up to the very top of the house. The casual visitor to Newburgh Priory would assume they had reached the highest point if they entered the attic rooms where the servants sleep. But this is not so. We pull aside a dull curtain in a cobwebbed corridor and climb another flight of steep stairs, emerging breathless into a narrow stone chamber built, it seems, into the very roof itself. I look around me as I place my hands on my hips, waiting for my breathing to slow. It is a bare, empty space, remarkable only in its construction: a vault among the rafters, a tomb in the sky.

'He is here?'

I nod once in answer, unwilling to say the words aloud.

'Good God.'

John Russell's voice echoes off the stone and I watch his words bounce and bend around the chamber. After they have faded away, we stand together in silence while I listen to the new, heavy knowledge sink into John like lead through water.

In the silence my thoughts wander from him to Father.

I feel him here with me, though there is no plaque or memorial, no sign or marker anywhere in the room to reveal his final resting place. Without such clues he may, perhaps, be left in peace. I see him even now in my mind, lying hollowed-out in the great state bed at Whitehall Palace, his rough hand in mine as he bade me live a long life, give a good account of him to my children, write my own history.

And so am I my father's keeper? Do I live my life looking back on another's, defending everything he chose to do? But what choice do I have? What the histories make of him, they will make of me, for what am I but a model carved from his clay, a brass rubbing made from his likeness, a postscript to his life's story? I should not have to be the caretaker of his name, I think; I do not have to be. Yet I know what my answer is, what my heart says whatever my head objects: yes, yes, a thousand times yes.

But though I will carry him with me always, yet I must go my own way now.

From Father in his last resting place, my mind travels on to Robert, lying in the Essex earth, his beautiful face turned from me for ever; his body, so young and vivid, so eager to know my own, now cold and still. I slip my hand into my pocket and feel for the familiar shape of his miniature, tracing its frame with my thumb as I summon him to me one last time.

I feel John turn towards me; find my other hand in his.

'Come,' I say quietly, 'let us go out into the fresh air. Thomas has promised us an afternoon hawking.'

'Wait, Frances. Your telling me this, bringing me here.

Can I hope . . . Does this mean yes?' His voice is slow and soft, his large hand warm.

I look back at him now, taking him in properly perhaps only for the first time: his eyes the blue of the fens, his russet hair just a few shades darker than Robert's, his kind, shy smile. I see myself too, a future self – a Cromwell living and loving.

I pause and gather Robert and Father to me like children, pressing them deep into my skin . . .

'Yes.'

HISTORICAL NOTE

Frances and John Russell married in 1663, a year before John inherited his father's estate at Chippenham, becoming Baron Russell. They had five children: one daughter and four sons, the second of whom they called Rich in memory of Robert. Writing to Harry when Robert died, Frances said that 'nothing in the world can repair my loss'. Yet she did find happiness again with John, as their spirited love letters show. Frances still enjoyed the lively company of other men (and Venetian ambassadors in particular): Thomas Fauconberg once teased his brother-in-law John Russell in a postscript to a letter by saying he should hurry back to his wife because Frances was being 'so courted by the Venetian ambassador' (not, sadly, Signor Giavarina but one of his successors in the office). Frances also remained friends with Jeremiah White, who later became chaplain to the Russell family.

When Robert left her a widow, Frances told Harry she 'hoped to get him for my husband that will never die'. Sadly, Providence had other plans and her second husband John died in 1670 after only seven years of marriage. Frances did not remarry but spent the next fifty years a widow, dying in old age in 1720 – the last survivor among her siblings and the only one to live to see the Stuart dynasty end for good with the succession of King George I of Hanover in 1714. One of Frances's descendants acquired Chequers Court, which later became the country house of the prime minister, and a substantial collection of Cromwellian portraits and personal items remains there today. (Another quirk of history is that the 'Cockpit' where the Cromwells lived when they first moved into Whitehall Palace was on the site of modern-day Downing Street.)

Frances spent much of her long widowhood with *Mary and Thomas* who, in contrast to her, enjoyed another forty years of marriage but never had children. Frances and Mary remained very close: Mary doted on and promoted the interests of Frances's children, helped Frances when she was in financial difficulty and left her a substantial legacy when she died. The marriage of Frances's daughter Betty to Thomas's nephew brought the two families even closer. Frances and Mary's love lasted to the end and they are buried together in Chiswick. Mary and Thomas were a devoted couple and flourished under the Restoration (the only Cromwells to do so), even receiving the Duke and Duchess of York at Newburgh in 1665 – we can only assume they did not climb up to the secret vault in the roof. Thomas became Ambassador Extraordinary to Venice and later a Privy Councillor, finally being made an earl by William III. He died in 1700, Mary in 1713 – a great curiosity at the court of the last Stuart Queen Anne, in part because she looked so much like her famous father.

By contrast, *Bridget* died only a couple of years after the Restoration, living long enough to see her and

Charles's baby dug up from her burial place in the Henry VII chapel in Westminster Abbey and thrown into a pit in neighbouring St Margaret's graveyard. Oliver Cromwell's mother Elizabeth, his sister Jane Desborough, General-at-Sea Robert Blake and the other prestigious figures who had been buried in the Abbey during the Commonwealth also suffered the same fate. Elizabeth Claypole is the only member of the family to remain undisturbed, possibly because she was overlooked by mistake. She still lies among the Tudor kings and queens. *Charles Fleetwood* outlived Bridget by many decades, marrying a third wife and living a quiet life at Stoke Newington until his death in 1692. His fellow army leader *John Lambert* was not so fortunate, however, suffering twenty years of imprisonment in various island fortresses around Britain until his death in 1684, by which point he was reputedly mad.

Overall, Charles II's treatment of the Cromwell family at his Restoration was lenient. Frances's mother, the *Lady Protectoress*, was allowed to live in peace with her son-in-law *John Claypole*, though a hostile press accused her of stealing and selling off valuable items from the royal collection, forcing her to petition the king for protection. She died at Northborough in 1665 and was buried in the village church. John Claypole married again in 1670, though he appears to have left his second wife later to live with a laundress. He died in 1688, sadly having outlived all of his and Elizabeth's children, none of whom had any children of their own.

Henry Cromwell too was left in peace to live quietly at Spinney Abbey in Cambridgeshire, close to Frances and John's home at Chippenham. There are stories of Charles II visiting him there when he went to Newmarket races, although we cannot be certain these are true. Letters between Frances and John also speak of a possible visit by the king to them at Chippenham – if he did go we must wonder what he and Frances made of each other, given their once intended marriage. Henry died in 1674, leaving six Cromwell children behind him. *Richard*, on the other hand, did not feel able to return to England until after twenty years of wandering exile in Europe – 'my solitary life' as he called it. His wife *Dorothy* had died without him ever seeing her again and, even when he returned to England, he was careful to see his children only occasionally. He did not return to his estate at Hursley but lived as a lodger in various modest houses, always under a false name. He died in 1712 as an ordinary, unnoticed, modest gentleman, having paid a heavy price of over half a century of lonely exile for a mere nine months as Head of State.

Richard never felt able to reclaim his Cromwell name, such was the power and fascination it exerted then and continued to do for many generations. Even in more recent times the name has provoked strong reactions from the powerful. In 1911 King George V blocked the request of his First Lord of the Admiralty, Winston Churchill, to name a battleship *Oliver Cromwell* and half a century later, our present queen vetoed Tony Benn's plans as Postmaster General to include Cromwell in a new set of stamps depicting all British heads of state from James I onwards, and the whole set was scrapped. Today, if you visit Cromwell's old Cambridge college, Sidney Sussex, meanwhile, you will find curtains on either side of his portrait in the hall; a precautionary measure designed to avoid embarrassment should a member of the royal family visit.

And if we do draw back the curtains, who is the Cromwell we find? Lord Protector Oliver Cromwell haunted the reign of Charles II as surely as the ghost of Hamlet's father did that of Claudius, providing an uncomfortable yardstick by which men of all political views measured the pleasure-loving king, whether it was in 'Old Noll's' ostensible successes in foreign policy or the energised industry of his court. Samuel Pepys – himself not immune to the pleasures of fine wine and women – bemoaned the 'ill condition' of the new king's court, its 'vices of swearing, drinking and whoring', reflecting on the 'bad management of things now compared with what it was in the late rebellious times, when men, some for fear and some for religion, minded their business; which none now do, by being void of both.'

But if Cromwell's regime was held up as a moral rebuke to the merry monarch's, it was not because it was the joyless, repressive military dictatorship of common myth. In fact Cromwell took pains to keep the army at a distance, particularly after the experimental rule of the Major-Generals was abandoned, and ruled conscientiously in constant collaboration with a strong Council and under the eye of Parliament (the first and last time in fact that a British head of state governed under a written constitution). The Protectorate became more traditional and monarchical with each passing year, attempting a return to the comfort of the ancient constitution while taking it in a new and modern direction. The regime, especially in its final years, represented the beginning of a softening culture after the fervour of the kingless

Commonwealth: a court full of poets and musicians; the return of masques and the first English operas; and marriages between former parliamentarian and royalist foes. In character, it was less stiff and formal than the court of King Charles I but more disciplined and competent than that of Charles II. At Cromwell's court there was drinking but not excessive drunkenness, sports but no gambling, romance without licentiousness. Life was luxurious but not decadent. Moderation and virtuosity were prized above all.

Women were central to this more relaxed and civilian court and not merely as ornaments but as people of agency. The upheaval of the Civil Wars had given women new opportunities to show strength and Cromwell's daughters were widely admired for their staunch characters. As one contemporary historian assessed Cromwell's sons and daughters: 'those who wore the breeches deserved the petticoats better; but if those in petticoats had been in breeches, they would have held faster.' Cromwell himself was devoted to his bold daughters and is known to have relied on their advice, particularly that of Elizabeth, with whom he was especially close. Although he held out against Frances's marriage to Robert, largely because of his concerns about the young man's character (and possibly his ill health), he took great care in all of his children's marriages to ensure there was emerging love and not merely the opportunity of a useful alliance: that was the Puritan way.

This Cromwell was not the dour, black-coated Puritan of popular imagination who killed a king and cancelled Christmas (neither of which charges can solely or truly be laid at his door); if in doubt, a cursory glance at the splendid portraits of him and his elegantly dressed wife and daughters is enough to dislodge the image largely created by the Victorians. Cromwell was a Puritan certainly, for whom his relationship with God was the guiding force of his life. But he believed passionately in toleration, hated persecution of any kind, and never sought to impose the way he lived a Christian life on others. If he loved God with an ardent intimacy, he also loved his family, his friends, fine conversation and lively debate, music (not performed in church where it was a distraction), thoroughbred horses, hunting, hawking, drinking and practical jokes. He was magnetic and charming with a ready, almost schoolboy, sense of humour and a remarkable talent for cultivating friends across social, political and religious groups; always the first to spot talent and to overlook a man's past if he could see his potential. 'No man knew more of Men,' said Cromwell's physician Dr Bate, and it was this quality, among many others, that made him such a phenomenally successful soldier and politician and inspired those around him to follow him with devotion.

So if it is time to revisit the Protectorate with fresh eyes, where are we to search for the remains of the Lord Protector himself? Does he lie in the secret vault in the roof at Newburgh Priory? While there is no contemporary evidence to support the claim, the legend that Cromwell's daughters rescued his body (either the intact body through a substitution on the night it lay at the Red Lion pub or merely the headless trunk retrieved from under the gallows) and buried it in the secret chamber at Newburgh persists. The vault exists and the family have never allowed it to be opened: not even at the request of

King Edward VII. But this story is one of many competing theories surrounding Cromwell's final resting place, the strongest of which suggests that his body lies at the site of Tyburn near today's Marble Arch, and that his head, having passed through many hands after it was blown down from its spike above Westminster Hall, is buried beneath the chapel of Sidney Sussex College.

We will probably never know the full truth. Whatever that is, however, one thing is certain: that Oliver Cromwell in death is as extraordinary as he was in life.

ACKNOWLEDGEMENTS

I was first captivated by the extraordinary Oliver Cromwell and his equally extraordinary times as a teenager and have been studying the Civil Wars and Interregnum ever since. For my introduction to the man whose life would shape my own, I must thank my parents: my father Julian for being an avowed roundhead and avid reader of military history and historical fiction and my mother Joanna, another history lover, for spotting the first seeds of my interest and nurturing them with love and encouragement – even taking me on research trips. Without their support of my academic career, I would never have been in the position to write this book.

At university I was immensely fortunate to study under Dr David Smith and Professor John Morrill and wish to thank them and my mentor Dr Gabriel Glickman for their brilliance and their belief in me. The Cromwell Association has provided me with another source of wonderful colleagues and fellow enthusiasts and I am particularly grateful to those experts who read and commented on early copies of the book. Any unintentional inaccuracies are of course all my own.

This book would not exist without my fantastic agent

Giles Milburn who pulled me from the slush pile and told me I could do this. He has shepherded me here and I am more grateful than I can say for his encouragement, good humour and brilliant advice and the efforts of his team at MMLA. My lovely publisher Victoria Oundjian and the whole team at Orion Fiction have been fabulous and I have loved every moment working with them. Special thanks must also go to my team at NRF – Ian Giles and Susanna Rogers in particular – for their support and enthusiasm for my writing endeavours.

I am very lucky to have a large, loving family and wonderful friends who have encouraged me for many years and shared in my delight at seeing The Puritan Princess come to life. Thank you all for your love and friendship. Finally, my deepest thanks are reserved for my two special boys. My little boy Theodore for being such a joy (and, crucially, a terrific sleeper!) and my wonderful husband Charlie for being my companion on every step of this journey: encouraging me, brainstorming and plotting with me, researching and editing my work, helping with author admin and looking after Teddy so I can write. Each day he explores the seventeenth century with me and leads me into historical worlds of his own.

I simply would not be a writer without him.

PROLOGUE

JANUARY 1636, THE FENS

I am always the first in my house to wake. Before Mother or Father, before my brothers and sisters. Before grand-mother who cannot sleep more than three hours together and never after five in the morning.

I even beat the cockerel in the barn.

She rises while it is still night and gives food to her household and portions to her servants.

I like that proverb. It is not just the sense of warmth, of bringing light out of the darkness or providing for loved ones that speaks to me. It is the word *She*. She rises. She acts. She meets the day first and on her own terms, restored by a few precious minutes of quiet. She sets the fire and lays the table, yes. But she lays out more than that: she shapes the day itself for her and all around her.

And what does she do next? More, even more. *She appraises a field and buys it; from her earnings she plants a vineyard. She girds herself with strength and shows that her arms are strong.* There are a lot of verbs in there. Women do not get many verbs. For once, just for once, the Lord speaks to us not of kings or prophets, of a rich man in a castle or a poor one at his gate. He tells of an ordinary woman. A woman whose *strength and honour are her clothing.* A woman who *opens her mouth with wisdom, and faithful instruction is on her tongue.* A woman whose *price is far above rubies.*

And so each morning I wake first and claim the day for my own.

Yet even so there are some things I cannot change. I cannot find the wages for a servant to help Mother. I cannot conjure bacon when our stock of salted meat runs so low nor stop the many-fingered frost crawling through the cracks in the windows. I place dried lavender on the kitchen table and mix the honey and herbs to flavour the porridge now warming on the hearth. But this is all I can do.

It has been a hard winter for us. Though Mother and Father do not like to admit their worries, we children have noticed each little economy as it has crept upon us. When the first beeswax candle stubs were replaced with the pungent tallow kind. When Mother started to take in our neighbours' linen for mending. When Father had to sell his hunter; a horse he loved almost as much as his children. But what use has a farmer for a thoroughbred which cannot work in the fields, even if he is a gentleman?

And the weather has done its worst. The cold has gone to Father's chest forcing him to wear a red flannel round his throat day and night. And the rain, so much rain. The winter floods have receded for now, but they have left destruction in their wake: mounds of muddy peat banked along the roads that criss-cross the fens, sodden fields and rotting fence posts. There is no time to lose if we are to nurse the land back to health in time for the next year's yield. Tenant farmers in these parts are soon ejected if they don't make their farms pay; whatever their good name, however illustrious their ancestors.

So each day, after taking our porridge in the pink dawn light, we are at our labours, Father anxious not to waste an hour of the short winter days. This morning, as the watery sun climbs above the wide, flat horizon, my hands tingle, frozen inside my gloves. Each fingertip has been unstitched so that I can use my fingers to work alongside my brothers. I sit with my little sister Betty chitting potatoes in the barn at the edge of the field while we watch their brown-coated backs bend over their work. Hours pass as we pick all but the best nobbled eyes off the potato tubers and place them rose-end up in long, narrow crates packed with straw.

I pause for a few moments, chafing my fingertips against each other. They smell sickly sweet with starch and are stained soil-black, the swirling grooves on each so ingrained I could use them to make prints on paper as I used to when I was a child. I look down at the wheat-coloured curls of my little sister Betty's head as it rests against my arm. At six years old – five years younger than me – she tires quickly. I will send her inside soon, I think. She can have some milk and a biscuit then help Mother with the mending.

Father is in good humour today at least, the black mood that claimed him last week has passed for now, though we never know when the storm clouds will gather again. He strikes up a song and I listen as the mixed trebles of my brothers join in, my eldest brother

Robert's pitch less steady than the rest as his voice is breaking into a baritone. Betty and I join in and we are quite the choir when a horseman appears on the ridge against the sky. From my vantage point I see him first and fall silent, Betty then each of my brothers following suit when they spot him, Father the last to cease. The rider stops at the nearest gate, his bay horse snorting frosted breath. Father stands up from the hurdle he is mending and holds a hand to the small of his back.

'You the tenant farmer here? Mister Oliver Cromwell?' The messenger calls to Father, leaning down into his saddlebag. 'I've a letter for you.'

We watch as Father plants his stake in the sodden soil and strides towards the man, his long boots squelching in the mud. He takes the proffered square of paper and thumbs it open, the seal cracking between his gloves. He reads, his face bent low over the page, his brow furrowed like the field he stands in.

It is a long letter.

Betty idly juggles two potatoes up in the air and I watch them spin, sprinkling soil on our skirts. But then a great, throated laugh takes our eyes back to Father and the potatoes tumble to the ground as we watch him clasp his arms around himself, his whole body shaking and sagging with a convulsion of laughter and tears.

'Boys!' He shouts when he can speak again. 'Robin, Olly, Dick, Harry!' Father calls them in age order and like hounds they bound towards him. 'Biddy, Betty!' He looks for us next.

We run to him them, potatoes spilling from our laps and rolling in every direction across the floor of the barn. I pick up my skirts and hurry into the field, Betty scampering ahead of me leaping the mountainous ridges of mud that are as high as her knees. When we reach Father, our brothers crowding around him, he sweeps Betty up in his arms and she clamps her muddy legs around his waist, nuzzling into the roughness of his thick working coat as I hang back, wishing it was me pressing my flushed cheek against his, before chiding myself for my sinful envy.

'News, my darlings! The best of news!' Father says at last. 'Praise God! My uncle, who you know died last month, has left me an inheritance: leases on a number of properties in Ely, a post as the tithe-collector for the dean and chapter of the cathedral, an income of some £300 a year. It is not a fortune, but it is enough, more than enough . . .'

His words tail off but I know what he means: enough for Father to climb back into the ranks of the gentlemen where he belongs. Enough to reclaim his status among the leading property-owners of the county. Enough for us to reverse the recent decline in our luck. It was four years ago when Providence began to frown on us and Father was forced to sell up and leave his native Huntingdon. Exiled from the town and his respectable life there, I watched him sink down in the world to the rank of tenant farmer – him, the grandson of the so-called 'golden knight' Sir Oliver Cromwell who had built the magnificent Hinchingbrooke house, favourite stopping place of old King James whenever he took to the Great North Road. Even our current King Charles had visited there as a boy and played at rough and tumble in the gardens with Father himself. Or so he claims.

But all that will change now. We can re-write our history.

Robin, my eldest brother, who at fourteen is almost a man himself, beams with joy and relief. As Father's heir, he will have most to gain from this elevation, though I know it will mean a great deal for all of us. For my brothers, university, perhaps a profession – Parliament even, if the King ever lets it convene again. For Betty and me, a better class of husband when the time comes. And for Mother, no more sewing by tallow candlelight.

'Oh my dears . . .' Father's voice returns, heartier than before and I can almost see his body strengthening. 'Come let's go and tell your mother, we'll roast one of the chickens to celebrate! And you sir', he calls to the bewildered messenger, 'you'll join us in a drink I hope? Raise a glass of wine to our future?'

He gathers us to him to walk back across the fields to the farmhouse, the horseman – smiling now – shadowing us along the road. The boys set off at a trot but Father takes only a few strides before pausing. 'This is God's work', he says so quietly only Betty and I can hear, 'and I will thank Him every day of my life.' Father touches his nose to Betty's and she smiles. 'God came to me when I was at my weakest, girls, did you know that? When I was at my most broken. And He bid me serve Him through my suffering. And I have – He knows how I have. And I never questioned His plan for me for all my doubts . . . But now, ha ha!'

Betty giggles and I find myself laughing too, giddy as Father puts an arm around me pulling me into his chest. My brothers hear our laughter and spring backwards to cluster around Father's legs once more, the older two

Robin and Olly grinning and clapping him on the back, the younger Dick and Harry skipping and clutching at his coat.

But Father has left us once more as he looks up to heaven, tears welling in his eyes. I tip my face to the sky to look where he does and a watery shaft of sunlight blurs my vision. I hear Father's deep voice once more, feel the words growing in his chest as his heart beats against my ear:

'Now I can serve God by my *doing* and not by my suffering alone. And what things I shall do in the world!'

Father's voice rings out sending a flock of starlings winging into the air, and the whole field resounds with our rejoicing.

READING GROUP QUESTIONS

1. 'For me, history has the same capacity as faith to teach, to inspire, but also to tempt, to mislead.' What did you know about Oliver Cromwell before and has this book changed your view of him?

2. The Cromwells are a close-knit family. How do you see the relationships between the siblings and with their parents? In what ways have their lives been transformed by Oliver's extraordinary career and how have they reacted?

3. 'We have been equals, partners, peers; a pair of playing cards, two sides of a coin.' Is the relationship between Frances and Mary the central love story of the novel? How do they show their love for each other?

4. Describe the character of Cromwell's court. What do you think life was like there? Did you notice similarities and differences to the other royal courts you have read about?

5. 'Father returns his thoughts from men to God, where I struggle to follow.' Frances and her father have different

attitudes, such as to faith and history, but also some similarities in their characters. How do they see one another and how do you see their relationship?

6. Frances feels the weight of her father's legacy and how it overshadows her: 'What the histories make of him, they will make of me, for what am I but a model carved from his clay, a brass rubbing made from his likeness, a postscript to his life's story?' Why do you think the women of Cromwell's family and other women in history are so often overlooked?

7. 'This is a new age for women and I want my part of it.' The Civil Wars ushered in new opportunities for women, yet their choices were often still constrained. What decisions do the female characters make in the novel and where are their life choices taken out of their hands?

8. 'God laid the title of king in the dust under our feet.' Cromwell says. From what you have read, why do you think Cromwell refused to become king? What do you think would have been different if he had taken the crown?

9. Unexpected and sudden deaths were more common in the seventeenth century. How do the characters cope with the losses of their loved ones? How does their faith play a part in this?

10. 'Our lives are our own once more,' Frances says at the end of the novel, feeling she has regained some measure of control over her own future. What has she learned and do you think she will be happy?

CREDITS

Miranda Malins and Orion Fiction would like to thank everyone at Orion who worked on the publication of *The Puritan Princess* in the UK.

Editorial
Victoria Oundjian
Olivia Barber

Copy editor
Susan Opie

Proof reader
John Garth

Audio
Paul Stark
Amber Bates

Contracts
Anne Goddard
Paul Bulos
Jake Alderson

Design
Debbie Holmes
Joanna Ridley
Nick May

Editorial Management
Charlie Panayiotou
Jane Hughes
Alice Davis

Finance
Jasdip Nandra
Afeera Ahmed
Elizabeth Beaumont
Sue Baker

Production
Ruth Sharvell

Marketing
Lucy Cameron

Publicity
Alex Layt

Sales
Laura Fletcher
Esther Waters
Victoria Laws
Rachael Hum
Ellie Kyrke-Smith
Frances Doyle
Georgina Cutler

Operations
Jo Jacobs
Sharon Willis
Lisa Pryde
Lucy Brem